Luc lifted her off h...
mouth against ...

"Are you sure about this?" His voice was raw.

"Yes."

Luc's lips traced the outline of hers, gentle at first and then harder to coax her mouth open.

A sharp stab of desire shot through her. She hadn't been kissed or held by a man in almost thirteen years. She moaned and kissed Luc back. Even though she was way out of her comfort zone, and he was way out of her league, she'd wanted to kiss Luc for years. And now he wanted to kiss her back.

"Catherine." His voice rasped her name in the lilting French way, and she moaned again. Whenever anyone else called her by her full name, it sounded prim and proper. The way Luc said it was sexy, as if she was a whole different woman; one who was daring and maybe even a bit coy.

She glimpsed his eyes, so dark blue they were almost black, before he lifted her into his arms like she weighed nothing and held her even closer. She wrapped her legs around his waist, and he groaned...

ACCLAIM FOR JEN GILROY

SUMMER ON FIREFLY LAKE

"Has charm to spare... The delightful supporting cast... and expertly plotted story add depth and richness to this tale, leaving readers eager for another visit to Firefly Lake."   —*Publishers Weekly*

"4 stars! Gilroy's second Firefly Lake novel encapsulates the quaint, busybody small-town feel and the slippery slope of friends becoming lovers quite well... Engaging... [a] fast-paced page turner."   —*RT Book Reviews*

THE COTTAGE AT FIREFLY LAKE

"Gilroy's debut contemporary is packed with potent emotions... [Her] protagonists tug at the heartstrings from the beginning of the story and don't let go. The strong group of supporting characters includes Charlie's sister, Mia, and her daughter, Naomi, whose stories are to be later told. Long on charm, this story invites readers to come in and stay a while."   —*Publishers Weekly*

"4 stars! Memories, regrets, and second chances are front and center in Gilroy's fantastic debut. The first book in the Firefly Lake series is complex and mired in secrets. The Vermont setting adds a genuine feel to the story, and the co-stars are highly entertaining. The homebody hero and world-traveling heroine must travel a long and bumpy road to happiness." —*RT Book Reviews*

"The story has all the elements in place to create an emotional and touching atmosphere. The pacing is steady and the writing is fluid, creating just the right amount of tension and emotion." —NightOwlReviews.com

"Jen Gilroy's *The Cottage at Firefly Lake* is a heart-stirring debut centering around forgiveness and second chances. Gilroy weaves a delightful story and I'm happy to recommend this book!" —OnceUponAPage.com

"This book is a lot of fun and is definitely for fans of Susan Mallery or Marina Adair." —KatyBooks.com

"*The Cottage at Firefly Lake* is Jen Gilroy's debut romance book, but you honestly can't tell. She effortlessly brings this wonderful tale of second chances to us in such a sweet and romantic way that you won't want to put this book down." —Escapingin2Books.com

"This is a sweet and heartwarming second-chance love story that is sure to make you both smile and cry! I felt many different types of emotions while reading it, and the fact that the author can evoke such emotions in her readers is tremendous! Readers who enjoy classy and sweet romances that are filled with heart will definitely pair well with this novel." —PrettyLittleBookReviews.com

Back Home at Firefly Lake

Back Home at Firefly Lake

JEN GILROY

FOREVER

NEW YORK BOSTON

Copyright 2017 © by Jen Gilroy
Excerpt from *The Cottage at Firefly Lake* copyright © 2017 by Jen Gilroy

Cover design by Elizabeth Turner. Cover copyright © 2017 by Hachette Book Group, Inc.

Forever
Hachette Book Group
1290 Avenue of the Americas, New York, NY 10104
forever-romance.com
twitter.com/foreverromance

First Edition: December 2017

Forever is an imprint of Grand Central Publishing. The Forever name and logo are trademarks of Hachette Book Group, Inc.

The publisher is not responsible for websites (or their content) that are not owned by the publisher.

The Hachette Speakers Bureau provides a wide range of authors for speaking events. To find out more, go to www.hachettespeakersbureau.com or call (866) 376-6591.

ISBNs: 978-1-4555-6961-8 (mass market), 978-1-4555-6693-8 (ebook)

Printed in the United States of America

OPM

10 9 8 7 6 5 4 3 2 1

For my husband, who long ago saw parts of me I'd either suppressed or didn't know were there, and whose steadfast love helps me do what I do.

And for Susanna Bavin, whose friendship, support, and indomitable spirit have gotten me through some dark moments in writing and life.

Acknowledgments

Thanks to my editor, Michele Bidelspach, who makes my books better, and the entire team at Grand Central Forever for their enthusiasm, hard work, and support of the Firefly Lake series.

I'm grateful to my agent, Dawn Dowdle at Blue Ridge Literary Agency, who continues to guide my career with skill, kindness, and compassion.

An appreciative shout-out to Jennifer Brodie, who helped me when I'd fallen into a "plot hole" with this book, and Hope Ramsay, whose discerning critique of an early part of the manuscript (which I won from the wonderful Ruby Slippered Sisterhood) made me think about the story in new ways.

As in the other books in this series, the dragonfly reference is for my Romance Writers of America (RWA) class of 2015 Golden Heart finalists, the Dragonflies. I'm glad you're part of my writing journey.

I'm also grateful for my many supportive friends in the Romantic Novelists' Association (RNA).

To Tracy Brody and Arlene McFarlane, thank you for the friendship, prayers, and all-round awesomeness in both life and writing.

To Susanna Bavin, thank you for the encouragement, "hwyl," wise advice, and always being there with a virtual cup of tea and fab biscuits.

As always, thank you to my husband, daughter, and Heidi, the sister of my heart, who put up with the highs and lows of my writing life with humor and grace, love me unconditionally, and who always believe in me.

And to all the readers who pick up this book and others in the Firefly Lake series. Thank you for reading and taking my characters into your lives and hearts. I'm so very grateful for each and every one of you.

Back Home at Firefly Lake

Chapter One

❦

"Next." The high-pitched, perky voice came from the woman behind the arena's reception desk.

Cat McGuire moved forward and wrinkled her nose. The pungent cocktail of stale beer, sweat, and hockey equipment invaded her senses. "Hi. I'm here to register my daughter for hockey." She glanced at twelve-year-old Amy beside her. Under the harsh, fluorescent light, Amy's dark-blond hair was limp and colorless, and above her Pittsburgh Penguins jersey her expression was sulky.

"Firefly Lake doesn't have any hockey teams for girls." The woman's tone was curt, her face unsmiling. She had long, highlighted brown hair and shiny pink lips, and wore a too-tight white sweater.

"But when I called before Christmas, the man I spoke to said we could register today in person." Cat dug her nails into her damp palms. "I told him Amy was a girl."

"That would've been the skate sharpening guy. He always gets mixed up. It doesn't matter, though, because girl or boy, this registration is only for kids five and under. The main hockey registration closed in September." She shuffled papers, brisk and officious. "No exceptions, not even for you." As the woman looked her up and down, faint recognition tugged at the edge of Cat's consciousness.

"Not even..." Cat stopped. "Stephanie?"

Stephanie Larocque, the girl Cat had envied and hated from kindergarten on, nodded and tossed her hair over her shoulders like she'd done in high school. "I heard you were back in town."

Cat didn't need to ask how. Although she'd been in Firefly Lake less than twenty-four hours, it was a small town and news traveled with the efficiency of a bush telegraph in the Australian outback.

"Then you also know I wasn't here in September." Cat tried to keep her voice even. She was an adult, Stephanie was too, and their school days were long behind them. "Are there any other options? Amy loves hockey."

"No." Stephanie gave her best cheerleader smile. "Rules are rules."

"Mom." Amy's voice was a whine mixed with an anguished wail. "It's bad enough you made me move to Vermont, but if I can't play hockey I'll die."

Cat's heart pounded. She had to fix this—and fast. "Sweetie, we'll work something out, I—"

"I can't have any kid dying on my watch." The voice was deep, male, and familiar. "Hey, Cat."

"Luc." Cat's head jerked up.

Next to her, Amy sucked in a breath.

The man who stood behind Stephanie smiled at them. The same easygoing smile Luc Simard had always given

Cat, the one that had graced a thousand sports pages. He still had the same hair, too, dark golden brown like maple syrup. "It's great news about the research grant. I never thought we'd see you back living in Firefly Lake."

Cat hadn't either, but desperate times called for desperate measures. If things worked out like she planned, she wouldn't have to live here permanently. Her stomach knotted. "Life can surprise you."

"It sure can." Luc's smile slipped and his blue eyes clouded.

Cat's face heated. More than anyone, Luc knew how life could throw you a curve.

"So what's the problem?" His voice was gruff.

"I..." Cat swallowed.

"The problem," Stephanie interjected, "is that Cat wants to register her daughter for hockey. I already told her we don't offer girls' hockey, but even if we did, registration for any child older than five closed in September." Stephanie's voice had the same smug tone as in first grade when she'd told Cat the whole class had seen her underwear. She glanced at Luc and her expression warmed. "It's nothing for you to worry about, sugar."

Cat blinked. Stephanie had the same mix of Vermont and Quebec roots she did. As far as she could remember, nobody under the age of seventy had ever called anybody else "sugar" around here.

"Hockey spaces fill up fast." Luc rested one blue-jeaned leg against the desk. "I hear Amy's a good little player." His gaze shifted from Cat to her daughter. "Your grandma has told me lots about you."

"She has?" Amy's eyes widened.

"Absolutely. She's real proud of you." Luc reached

over Stephanie's head of pageant hair and scooped several sheets of paper from the desk. "The girls here are into figure skating, not hockey, but there's nothing to say a girl who wants to play hockey can't. Since Amy's only turned twelve, if you give the go-ahead, she can play on the boys' team. One more kid won't make a difference."

"But…but…" Stephanie stuttered. "It says right here, no exceptions." She waved a blue binder. "You could get me fired. I need this job and—"

"You won't get fired." Luc's gaze swiveled from Stephanie to Cat and held. She trembled and her breath quickened. "No exceptions unless at the coach's discretion. Since Coach MacPherson fell off a ladder hanging up decorations for a New Year's Eve party and broke his leg in three places, I'm filling in. In this case, I'm making an exception." He quirked an eyebrow, and his smile was sweet and way too sexy for comfort.

"Mom?" The yearning in Amy's voice punched Cat's chest. "Please? You promised I could play, no matter what, remember? It's not as if there's anything else here for me." Her face was white, her expression strained and etched with desperation.

Cat *had* promised, and she'd already taken Amy away from the only home she remembered, her team, and the hockey tournament. She drew in a breath. "There's family here and a good school for you." Cat had to get Amy back on track academically. And she had to give them both a better chance for stability and future financial security.

"School's a waste of time for me." Amy stared at her feet, but not before Cat caught the flicker of uncertainty in her light blue eyes, as well as the fear.

Her stomach clenched. Had she put that look in Amy's

eyes? "I guess you can play with the boys, at least for now." She forced the words out and glanced up at Luc. "Thank you." The backs of her eyes burned. Luc was still kind, and although he hadn't been a real part of her life for years, he'd slipped right back in to looking out for her like he always had.

"Mom!" This time, Amy's voice was an excited yelp. She jumped up and down, and her winter boots squeaked on the scuffed tile. "You're amazing. He's amazing. This is the most amazing thing that's ever happened to me. I promise you won't regret it."

Cat regretted it already, but she couldn't deny Amy something that would make her this happy and help her feel good about herself, too.

Luc pivoted away from Stephanie with surprising grace, and Cat's tongue got stuck to the roof of her mouth. She always forgot how big he was, and how he filled whatever space he was in and seemed to suck the air out of it—at least her air.

"Since there's a line of folks waiting to do whatever it is they need to do before we close, you go on and help them, and I'll handle Amy's registration." He smiled again, and Cat's heart skipped a beat.

"I...you..." Stephanie's face was a mottled red.

"Sometimes everyone needs a helping hand. No man or woman is an island." Luc's blue gaze drilled into Cat, the same blue as his crewneck Henley. The T-shirt molded to his broad chest and powerful forearms before it dipped below the waistband of his jeans to rest against...

Cat's hands tingled as warmth spread through her chest. She wouldn't go there. Not with anyone, but especially not with Luc. As toddlers, they'd gone to the same playgroup and attended the same birthday parties. He'd seen her with cake on her face and ice cream in her hair. He'd been her lab partner in chemistry senior year, and he'd rented her old bedroom in her mom's house for the past four months.

In all that time, he'd never looked at her, except as a friend of the family. The kid with the thick glasses who'd skipped fifth grade, and who was so bad at sports she was the last one picked for any team except when he took pity on her.

In their small-town world, Luc had been a god. The kind of guy who'd dated the pretty, popular girls. Even if Cat had been the kind of woman for a man like him, having feelings for him would be wrong on so many levels. Her life had changed almost beyond recognition since high school, but it hadn't changed enough for that.

Luc opened the metal gate separating the reception desk from the arena foyer and waved Cat and Amy toward the cubbyhole that served as the coaching office. Even before Jim MacPherson's accident, the hockey program had been in chaos, so one more kid truly wouldn't make a difference. Even if it had, though, making that exception would have been worth it for the expression on Cat's face. Relief, gratitude, and something he didn't want to put a label on but that touched an emotion he'd forgotten he could feel.

As for Amy, he might not know much about kids, but her longing was palpable. She clearly needed to play hockey almost as much as she needed to breathe. "Take a seat." He gestured to the two chairs in front of the coach's desk, now his desk at least until the end of the season.

Cat nudged her daughter, who continued to stare at him like he'd sprouted an extra head.

"You...you'll be coaching me...like for real?" Amy's voice stuttered.

"Sure." Luc moved a stack of paperwork and several fishing magazines aside to make a clear space on the desk for the registration package. "You think you can handle that?"

"Yeah." Amy leaned forward. "You played in the NHL. You played for Tampa, and Chicago, and Vancouver, and Winnipeg. You were on the US Olympic team and World Juniors and you..." She stopped as Cat gave her a silencing look.

And Luc had the scars to prove it, not only the physical ones but also those that couldn't be seen. "I retired after last season, so now I'm just a regular coach." He pulled a plastic portfolio from atop a pile. "Why don't you take a look at some of the player information while I talk to your mom? You can see the uniform, and there's a bunch of pictures from games."

Amy gave a quick nod and took the portfolio he held out.

Luc sat in the battered black vinyl chair and studied the woman across from him. Cat still had that serious look she'd had as a kid, and she wasn't much taller than when she'd joined his sixth-grade class, almost two years younger but a whole lot smarter than everyone else. But she'd been a sweet kid, and he'd looked out for her when he could. He'd never have expected her to produce a hockey player, though. It must have something to do with Amy's dad, a guy who'd never been in the picture and, unusually for Firefly Lake, nobody ever mentioned.

Cat glanced at her daughter, and her mouth tilted into a smile filled with so much love that Luc's heart caught.

He cleared his throat. "I feel bad you and Amy aren't staying at Harbor House with your mom. I already told her I can find another place to rent until the house I'm having built is ready."

"Of course not." Cat's face went pink, and she tucked a strand of blond hair behind one ear. Why had he never noticed she had pretty ears? "Even if you weren't staying there, Amy and I would still need our own space. Besides, I wouldn't think of inflicting my cats on Pixie." Her expression changed. Not defensive exactly, but watchful and tinged with apprehension.

"That little dog sure rules the roost at your mom's place." An unexpected prickle of sexual awareness whipped through him. Cat had a pretty face, too. Big blue eyes behind almost invisible glasses, delicate features, and a classic oval face. Why had he never noticed all that about her, either?

"I sublet my place in Boston and rented an apartment above the craft gallery on Main Street. I got a great deal on rent as part of helping the gallery owner. The winter months are quiet, but the gallery owner has a few buying trips coming up, so he needed to hire somebody to look after the store." She glanced at her daughter again and her face softened. "Like I tell Amy, everything works out somehow. You have to keep the faith."

Clearly, Cat was a glass-half-full person. The kind of person he used to be before he lost his wife and his hopes and dreams along with her.

Luc took a bulging folder from the bottom desk drawer and got his mind back on hockey, where it belonged. "The practice schedule is in here, along with the game dates and all the other information you need. The parent volunteer roster is already set, but if you want—"

"No." Cat's voice was laced with what might have been panic. "I'm not really a hockey mom. I help out when I'm needed, but..." She took the folder from him and set it on her lap on top of a bulky black tote. "I want to help Amy get settled at her new school first. It's hard to change in the middle of the year."

"Of course." Luc's heart gave a painful thud. His mom had been a big hockey mom. Like his wife would have been if she'd had the chance.

"Thanks." Cat's smile was sweet and genuine. It shouldn't have been sexy but somehow was.

Luc tented his hands on the desk and tried to work moisture into his dry mouth. As far as women were concerned, he was off the market indefinitely and by choice. He shouldn't look at Cat's straight, blond hair and wonder how it would feel as it slipped through his fingers. And he definitely shouldn't wonder about her petite figure beneath her chunky gray sweater and tailored black coat. Despite all the women who'd made it clear they'd be interested in whatever he offered, Luc wasn't offering anything. Once the construction crew finished his new house in the spring, coaching and working alongside his dad and uncles at Simard's Creamery would be his life— his whole life.

"Your mom's real excited about your brother's wedding." He changed the subject with an effort. "She says it's so romantic that Nick and Mia are getting married on New Year's Eve."

"Yes." Cat smiled, and damn if the soft curve of her

rosy lips didn't take Luc's thoughts right back to where they had no business going. "It's great to see Mom so happy, and Nick and Mia, too. With Mia, it's like I'm getting another sister."

"Nick's been a good friend to me." And that was even more reason why Luc shouldn't think about Cat like he'd been thinking about her. A guy didn't have those kinds of thoughts about a buddy's little sister.

Luc dragged his gaze away from Cat's mouth to stare at the frost-fringed office window. The tall pine trees outside were etched in white, and the open field behind the arena slept in a blanket of snow as it sloped in a gentle hill to the shore of the ice-covered lake. In the distance, wisps of wood smoke curled from chimneys in the small town of Firefly Lake cradled between the dark-green Vermont hills.

Home, family, and community. Everything Luc needed to get his life stable and back on track was right here. Apart from his wife and professional hockey, everything he'd ever wanted was here, too.

"The uniform's great." Amy's excited voice brought him back to the present. "Does Mom need to fill out some forms and pay?"

"Yeah, she does." Luc's voice hitched.

"While I do that, why don't you go out to the rink?" Cat dug in her tote and pulled out a folded bill. "You can get yourself a hot chocolate and watch the figure skating practice."

"Mom." Amy made a disgusted face. "Figure skating's for girlie girls."

"Before she switched to hockey, my wife started out as a figure skater." Luc pushed the words out through lips that were all of a sudden numb. When it came to sports, Maggie had been as driven as him and as competitive. Between his failings and hers, he hadn't been with her when she needed him most. "My mom was a figure skater, too. You have to be real fit to do those routines. Unlike in hockey, you aren't wearing gear to protect you from falls, either."

"Sure, but you'd never get me into one of those costumes." Amy gave him a dimpled grin. "I had to wear sequins for a school play once. I never itched so much in my whole entire life. Can you imagine skating in one of those outfits?"

"Nope." The force of Amy's smile kept the memories at bay and, despite himself, Luc managed a smile back. "Go on, we won't be long."

"Okay." With another grin, Amy took the bill from Cat and tucked it into the front pocket of her jeans.

When Amy had left, shutting the office door behind her, Luc turned back to Cat. There was no mistaking the sympathy in her eyes.

"It must be hard to talk about your wife. Amy's still a kid, so she doesn't think before she speaks."

"Life goes on." His voice caught again. Maybe it did for everyone else, but his life had stopped two years ago. Although he went through the motions and did what his family and everyone expected, the biggest part of him was numb. Until today, he'd been fine with that numbness. Then Cat had poked through it with her big blue eyes and a smile that was like a warm hug on a cold day. He cleared his throat. "What's up?"

"Nothing...I..." She fiddled with the strap of her bag. "Until my grant money comes through after New

Year's, money's a bit tight. Amy needs new skates, and with our move, the holidays, and the wedding and all, I wondered...can I buy a secondhand pair anywhere?"

Luc's throat closed as guilt needled him. If money was that tight, Cat and Amy should be staying at Harbor House, rent-free. Except they weren't, and he couldn't shake a sense it had something to do with him.

"Len's Hardware on Main sells used gear, but it goes fast." Although there was money in Firefly Lake, folks were thrifty New Englanders who could sniff out a bargain at twenty paces.

"Oh." She pulled out her checkbook. "Amy will have to make do—"

"Hang on." He stood and came around the desk to sit beside her in the chair Amy had vacated. "I can wait for the hockey registration fee. Put that money toward new skates instead. Len sells those, too, and he gives a discount to local kids. Show him Amy's paperwork so she'll qualify." In the meantime, he'd square the registration fee with the arena manager. Cat would never have to know.

"Really?" Cat's cheeks reddened. "That would be great. I don't want to ask my mom or Nick. They'd both help me out, no question, but..." She gripped her bag and slid down in the chair.

Luc's heart squeezed. She was embarrassed to ask her family for help, like he'd have been embarrassed asking his. Except, that would never be an issue because he had more money than he could spend in one lifetime. Money to finance the creamery expansion his dad had talked about for years, and to send his folks on that cruise they'd hankered after but could never afford because of the cost of raising four kids and putting most of them through college. Money for everything except what mattered most—taking care of his wife and their child like he'd planned.

"Pay for the hockey registration when your grant comes through." He tried to smile. "I know you're good for it."

"Thanks." Cat's voice cracked and she took one hand away from her bag to rub it across her face. "Hockey means everything to Amy. I want her to be able to play, but she's growing so fast right now."

"Hockey's an expensive sport." He slid an arm around her shoulders and gave her a little squeeze. The same kind of friendly squeeze he'd given her all those times back in high school when she'd saved his butt in chemistry. Before today, however, his fingers had never tingled when he'd touched Cat. His body had never heated, either.

Cat started and pulled away at the same instant he did. "Hockey can be a dangerous sport, too, and now Amy will be playing with boys. She hasn't played with boys since she was seven. She could get hurt."

Like he had, hurt so bad it had ended his career. "Amy's playing minor hockey. At her age, there is a rule about no body checking." He tried to make his tone reassuring. "I promise I'll keep a close eye on her." It was his job as her coach, and he'd do the same for any kid. It had nothing to do with the strange and unexpected attraction he all of a sudden had for this woman he'd known his whole life, whom he'd never really looked at until today.

A woman who wasn't Maggie. Luc's stomach clenched in a tangled lump of guilt and grief, tied tight with a slippery ribbon of disloyalty. Maggie was never coming back, but that didn't mean Luc could forget her. Or that he wanted to.

Chapter Two

❦

Cat pressed the bell-shaped cookie cutter into the rolled-out dough and reminded herself to breathe. It was only her third day back in Firefly Lake. Once Nick and Mia's wedding was over and she and Amy were more settled, life would be normal again. At least a new version of normal.

"Who'd have thought we'd end the year with a wedding?" From the scrubbed pine table in Harbor House's spacious country kitchen, her mom gestured with a wooden spoon. "I can't remember the last time I was so excited. When did my whole family ever come here for New Year's?"

"I don't know." Cat replaced the bell with a cutter shaped like a wedding dress. "When I was a kid, maybe." Before her dad had left and hadn't come back. Her chest got tight. As soon as she finished this last batch of cookies, she could go home for a few hours before the wedding rehearsal. If she was in her own little apartment, despite the boxes still piled everywhere, she wouldn't feel so on edge, caught up in a vortex of memories as relentless as mosquitoes in a Vermont summer.

"What if your aunt forgets to bring the necklace with her?" Her mom's blue eyes were worried. "It's not like she'll have enough time to drive all the way back to Montreal to get it at the last minute."

"You already texted her twice this morning, but if you want, Amy and I could meet her at the Canadian border to make sure she has it." And if she was driving the road north, Cat could try to pretend for a few hours that her problems were far behind her. However, although being in Firefly Lake made her remember things she'd vowed to forget, those things were rooted in life, not geography. No matter how far or how long she drove, she couldn't escape them.

Her mom's laugh rippled out. "You always were my helpful girl." She joined Cat beside the wooden pastry board made by an uncle many generations removed. "I want everything to be perfect for Nick and Mia. Every bride in my family, since your great-grandmother's day, has worn that pearl necklace."

"The wedding *will* be perfect, and Mia will look beautiful with or without the necklace." Cat wrapped an arm around her mom's thin shoulders. "For all Nick cares, Mia could wear a T-shirt and yoga pants to marry him."

Her mom laughed again. "Thankfully, Mia has more sense. She's like another daughter to me, and I've never been able to help plan a wedding for one of you kids before." Her mom put a hand to her mouth. "I'm sorry. Not that you...you know what I mean."

"It's okay. Marriage isn't my thing, but it is for Nick."

And Cat would be there for her big brother like he'd always been there for her. "Maybe someday Georgia will settle down and give you a chance to be a mother of the bride."

Her mom's expression was wry. "I doubt your sister will ever settle down or do anything as conventional as get married, but seeing your brother so happy is a dream come true. As is having you and Amy in Firefly Lake, although I still don't see why the two of you can't stay here with me, at least until you find your feet. Even if Georgia sticks around for a while, this house is more than big enough for all of you. Ward travels so much he isn't here for more than a few weeks at a time. And Luc's so quiet, you'd hardly know he's around."

Cat bit her lower lip and sprinkled flour across the board. She liked Ward, her mom's partner, but it would still be weird to live in the same house with him. As for Luc, her mom was wrong. Thanks to that hyperawareness she'd always had where he was concerned, she'd know exactly where he was. As Amy's coach, she'd already see way too much of him. She didn't need to bump into him on her way to brush her teeth or when making a cup of tea.

"It's not you, or Ward, or Luc. Amy and I need our own place, that's all. Besides, I need a space where I can work." She gripped the rolling pin to stop her hands from shaking. She was a grown-up. Although she loved her mom and didn't want to disappoint her, if she moved back to Harbor House, a part of her might become that little girl she'd worked so hard to leave behind.

"I understand." Her mom gave her a sad smile before she slid the sheet of cookies Cat had cut out into the oven.

"Are you sure Amy doesn't want to be a junior brides-maid? She'd look so sweet in one of those pink dresses Mia chose for her girls." Her voice brightened. "Mia ordered one in Amy's size in case she changed her mind."

Cat bit back a sigh. "Amy's happy handling the guest book. It would've been a battle to get her into any dress, unless it somehow incorporated a hockey jersey." If only she understood Amy better, she could help her more, but she didn't, and most of the time she was parenting by trial and error. By the time she figured out what Amy needed, her daughter had moved on and there was a new challenge.

"Girls of Amy's age need to be able to make some of their own decisions. It gives them confidence. That's how I tried to raise you and your sister, anyway." Her mom's expression was hesitant.

"You were a great mom to us. You still are. I should tell you so more often." Cat's voice hitched. Although she was doing fine now, her mom's cancer diagnosis had rocked their family to the core and reshaped it into a new pattern. A better one, though, because although Cat still ached with the knowledge of what she could have lost, for the first time in years she and her brother and sister were really talking to each other, as well as to their mom.

"You have a lot of years left to tell me." Her mom's eyes twinkled beneath the soft waves of silver hair that brushed her eyebrows. "I'm going to call your aunt. Josette has always been scatterbrained. If she doesn't put that necklace in her purse while I'm talking to her, I'll be sending you to the border for me for sure."

After the kitchen door shut behind her mother with a gentle whoosh, Cat looked out the window above the counter into the winter wonderland beyond. It had snowed again overnight, and the trees near the house were gowned in white like a quartet of statuesque brides. She shivered and turned back to check the oven temperature. She could handle living in Firefly Lake again for a little while. And no matter how long it took, she was here for Amy and her mom, too.

The back door banged open and frosty air whirled into the kitchen. "Gabrielle? I went out to the tree farm and got those spruce wreaths for the church doors. I left them on the porch until...oh, Cat." Luc's cheeks were tinged red with cold, and he stamped his snowy boots on the mat inside the door.

"Mom went to make a phone call. She should be back soon." The timer dinged, and Cat grabbed a pair of oven mitts. "Amy took Pixie for a walk, and Nick's in Burlington picking up Georgia from the airport."

Too much information. Georgia, the baby of the family, was the chatterbox, while Cat had always been the quiet middle child. She shut her mouth fast, then opened the oven door and bent to slide out the cookie sheet to hide her face.

Luc pulled off his boots and slung his parka on a kitchen chair before he padded across the kitchen toward her in his sock feet. "It sure smells good in here."

Cat's stomach flipped and she fumbled with the cookies. A wedding bell slid off to land on the tiled floor.

"Oops." Luc scooped it up and ate it. "Five-second rule."

"These cookies are for the wedding rehearsal party." Cat moved cooling racks aside to make space for the new batch.

"Oh, sorry." Luc gave her a smile that was a little bit rueful and way too endearing. The same smile he'd given her all those years ago when he'd sat on her Care Bear at playgroup. The pink Cheer Bear that had gone everywhere with her and helped her to look on the bright side, no matter what.

"It's too bad your folks are away." She lifted cookies off the sheet with a spatula, giving the simple task more concentration than it needed.

"Yeah, inconsiderate of my sister to give birth in the middle of the holidays, wasn't it?" His laugh rumbled before he sobered. "Mom's sad about missing the wedding, but nothing can compete with her first grandbaby. She and Dad were on a plane heading to San Francisco almost as soon as my sister went into labor. Mom's wanted to be a grandmother for years."

"So I hear." Like Cat's mom wanted more grandchildren, and Cat wasn't in a position to give them to her. Her heart compressed as she put the last cookie on a rack, ready to join the feast of treats her mom and Mia, her sister-in-law to be, had been baking for days. Not only sugar cookies but oatmeal chews, brownies, Scottish shortbread, and her favorite sweet maple bars made with her mémère's Quebec recipe.

"It must be tough being a single mom." Luc picked up a dirty mixing bowl and rinsed it in the sink.

"I've never not been one." She gave what she hoped was a nonchalant shrug. "I had a good example in my mom." And like her mom, she'd made the best of things because she'd had no choice.

"Still, the way you juggled classes and earned all those degrees along with caring for Amy can't have been easy."

He turned off the tap and started loading the dishwasher. "I bet you're the first person from our high school to get a PhD, let alone from Harvard. That's huge."

Except, books had been Cat's escape from the real world. Unlike people, books were safe, and maybe she'd studied history because everything had already happened and couldn't be changed. It couldn't hurt her, either.

She manufactured a smile. "Aren't you the first person from Firefly Lake to make it as a professional athlete? That's huge too." Amy couldn't stop talking about how Luc would be coaching her, a guy who'd played Olympic hockey, like her daughter dreamed of doing.

"All I ever did was shoot a puck across a sheet of ice." Luc's arm brushed her side as he moved away from the dishwasher, and heat flashed through Cat's body. "Not like you. You're a teacher and you write about important things and important people. I bet you know more about the history of Vermont women than anyone. That's our history, my family and yours."

"You read that newspaper article, didn't you?"

"It was hard to miss." He gave her that smile again that turned her insides to mush and made her forget about scholarly things. "Especially since your mom cut it out and framed it. You didn't see it there on the living room mantel?"

Cat shook her head. "I came in through the back door."

The article had taken up half a page in the *Kincaid Examiner*, the newspaper in the town twenty miles away that also covered Firefly Lake news. As well as talking about the research grant and pretty much everything she'd ever done in school from first grade on, the article had featured a picture of her in her academic robes when she'd been awarded her PhD. Why had her mom shared that particular picture with the reporter? All Luc and everyone else would see was that Cat McGuire was still the brain box she'd always been—still the girl who didn't fit in at Firefly Lake.

"Your mom's proud of you. As for your job, you're lucky. You can do it for as long as you want to." His smile slipped away.

She could if only she could find something permanent and didn't have to rely on temporary contracts. "I guess so."

From Luc's perspective, though, she *was* lucky. Her job was quiet and safe. When she wasn't teaching, she spent her life in libraries and archives. An errant book wouldn't end her career like a dirty hit had ended his. Yet, these days, permanent university jobs for people with humanities PhDs were as scarce as NHL players over thirty-five. Maybe she and Luc had more in common than she thought.

"It must be hard not playing in the league this season." She took the empty cookie sheets he held out and made sure her fingers didn't brush his.

"It's life." He grabbed paper towels from the holder, wiped the counter, and avoided her gaze. "Even if I hadn't blown out my shoulder, I'd have had to retire in the next year or so anyway. It's time I helped with the creamery. Mom and Dad sacrificed a lot for my hockey and they aren't getting any younger. They're glad to have me back. I'm spending this winter learning the business."

"I'm sure you'll do well." Luc did everything well. Not only was he a superb athlete, but he was a good student, class president, and everybody's friend. The kind of all-rounder that women, as well as college admissions committees, loved.

She swallowed hard and shoved the last cookie sheet into the dishwasher. She had oodles of academic skills and had gained parenting savvy because she had to. But as far as relationship skills went, she was stuck batting zero—a streak that wasn't likely to change anytime soon.

Half the people were talking in French, and Amy's mom was jabbering away along with them, huddled with her grandma and a tiny, gray-haired woman Amy was supposed to call Aunt Josette.

Amy edged around the buffet table and out of the big dining room at Harbor House, a plate heaped with food balanced in one hand and a can of soda in the other. If she could make it across the living room and into the little alcove with the TV, she could catch part of the Pittsburgh-Edmonton game.

"Amy?" Her aunt Mia, who was marrying her uncle Nick the next day, stopped her beside the piano. "Where are you off to all by yourself?"

"Finding a place to eat." Amy tried to look innocent. Her mom had asked her to make an effort, but how could she be expected to talk to people who couldn't be bothered to speak English? "The dining room's packed."

"With lots of relatives you only just met and most of them speaking a language you don't understand." Aunt Mia smiled. Not only was her new aunt gorgeous, she was kind, and Amy already loved her. "Why don't you join Kylie in here?" She gestured toward the alcove where Amy had been headed. "After the rehearsal, she needed a break, too."

With a grateful look at her aunt, Amy slipped into the small space and perched on the end of a sofa. Kylie, Uncle Nick and Aunt Mia's foster daughter, was sprawled on the other end playing a game on her tablet.

"Hey." Kylie gestured to a plate piled high with brownies and assorted cookies. "Help yourself. I stocked up."

"Thanks." Before today, Amy had only met Kylie once, but she liked her. Kylie had worn jeans and a sweater to the wedding rehearsal—normal, everyday clothes. Her blond hair was pulled back in a messy ponytail and it was normal hair. If the scattered plates were any indication, she also ate like a normal girl.

"Do you speak French?" Kylie set her tablet aside and popped a brownie into her mouth.

"Nope." Getting English right was enough of a challenge.

"Me neither." Kylie swallowed a chunk of brownie. "I have to learn Spanish at school this year and like why?" She rolled her eyes.

Amy started to smile, then stopped. Her mom already spoke English and French and wanted to learn Italian for fun. She also said knowing other languages was important in understanding other cultures. Amy would have agreed with her if languages—and everything except hockey—hadn't been so hard for her to learn.

"I know." Kylie grinned and her green eyes twinkled. "Mia and my dad would be pissed if they heard me say so, but you have to admit that learning a foreign language in Firefly Lake is about as useless as learning geometry. And geometry's useless anywhere, unless you're a math genius."

Amy liked this girl more and more. "Your dad, do you mean my uncle Nick?"

"He's the only dad I know. I sort of adopted him." Kylie dug in the pocket of her jeans for a pack of gum and held it out. "Unlike Mia, he doesn't have any other kids. Since I never had a dad, it works out great."

Amy took a stick of gum and set it on the side of her plate. "I don't have a dad, either." And she'd only seen one blurry picture of him, so that didn't count. She didn't have a dad in any of the ways that were important.

"That sucks." Kylie gave Amy's arm a rough pat. "Do you want a dad?"

"I don't know." It had always been just her mom and her, but lately it was like something was missing. Amy couldn't miss what she'd never had, though, could she?

"Even though he's still learning about it, Nick's a great dad." Kylie leaned closer. "Since he and Mia aren't gonna have any kids of their own, I'll always be the only one he has that's all his. He says that makes me extra special. Now you're living in Firefly Lake, I bet he'll come to stuff at school for you. He's good that way."

Amy's chest knotted. Nick was a great uncle, too, and no matter how busy he was with his job as a lawyer, he still called her every few weeks and remembered her birthday. Whenever he came to Boston on business, he took her to a hockey game, to see a movie, or out for a burger. But by this time tomorrow, he'd have his own forever family—Mia and her two daughters, as well as Kylie.

Her mom might say she didn't need a dad, or that no dad was better than a bad one, but Amy knew better. A lot of who she was came from that dad who'd died before her mom could tell him she was pregnant. Since she couldn't have him back, maybe she needed to find someone else like Kylie had.

She dug her fork into the pasta salad her mom had made especially for the rehearsal party. It was Amy's favorite, and her mom didn't have time to make it very often. "When you said that you adopted Nick, what did you mean exactly?"

If Amy figured it out, maybe she could do the same thing. And she had the perfect guy in mind. Coach Luc would be even better than Uncle Nick, at least for her.

Chapter Three

❧

Fourteen years ago, Luc had said the same vows that Nick and Mia had made to each other earlier, and he'd meant every word of them. But death had parted him and Maggie a lot sooner than either of them could have imagined.

He took a long pull on his beer and scanned the ballroom at the Inn on the Lake, the Victorian hotel outside town nestled beside Firefly Lake. Twinkling white lights were strung from one side of the room to the other, and a big spruce decorated in white and silver stood guard by the head table. Nick and Mia had cut their wedding cake in front of that tree half an hour ago. As soon as they left, he could leave, too. And put the memories that had needled him all day back where they belonged.

"You look like you're coming down with something." Liz Carmichael, an older family friend with a reedy, Vermont lilt and bleached blond hair piled on top of her head in a complicated twist, who worked at the North Woods

Diner, slid into the empty chair next to his. She eyed his uneaten piece of cake and frowned. "I thought you looked peaked in church, and you look even worse now. Your skin's real pasty. I'd have texted your mother, but Chantal's so excited about your sister's baby I didn't want to worry her."

"I'm good." Luc tried to smile. "I'm just tired. Between the creamery and coaching, I'm working a lot."

Liz covered his cold hand with her warm one. "This wedding must make you think of your Maggie. As I said to your mom back then, Maggie was the sweetest bride I'd ever seen, and the two of you were so happy. You had a perfect match with that girl. It was a real tragedy what happened."

"Yeah, it was." All of a sudden, Luc found it hard to breathe.

"Even so, neither Maggie nor your mother would want you sitting here moping." Liz gave his hand a comforting squeeze.

"I'm not moping." That was what little kids did. He was a thirty-five-year-old man doing his best to move on with his life.

"So, why haven't you eaten your cake?" Liz's brown eyes were kind. "You hardly touched your dinner either, and your folks didn't raise you to let good food go to waste."

Luc let out a shallow breath. He cared about Liz and, apart from his family, she knew him about as well as anybody did. However, one of the disadvantages of living in the small town where you'd grown up was that people had long memories and didn't hesitate to look out for you, even when you didn't need it. "I'm not hungry."

Liz dug in her sparkly evening bag and brought out a package of saltine crackers wrapped in cellophane. "You shouldn't be drinking on an empty stomach. Here, you used to gobble up these crackers when you were little. If you're feeling queasy, they'll settle your stomach lickety-split." She pushed the package into his hand.

In Luc's world, one beer didn't constitute drinking, but he took the crackers and made himself smile. "Thanks, but I'm not queasy, either. I'll eat something later. There's a fridge full of food from the rehearsal party at Gabrielle's house. I won't starve."

From the dance floor with his new wife, Nick raised a dark eyebrow and grinned. His friend looked happier than Luc had ever seen him. Yet, although Luc was glad for Nick and Mia, their happiness made him remember, in painful detail, everything he'd lost.

"Liz?" Cat appeared at the older woman's side. In her filmy, dark-red bridesmaid's dress she looked younger and less serious than usual. "There's a man over there who I bet would like to dance with you. Why don't you ask him?" Over Liz's head, she gave Luc a half-smile.

"Who?" Liz turned toward Cat, and Luc slipped the crackers into his jacket pocket.

"My new landlord, Michael Kavanagh." Cat's smile widened.

"Why would he want to dance with me?" Liz's tone was disbelieving. "He owns the gallery, and that artsy-crafty stuff is way beyond me. You know that painting he's got in the window, the one with those red and black streaks and yellow tape? It's as good as a crime scene in the middle of Main Street, but he's asking a thousand dollars for it."

Cat patted Liz's shoulder. "I don't like that painting

either, but Michael's planning a quilting exhibition for the summer and he wants your help because you're the best quilter in Firefly Lake. He says quilting is an art as well as a craft. He also told me you make the best coffee in town and your bran muffins are perfection." Her blue eyes sparkled, and Luc caught his breath at how that sparkle transformed her face.

"I've known Michael since high school, but he..." Liz put a hand to her hair and smoothed it. "I...he sure was a good dancer back in the day."

"You're a good dancer, too, so go on." Cat's expression softened. "It's only one dance, isn't it?"

"I guess so." Liz gathered up the skirt of her party dress and moved toward Michael, who sat at a table by himself near one of the big windows that overlooked the frozen Firefly Lake.

"Thanks." Luc looked up at Cat, tiny even in her heels.

"Liz is a nice woman, and she'd have made a wonderful mom, but you had the same look on your face Nick gets when she bears down on him. Cornered and in need of rescuing." Cat's chuckle was throaty and engaging. "Besides, Michael loves to dance and, although I've only been here a short time, he's always over at the diner. One man can only drink so much coffee or eat that much bran, if you get my drift."

"You're a nice woman, too." And when Luc was around Cat, he felt a bit like the man he used to be.

"I like making people happy."

"You always did." Funny how he'd forgotten that about her. He gestured and Cat sat beside him.

"I grew up with the Care Bears, remember?" Her face got a wistful expression.

"I sure do. How's Cheer Bear doing these days?" That soft pink bear was as much a part of the little girl he remembered as her glasses, long blond hair, and the stack of library books she'd toted around with her everywhere.

"He's fine." She put a hand to her mouth.

"Don't worry, your secret's safe with me. I probably have a few old G.I. Joe figures around somewhere. My mom kept a lot of stuff for those grandchildren she was hoping for." And now his kid sister had a baby boy, the best holiday gift ever, his mom said when he'd talked to her earlier.

He glanced toward the dance floor. Nick still had Mia wrapped in his arms. Gabrielle danced with Ward, and Mia's sister, Charlie, was cuddled up with her husband, Sean, who owned the marina where Luc kept his boat. Even Cat's sister, Georgia, was attempting to teach a waltz to Josh Tremblay, who ran the local plumbing and heating store.

"Hey." He took a deep breath. "Do you want to dance? Everyone else is, and if we don't join in, they'll think we're unsociable." In Firefly Lake, being unsociable, if not a certifiable crime, was enough to make people talk and maybe even call you an "odd duck."

"I'm not really a dancer, but sure...okay." Cat worried her bottom lip.

"I won't step on your feet. Back when she thought she might turn her kids into figure skaters like her, my mom taught my sisters and me how to dance." Luc got up and held out his hands.

After several seconds, she put her hands in his. Like the rest of her, Cat's hands were small and, as they moved onto the dance floor, Luc's breath got short. Maggie was the last woman he'd danced with, and that had been at a wedding, too. As he'd held her, Maggie had tucked her head into the crook of his shoulder, and Luc knew he'd love her forever. No other woman could ever come close.

"Luc?" Cat peered at him. Without her glasses, her eyes were even bluer. "We don't have to dance. Nick and Mia will be leaving soon, and I need to get Amy home and into bed. She's had a long day."

He pulled himself back to the present with an effort. "It's fine. I want to dance with you." As she'd told Liz, it was only a dance.

He drew her into his arms, her slight figure so different from Maggie's strong, athletic frame. While his wife had reached his shoulder, the top of Cat's shiny, blond head barely grazed the middle of his chest. His heart tripped at her nearness, and he smelled flowers. Roses, but with an unexpected citrus tang.

"Nick and Mia have had a happy day." Cat's words were a soft murmur, and the bare skin of her shoulder was smooth and warm beneath his hand.

"They sure have." And as he'd watched his friend say his vows, Luc's heart had contracted. Nick's first marriage had ended in divorce, but with Mia he'd found a second chance. However, Nick hadn't left part of his heart beneath a pink granite stone on a dreary November day, and he hadn't lost a part of himself he'd never get back.

As Natalie Cole crooned "Unforgettable," Cat stumbled against him. "See, I told you I'm not a good dancer."

"You just need more practice." Luc steadied her as his mouth went dry. Even though he might want to, he couldn't be the one to give her that practice, but, in the darkness of the dance floor, illuminated only by those little white lights, all the reasons why holding her like this was a bad idea evaporated. Cat was soft, warm, and alive. With that warmth, some of the ice that had encased his heart for the past two years melted, and his body hummed with an almost-forgotten awareness.

The music stopped. Then noisemakers blared and streamers and balloons fell from the ceiling. All around them, laughter and cheers echoed, and outside the ballroom window fireworks lit up the night sky in brilliant technicolor.

"Happy New Year, Luc." Cat tilted her head to look at him.

"*Bonne année*, Catherine." His voice was husky, the intonation of the French words he hadn't spoken for years instinctive. His hand trembled as he brushed her back, and he sucked in a harsh breath.

Her body quivered as she rested her head against his chest. "What are we doing?" Although her voice was low and despite the cacophony, he heard every word.

"I don't know." His heart shifted and all the nerve endings in his body stirred and tingled. But even though he might not know what this was, he knew he had to stop before it went any further.

"Today's been a cross between my biggest nightmare and every cheesy family holiday movie I've ever seen." A sparkly silver hat perched lopsidedly on Georgia's head, and she grinned at Cat, who collected the mountain of dirty plates scattered around the living room at Harbor House in the wake of their mom's New Year's Day buffet brunch. "Wall-to-wall relatives. I ate so much I'm about to burst, and what's with the dog in a dress?"

"Mom got Pixie a special holiday outfit." Cat plucked the Maltese from the nest she'd made out of Aunt Josette's mohair sweater. "I know it may seem unusual but—"

"Unusual." Georgia snorted. "It's downright weird."

"Says the woman who's spent the past six months on top of an Indian mountain chanting most of the day." Cat gave Georgia an answering grin. "She who lives in a glass house should not cast stones."

"It was a retreat and yoga center, and I wasn't chanting, at least not all of the time. I was meditating." Georgia's voice was unexpectedly serious. "You should try it. It helped me figure out a lot about who I am and what I want in life."

"I already know that." Cat's stomach knotted. It was taking her longer to get what she wanted than she expected, but she had a plan. And that plan was based on who she was and what she'd worked toward for years.

"Dressing up Pixie aside, Mom's looking good." Georgia glanced toward the dining room. "She and Ward sure looked all loved-up dancing at the wedding last night."

"They are and Mom *is* good. Seeing her now, I can't believe she was so sick." Cat folded the sweater in a jerky motion. "Having everyone here for the wedding and New Year's is a special gift for her." And for Cat, too, because twelve months ago, she'd worried that her mom wouldn't see another new year.

"It is." Georgia's tone softened. "There sure have been lots of changes while I've been away. Nick's a married man, to a woman who looks like a supermodel, no less, and he's an instant dad to three girls. Mom's got Ward in her life, and Amy's grown so big I hardly recognize her.

And here you are back in Firefly Lake all cozy with Luc Simard."

Despite the new tattoo on her forearm and longer hair, her sister hadn't changed a bit, and the two of them had slipped back into their relationship as if they'd never been apart. Like when they were younger, the instant Cat let down her guard, Georgia landed with military precision on the subject Cat least wanted to talk about.

"I have no idea what you mean." She hugged the sweater to her chest. "Luc's coaching Amy in hockey, and he's living here at Harbor House while his own place is being built. Nothing more."

"So why were the two of you also looking pretty loved-up on the dance floor?" Georgia's blue eyes, a dark blue like Nick's and their dad's, sharpened.

"We had one dance. Everybody else was dancing, so it would have been rude to not join in. Luc only asked me to be polite." Except, for a few minutes, the way he'd held her was intimate and right. Then he'd tensed, moved away, and, as soon as the New Year toast was over, muttered an excuse and left Cat strangely bereft.

"A real hero, isn't he?" Georgia's voice shook with suppressed laughter.

Cat rolled her eyes at her sister. "Even if he weren't still grieving his wife, Luc and I have nothing in common. Look at him. He's a jock, and I'm out of breath after a gentle bike ride."

"You used to have a crush on him."

"When I was in middle school maybe." Because Luc had looked out for her and protected her from the kids who'd teased her because she was smaller and awkward at sports and being so good at school had set her apart. "Like you had crushes on boys. You danced with one of them last night."

"Please." Georgia made a face and gave a way-too-casual shrug. "Josh Tremblay's still cute, sure, but he didn't know I existed back then. Now, though, he's so not my type. Can you see me with a guy who manages a plumbing and heating business? He has a kid, too, so he must have a lot of baggage going on."

"He's a good guy to know if your furnace fails in the middle of January or your basement floods at three in the morning. He also does a lot for Mom around this house, and I'm sure he doesn't charge her for most of it." Cat's breath hitched. "And so what if he's a dad? From what I've heard, he's a fine man. It's not like any of us get to our thirties without some baggage. You need to be practical."

"And you need to live a little." Georgia scooped up Pixie and eyed Cat over the dog's head. "If you want my opinion, Luc would be a very good guy to live a little with."

"Georgie…" Cat tried to keep the frustration out of her voice. "My life's okay, really. With the research grant, I won't have to teach for the next two semesters, so I can finally finish my book. If I finish the book and write a few more articles, I'll have a better chance of getting a permanent job. And Amy needs me even more than usual right now. School's hard for her, like it was for you, and now she has to cope with a new school. I want to help her all I can."

"You're a good mom. You're also good at your job and you're responsible." Georgia's voice was flat and she fiddled with Pixie's collar. "You're everything I'm not. I had no right to tease."

"You're a lot of things I'm not. Good things. You're spontaneous and fun, and you wear your heart on your sleeve." Cat set the sweater on a side table and reached around the dog to give her sister a hug. "It's the wedding and a new year. Too much emotion. I'm glad you're home, Georgie."

"Me too." Georgia set Pixie back on the footstool and returned Cat's hug. "I'm sticking around, at least for a while. I talked to the night manager at the Inn on the Lake, and they're looking for another fitness teacher at the spa. If I apply, I might have a good chance of getting the job."

"That's great." Cat held her sister tight, as if she could somehow also bridge the years they'd been apart.

"It's not fair for Nick to always have to keep an eye on Mom. Even before you moved here, you came up from Boston every few weeks. I should do my share." Georgia's voice caught. "Besides, I missed you guys, you know?"

"We missed you, too." Although coming back to Firefly Lake wouldn't have been what Cat would have chosen, maybe the grant had come at a good time.

"Did you talk to Dad before the holidays?" Her sister's generous mouth narrowed. "Nick didn't invite him to the wedding, and that must have hurt."

"Like Dad hasn't hurt us?" Cat's mouth went dry. "I didn't talk to him, and I don't want him to be part of Amy's life. I don't trust him." Her voice faltered, and her body got that familiar numb heaviness.

"I think he's sorry for what he did." Georgia twisted

her hands together. "Nick may not have wanted him at the wedding, but he still talks to Dad every few months."

"Nick can do what he wants. So can you." Cat pressed a hand to her chest. "I don't want anything to do with Dad."

"I guess there would have been a lot of talk if he'd turned up at the wedding." Georgia's voice was soft and, for her bubbly sister, almost tentative.

Cat bit back a harsh laugh. "It'd have ruined Nick and Mia's day. Mom's family would have run him out of town for how he treated her, and that's before the folks in Firefly Lake he cheated out of money got hold of him. The only reason Nick talks to Dad is because it reminds him of who he doesn't want to be."

And Cat didn't need that reminder. Her dad had left exactly three months before her seventh birthday. She'd grown up without him, and she wasn't in any danger of becoming like him. The only thing his desertion had done was make her more independent and resilient— determined to not count on anyone, especially a man. She straightened her shoulders and sucked in her cheeks.

"Nick could never be like Dad." Georgia's lower lip wobbled like it had when she was little.

"Of course not." Cat's voice was sharper than she intended. She stopped and took several breaths. "What I meant is I think Nick needs closure, especially because he's now a dad. You were so young when Dad left, you don't remember as much, but Nick was older and he and Dad were close. Nick looks a lot like I remember Dad looking, too."

The charming, handsome man who'd called Cat his little princess and whom she'd idolized. The man who

thought she was smart and pretty and told her she could
do anything she set her mind to. Which she had, and she
hadn't needed him to do it, either. She stared at her hands.
Even though she was an adult, the years hadn't dimmed
those childhood memories or made them any less painful.

"I can't talk to him, Georgie." She swallowed the lump
lodged at the back of her throat.

"I think I should, but I can't seem to either." Her sister
gave Cat a sad smile. "But maybe because of him, here
we are both in our thirties and still on our own."

"I'm single because I want to be." Cat's stomach
churned. Maybe if she said it often enough, she'd believe
it. The same way she told herself those bewildering feelings for Luc were nothing more than the residue of her
childhood crush. Her heartbeat was loud in her ears.

"I'm single because no guy would put up with me. I'm
too spontaneous and fun." Georgia's laugh was hollow.

"No, you're not." She made her tone bright. "Someday
you'll meet someone who appreciates you and—"

"Mom?" Cat swiveled at Amy's voice. "Coach Luc's
organizing a road hockey game. You have to come and
play. You too, Aunt Georgia." Her daughter's tone was
hopeful.

Although Cat had planned to spend the rest of the afternoon with a book and a box of Lindt, she couldn't
let Amy down. After all, if she was truly going to help
her daughter, Amy needed to see firsthand something Cat
wasn't good at.

"Sure, honey. I'll be right there as soon as I put on
some warmer clothes." If she could find them, knee pads
and a bicycle helmet might also come in handy.

"I should check on Mom. She and Aunt Josette probably need help with the dishes and..." Georgia's voice trailed off as she sidled toward the dining room.

"Oh, no you don't." Cat took her sister's arm in a firm grip. "If I'm going out there, you are too. No excuses."

"I was in India only a few days ago. It's a very hot country." Her sister gestured to her gauzy, beaded top. "It's freezing outside. I'll catch a cold."

"You catch a cold from a virus, not from being outside in the winter. I'm sure Mom has a pair of long underwear and a sweater you can borrow." Cat steered Georgia in the direction of the stairs. "We Vermont girls are tough."

And Cat would need every bit of that toughness to pick up a hockey stick in front of Luc. The man who'd taken off after their dance last night like he was chasing a breakaway puck in the last minute of the Stanley Cup final.

Chapter Four

❧

Luc had missed this crisp, pine-scented air and the sharp crunch of snow under his boots. He'd also missed the clear blue of the sky, like an overturned bowl above his head, and how the sun glittered off the rolling white landscape. And down to his bones, he'd missed this view of the town of Firefly Lake laid out below Harbor House like a gingerbread village nestled between icing sugar-dusted hills.

He'd spent the last two years of his NHL career in Winnipeg, so it wasn't like he hadn't had winter in abundance. But he hadn't had this kind of winter. Or maybe it was this kind of day. One that took him back to his childhood, when he'd pulled his sled down this same street and skated on the rink his dad had made in their backyard every winter. A day where, thanks to Gabrielle's Quebec family, there'd been the same cheerful babble of English and French he'd grown up with. The same *tourtière* too, the succulent meat pie snug in its golden-brown pastry that was as much a part of his album of holiday memories as pond hockey and ice fishing.

"My mom will be right out." Amy skidded to a stop beside him, bundled up in a blue ski jacket, matching pants, and a fluffy white hat and scarf. "You need to go easy on her, though, because she's not real athletic. Maybe we could help her score a goal? What do you think?"

"Sure." Luc smiled at the girl who, even at twelve, was already taller and sturdier than Cat.

"I absolutely can't wait until next Saturday." Amy's crooked smile made Luc smile back.

"Why?" Whenever he'd thought about having kids, he'd imagined rough-and-tumble boys, but there was something about this girl with her button nose and passion for hockey that touched a part of him he hadn't known was there.

"My first practice with you, of course." Amy looked at him with a trusting expression. "I didn't want to move here because of leaving my team in Boston, but being coached by you makes up for a whole lot. I still can't believe it."

Luc couldn't either. He'd agreed to help Coach MacPherson as a favor last August, but, all of a sudden, he was running the whole show. "This is my first time as a head coach."

"You'll be great." Amy waved away any objections he might have made. "I bet the kids will listen to everything you say because you played in the NHL and the Olympics. If they don't, I'll take care of them."

"Thanks." He pushed down the laugh because there was something sweet about this girl wanting to stand up for him.

"I mean it. My mom says you have to stop the bullies and tell other people what's happening." Amy's light blue eyes clouded and her chin trembled. "Like you did with that guy who hit you. He got suspended and fined. You have to speak out, even if you're a kid, or it's hard, and you feel stupid."

The hit from a brash young enforcer had ended Luc's career. Or maybe it was the last hit in a career full of hits that had made the difference. His chest got heavy. He'd never know and, no matter how much he relived what had happened—all the could haves, might haves, and shoulds—it wouldn't change the outcome. "Your mom's right." Luc would like to take care of the boy or girl who'd put the sad and almost defeated look in Amy's eyes. "If anybody on the team here doesn't treat you right, you have to tell me, promise?"

"I promise." She tugged her hat over her eyebrows. "Here's Mom now." Her voice was a high-pitched whisper. "You remember what I said about the goal?"

"Sure." He bumped his stick against Amy's, then sucked in a breath as Cat came toward him. The sun turned the hair beneath her knit cap into a band of gold and, in her white parka topped with a pink scarf, she was a sexy snow queen instead of the familiar Cat McGuire he'd known all his life.

"Coach?"

"What?" He dragged his attention back to Amy.

"Are you okay?" Her voice was quizzical.

"Fine. I must have eaten too much of that *tourtière*." He tried to laugh and failed. "Your grandma's a fantastic cook."

"My mom made the *tourtière*, not Grandma." As Amy

studied him, something flickered in her eyes that Luc couldn't read.

"Then she's a fantastic cook, too." Luc bent his head to check the tape on his stick.

Cat was not only smart, she was beautiful and could make a traditional French Canadian meat pie as good as his mom's, maybe even better. Although a big piece of his heart might be dead and buried, the rest of him wasn't, given how he'd reacted to her over the last few days. She unsettled him more than any woman since Maggie, but in a whole different way than Maggie had.

"Amy says you want to play some hockey?" Cat's expression was as resolute as it was scared. "You probably remember I'm not really sporty."

"It's only a fun game. We'll take it easy." He tried to make his tone reassuring, even as his pulse sped up. "Your mom's cousins are playing, and those guys are in their sixties and seventies."

"One of those guys was a champion speed skater in his day, and another's so competitive his wife won't even go out for a friendly night of bowling with him." As Cat shook her head, the pom-pom on her hat bounced in a way that was both cute and sexy. "Appearances can be deceiving."

And wasn't that ironic, because Cat's appearance had deceived Luc for years. Or maybe he'd never really looked at her until this week. He grabbed a hockey stick from the pile stacked under a tree and handed it to her. "You can be on my team. Since Nick's already left on his honeymoon, I'll look out for you."

If he looked out for her like he always had, like she was Nick's kid sister, he could ignore her surprisingly curvy butt outlined in dark jeans beneath the hem of her jacket. He could also ignore her smile that was sweeter than any of the treats that had graced Gabrielle's New Year's table. And he could make himself forget how Cat's soft blond hair lit up his world more brightly than any of the candles that had decorated Nick and Mia's wedding reception.

"You've got your work cut out for you." Georgia, a tall brunette, who was a younger, feminine version of Nick, jogged down the walk and stopped at Cat's side. "Cat's the only person I know who can get hurt even watching sports. Remember when she went to get snacks at Nick's high school basketball game and tripped over Mom's purse? She fractured two toes." She flashed her sister a teasing grin. "That kept her out of gym class for the next month, which, for Cat, was a good thing."

Cat looked half amused, half irritated. "Some people aren't naturally athletic. I'm one of them."

"There's a sport for everyone. A lot of folks just take longer to find theirs." Luc turned Cat's hockey stick the right way around, and her gaze caught his and held.

Maybe it was New Year's magic or being back in Firefly Lake in the winter after all these years. Or maybe it had nothing to do with the season or the place and everything to do with the woman. But in that instant, and as Luc met Cat's steady blue gaze, almost everything he thought about himself and what he wanted imperceptibly shifted and changed—maybe forever.

Cat brushed fluffy snow off the garden bench that she, Nick, and Georgia had given their mom for her sixtieth birthday, then set her mug of tea on one of its flat, broad arms. She'd gotten through both the wedding and a big family New Year's, so maybe the ghosts of her past were well and truly banished.

She looked at the chubby moon that cast silver light across her mom's garden and threw the dark trees near Harbor House into sharp relief. At the bottom of the terraced gardens, snow had drifted across the frozen lake to form peaks and furrows like the whipped cream atop Aunt Josette's old-time Quebec sugar pie.

Sitting on the bench, she let the night soak into her. It was colder here than in Boston, and quieter. No sirens for a start, but no other traffic noise, either. It was so still that when the clock on the town hall struck eight, the sound reverberated off the dark hills. Cat's breathing slowed. Nick was happy with Mia. Her mom was healthy and happy with Ward, and if Amy wasn't happy yet, she was at least settling in better in Firefly Lake than Cat had expected.

Only because of Luc. The thought skittered away. She should be glad Luc could help her daughter.

"I thought you'd still be in front of the fire with a book, not out here."

Cat started at Luc's deep voice behind her. "Too many of my relatives decided the perfect place for them to play Monopoly was by that living room fireplace. I'm taking a breather." She tried to laugh. "What are you doing?"

"After the third card game, I went for a run to work off some of the food your mom and aunt insisted I eat." He sat beside her and grinned. "I've never met a card shark like Amy. That kid's a fiend. If we'd been playing for real money, I'd have lost half my investment portfolio. I left before she cleaned me out entirely."

"Sorry." A laugh bubbled up and escaped before Cat could stop it.

Luc laughed too. "Don't be. She's a great kid. I'm looking forward to seeing her on the ice. Even playing road hockey, she was impressive." He shifted on the bench, and his legs were long and lean in black athletic pants. "You did great, too."

"Not great, but I did okay because you helped me." Cat's mouth went dry and she pulled her gaze away from Luc's muscular thighs. "You even distracted the goalie to let me score that goal." She picked up her tea to steady her hands. "I had fun, though, and sports are never fun for me. I was the kid who read a book in the outfield when we played baseball in elementary school. I always hoped some superjock like you wouldn't hit the ball my way."

He looked at her in disbelief. "I see I have to take you in hand."

Cat gulped a mouthful of hot tea and choked. It had been too long since she'd talked with a man about anything but work. That was the only reason why a perfectly innocent comment made her heart bang against her ribs so loud she was sure he could hear it. Luc meant he could help her as a friend, not that he wanted to put his hands on her, literally.

"Hey." Luc thumped her back. "Are you okay?"

"Yes." The word came out between a sputter and a cough.

"Here, you don't want to burn yourself." He took her mug and set it back on the arm of the bench. "You never had a chance to be good at sports. I'm not judging you."

"I know." Her voice was husky and she coughed again. She'd judged herself, and maybe she'd overcompensated with academics because school was the only thing she was good at. Unlike Nick, who hadn't seemed to try but still sailed through school and was good at sports, too. Or Georgia, who'd barely scraped through school, but who'd excelled at gymnastics and dance and never cared what anyone thought of her.

And unlike her dad, who'd been the high school football hero and whose name was undoubtedly still on all those shields in the glass case outside the principal's office. Not only football, but he'd played baseball and hockey, and he'd been a daredevil on downhill skis. Back then, if there was an athletic trophy in Firefly Lake to be won, her dad had won it. He'd been a winner in everything, except when it came to his family. Her throat got scratchy, and she curled her hands inside her wooly mittens until her fingernails dug into her palms.

"Hey." Luc patted her shoulder. His touch lingered, and despite the barrier of his gloves and her parka, her body tingled. "Even if you don't get hurt like I did, most professional athletes have a pretty short career. Then you have to figure out what you want to do with the rest of your life." His voice got flat and he stared into the distance.

That was why Cat wanted something different for Amy. Something safe, secure, and ordinary. "You have a college degree, and you had a job waiting for you at the creamery to fall back on."

Amy might not be able to make it through high school, let alone college. And the only family business for her to fall back on was a small-town law office. Although Nick had turned McGuire and Pelletier around, it wasn't on the scale of Simard's Creamery, which had customers all across New England.

"I'm one of the lucky ones. My folks insisted I finish college before I played in the NHL, and they also built a thriving business." There was a smile in his voice. "As they never cease to remind me, in case pro hockey made me soft and I forget to appreciate the value of doing a day's hard work in the real world." He stopped and reached between their feet to scoop up a handful of snow. He packed the snow into a ball, then handed it to her. "Here."

"What?" She held the snowball gingerly in the palm of one mitten.

"No time like the present." He got to his feet and moved away from her to the edge of what, in summer, was a flagstone terrace. "Throw it to me."

"You want to have a snowball fight?" She stood and her stomach flipped. It was like fourth grade all over again.

"No, I want to teach you how to throw a snowball and try a whole bunch of sports so you never have to feel like sports aren't for you. Come on. It'll be fun." His blue eyes were soft in the moonlight, like they'd been all those years ago when he'd picked up her scattered books, zipped them into her pink Care Bear backpack, found the hat the snowball-wielding bullies had grabbed off her head, walked behind her all the way to Harbor House, and then waited until she was safely on the porch.

Her eyes burned. "Nick taught me how to throw a ball." Her big brother had played with her every day for months the year after their dad left. To try to help her fit in, to make her feel special and loved, and to help her forget what she'd lost.

Luc's firm lips tilted into a lopsided grin. "When you threw that birdseed at Nick and Mia when they came out of the church yesterday, you hit the minister right on his bald spot."

"Well..." Her cheeks heated and she sucked in a breath of frosty air mixed with musky male.

Luc had paid attention to her, even though he'd caught her in a klutzy moment.

"You need a refresher course in ball throwing for beginners." Luc's tone teased her. "Besides, it was only thanks to you I passed chemistry our senior year. I missed you once I got to college. Let me return the favor."

Cat's heart pinched. She'd missed Luc, too, but not in the way he'd missed her. To him, she was a lab partner and family friend. Whereas to her, he'd been friend, protector, and first crush rolled into one.

She tossed the snowball toward him, but it went low and hit a patch of ice to shatter on the terrace between them. "See? I'm a hopeless case." She tried to laugh, but the sound was tinny.

"Of course you're not. What would you say if one of your students said something like that?" Luc jogged over to her, another snowball already in hand.

"That's different." She took a step back and bumped into the bench.

"Different how?" Luc tucked the packed snow into her right mitten and held it tight. "In sports or school, you won't succeed unless you keep trying and learning from your mistakes. When it comes to snowball throwing, uplift also helps." His hand guided hers and, like magic, the ball of snow hurtled through the air and came to rest, still intact, on top of a hedge.

"How did you…" Cat flexed her hand in his, then pulled it away.

"I didn't." Luc's smile made her smile back. "We did. Now you try by yourself. The snow's perfect tonight. Wet, but not too wet, and with exactly the right amount of crispness."

There were different types of snow? How had she grown up here and not known that? Cat scooped up another snowy handful and shaped it into a ball. Maybe it was a silly game, but it was also surprisingly fun. After her dad left, she'd had to grow up fast. Then, between raising Amy and school, she hadn't had time to be carefree. "Like this?" She held the snowball out for his inspection.

"Perfect, an A plus." His voice teased her. "Since you're such a competitive type." His eyes gleamed bright blue.

"I'm not." Her heartbeat sped up.

His laugh warmed her. "You have to be competitive to get into Harvard, let alone earn a doctorate. That perfect GPA in our little academic pond was only the start. You should be proud." He jogged toward the hedge, then turned to face her again.

"Yes, well…"

He had a point, but it was only when she got to Harvard that she'd had anybody to compete with.

"Come on. I want to see you throw that snowball."

She tensed before she let the ball of snow fly in a high arc, glittering white in the moonlight. "I did it. See, I…" She clapped a hand over her mouth.

The snowball missed its mark and hit the top of Luc's head, to send a snow shower over his face.

"I'm sorry." She darted to his side. What if she'd broken his nose? Or a tooth? She'd packed that snow pretty hard. It wasn't like hitting kindly Reverend Arthur with a handful of bird seed. She'd hit an Olympian, an NHL all-star, and Firefly Lake's hometown hero. While her research grant had merited a half page inside the *Kincaid Examiner*, Luc Simard was front-page news. His name was even on the "Welcome to Firefly Lake" sign outside town. He was as good as a tourist attraction.

His shoulders heaved and he grunted.

She grabbed his arm and held on to what felt like a solid tree trunk. People didn't always pass out after a blow to the head, did they? "Come and sit down. I'll—"

"No." Luc's shoulders shook harder and what she'd thought was a grunt turned into a laugh so deep and sexy her legs shook.

"You might have a head injury." She clutched his arm tighter.

"From that little tap?" He brushed the last of the snow off his face and his eyes twinkled at her. "Even if you'd put some weight into the throw, you don't have much weight to throw around."

Cat yanked her arm away. "I did so put weight into it. I'm stronger than I look."

"I know you are." His laughter stopped like a candle flame that had been snuffed out. "You're a strong woman, and I'm not talking about physical strength."

"You aren't?" She stared at him, mesmerized by how the moonlight sculpted the blunt angles of his jaw and deep-set eyes.

He shook his head, and when he spoke again, his voice was gruff. "Life has thrown a lot more at you than a few snowballs." He reached out and brushed snowflakes off her coat, his hand lingering near her shoulder before it moved upward to cup her chin. "You never gave up, and I think there's more to you being here than that research grant."

"How…" His fleece glove was soft against her chin, and her skin heated.

"Why else would a high-flier like you move back to Firefly Lake?" He bent toward her. "Sure, you won that grant, but if you'd really wanted to, you could have stayed in Boston and made a few research trips." His warm breath ruffled the tendrils of hair beneath her hat. "But instead, you uprooted your whole life to live in an apartment on Main Street and help Michael out in the gallery."

"I need time to finish my book." It was her stock answer that most people didn't probe further.

"And?" His thumb traced the line of her jaw in a light but sensual caress.

"Amy was having a tough time at school. Firefly Lake Elementary is smaller, and she'll get more individual attention." Cat's mouth went dry as his hand continued its gentle exploration. "As for my mom, she was so sick. We could have lost her, but we didn't. I want to be there for her more than I have been." Her mom's illness had made Cat realize how fragile life was and what her family meant to her.

Luc's hand fell away from her face and he took a step back. She flinched and smoothed the downy front of her parka. "You're a good mom." A shadow flitted across his face, and, for an instant, his expression was troubled. "A good daughter, too." He cleared his throat. "And a good friend. You've always been a good friend to me. Maybe I've never told you that before, but I should have."

"I..." She drew in a sharp breath.

"Thanks for being my friend and making the wedding and everything easier." He stared at her for several endless seconds before he turned away and slipped through the squeaky gate in the hedge into the darkness beyond.

Cat stumbled back to the bench, her legs like jelly. Below Harbor House, Firefly Lake was white and mysterious in the moonlight. Far above, the stars glittered in the inky sky as timeless and unreachable as wishes. "If wishes were horses, beggars would ride." The words of the old nursery rhyme came back to her with the sharpness of a taunt.

She'd been wrong. She hadn't banished the ghosts of her past after all. They were still there as large as life. She'd be foolish to let herself think about what might have happened if Luc hadn't turned away. Or let herself wish for something—and someone—she couldn't have.

Chapter Five

❧

Luc cradled a travel mug of coffee between his hands and leaned against the weathered boards that encircled the ice at Firefly Lake's arena. The place didn't generate the same excitement it had when he was a kid, when the game that had become his life had only been about having fun with his friends, but it was still special. And on this January Saturday morning, like it was back then, hockey practice was still a community event.

He scanned the parka-clad people who packed the battered bleachers and the hum of conversation hushed. He was the coach all right. Although he might be an assistant coach in name, he was here to fill Jim MacPherson's shoes. And although his hometown crowd was friendly, they still had big expectations and were looking to him to deliver. Luc stuffed his hands into the pockets of his sweats as a group of little kids exited the ice beside him in a wobbly line, their skates stiff with newness.

"Takes you back, doesn't it?" Scott Callaghan, the other assistant coach, stood at Luc's shoulder. His hazel eyes twinkled behind rimless glasses and, with the helmet that hid how his sandy hair had thinned on top, he looked a lot like the kid Luc remembered from all the childhood hockey practices they'd shared. He still had that same eager, puppy-dog attitude to life, too.

"It sure does." On the other side of the boards, Scott's wife reached out to steady a tiny girl in a purple snowsuit who'd spent most of her first learn-to-skate lesson on her butt. With his and Maggie's genes, their kid would likely have taken to skating like a natural, but that was another one of those things he'd never know.

"I'm glad you're here to cover my ass." Luc turned away from the little kids and shoved the fragments of what might have been away. "MacPherson's coached for at least twenty years. He's a pro."

"Like you aren't." Scott swatted his arm. "It's not as if you didn't cover my ass back in the day. Who helped me with my wrist shot when my dad and everyone else thought I'd be stuck on the bench for half a season?"

"There was only one of you." Luc swatted back. "Coaching a team is a whole new gig." And Luc was well aware of his limitations.

"Don't sweat it." Scott's tone was warm. "You've taken the coaching training and you're registered with USA Hockey. Although MacPherson's more experienced as a coach, he only played college hockey, not the Olympics or the NHL. The kids look up to you for that alone. I teach sixth and seventh grade. I'll handle anybody who gets out of line." He raised his eyebrows and gave Luc a knowing look. "Your halo is pretty shiny around here. You wouldn't want it to get tarnished, now would you?"

"Cut the crap." Luc let out a breath in an icy cloud. "Most of these guys aren't even thirteen yet."

Scott snorted. "Exactly, bro. I knew you were a fast learner." He grabbed a clipboard from the top of the boards and made a note. "Even though the parents want their kids to win games, minor hockey's about having fun and skill development. There aren't any bench warmers on this team."

"Is that your way of telling me to stay humble?"

"Maybe, but unlike some guys, you never believed your own PR." Scott chuckled. "What about that new girl, Amy McGuire? I hear she's hockey crazy."

"She's Cat's daughter." Luc hesitated. Even though he'd been tempted to kiss Cat, she was a friend. It must have been a temporary bout of insanity brought on by too much of her aunt Josette's lethal eggnog. Yet, despite having his back to the bleachers, Luc was aware of Cat nearby. It was in the little prickle of the hairs on the back of his neck and how his fingers tingled inside his gloves. "Amy played on one of the top girls' teams in her age group in Boston. Her mom's worried about her playing with the boys here. From the little I've seen of her off the ice, she's a feisty kid, so she should cope fine, but can you help me keep an eye on her?"

"Sure. You need eyes in the back of your head with this group." Scott glanced at the players, who milled about on the ice. "Amy's number five, right?"

"Yep." Luc didn't have eyes in the back of his head, and he might be way out of his depth. Maybe this hockey program wasn't in chaos. Maybe chaos was its normal state, and Jim MacPherson was the only guy standing between order and complete anarchy. He scanned the bleachers again and nodded at his first coach, who sat two rows back from center ice. The guy was well into his eighties, but he still came out to every game and most of the practices and wasn't backward in offering advice.

"Here goes nothing." He drained his coffee and set the mug on top of the boards. Then he sucked in a breath of frigid air and brought the coach's whistle to his lips.

"Here goes everything." Laughter lurked in Scott's voice. "Behind that pretty-boy face, you were always a lot smarter than you looked."

With a bunch of kids and their folks in earshot, Luc couldn't tell his friend where to shove it. "Let's warm up," he said instead and clapped his hands. "Forward skating in groups of three."

"No pushing or talking." Scott gave Luc a sideways smile before he turned to the kids in their green and white hockey jerseys.

"Now let's see you skate backward, also in groups of three." Luc glanced at Scott, who made more notes on the clipboard. When he nodded, Luc demonstrated. "Show us some speed and then stop."

Scott encouraged and corrected in turn. Steel skate blades whooshed against the ice, and the sound echoed up into the dark rafters, where several championship pennants fluttered, their once bright blue faded to a tired gray.

"You're the pro, Callaghan, not me." Luc grinned. "If we didn't go way back, your coaching skills would seriously piss me off."

"Watch and learn, hotshot." Scott grinned back. "You think you didn't piss me off back then?" His expression sobered. "You're the spark this hockey program needs. Despite the summer tourists, the past few years since the feed plant closed have been tough around here for a bunch of folks. If MacPherson hadn't gotten local businesses to chip in, some of these kids wouldn't be able to play. Having someone like you coaching their team gives these kids hope. From what I see in my classroom, hope's something a lot of them don't have much of right now."

Despite his fame and the money that went with it, Luc was all too familiar with losing hope. And how it meant you could also stop dreaming and believing in yourself. He swallowed the sudden rawness in his throat. The past was dead and buried, ditto his happy ending. He'd resolved to not think about what might have been.

"You're still a stand-up guy, Callaghan. MacPherson is, too." And Luc was determined he wouldn't let either them or these kids down. "Most of these guys can skate okay, but their passing and puck handling need work. Are you ready to take them through the drills we talked about?" He rubbed his right shoulder and winced.

Scott's gaze zeroed in on Luc's shoulder. "Okay, but..." He hesitated for several endless seconds.

"I'm fine." Luc bent to tighten an already-tight skate lace—and avoid the compassion in his friend's eyes.

"Your shoulder's fine, sure, at least for this kind of workout." Scott dug in his jacket pocket for a puck and sent it spinning down the ice. "And the rest of you will get there." He cleared his throat and when he spoke again, his voice was gruff. "Maggie would be real proud of how you're doing. You're moving on with your life. With this coaching, you're giving back like she did."

Luc gave a jerky nod and sprinted after the puck, his

leg muscles pumping in the rhythm he'd spent most of his life perfecting. How could he think about moving on in anything but the most superficial way? He caught the rubber disc near one of the goal creases and swiveled to a light smattering of applause. That prickle of awareness was back and, when he lifted his head, Cat stared at him. Perched on one end of a bleacher, she wore the same angelic white parka as when they'd played road hockey on New Year's Day. The pink blanket that covered her legs matched the pink in her cheeks and, even at twenty feet, he couldn't miss the gentle curve of her Cupid's-bow mouth.

She held his gaze a fraction longer than necessary, then dropped her head and turned a page in the book that rested on her knees.

Luc fired the puck back to Scott. He couldn't blame whatever this feeling was on Josette's eggnog, a moonlit garden, or temporary insanity. But even if he'd wanted to, he couldn't start anything with the mother of a child he was coaching.

"Okay, let's do a passing drill." He skidded to a stop at center ice and faced the boys and Amy. "We need to work on your accuracy and speed."

Fifty minutes later, Luc rounded the ice one last time and glanced at the clock in the end zone. The practice had flown by, and he'd even earned several approving nods from his old coach.

"Well?" Scott balanced a stack of pucks on top of the boards, where white paint had peeled away to expose raw lumber beneath.

"Thanks." He clapped a hand on his friend's shoulder.

"For what?" Scott arched a sandy eyebrow.

"When MacPherson was here, and I was only helping out, these guys went easy on me." Or maybe, and despite his newly minted coaching certification, he had no coaching skills and he should stick with his day job at the creamery. Either way, he had a new respect for teachers everywhere, starting with the man in front of him.

Scott laughed. "Don't you remember puberty? All those hormones bouncing around sure make life interesting."

Although those awkward adolescent years were thankfully now a hazy memory, if this practice had shown Luc anything, it was that coaching minor hockey wasn't for the faint of heart. Between the antics of the kids on the ice—including breaking up several fights between guys who'd hated each other's guts before they'd ever laced up their skates—and dealing with parents in the stands, who didn't hesitate to add their two cents' worth, he wasn't sure how much real coaching he'd actually done. However, he was as drenched in sweat as if he'd played a league game that had gone into double overtime.

"Tell me we weren't like these kids at that age." Luc gathered up some scattered sticks and waved a few straggling players toward the locker room.

"No can do." Scott's grin was rueful. "And you were worse because you were competitive as hell and skated circles around the rest of us. Growing up with you, it's a wonder I wasn't scarred for life."

"Yeah, right." Luc laughed because Scott was the most balanced guy he knew. Easygoing, but able to kick ass when he needed to, as well as a devoted husband and dad.

"Amy McGuire reminds me a lot of you. Heaps of natural athletic ability, as well as that sixth sense you always seemed to have on the ice, like you knew where the puck was even when you couldn't see it." Scott bounced a puck toward him and Luc caught it one-handed. "She'll be bored with this team. You should give her extra coaching."

"I doubt Cat would go for that." He glanced toward the stands, but Cat's spot in the bleachers was empty. "She's focused on getting Amy settled at school."

And although Cat hadn't said so, Luc suspected she wasn't as keen on hockey as Amy, or as ambitious as most hockey parents were. Amy had enough ambition of her own, though, and when it came to hockey, she was as driven and focused as Cat had been with academics.

"You should still sound her out. Imagine if Amy turned out to be the next big one in US women's hockey. You could play a hand in developing her career." Scott's voice softened. "Think about it. Wouldn't any parent jump at the chance to have you give their kid one-on-one attention?"

Except, as much as Luc wanted to think of her that way, Cat wasn't any parent. She'd sat in the stands with her head in a book for most of the practice. Although she'd looked up occasionally, she'd trusted her daughter and the coaching team to get on with their jobs. But Scott was right. Amy had a special spark a kid either had or didn't, and no amount of work could develop.

Luc had thought about Cat way too much lately. Instead, he should be thinking about her daughter. How he could nurture Amy's talent and maybe make a big difference in her life—the kind of difference Maggie had made with the girls she'd coached; a difference she'd have wanted him to make, too.

Two days later, Cat smoothed one end of the quilt that hung on the rear wall of the Firefly Lake Craft Gallery. From the small town nestled between the green hills, to a covered bridge and a moose family at the edge of a snow-covered lake, the colorful and intricately sewn pieces of fabric captured the Vermont where Cat had grown up. The place that had pulled her back.

She moved behind the vintage teacher's desk, sat in the swivel chair, and powered up her laptop. Although a craft gallery in name, the spacious, light-filled store displayed a range of art too, as well as pottery, handmade furniture, textiles, jewelry, and glass. Outside, snow drifted in lazy flakes from a muted gray sky, and across Main Street, cozy yellow light shone out between the ruffled café curtains at the North Woods Diner. The soothing notes of a flute concerto came from Michael's CD player on the old kitchen dresser by the desk.

"Have you settled in okay?" Michael's deep voice resonated behind her.

Cat spun around to face her boss, who stood in the doorway of the small stockroom at the rear of the gallery. "Fine. The apartment's comfortable and has everything Amy and I need. You should be charging me a lot more."

"Why?" Michael moved across the gallery toward her and gave her a quizzical smile. "It's not like I need the money or am saving what I do have to pass it on to anyone." His thick hair was pure white, but even in his mid-sixties, he still stood tall and straight. "My wife died before we were blessed with kids, and I don't have any other close family." He stacked several art magazines and avoided Cat's gaze.

"I'm sorry." Cat twisted her hands together. Life often wasn't fair, but this sweet man deserved better.

Michael stared at the neat pile of magazines like he didn't see it. "It is what it is. My wife and I wanted to go to Australia something bad. We had this idea we'd backpack there after college, but we never did." His shoulders drooped. "Then we said we'd do it when we retired, but she got sick and..." He stopped and swallowed. "I'm too old to backpack now, but even if I weren't, I don't have the heart to go alone. Even the animals in the ark went two by two. I'd feel like the odd one out." His voice was thick with sadness.

"Hey." Cat's heart pinched as she got to her feet. "There's no way you're too old. Maybe you could travel with a friend. There must be senior backpackers." She patted his sweater-covered arm. "Why don't you go over to the diner? Amy went there after school to make gingerbread with Liz. I'll look after things here."

"Gingerbread, huh?" Michael raised his bushy, white eyebrows. "Liz's Vermont gingerbread is like my grandmother used to make."

"Go on." Cat grabbed Michael's coat from a hook on the wall near the desk and held it out.

"You're not trying to get rid of me, are you?" He shrugged into the coat and wrapped a scarf around his neck and ears.

"Of course not." But with Amy occupied in baking, and if Michael was where he only needed an excuse to be, she could work on her book in between the few customers who ventured out into the cold and snowy afternoon.

Michael pulled a pair of gloves out of his coat pockets. "You're like your mother, you are. She always fancied herself a matchmaker, and the apple doesn't fall far from the tree. It was you who sent Liz over to dance with me at Nick and Mia's wedding, wasn't it?"

Cat laughed. "You both like to dance, don't you? So really, I did you a favor."

"You're half Irish and half French, and that's a dangerous combination." Michael winked, then gave her a mock glare before he opened the door and disappeared into a flurry of snow.

An hour later, Cat's phone rang and she hit Answer, one eye on the laptop screen. "Hey, Mom. Are you and Ward still on for supper with us tonight? Amy's making dessert and—

"Is Amy with you?" Her mom's tone was sharp with anxiety.

"No." Cat gripped the desk. "Amy's at the diner with Liz."

"She was, but now she's not." Her mom's voice shook. "I stopped in here for a few minutes to pick up a pie, and Amy was at a table near the door. I asked Liz about taking a cutting from one of her ferns. We only turned around for a minute, but when we turned back again, Amy was gone."

"Gone?" Cat's mouth went dry. "Where would she go? Did you check the bathroom?"

Cat had talked to Amy about stranger danger from the time her daughter was old enough to understand. She'd never have gone off with someone she didn't know or gotten into a stranger's car. Icy tentacles of fear curled up from Cat's stomach to catch in the back of her throat and mingle with the sickly smell of the berry-scented candle that only five minutes before had seemed homey.

"We checked both bathrooms, as well as the little office off the kitchen. We've looked everywhere." Her mom's voice caught. "Liz is calling the police, and Michael will check along Main Street. If I hadn't distracted Liz, Amy wouldn't have—"

"It's not your fault." Cat shoved the chair away from the desk and grabbed her keys and purse. "I'll check the apartment. Maybe Amy came home and went up the outside stairs instead of coming into the gallery first. If she's not there, I'll be right over."

Her heart thudded against her ribs and it took two tries to blow out the candle. Where could Amy have gone? And why?

Cat locked the gallery door and stumbled up the side staircase to the dark apartment. Empty. She tasted bile and pressed a hand to her stomach. She'd moved to Firefly Lake because she was desperate to help Amy, the person she loved more than life herself. But had the move only made things worse?

Chapter Six

✤

After leaving the creamery, Luc turned off Main Street onto Lake Road and slowed his pickup truck to a crawl behind a lumbering yellow snow plow. It was snowing too hard for there have been much progress for him to see on his new house today, so maybe an hour at the gym would get the kinks out of his shoulder and Cat out of his thoughts. Even the drawings for the plant expansion and details of the new equipment he was financing hadn't captured his attention like they should have.

He glanced at the window of Firefly Lake Flowers. A woman he recognized from high school waved at him over a bouquet of red roses. Did Cat like red roses? Luc braked hard as the snow plow bumped to a stop. *What am I doing?* It didn't matter what flowers Cat liked because he wouldn't be giving her any, especially not from there. Unless it was for his mom or one of his sisters, the details of any order he placed would be all over town in less than an hour.

He pulled out around the plow and, through the swirling snow, spotted the gym ahead to his right, with the arena on the corner. He signaled, then caught a flash of blue in the windswept, almost empty arena parking lot. Judging by the flowered backpack slung over one shoulder, it was a girl, and she was young. He didn't know much about kids, but he did know they didn't wander around by themselves, especially in a snowstorm when dark was drawing in. He flipped off the signal and headed to the arena instead, keeping her in sight.

As soon as the slight figure reached the arena's double doors and pushed back her parka hood, Luc recognized Cat's daughter. Although it was a darker blond, almost brown, Amy had the same silky, straight hair as her mom. The same walk, too. A brisk and determined stride that told the world the woman, and the girl, were going places.

After Amy disappeared inside the arena, Luc parked beside a snowbank, grabbed his phone and his skate bag, and followed her. He didn't have Cat's number, but, once inside the deserted lobby after Amy disappeared through the door that led to the ice, he texted Gabrielle. Then he slipped into the rink, eased the door closed behind him, and ducked behind the bank of bleachers to lace up his skates. Through a gap in the seats, he kept one eye on Amy. She sat on the home team's bench and pulled a pair of skates out of her backpack.

Stephanie came out of the restroom and her usually sharp expression softened. "I didn't expect to see you here today."

Luc pressed a finger to his lips. "Here." He pulled out his wallet and handed her a couple of bills. "For the ice time."

She glanced at the ice as Amy glided toward the center with her arms outstretched. "What's she doing here?"

"I don't know, but while I find out, can you get Cat's number from Amy's registration form and call her? I already texted Gabrielle."

"Sure thing." Stephanie disappeared back into the reception area. She still had that sway to her hips and the same tight jeans she'd been known for back in high school. Then, a lot of guys found her sexy, but Luc never had. He still didn't.

He turned back to the ice and his breath caught at the joy on Amy's face. When had he last experienced that kind of joy, let alone showed it? After Amy cruised past center ice for a third time, he stepped from behind the bleachers and swung his legs over the boards.

"Coach." She skidded to a stop, then fell over in front of him. Ignoring his outstretched hand, she scrambled to her feet, her face as red as the sweatshirt beneath her coat. "I was only...what I...well..." She crossed her arms over her chest.

"Skating?" Luc smiled at her.

The expression on her face was defensive, scared, and so vulnerable it would've broken his heart if he'd had one left to break.

"Sort of." Amy's lower lip wobbled. "It's hard to explain."

"Try me. We can skate while we talk." He kept his voice gentle so she didn't think he was mad.

Amy's pointed chin jerked. "My mom doesn't know I'm here." She raised her head and the pain in her still childlike blue eyes sliced through him.

"Why not?" Luc pushed into a glide and Amy followed.

"I was at the diner with Mrs. Liz and my grandma came to talk to her. They turned their backs and before I knew it, I left and was halfway here. I was thinking about school and..." Her voice wobbled along with her lip.

"You happened to have your skates with you?" Luc's breathing eased as his blades caught the smooth ice.

"I take them everywhere with me." Amy sniffed and wiped the back of her hand across her face. "I'm really dumb at school, pretty much in life, really, but when I skate, it's like I'm the person I'm meant to be. Hockey's the only thing I'm good at. Since we moved, it's the only thing that's sort of the same. And these skates are new, so they're really special. Having them nearby helps, you know?" Her voice rasped.

Even though he was almost twenty-five years older than Amy, Luc got that need to skate. Like her, he pretty much took his skates everywhere, too. But unlike her, he'd been good at lots of things besides hockey. He'd also grown up in a family with two parents who loved him, and, until he left for college, he'd never had to move.

"I don't think you're dumb at all." His phone buzzed to signal an incoming text and he pulled it out of his jacket pocket. "You're a card shark for a start. Anybody who's as good at cards as you must be pretty smart."

"Nobody played cards at my old school." Amy's tone was glum.

"That doesn't mean somebody here won't. You can always ask." He read the text from Gabrielle and put his phone away. "When I saw you come in here, I texted your grandma. She just texted me back to say your mom is on her way."

"Mom's sure going to be mad." Amy's eyes got shiny, and Luc's heart ached. He wished he could tell her everything would be okay, except he couldn't. If he hadn't been able to make things okay for Maggie and their baby, how could he promise they'd be okay for this girl he barely knew?

"When Mom finds out I snuck in here…" Amy's voice roughened. "And I ran off. I've never done anything like that before."

"Don't you think your mom must have been pretty worried? Your grandma and Liz, too. I bet half the town has been out looking for you." He kept his voice soft because she was already beating herself up for what she'd done. He didn't need to make her feel any worse. This wasn't about being her coach. It was about being her friend.

"I wasn't thinking." Amy stumbled on her skates, and Luc reached out to steady her. "I miss Boston and my old team. And school scares me. I think all the other kids hate me."

"Why would they? You haven't even been there a week. You got along at hockey practice all right, didn't you?" If she hadn't—if any of the guys had said something to her—he'd make sure it never happened again.

"Sure I did, but they're boys. You don't know anything about sixth grade girls." Her voice held a note of defeat that wrenched Luc's heart even further. "It's not like I have to do anything. Maybe they think I look weird. Or maybe I said something they think is weird. Most girls my age, except for a few of my old teammates, it's like they're part of some secret club. If you don't know the code..." She made a chopping motion across her throat.

Luc didn't know anything about girls, sixth grade or otherwise, but he knew about hockey and he had to talk to Amy about something that had been on his mind since practice, ever since Scott's casual comment that maybe wasn't so casual. "Were you a bit bored with the team here? You've played more hockey than those guys."

Amy shrugged. "You were great, but... I don't know, I..." She glided to a stop and looked at him. "I didn't feel like I fit in, and hockey's the only place where I ever fit. Mom loves me, but I bet she wouldn't have asked for a daughter like me if she'd had a choice."

Luc stopped too. "You're the most important person in your mom's life. She wouldn't trade you, even if she'd had a choice." That was the kind of person Cat was and anybody could see how much Amy meant to her.

"I'm not anything like Mom." She pulled a tissue out of her coat pocket and rubbed at her face. "Or anybody else, either."

"Why would you want to be like anybody except yourself?" That was what his folks had told him when he was Amy's age and it had always made him feel good. "Forget about what anybody else says or thinks."

"I guess so, but maybe I'm like my dad. I don't know, though. He died in a farm accident before I was born and Mom never talks about him." She studied the toes of her skates.

"Amy, I..." Luc bit his lower lip. If he'd thought he was out of his depth with coaching, he was even more out of his depth here.

"It's no big deal." She shrugged. "You don't miss what

you never had, do you?" The forced perkiness in her voice didn't hide the uncertainty—or the pain—lodged deep in her eyes. "Hey, before Mom gets here and grounds me for the rest of my life, maybe I could practice some drills with you?"

"Sure." He let out a breath.

Drills were good. They were logical and unemotional. They didn't make you think about things you didn't want to think about. Amy was a kid, so she couldn't know how what you never had ate away at you until you were a hollow shell of the person you used to be; one who couldn't open yourself up to life or other people like you'd done before.

And because she'd lost her dad before she was born, she also couldn't know how life could change in an instant, a hideous and irrevocable turning point against which you measured everything that came after it.

Cat ran into the arena lobby. The coat she hadn't taken the time to button flapped open and her boots clattered on the tiled floor.

"Where's Amy?" She slowed as she passed Stephanie behind the reception desk.

"On the ice with Luc." Behind the camera-ready makeup, there was unexpected compassion in the other woman's eyes.

"Thanks." Cat flung the word over her shoulder in a breathless pant, already halfway to the rink.

She barreled to a stop at the boards. Amy and Luc were at the far end of the ice near a goal crease. Her daughter laughed at something Luc said and her thin face was animated in a way it hadn't been in weeks.

Cat's heart gave a sickening thump. Amy hadn't looked happy in Boston, either, but would she have been happier if Cat hadn't uprooted them to move to Firefly Lake? Had she made a terrible mistake? Maybe if she'd helped Amy more at school, she'd have kept her grades up. Had her place on the team been as much at risk as the coaches said? Could Cat have tried harder to find another option? Maybes, might haves, could haves...she had to stop second-guessing herself.

"Amy?" Her voice was a hollow echo in the empty arena. She pushed open the gate and edged onto the ice, curling her fingers inside her mittens.

Her daughter turned and the smile slipped off her face. "Mom?"

"It's okay." Cat held out her arms and, with a half dozen glides, Amy skated into them.

"I'm sorry." Her daughter's words were a muffled gasp against Cat's coat. "I was dumb. I didn't mean to make you worry, or Grandma and Mrs. Liz, either." Her shoulders heaved.

"Not dumb, never dumb." Cat smoothed Amy's hair and held her tighter. "But maybe you didn't think. When your grandma and Liz couldn't find you, and you weren't in the apartment...I was so scared." She choked back a sob. "I love you so much, sweetie."

"Since everything's okay, I'll head out."

At Luc's deep voice, Cat looked up. On skates, he towered over her even more than usual.

"You...I...thank you...if you hadn't found Amy..." Cat tasted the fear at the back of her throat. Her daughter could have been kidnapped or killed. Or she could have gotten lost in the snowstorm and frozen to death.

"Hey." Luc moved around Amy. "You're as white as the ice. Come, sit down." With a gentle pressure and without dislodging Amy from her arms, he guided them both to one of the team benches and sat beside her. "I was on my way to the gym when I drove past a kid alone in the parking lot. I didn't know it was Amy, but something didn't look right, so I checked it out."

"Thank God you did. Amy?" Cat cupped her daughter's chin. "I'm not mad, but if Coach Luc hadn't been around, you could have gotten into real trouble."

"I know." Amy's voice was small. "I made a mistake, but all of a sudden I had to skate and that's all I could think about."

Cat exhaled. "When we get home, we'll talk about how to make better choices, but for now, what do you say to your coach?"

"Thank you." Amy turned her tear-streaked face to Luc. "I made you miss your workout. Will you bench me?"

"No." Luc gave Amy's arm a rough pat. "You haven't even played a game for the team yet, so how could I bench you? I can give you some extra drills and laps, though."

Amy's expression brightened. "I can start now. I mean, if you want me to?"

"Great. Five laps of the ice, then go through those two drills we worked on." He hesitated before turning to Cat. "If that's all right with you."

"Go on." After Amy sped onto the ice, she eyed him. "You know that laps and drills aren't exactly a punishment for her?"

He gave her a tip-tilted smile that squeezed her heart.

"Amy's having a tough time. I don't want to make it any harder for her. Besides, she might as well use the ice time."

"You paid for ice time?" She dug in her purse for her wallet. Paying him back would pretty much wipe out this week's grocery money, but her mom had given her lots of holiday leftovers and all the lean years had taught Cat how to stretch a food budget.

"Forget it." Luc put his hand over hers and, even through her mitten, her skin tingled. "I enjoyed skating with Amy."

"But…" Cat's voice was husky. Ice time was pocket change for him, so why was it hard for her to accept a kind gesture? Maybe because she'd always paid her own way and never let her mom, Nick, or anyone else help her out, even when she might have needed it.

"Put your money away." He grinned. "No man or woman is an island, remember?"

"Thanks." She pulled her hand away from his to fumble with her bag.

"See. That wasn't so hard, was it?" His voiced teased her. "Besides, I want to talk to you about Amy, and those drills will keep her occupied for a while."

Cat's heart thudded hammerlike against her ribs. How many times had someone said they wanted to talk to her about her daughter? Even before Amy was old enough to toddle, Cat had sensed she wasn't the same as other kids. Behind her big blue eyes and cherubic face, her little girl was wired differently. Although teachers and coaches over the years had tried to understand Amy, most of them didn't, at least not enough to truly help her.

"What about Amy?" She stared at the ice and her

daughter skating at speed, her hair flying out beneath a helmet.

"She's a special girl." Luc's expression didn't look like he was judging. Instead, he seemed almost excited.

"Yes." Cat had also lost count of how many times she'd heard the word *special*. Back when people had applied it to her, and now with Amy, it was never as good as it sounded.

"I mean it. She's a smart and savvy little hockey player with heaps of potential. She's also hardworking and focused. From what the other assistant coach and I saw on Saturday, she could be the kind of kid who comes along once in a generation."

"Really?" Cat gripped the edge of the bench. Although Amy's coaches in Boston had said she was good, there were lots of good players on her team. Cat had never gotten the sense her daughter stood out.

"I mean it." Although Luc's blue gaze was warm, it was also determined. "I want to give her extra coaching. The team here won't stretch Amy enough, and these next few years will be crucial for her development."

"She's only twelve." She gripped the bench tighter. Although she wanted the best for Amy, the best cost money. When it came to hockey, she could barely afford new skates, and no sport was as important as what Amy needed at school.

"Hockey's a fun sport for kids, but if they're any good, it can also become a business. For girls like Amy, there are summer hockey schools and elite teams. When she gets older, she might even be on track for a college scholarship like I had." His gaze softened. "Nobody's ever talked to you about anything like this?"

"No." She blinked away the burning sensation behind her eyes. "Amy has dyslexia. Back in Boston, some of the other kids bullied her because of it. Hockey helps her feel good about herself, but she needs to focus on school, too. Some of the teachers here are specialists in teaching dyslexic students." And Amy would get the kind of help for free that Cat couldn't otherwise afford.

"You won't get any argument from me that school's important, and I'm not minimizing Amy's academic challenges, but lots of athletes are dyslexic." Luc studied her for a beat. "I want to help her. Will you let me?"

"I…" Her legs shook and she pressed her knees together.

"I wouldn't charge you anything. You and Amy are like family. Call it paying it forward." A faint flush tinged his cheeks.

Cat hugged her purse. For Amy's sake, could she be beholden to Luc? If he gave her daughter private coaching, he'd become an even bigger part of both their lives, and she already thought about him more than she should. But how could she deny Amy something she'd want more than anything? If she ever found out Cat had said no to this chance, her daughter might never forgive her. Luc's blue gaze matched his words. Steady, honest, and nothing for Cat to be scared of. All he wanted was what was best for Amy.

"That's really generous, but…" She stopped and looked at the rapt expression on her daughter's face. She and Amy wouldn't be in Firefly Lake forever. Any extra coaching would be temporary. "Okay." Cat made her mouth shape the word even as her stomach knotted.

"That's great." His grin was open and boyish. Unlike

her, he didn't question every choice he made or hesitate when he had to step into the unknown. And unlike her, he hadn't once made a bad choice that had altered his whole life. "You won't regret it. Given what Amy put you through today, do you want to tell her now or wait?"

"I'll talk to her when we get home." Cat needed to impress on Amy that by running off, she'd frightened everyone half to death. The extra coaching was only because Luc thought she had talent. "If you give me your number, Amy will probably want to call you later." She told herself she was asking for his number for her daughter and not because he was surprisingly easy to talk to.

"Sure, give me yours, too." He pulled out his phone and gave her a wry smile. "I hope I don't ever have to send you a text like the one I sent your mom earlier."

Cat's hand trembled as she rummaged in her purse for her phone. Luc had been a good kid, and he'd grown up into a good man who did the right thing and didn't expect anything in return—especially not from a woman he'd always looked out for like an extra sister.

But his giving Amy extra coaching would change things in a way Cat already regretted.

Chapter Seven

❧

Two weeks later, Luc left the wood-paneled conference room at the Inn on the Lake and headed into the lobby. Dominated by a massive fieldstone fireplace and with welcoming sofas, low tables, and soft lighting, the space managed to be both impressive and cozy.

When he'd moved back here, he'd wanted to become a real part of the community and give back to the town that had given him his start in life. But helping others had helped him, too. Not only had it eased the ache in his heart, it had given him a sense of home that, like this inn, brought comfort and unexpected calm.

"Having you join us has sure given the Rotary Club a boost." Nick clapped him on the shoulder and grinned. "We've never had so many people come out for one of our monthly lunches before. You'll have to get involved in the Chamber of Commerce, too."

"Happy to." And Luc was happy, or at least what he told himself was his new version of happy. Not as happy as Nick, who still wore the glow of his Barbados honey-moon, but as happy as he could ever be after losing the love of his life.

"I hear you're giving Amy extra coaching." Sean Carmichael, Nick's brother-in-law, joined them in front of one of the lobby's soaring windows that overlooked the winter world beyond. "Some folks are sure pissed the new girl in town is getting special attention." He chuckled. "I think it's great, though. It's also given my wife the idea that Firefly Lake should get behind girls' hockey so our daughter can play when she's old enough."

Although a lot of things had changed since Luc was a kid, the rivalry between hockey parents clearly hadn't. Despite any noses that were out of joint, he stood by his decision to help Amy. "That girl has a sense of the ice like no other kid I've ever seen, but if there are other girls around here who want to play hockey, bring them on. Maybe we could have a demonstration at the winter carnival next month." Luc had volunteered to give time and money to the carnival the Rotary was organizing. "I know lots of women players. Maybe a few of them would be able to come here and help out."

"We got lucky. We have to pay it forward." Maggie's words echoed in Luc's head. He could almost see the sparkle in her brown eyes and the generous curve of her mouth, with the tiny scar on her upper lip. His mouth went dry.

"That's a terrific idea. I bet Amy would love to take part. It would help her get settled here." Nick beamed at him. "I have to get back to the office, but why don't you join us for dinner at Mom's on Sunday? We can talk more then. The whole family will be there, Cat and Amy too."

Luc's chest constricted. "Well..." He tried to avoid family dinners, even families that weren't his, because they reminded him of Maggie and the empty space at the table that would never be filled.

"Come on, you live at Harbor House anyway, and you have to eat." Of course, Sean, the poster guy for happy families everywhere, had to jump in. "You can talk to Charlie. If you get a few high-profile women players to come here, I bet she could arrange media coverage."

Charlie, Sean's wife, was a journalist and, along with her sister, Mia, was one of the nicest women Luc had ever met. They were both kindhearted, and neither one of them ever missed an opportunity to promote good causes. If a cause meant they could also promote the virtues of Firefly Lake, it was even better. In a lot of ways, they reminded him of Maggie, which was why, although he was friendly, he also kept his distance from them.

"Dinner...I guess so." Luc balled his hands into fists.

Gabrielle's boisterous New Year's brunch hadn't been as hard as he'd expected. Why should Sunday dinner be different?

It shouldn't be, except for the two men who stood in front of him. Neither Nick nor Sean and their families had been there on New Year's Day, so they wouldn't have picked up on any of the undercurrents between him and Cat. However, Charlie and Mia were sharp—too sharp. And without her loud and loving French Canadian family around, and with Nick and Mia happily married, Gabrielle would have more time to focus on other members of her family, Cat and Amy in particular.

"Great, see you at six on Sunday, and bring an appetite. You'd think Mom expected an invasion over the holidays. The freezer is still stuffed with leftovers, so if you don't help us out, we'll be eating turkey until Easter." Nick clapped Luc's shoulder again, then he and Sean headed across the lobby toward the hotel entrance.

Luc looked out the window and, in the sudden silence, classical piano music tinkled through unseen speakers. By the edge of the lake, near what in summer was the inn's boat dock, snow had been cleared to make a skating rink that glinted silver-white in the midday sun. Above the music, a laugh rang out like a chime of sleigh bells. He turned away from the window and caught his breath.

Cat stood near the reception desk with Georgia, who wore workout clothes. Although her sister's outfit was more revealing, it was Cat that Luc's gaze was drawn to. Today she wore a pair of black pants and a soft pink sweater that hugged each one of her sweet, womanly curves. His body reacted and guilt speared him, even as he moved closer to her like a magnet pulled by steel.

"I do get—Luc?" Cat stopped midsentence and stared at him with those beguiling blue eyes of hers.

"I didn't see you two at the Rotary Club meeting." He cringed like the teenage boy he'd once been. It had been so long he'd forgotten how to make small talk with women. Or maybe it was only one woman. Cat and Georgia hadn't been at the meeting. There was no way he'd have missed Cat if she'd been in the same room as him. Even when she sat in the bleachers at Amy's coaching sessions, he was aware of her every move.

"The Rotary Club is for stuffy business types like you and Nick." Georgia gave him a cheeky grin. "I'm teaching exercise classes at the health spa, and Cat's holed up in the Inn's archives. I just told her she needs to get off her butt and go outside in that gorgeous sunshine. Poring over those musty papers all day long will make her vitamin D deficient."

"I do go outside." Cat's cheeks were as pink as her sweater. "And those musty papers are an important part of Vermont's history. Do you know how many local people this place has employed over the years?"

"No, but you do, so we can all rest easy." Georgia's voice was teasing. "You'll also write about it in fancy articles with lots of big words I'll try to read because you're my sister and I love you."

"I love you, too, but you're impossible." Cat ruffled Georgia's curly, dark hair.

Luc looked between them and tried to hide a smile. "I took a few history electives in college. Like one of my professors said, if you don't understand the past, how can you build a better future?" It was something that made sense to him on more levels than Luc wanted to admit, especially when it came to the new feelings Cat stirred up in him, feelings that had given him more than a few restless nights since Nick and Mia's wedding.

Cat gave him a surprisingly mischievous smile. "I always knew you had hidden depths."

His body throbbed as if to remind him of those depths, and he stuffed his hands into his pants pockets.

"But does he read books?" Georgia winked.

"Sure I do." He teased her back like he'd done when she was little. She'd been a cute kid who'd grown into a stunning woman. Even though she was the kind of woman he should have been drawn to, he wasn't and, unlike Cat, he had no problem thinking about Georgia like a sister.

"What kind of books?" Cat tilted her head and the soft curve of her neck made his pants even tighter.

"Mysteries and thrillers mostly, or books about sports." Books that had helped pass the time when he was on planes or in hotel rooms on road trips with the team. Or that now kept him company in the vast emptiness of Harbor House after Gabrielle had gone to bed and there wasn't anything worth watching on TV.

"Cat reads historical fiction, where nobody ever plays sports." Georgia's sigh was as dramatic as that over-the-top kid she'd once been. "Her e-reader is absolutely stuffed with—"

"Georgie." There was a flicker of irritation in Cat's voice. "Don't you have a class to teach? Stressed-out people to calm with downward dog or whatever?"

"Sure, but that book with the duke guy by Eloisa what's-her-name was great and I—"

"Don't, Georgie, please?" Cat's voice wobbled. Slight, but still there and Luc's heart twisted. "Just go to class."

When Georgia had disappeared down a hallway beyond the reception desk, Cat gave a half shrug that didn't mask the bleakness in her eyes. "Georgia has always liked to tease me."

And although Cat would never admit it, some of that teasing had hurt her sensitive soul. "You read Eloisa James. What's the big deal?"

"You know who she is?" Her eyes widened.

"My mom's a big fan of her books." He tried to keep a straight face. "I got her a signed copy of Eloisa's latest for her birthday. Mom said I was her favorite son."

"You're her only son." Cat's lips twitched.

"If you want, I can get you a signed copy, too. Eloisa

and I are buddies." Despite his best efforts, he couldn't hold back the laugh.

"You're not." Cat put her hands on her hips and gave him a teasing grin.

"I'm sure she'd remember me. I bet not too many guys turn up for her signings." And he'd been like a fish out of water among all those women at the bookstore, especially when some of them had recognized him and he'd ended up posing for fan pictures.

"But you did, because a signed book meant a lot to your mom." Cat's voice became soft. "That's sweet."

"I'm a guy and I'm a hockey player. I'm not sweet." His mouth went dry because when it came to Cat, maybe he was. Although it made no logical sense, if she really wanted something, whether it was a signed book by her favorite author or something bigger, he'd do his best to get it for her.

"Sure you are, but I won't tell anyone." Cat's pretty laugh rippled out. "I should get back to the archives and—"

"Wait." Luc's heart thudded. He didn't want her to go. He liked spending time with her. Not only that, he liked making her laugh and finding out more about what made her tick. *Because she is a friend.* Even though that was what he kept telling himself, the words sounded at best tired, at worst false. But he was still mourning Maggie. There no way he was ready for a relationship, so what was with the buzzing in his head and shakiness in his legs? "Georgia's right. It's a beautiful day and you're stuck inside. Want to play hooky with me for an hour and go skating?"

"Skating? Do you mean on the lake?" Cat's laughter

stopped and an expression flashed across her face that looked a lot like fear.

"Sure, why not?" Why would anyone who'd grown up in Vermont be scared of skating?

"I don't have any skates." Her voice was high-pitched and nervous.

"You can rent them here, along with outdoor gear. I talked to the Inn manager at lunch. She said they're starting to push winter sports to attract tourists all year." He kept his tone low-key with no pressure. At least not overt pressure, even though all of a sudden he wanted to skate with Cat more than he'd wanted to do anything in a very long time.

"I don't skate." She worried her bottom lip.

"Not ever? Not even with Amy?" That was something else that didn't make sense. Why was Amy so hockey crazy if Cat hadn't ever joined her on the ice?

"I went once with my dad, but after that, no." She fiddled with the cuff of her sweater and avoided his gaze.

"Oh." Luc paused. Nowadays, Cat's dad, Brian McGuire, was almost forgotten. But when Luc was a kid, Brian had skipped town after embezzling money from the family law firm, and the scandal had taken years to subside.

"I can teach you to skate. I bet you're a natural." She might not be athletic, but Cat had an innate grace to her.

"I…I…" She tugged on one of her delicate silver earrings.

"You're not a real Vermonter if you don't skate. Besides, the arena has family skating on Friday nights. If you learn, it's something you and Amy could do together. I bet she'd love it. Skating outdoors is even better, though." Although he couldn't remember the last time he'd skated on an outdoor rink, it was probably right here in Firefly Lake.

"What if I fall?" Her voice was uncertain.

"Everybody falls sometimes, but I can teach you how to fall so you won't hurt yourself and help you get up again." Which would give him the perfect excuse to touch her. Luc's body flooded with warmth and his fingers tingled. "It'll be fun, I promise. Trust me?"

She raised her head and her rosy lips parted. "Amy's always trying to get me to skate." She gave him a smile that was tentative but determined. "I guess it's time I tried."

In the wooden warming shelter by the lake, Cat clutched the tops of the white figure skates with fingers that were chilled, even inside her gloves. Her heart raced and she pressed a hand to her chest. Luc asking her to trust him didn't mean anything important, even though her dad had said those exact same words to her so many times she'd lost count. Yet, despite all those promises, he'd still walked out of her life and hadn't come back.

She wouldn't think about that or about Amy's dad, either. She'd moved on years ago. The past was done, and if she hadn't dealt with it, she'd accepted it. That had to be enough.

"Here, I'll help you." Luc crouched in front of where she sat on the low plank bench—big, male, and oh-so-enticing. "We've got the lake to ourselves this afternoon." He already had his skates on, a larger version of the ones Amy wore. In his black parka with a black headband covering his ears, he could have stepped out of an "Experience Winter in Vermont" tourist brochure.

Cat stuck her left foot into what she hoped was the left skate. Maybe it was good there was nobody else around. She wouldn't have an audience while she tripped over her feet—or him. She licked her lips and tried to focus on tying a bow with the lace.

"That's right, pull it tight." Luc ran his gloved hand over the boot of her skate. "Minnie Mouse socks?" He quirked an eyebrow.

"Amy's cast-offs. Her feet were bigger than mine a few years ago." Her face heated. Not only was she as short as a kid, the socks made her look like one. She wedged her right foot into the other skate and laced it tight.

"Cute." Luc patted Minnie's jaunty bow. Cat's stomach fluttered and her palms got damp. He scrambled to his feet and held out a hand, as comfortable on those thin skate blades as he was in shoes or boots. "Put one foot in front of the other like you're marching." Luc helped her move onto the ice and demonstrated.

"Like this?" Cat held her breath, lifted one skate up, and put it down fast.

"Perfect." His tone was warm. "If you feel like you're going to fall, try to go forward so you can get up from your knees." He showed her.

Cat knelt on the ice, then gingerly stood up again.

"Now try that marching thing once more."

Even though her muscles quivered, she took several tentative steps. Not only were her skates disconnected from the rest of her body, she seemed to have acquired several extra arms and legs she didn't know what to do with.

"You're doing great." There was a gentle smile in Luc's voice.

Cat inched ahead again. Under her skates, the milky-blue ice was as smooth as glass. Beneath it, though, was the same friendly Firefly Lake that she'd swum in each summer of her childhood.

"I'm skating, sort of." She ventured a quick glance upward. A hint of beard stubble grazed Luc's jaw, and he was so close she smelled the clean, woodsy scent of his aftershave.

"You sure are. Skating's harder as an adult if you didn't learn as a kid, but if you relax, it's easier." A slow smile spread across his face as he held her gaze.

As if relaxing around him—or on skates—would ever be easy. She swallowed and focused on her feet again.

He took both her hands in his and pushed backward so Cat glided along with him. "We'll head a little farther out to enjoy the scenery." His voice was solid and reassuring.

When she looked up again, tall pine trees stood guard along the shore beyond the inn. Overhead, the sky was a brilliant blue cradled by green hills dusted with snow-like filigree. "I'd forgotten how beautiful winter is here." Secure in Luc's grasp, she inclined her head toward the small island that formed a rocky, tree-girdled bump in the middle of the lake. "When I was little, we used to take a boat out to that island and picnic."

"I did that with my family, too. My granddad and I pretended we were deserted mariners like Robinson Crusoe." Luc picked up speed, and the wind lifted Cat's hair beneath her hat. "The crew is building my new house in the curve of the lake beyond the inn. That land used to belong to my grandparents. When they passed, each of their grandkids got a share. It's where I've always wanted to live. See?" He took one hand away from hers to point to where a roofline dipped into the trees near the shore.

Cat squeaked and grabbed his hand again.

"Don't be scared." He glided to a stop, and she bumped against him. His blue eyes shone, and she licked her lips.

"I'm not." At least not much. The flutter in her stomach wasn't nerves, exactly. It was more being alone with Luc in the middle of this vast, white wilderness that was like a snow globe come to life—both a landscape and a man that were and weren't familiar. She gulped and as her knees went weak, she reminded herself to breathe.

"My property goes right down to the lake shore. If I want, I can have a skating rink outside my back door." His deep laugh rumbled. "Remember the rink my dad made in my folks' backyard every winter? It must have been tough on my mom, with all the neighborhood kids tracking in and out of the house wanting snacks and the bathroom for weeks on end, but she never complained."

"Your parents are great." Although her mom had done her best, the Simard family was the kind Cat had longed for growing up. The TV movie kind of family with two parents who loved each other and weren't afraid to show it. Not a family like hers that people talked about in hushed voices at the grocery store. Back then, she'd vowed that if she ever became a mom, her kids would have a different life. Instead, she'd ended up a single parent and hadn't even managed to give Amy a real family—no father and no brothers or sisters, either.

The familiar pain rippled through her as she clutched Luc's hands and he towed her around the makeshift rink in a big circle. "Skating's not so hard, is it?" There was nothing but gentle encouragement in his voice. No teasing, only a rock-solid belief she could do this that helped her believe it, too.

Cat risked another glance upward and bumped into his parka, her nose barely reaching the midpoint of his chest. "I'm holding on to you in a death grip." And despite their winter clothes, every nerve end in her body stirred with his nearness.

He squeezed her hands through their gloves. Despite the cold weather, her body was warm. "It takes time to get used to the feeling of the ice. Seeing as you're so convinced you're not the athletic type, how did Amy get into hockey?"

Cat tried to focus on his question and not how his voice resonated like a caress. "She went skating with a friend from Harvard and her son. We traded babysitting duty so we'd both have time to study. As soon as Amy saw a group of boys playing hockey, she wanted to try it too. Once she did, she never looked back, so I tutored to earn the extra money to pay for her hockey program." When Cat looked back on them, those years were a caffeine-fueled blur of late nights that had melded into endless days when she'd barely managed to put one foot in front of the other.

"Amy's lucky to have you as her mom." Luc's voice roughened. "Not many parents would have done what you did."

"I did what I had to." Like she always did. Her chest got tight. Between Amy and school, it sometimes seemed she'd missed out on her twenties and had forgotten how to have fun. "What do I need to do next?" If she changed the subject, maybe Luc wouldn't see her hurt or regrets. She made herself give him a sunny smile.

He slowed to a stop and let go of her hands. "Like you did before, put one foot in front of the other and move toward me."

Cat lifted her right skate up and put it down again. "I don't know how to stop."

"You won't go fast enough to have to stop. Besides, I'll be right here in front of you."

"What if I knock you over?" Her ankles buckled, and the skates rolled inward before Luc snagged her arm.

"Two-hundred-pound guys used to knock me over whenever I stepped onto the ice." His laugh was rich and sexy. "For some of them, it was part of their job description to take me out. I'm not worried about a little bitty thing like you."

She should have been offended, but something in Luc's tone when he said "little bitty thing" made it an endearment, rather than a variation of the taunt about her small size she'd heard all her life. "Like this?" Cat's skate blades propelled her across the ice toward him.

"You've got it, but hold out your arms to help keep your balance."

Cat raised her arms like he showed her and moved forward again.

"Don't forget to breathe." Luc glided backward but stayed in arm's reach. "You've got it. Looking good, Minnie." He grinned, a crooked tilt upward of his mouth that turned Cat's insides to jelly.

"Minnie?" She clenched her hands briefly and looked at her skates that seemed to have taken on a life of their own.

"Your socks." Good-natured teasing and something darker that skittered along her nerve ends edged his mellow voice.

"Amy's, remember?" She lifted her head and her breathing quickened. The man she'd known her whole life still glided in front of her. Except, his teasing had a sensuality that had never been there before. "I...I..." She stuttered as one of her skates caught a ridge in the ice.

"Watch your toe pick." Luc reached out to balance her, and his touch lingered on her arm.

She nodded, her initial fear replaced by an unfamiliar excitement that swirled and fizzed, making her light-headed. "I'm skating. I can't believe it. Amy won't, either." Cold air kissed her cheeks, her body was relaxed, not stiff, and she inhaled deeply as she held her arms out wide and let her skates carry her farther forward. Firefly Lake in winter had its own smell, a timeless blend of crisp snow, spicy pine, and smoke from a hundred fireplaces.

"You sure are." Luc clapped his hands and the sound reverberated in the white stillness.

Cat did another step-and-glide combination and finished with an impromptu twist that brought her closer to him again.

"You're still feisty, too." Humor lit his blue gaze. "I always liked that about you, Minnie."

Her pulse raced and butterflies took flight in the pit of her stomach. "If you keep calling me Minnie, I'll have to find a name for you."

"Go ahead." He spun in a circle. "Minnie fits you. Not only is she feisty and smart, but she's cute and a whole lot sassy, too."

This was Luc. If it had been any other man, she'd have thought he was flirting with her, but Luc had never flirted with her. And even if Cat had been the kind of woman that men flirted with, she'd forgotten how to flirt back, if she'd ever known.

"Thanks." Her voice was stilted in her ears, and she raised a gloved hand to her mouth.

"Minnie's also kind." His voice got low. "She's loyal and always sees the good in others, no matter what."

"I..." Her lips parted, but she couldn't find the words she wanted to say.

"It's true. Even when kids used to push you into snow-banks and take your books, you didn't let it get you down for long. You said they must have problems nobody knew about. That stuck with me. You might have been small, but you sure were mighty. You still are."

The respect in Luc's voice humbled her, even as his words settled deep in her soul. "I...you..." Her skates slid out from under her, and she toppled onto the ice to land on her butt. "Oh." The breath whooshed from her lungs.

"Are you okay?" Luc was on his knees beside her in an instant. His eyebrows and lashes were tipped white with frost, and the world telescoped to the size of a miniature portrait.

"I'm fine." The padding in the ski pants they'd rented along with the skates had cushioned her fall, so it was her dignity that was hurt more than anything.

"Maybe we need to practice that falling technique again." Luc's mouth moved, and Cat followed the pattern of his firm lips, mesmerized. "Let yourself fall forward, remember?" He pulled her to her knees to face him. "Up you go."

"Okay, I..." She slipped and pitched toward him.

He caught her before she hit the ice again, and his

strong arms held her tight. "That's the way to fall." His breath made a cloud in the cold air, and Cat's body shook, more with the shock of his closeness than the near fall.

"Is it?" She leaned into him, hyper aware of his touch.

A truck rumbled by on the road behind the inn and faded. In the silence, her heart hammered in her ears.

"Textbook." He lifted her off her skates and up his body, then pressed his mouth against her jaw. His lips were warm against her cold skin, and she gulped. He moved his head back a fraction of an inch and there was a question in his eyes. "Are you sure? I . . ." His voice was raw.

"Yes." She angled her face back toward his.

Luc's lips traced the outline of hers, gentle at first and then harder to coax her mouth open.

She went limp in his arms and a sharp stab of desire shot through her. She hadn't been kissed or held by a man in almost thirteen years. After Amy's dad, she'd been so afraid to trust anyone that she'd steered clear of men until it had become a habit, instead of a choice. And apart from Amy's dad, she wasn't one for a spur-of-the-moment hookup, so on those rare occasions she'd considered getting close to a guy, she'd always stopped herself. Amy came first, and she didn't have time for a relationship.

She moaned and kissed Luc back. Later, she'd analyze why this wasn't a good idea and berate herself for her lack of willpower. Not now. Even though she way out of her comfort zone, and he was way out of her league, she'd wanted to kiss Luc for years. And now he wanted to kiss her back.

Cat wriggled out of her gloves and lifted a hand to his

face, where beard stubble scraped her palm. She brushed his bare skin with her fingers and twisted even closer.

"Catherine." His voice rasped her name in the lilting French way, and she moaned again. Whenever anyone else called her by her full name, it sounded prim and proper. The way Luc said it was sexy, as if she was a whole different woman; one who was daring and maybe even a bit coy.

She glimpsed his eyes, so dark blue they were almost black, before he lifted her into his arms like she weighed nothing and held her even closer. She wrapped her legs around his waist, and he groaned. Then his mouth captured hers again, warm, insistent, and everything she'd ever dreamed a kiss from him would be.

He tugged at her hat and pulled it off. Then his gloves were off too, and his fingers tunneled through and beneath her hair to slide along her neck and collarbone, his touch both gentle and insistent.

Cat arched against him as her tongue danced with his. She tasted coffee, winter, and him, and it was so good she couldn't help it. She moaned again and he did too, guttural and aroused.

It was a sound that touched every part of who she was and changed her. In all those years of raising Amy, she'd experienced life secondhand, safe behind the barriers she'd painstakingly constructed. But this was raw and so honest that if she wasn't careful, it could end in heartbreak. One kiss from Luc was all it took to tear down her defenses and peel away the careful layers she'd constructed around her heart to leave her way too vulnerable.

Then Luc yanked his mouth away, and her body cooled

as if the ice beneath her feet had fissured to plunge her into the frigid water below.

"I don't know what came over me." He set her back on her skates and took a step back. "Coaching... Amy... I..." He scrubbed a hand across his face.

"Yes... Amy." Cat fumbled for her gloves and hat. "I don't know what came over me, either."

Except, she did, and she was even more like Minnie Mouse than Luc thought. Although she'd denied it for years, like Minnie, she was a hopeless romantic. It was in all those historical romances on her e-reader. It was why *Kate and Leopold* was one of her all-time favorite movies. Even her favorite color, pink, was the color of romance and unconditional love.

But being a romantic had led her to make bad choices. She yanked on her gloves and then jammed the hat back on her head. Luc wasn't her Mickey. He wasn't a real-life version of one of those book boyfriends she'd let herself dream about. Real life couldn't live up to fiction, and Luc definitely wasn't a hero for her starry-eyed happily ever after. No matter how much she wanted him to be.

Chapter Eight

Sunday dinners had gone out of fashion in lots of places, but not in Firefly Lake. Luc sat near the middle of the long table in the big dining room at Harbor House, surrounded by Gabrielle and her immediate and extended family. A fire crackled in the fireplace and a tall grandfather clock chimed each quarter hour.

His gaze landed on Cat, who sat across from him, her head down and intent on her turkey stew. The light from the chandelier reflected off the silky blond hair that brushed the delicate curve of her cheek. Although she'd avoided him all week, he still remembered, with perfect clarity, how that hair had slipped between his fingers and the softness of the skin of her face under the pads of his thumbs.

Given that his heart was supposed to be buried with Maggie, it was bad enough he'd kissed a woman who wasn't his wife. But he'd kissed Cat, who wasn't only Nick's little sister, so almost like family, but the mother of a child he was coaching. Although the coaching handbook didn't specify that relationships between coaches and parents were against the rules, once he was back on his feet, a straight-laced guy like Coach MacPherson would have plenty to say about Luc getting cozy with the parent of a kid on his team—not least because some folks already thought Amy was getting special treatment.

Then there was Gabrielle. For an instant, the dining room spun. Not only was Luc living in her house, but Gabrielle was one of his mom's best friends, and Cat was her daughter. You didn't mess with your mom's friend's daughter unless you were serious. Although he couldn't be serious about Cat, that kiss had been serious all right. And despite his better judgment, he wanted to kiss her again, preferably without a whole lot of clothes between them. He scooped up a spoonful of fragrant stew and suppressed a groan.

"Are you feeling okay, buddy?" On Cat's right, Nick dragged his attention away from Mia long enough to eye Luc with curiosity. "There's a bad flu going around. Half of Mia's fifth grade class was out on Friday, weren't they, angel?" He turned back to his wife with a besotted expression.

"They sure were." Mia gave Nick a smile filled with so much love and happiness that Luc's stomach coiled. "We're lucky none of the girls have gotten it so far. It comes on all of a sudden. You can be fine one minute, then sick as sick the next."

Kind of like how he'd kissed Cat. One instant he'd been picking her up off the ice like he'd have done with anybody, and then the next he'd had his mouth fused to hers like a man possessed. "I'm fine." At least he *was* fine as far as the flu went.

"As well as those women's hockey demos you're organizing for the winter carnival, I hear you're starting up a girls' hockey program." Beyond Nick and Mia, Charlie zeroed in on Luc. "That's so fabulous." Her brown eyes twinkled as she smiled at Sean, the two of them, with baby Lexie banging a spoon on her highchair tray between them, another picture of marital bliss. "We'll sign Lexie up as soon as she's old enough. It's not fair her big brother can play hockey and she can't."

"I didn't say I was starting a program for girls." While he'd been away from Firefly Lake, Luc had forgotten one very important aspect of small-town life. News took on a life of its own. While something—like a girls' hockey program—might start out as a vague, half-formed idea, in the blink of an eye, it morphed into accepted fact. "I've arranged for a few women players I know to come here and give demos at the carnival. It's a big step between that and a girls' hockey team."

"Not really." At the far end of the table by Gabrielle and Ward, Amy's expression was earnest and way too trusting. "I talked to a few girls at school. They said if you're coaching, they'd give hockey a try. They don't want to play with boys, but if there was a girls' team, it would be different. Besides, it's not just any women players. The ones who are coming here played in the Olympics."

"See?" Charlie grinned at him, and Lexie dropped her spoon on the floor with a clatter. "All the girls around here need is a chance and some positive female role models."

"I think it's a great idea." Cat finally raised her head

from her plate. "Since I worry about Amy getting hurt when she's playing with boys, if you take the lead on a team for girls, it would be a step in the right direction."

"Exactly." Mia beamed and squeezed Nick's arm. "We'll sign up our girls. Maybe not so much Naomi, but I bet Kylie and Emma would really take to it." She glanced down the table and sixteen-year-old Naomi, thirteen-year-old Kylie, and nine-year-old Emma looked back at her with matching expressions of horror.

"It's wonderful." Gabrielle chimed in. "There aren't a lot of sports programs for girls in Firefly Lake, and by starting one, you'd be doing a real community service. It's a shame Georgia had to work tonight, but if she were here, I'm sure she'd agree. She was such a sporty girl, but there weren't many opportunities for girls like her when she was growing up." She turned to her granddaughter. "Think of Amy. It would mean the world to her to have other girls here to share her sport with. She'd make new friends."

Luc let out a breath. Amy needed friends, but a girls' hockey program was a huge commitment. "It would take time to build a girls' program. It's already the end of January. Even if we decided to go ahead, apart from a few trial sessions, nothing much could happen until next fall." Luc looked at Nick, Sean, Ward, and Sean's teenage son, Ty. Surely the male contingent at the table would back him up? "It would also take money. Maybe we could get volunteer coaches, but there would still be money for the ice time and basic equipment. If the girls played in tournaments, those would cost, too."

"I'm sure the Rotary Club would help, but tournaments wouldn't be this year, maybe not even next." Sean made a funny face at Lexie, who giggled. "I'll coach for nothing, and Ty will too, won't you, son?"

"Sure thing. I'm already refereeing, and I'd like to earn a coaching certification." Seventeen-year-old Ty smiled at Naomi, as if to remind Luc he was the only guy at the table who wasn't coupled up.

"You can count on me, too," Nick said. "I want to set a good example for our girls. In Amy's case, you coaching her is about potential, but all girls should have a chance to try hockey. Who knows, maybe there are more girls out there like her."

Luc swallowed a laugh. Nick had only been an official stepdad to Mia's daughters for a few weeks and a foster dad to Kylie a bit longer, but he'd taken to the role like he'd done it since all three girls were born. As for there being any other girls like Amy in Firefly Lake, Luc doubted it. The more he worked with her, the more he was convinced she had a rare talent.

"I never played hockey, but I can help with fundraising." Ward looped an arm around Gabrielle's shoulders. "I could even make a short film about it, a fly-on-the-wall documentary. I bet Vermont Public Radio would be interested. What do you think, Charlie?"

"Leave it with me." Always the journalist, Charlie pulled out her phone and tapped at it.

So much for the supposed solidarity of testosterone. Even before Maggie, Luc had supported women's hockey. Coaching Amy was a way of giving back, as much for Maggie as himself. But he'd come home to Firefly Lake for a quiet life. There might not be lots of excitement or any great joys for him here, but there wouldn't be any complications, either.

When Coach MacPherson had asked him to help out with the minor hockey program last summer, Luc hadn't thought twice before signing on. The team was established, so all he'd have to do was turn up and coach a bit. If there were pushy parents or any other issues, MacPherson dealt with them. But then Coach Mac had gotten hurt, Cat and Amy had turned up, and all of Luc's complications had started. And by innocently volunteering to help the winter carnival, he'd been roped into starting a girls' hockey team where there'd never been one before, and where folks were already riled about the one girl he was coaching. It sure wouldn't be quiet, and it had a whole lot more complications waiting to happen.

He eyeballed Cat. "You realize, don't you, that even if we start a girls' team here, Amy's too advanced to play on it? She needs to play with girls who'll challenge her."

"Of course she can't play with girls who have no hockey experience." Cat eyeballed him right back. "But at least she wouldn't be the only girl in fifty miles who plays hockey, and maybe she could help you out with coaching. Teaching others to do something you're good at is an important part of skill development. You remember how I tutored you? You passed chemistry, and I learned something about teaching while I was still in high school. It was a win-win situation."

"I agree, but..." Luc gritted his teeth. Cat had gotten it in one. Helping coach other girls would give Amy confidence. From what he'd seen so far, confidence and self-belief were the only areas where she was weak. As her coach, and despite his entirely unprofessional attraction to her mother, it was his duty to help Amy in any way he could.

Cat's mouth turned up into a teasing smile. The same mouth that had been warm and oh-so-inviting as it had opened under his. "Even though it's not the case now, Firefly Lake has a rich history of women's winter sports. The archive over at the inn has some great photos."

"That's terrific." Luc stopped and shifted in his chair.

The woman was killing him. Even though there was nothing remotely sexy about the words coming out of her mouth, it was *her* mouth. His nerve endings tingled, and he tried and failed to tamp down the unexpected rush of desire. The same desire that meant he'd scooped her into his arms out on the lake to fit her body against his. Then her legs had gone around his waist and he'd been lost, the rush of sensual feeling overruling his usual good sense.

Cat's smile turned smug. "There were even some women hockey players here. A group of mill workers from Firefly Lake played against another women's team from Quebec in the nineteen thirties."

"I bet most people don't know anything about that. I sure didn't." Luc swallowed the excess saliva in his mouth. Hockey. He had to focus on hockey and the carnival, not on her rosy lips or the kissable dent at the base of her throat. "Why don't you use those pictures to make a storyboard display for the carnival? We could put it up in the arena lobby. It would be great PR, don't you think?"

The change of topic didn't help. Maybe it had even made things worse because now everyone around the table, even baby Lexie, stared at him and Cat. And Gabrielle's eyes had a shrewd gleam before she flicked a glance at Nick.

"I guess I could pull something together." Cat gave

him a too-bland smile before she crumbled the bread roll on her side plate.

"Why don't I drop by the inn and check out those photos with you?" He gave her an even blander smile in return. "Since everyone's so keen to start a girls' team, I should find out about the women who came before. They're the pioneers for girls today. Girls like Amy." He sat back, and his body flooded with a warmth that came from her, not the fire in the grate. Two could play a game of verbal banter, but, all of a sudden, and despite everyone watching, that banter had turned into something else— something that felt a whole lot like foreplay.

"Well, well." Nick glanced between them and, although his voice held a laugh, it also held more than a hint of warning.

Luc's desire faded along with the banter. "If folks want me to coach hockey, I'll coach hockey. Girls, boys, senior citizens, anybody." Okay, that was a lie. His ears got as hot as if his mom had been there to call him on it. Coaching a group of almost-adolescent boys and Amy was a big enough challenge. He was coping, barely, and only thanks to a lot of help from Scott. How would he manage a bunch of girls?

"You're messing with me," Cat said. Her sweet blue eyes narrowed behind those glasses that made her sexier than any woman he'd met before or after Maggie. But she was also smart and she had his number, so she was messing with him, too.

Luc twirled his spoon in the dregs of the food that congealed on his plate. Messing with his body he could handle, and maybe even messing with his brain. But it was the messing with his heart and soul that he couldn't risk, not now and not ever. He had to ignore that sizzling kiss between them and move on. It was a momentary lapse in judgment on both their parts that meant nothing.

Or so he'd tell himself the next time he woke in the early hours of the morning and it was Cat he yearned for, and her tender touch his body craved.

Qualifications for a dad. Amy slipped the piece of lined paper out of the back of her math textbook to check the list she and Kylie had made after dinner at her grandma's house the night before. *Thinks you're the best, does stuff with you, and helps out around the house.*

She tightened her grip on the pencil as she read the words that Kylie had written. Amy guessed that helping out was important, but since it had only ever been her mom and her, she didn't know for sure. But Kylie did, because Uncle Nick was now her dad, and she said Aunt Mia liked it when he cooked.

Likes to cook? Amy added a question mark beside that one. Did Coach Luc like to cook? How could she find a way to ask him? Her insides quivered.

Curled up in one of the armchairs in the living room of the apartment she was now supposed to call home, Amy twirled the pencil and looked at her mom in the circle of light cast by the lamp on her desk. Darcy, their elderly tabby cat, slept at her mom's feet while Bingley, Darcy's equally elderly brother, groomed himself on her lap. Her mom stared at her computer screen and, although her lips moved, no sound came out. Her forehead had a crease in it like it did when she was thinking hard about something. Or she was worried about money, work, or, most of all, Amy.

Amy bit back a sigh, then bent her head back to the notebook paper. *A good dad would help my mom so she wouldn't worry as much.* She squinted and bit her lip. No matter how hard she tried, the words she wanted never came out the right way on paper. Although she tried to not show it, her mom also worried about that.

Most important of all, though, a dad would need to love her more than anything. She wrote *LOVE* in big letters and drew a heart around it with her red pencil crayon. Her mom's love was the one thing she always had enough of. And now she had her grandma, Aunt Georgia, and Uncle Nick and Aunt Mia and their kids—a whole family of love right here in Firefly Lake.

"How's your math homework coming along?" Her mom's voice had a worried edge to it that matched her worried expression.

"Fine." Amy shoved the paper with her dad list back into the book. "Coach Callaghan's a good teacher." From what she'd seen of him, he was also a great dad. "The teacher helping me with reading is good, too." For the first time ever, the jumble of letters that everyone else could read so easily had begun to make some kind of sense to her.

"That's great, honey." Her mom's smile warmed Amy inside and out. "I'm so proud of you." She pushed away from the desk and scooted her chair on wheels closer to where Amy sat. "I know you didn't want to move here, but everything's working out okay, isn't it?"

"Whatever." Amy shrugged.

School anywhere would be bad, but the one here was better than the others she'd gone to. At least she didn't have the sick feeling in her stomach she used to get every

morning before school back in Boston. And even though
the hockey team was lame, Coach Luc made up for it. But
despite all that, Firefly Lake wasn't home. She sounded
different than the other kids, and she felt different too, in
a whole new way than she had in Boston. For a start, she
was the only girl who played hockey, but more than that,
she was the only kid in the entire school, maybe even the
whole town, without a dad. Even the kids whose parents
didn't live together had a dad somewhere.

"I'll have finished my book and those articles about the
inn by June, and if they get published, that could really
open doors for me." Her mom's smile was bright and her
voice was encouraging. "I bet a permanent job is right
around the corner. Life will get easier, I promise. If I'm
really careful with this grant money, maybe we can even
take a vacation this summer."

Amy gave a jerky nod and tried to smile back. She
wasn't a little kid anymore. The truth was right in front
of her, and it wasn't pretty. Even for someone as smart
as her mom, there weren't a lot of history professor jobs
out there. It was all her mom and her friends talked about.
She swallowed hard. Maybe she should add "has a good
job" to her list of dad requirements.

"We could go to Florida." She hunched in the chair.
"I'd love to go to Disney World."

"Florida in summer would be way too hot and humid."
Her mom's smile slipped away.

"You like hot weather." Amy could get into this game
of pretend because that was all it was. Kids like her didn't
get to go on fancy vacations. "You met my dad in Florida,
didn't you, on spring break?" She scooped up Bingley
from her mom's lap, and the cat let out a loud meow.

"Yes, in Fort Lauderdale." Her mom moved back toward the desk. "Look, you need to finish your homework so we can read together before bed and—"

"Why don't you ever talk about him?" Her pulse sped up. Amy needed answers to questions, important questions, but her mom always brushed her off or changed the subject like she was a baby. Now that she was twelve, though, she was too old to be distracted or fobbed off with half answers.

"There's nothing to talk about." Her mom rifled through pages of her book manuscript. "Like I've told you, he died in a farm accident before I knew I was pregnant with you."

"He must have had a family somewhere." Amy took a deep breath. "Did you go to his funeral?" Even though she didn't want it to, her voice shook.

"No." In the pool of light from the desk lamp, her mom's blond hair shone like the hair of the Cinderella doll Amy had gotten one Christmas when she was little. Back when she still believed in princesses and the kind of magic fairy godmothers could make. "He was from a small town in Minnesota. The funeral was there. I didn't find out he'd died until afterward."

"You could have still gotten in touch, especially after you had me." Her breathing got noisy, and she flexed her fingers against Bingley's warm sides. "I've only seen one blurry picture of him." Her dad had been a big guy with shaggy, dark-blond hair the same color as Amy's and, in the picture, he wore a University of North Dakota T-shirt and black shorts. He was in the middle of a group of college kids. Her mom was there too, but she was off to one side, like she'd ended up in the picture by mistake. Behind the group there were sand and a few spiky palm trees against a bright blue sky.

"Jared isn't your dad, except in name." Her mom's voice was as tight as her expression. "Even if he'd lived, I doubt he'd have been around for us."

"You don't know that for sure. What about my dad's folks? Did he have brothers and sisters?" Her thoughts spun.

"He was an only child, and his mom died when he was a kid." Her mom fiddled with the zipper on her hoodie. "His dad was in the military, and he was raised by an aunt and uncle. Sweetie, it's always been enough, just the two of us. Why the sudden interest in your dad? Believe me, if your dad all of a sudden leaves his family like mine did, it would be better to not have known him in the first place."

Like the mysterious Jared, her mom's dad was someone else nobody ever talked about. Not even her aunt Georgia and she talked about everything. "Being here in Firefly Lake with your family makes me feel like there's this whole other part of me that's missing. As if...like maybe...you're ashamed of me." Amy's face got hot and she gripped her sweatshirt.

"No, honey." Her mom got out of the chair and came to crouch at Amy's side. "I've never been ashamed of you, not once. I don't want you to ever think that. Getting pregnant with you wasn't planned, and although at first I didn't think I was ready to be a mom, from the minute I held you, I couldn't imagine my life without you." Her voice was tender, and she took Amy's hand, but instead of being warm and comforting like it usually was, her mom's hand was cold and shook a bit.

"Oh." Amy pressed her lips together until her jaw hurt.

She let her hand lie in her mom's without squeezing back. She wasn't as dumb as the kids at her old school had said. Maybe her mom wasn't ashamed of her, but it sounded like her mom had made a mistake—a big one.

"Was my dad even important to you?" Her body tensed and her palms got sweaty. As far back as Amy could remember, her mom hadn't dated, so she couldn't imagine her hooking up with some random guy. "You've never even told me his last name."

Her mom's eyes glistened. "You're the most important person in my life. You always have been, and you always will be. There are lots of ways to make a family, and you're my family. We don't need Jared or anyone else."

Which wasn't an answer, not a real one anyway. Amy's eyes watered and she blinked. Maybe they didn't need Jared. He could have been a real loser, and even if she had a grandfather or other relatives somewhere in that state with all those lakes, it wasn't like she could track them down, at least not when she was still a kid and didn't even have a last name. For a few seconds, it was hard to breathe and she was dizzy. Then she straightened, and all of a sudden she had a sense of purpose she'd never had before.

Her mom might not need anyone else, but Amy did. Someone like Coach Luc could help her with hockey, too. Although her mom had never actually come right out and said so, it was pretty clear she worried about Amy playing hockey. Coach Luc would be the perfect guy to make her mom see she had nothing to worry about.

Amy picked up her math textbook again and stared at the page of problems without seeing them. Her grandma said that Coach Luc was still sad because his wife passed, but Amy had seen how he looked at her mom. He liked her; she was sure of it. As for her mom, she liked Coach Luc, too. Why else would she turn red whenever he was around? She also combed her hair and put on lip gloss before hockey practice, and she'd never done anything like that back in Boston.

Maybe she and her mom could help Coach Luc with that sadness her grandma talked about. She had to forget about Jared without a last name and think about what she might be able to have, not what she didn't.

When her mom had gone back to tapping on the computer, Amy pulled out her list again. She added two more things. *Must play hockey.* She glanced from Bingley, who dozed on her lap, his deep throaty purr a comforting vibration against her stomach, to Darcy, who was still curled up under her mom's desk. *And like cats.*

Chapter Nine

❧

Two rows back from center ice, Cat shifted on one of the arena's wooden bleachers and raised a hand to her mouth to cover another jaw-cracking yawn. Why had Luc and Scott added this extra practice Friday after school? All week, night after night, she'd lain awake until the rosy light of the winter dawn had slipped through the slats in her bedroom blinds, the quiet pressing in on her. Thanks to the questions Amy had asked about the man who'd fathered her, the feelings Cat had locked away long ago had come tumbling out like the mythic evils from Pandora's box.

"Hey, Muppet." The bleacher creaked as Nick sat beside her.

"Hey, yourself. What are you doing here?" Cat huddled into her coat. The arena was like a walk-in freezer. Why would anybody be here unless they had to?

Nick handed her a thermal mug. "I got out of court early, so I thought I'd drop by and watch hockey practice.

I haven't seen Amy in action for a while, and if I'm going to help out with that new girls' team someday, I figured I better refresh my memory of what it's all about."

Cat eased the lid off the mug and inhaled the scent of steaming, maple-cinnamon latte. "How did you know I needed this?"

"Because you've been looking bad the past few days." His eyes narrowed. "Please tell me you're not working nights."

"You do." In his own way, her brother was as driven as she was.

"Did." Nick's smile was both loving and smug. "Thanks to Mia, I'm a reformed man. I'm even thinking about giving up my work for the firm in New York to go full-time at McGuire and Pelletier. Although I'd have to take a pay cut, it's not fair on Mia to single parent when I'm gone. Besides, I miss a lot during the weeks I'm in the city."

If her mouth hadn't already been open for another yawn, Cat's jaw would have dropped. "Who are you and what have you done with my brother? When did you become happy with the life of a small-town attorney?"

"When I became happy, period." Nick handed Cat one of her favorite cheddar and apple muffins in a paper bag from the Daily Bread Bakery. "There are more important things in life than work, but I only recognized that when I stepped off the fast track for a while."

Cat flinched as a player bigger than any twelve-year-old boy should be crashed into the boards in front of them.

"Amy wasn't even near him." Nick patted her arm.

"Not this time." Each and every time her baby girl

skated onto the ice, Cat wanted to haul her back, but she couldn't. She had to respect Amy's choices like her mom had respected hers.

"Relax. Luc won't let her get hurt."

"Amy's more than capable of getting into trouble all by herself. The instant she puts on her skates, she's fearless. She's so competitive, too." Cat wrapped her hands around the warm mug to stop her fingers from trembling.

"She's a lot like you." Nick's voice was even. "Didn't you always go after what you wanted?"

Cat's heart gave a sickening bump. She had and, except for once, it had worked out just like she'd planned. Although she'd wanted Amy's dad, he hadn't wanted her back. Getting her into bed had been a game to him, nothing more than a bet with his friends. For a smart girl, she'd been stupid, and Amy was the result.

"Hockey's different. It's so rough." Her gaze drifted to the ice. Luc stood at the far end, by one of the goal nets, with Amy and two other players. The hockey moms clustered near the boards watched his every move like fluttery Regency debutantes.

"It's also a world you don't know much about, isn't it?" Nick covered her hand with his. "I get it. I haven't been a dad for long, but now that I've got Mia's girls and Kylie in my life, it seems like there's danger everywhere I look. As for teenage boys, don't get me started." He gave a wry laugh. "Mom says it's payback time for the hell I put her through in high school."

"Amy's all I have." Cat gulped a mouthful of latte and the hot liquid burned her tongue. "If she'd chosen swimming or ballet or even soccer, I could understand it more, but hockey...it..." She pressed a hand to her throat.

"Did Amy's dad play hockey?" Nick's voice was carefully neutral.

Cat started. First Amy and now Nick. Her brother had never asked her about Jared before. Even her mom hadn't. Nobody in her family had judged or questioned her when she'd announced she was going to be a single mom. They'd respected her privacy then, so moving back to Firefly Lake didn't mean her life was all of a sudden an open book.

"He played college hockey." Her breathing got short and she clenched her hands. "And I don't want to talk about it." If he hadn't gotten himself pinned beneath his uncle's tractor, Jared had been on his way to the NHL. And as she'd found out way before the day that irrevocable blue line had appeared on the pregnancy test, he'd also been on his way to a big, white wedding with a fiancée who wasn't her.

"Fair enough, but being with Mia has shown me it helps to let things out." Nick's tone was warm. "If you ever want to talk, I'll try my best to listen."

"Thanks." Cat's eyes smarted and her throat got thick.

"So, what's with you and Luc?" Her brother's voice changed, and the warmth was replaced with a razor-sharp edge that reminded Cat why he was such a good attorney.

"Nothing." Cat gave what she hoped was an unconcerned shrug. It was true. Her feelings for Luc were nothing more than the remnants of that crush she'd never really outgrown.

"He was flirting with you at dinner last weekend."

"That's ridiculous." Cat focused on the ice to avoid her brother's way-too-intent gaze.

"Mom, Mia, and I all imagined what was going on?"

Nick's voice roughened. "Luc's a good guy, but we don't want you to get hurt."

"No chance of that." Cat tried to laugh, even as her gaze was drawn once again to Luc. Now she knew exactly what his powerful arms felt like wrapped around her and the strength in the sheltering curve of his broad shoulders. She shivered, but this time not from the arena's arctic chill. "I don't need a man in my life right now."

"Sure you do, Muppet. You just don't know it yet." Nick got to his feet. "I have to get home. Mia's school choir's singing at some party at the curling club tonight, so I'm in charge of dinner." He studied her for several endless seconds. "Give Amy a hug for me. Tell her she looks good out there."

"I will." Cat stood beside him and gulped a lungful of cold air. "Thanks for the coffee and the muffin."

"No problem." Still Nick studied her. He looked like their dad as she remembered him, but, unlike her father, her brother had never let her down. She laid one hand on his back and pulled him into a hug.

He hugged her back, and her eyes got damp. Then he clattered down the bleachers, and her gaze met Luc's across the arena and held. Her heart lurched, and her body shook with an unfamiliar emotion, a soul-searing sense of connection to this man that was new.

She looked away first and fumbled with her bag. Her life back in Boston was stressful, sure, and she'd never had enough hours in the day, but it had never been this confusing mix of uncertainty, excitement, hope, fear, and everything in between. She'd known who she was and what she wanted, and her life had stretched out before her in a linear path. But now, and although she'd only been

back in Firefly Lake a little over a month, her world had
turned topsy-turvy and that life path bent and twisted.

Luc skated over to the boards and gestured to her, and
the hockey moms turned as one to stare.

Avoiding the other women, she moved toward him on
legs that were like rubber. She wanted a permanent university job. She needed that security for herself and Amy.
That was why she was working so hard on her book. And,
along with Amy, that was why she couldn't let herself get
distracted by Luc or anything else. "What's up?"

"Amy has a lot of questions about women's hockey. If
it's okay with you, I thought we could talk over dinner at
the Pink Pagoda." He rested one arm on the gate to the
ice, so close she caught the musky scent of his aftershave
mixed with the cool smell of the ice. "I haven't been there
since high school, and Amy says you love Chinese food."

Back in high school, the Pink Pagoda, a little restaurant two blocks down Main from the gallery, was where
the popular kids went on dates. In the small world of Firefly Lake, it was exotic, foreign, and, as far as Cat was
concerned, it might as well have been in China for any
chance she'd had of going there with a boy.

"I…uh…"

Amy appeared behind Luc. "Please, Mom?"

"I made meatloaf earlier, honey." Even as she said the
words, she could almost taste the steamed pork buns the
Pink Pagoda was famed for and smell the delicate jasmine
tea—scents that wafted out onto the street year-round to
entice customers in. Her mouth watered.

"You can freeze the meatloaf, can't you?" Her daughter's voice was pleading. "We hardly ever eat out. I'm the
only kid in my class who hasn't been to the Pink Pagoda."

Restaurant meals were a luxury Cat couldn't often afford. Her stomach lurched.

"My treat." Luc's voice was smooth. "Maybe your mom and Ward would like to join us."

"Grandma and Ward are going out for a meal and to a movie tonight. They have a date." Amy's smile had the dimple at the corner that Cat could never resist.

Cat's stomach lurched again. "I don't…"

"If you two don't join me, I'll have to eat all alone in an empty house." Luc's tone teased her. "Besides, I bet I ate half of that *tourtière* you made at New Year's. I owe you."

"No, you don't." Owing people led to trouble. She stuffed her hands in her coat pockets, all the while conscious of the hockey moms' covert looks.

"Maybe not, but your daughter's pretty persuasive." His mouth twisted into a toe-curling grin that, in its own way, was just as irresistible as Amy's.

Cat glanced at her daughter again. Amy's face was the picture of innocence, but there was a look in her eyes that Cat didn't trust. That persuasiveness came with an agenda. Although Cat didn't know what it was yet, she intended to find out. Starting with dinner at the Pink Pagoda.

"My fortune cookie says that if I follow my heart, good luck will come my way." At the top of the stairs leading to the apartment above the gallery, Amy thrust the tiny piece of paper at Luc. "Do you think that's true?" Her sweet blue gaze was fixed on him.

"You can't go wrong if you follow your heart." His gaze swung to Cat, who unlocked the door. Slim jeans outlined the curve of her butt, and her hair was fluffed out over her coat collar. His chest tingled. He swallowed and took a step back on the small landing. "As for good luck, sure, you never know what's around the corner." Even though it might be something that would knock you flat and turn your life upside down, Amy wasn't him. She was only twelve and had her whole life ahead of her.

"Excuse the mess. I wasn't expecting company." Cat opened the apartment door and flicked on a light.

"If it's a problem, I can—"

"Of course it's not a problem. Mom's a neat freak, that's all. She thinks the place is a mess if a few cushions are out of place." Amy grabbed his hand and tugged him into the entryway. "You have to see my trophies and hockey card collection."

Luc ducked his head by instinct, but the apartment had high ceilings and was more spacious than he'd expected. Given that Cat and Amy had only moved in after Christmas, it was also more homelike with a few plants, pillows in pastel colors on the dark blue sofa and two chairs, and a mix of family photos and vintage prints displayed on small tables and hung along the neutral-colored walls.

He slipped off his boots and handed his parka to Amy, who put it on a coat stand. "Your place is nice."

And it was a whole lot more comfortable than his bedroom at Harbor House which, apart from his bed, dresser, and treadmill, was four bare gray walls with a stack of boxes he hadn't bothered to unpack piled in a corner. Like his life, the room was on hold.

"Thanks." Cat hung her coat on the stand, too. "I inherited some things from Mom's family and picked up other pieces at auctions and flea markets. Each one comes with a memory." Her laugh was light, almost embarrassed.

"It's cozy." He'd gotten rid of most of the furniture he and Maggie had shared because the memories were too painful. He didn't want to see the kitchen table where she'd drunk her morning coffee. Or picture her on the leather sofa, curled into his side to watch a hockey game. Except, even without the furniture, the memories were still there, and his new house would be a place to live, not a home. His chest got that familiar tight heaviness.

"Mom's great at fixing old stuff up. She says it's good for the environment and saves money, too." Amy gestured him into the combined living and dining room. Two tabby cats, like a pair of bookends, poked their heads out from under one of the chairs.

"Amy..." Cat gave her daughter a warning look.

"What? You say that all the time." Amy hopped in her sock feet in front of him. "These are our cats, Darcy and Bingley. They're real old, at least for cats. Almost as old as me. Mom rescued them when they were little kittens. They're super friendly. Here, pet him." Amy scooped up a bundle of mottled brown fur and thrust it into Luc's arms.

He grabbed the cat's hind legs and tucked the animal into his chest. Darcy or Bingley, he had no idea.

"You like cats, don't you?" Amy's eyes were all of a sudden serious.

"Sure. I've never had a cat, but they're okay." And after an unexpectedly intimate dinner at the Pink Pagoda, he couldn't deny it any longer. He also had a crazy thing for a woman whose nickname was Cat.

"Great." Amy gave him a big smile, like he'd passed

some invisible test. "What about cooking? Do you know how to cook?"

"What's with all the questions?" Cat came into the living room. She'd taken off the bulky sweater she'd worn at dinner, and her blue T-shirt cupped small but perfectly proportioned breasts. "Why does it matter if Coach Luc likes cats or cooks?"

"I'm curious. You say curiosity is good." Amy's sober expression was at odds with the mischievous twinkle in her eyes.

"Not when it involves asking people personal questions." Cat turned to Luc. "You don't have to answer her."

"It's fine." It wasn't like Amy had asked him anything really personal or important. "I'm an okay cook because my mom said no son of hers would grow up not knowing how to fend for himself in the kitchen."

"That's good." Amy eyed the purring ball of fluff in Luc's arms. "Bingley really likes you. He sleeps on Mom's bed. Would you have a problem if a cat slept on your bed?"

"Amy." Cat's voice was a strangled sound. "Go get your hockey trophies and card collection. That's the reason Coach Luc's here, remember?"

"Sure." Amy looked at him. "Mom also has her old Care Bear on her bed. Do you want to see?"

"Amy Gabrielle McGuire." Cat's face flushed pink, and she took her daughter by the shoulders and walked her out of the room.

When Cat returned to the living room, her cheeks were no longer a soft pink but dark, tomato red. "I don't know what's gotten into her."

"Don't worry about it." The laugh Luc had tried to suppress escaped. "Bingley and Darcy?" He glanced from the cat still snuggled in his arms to the other one that had plunked itself near his feet.

"*Pride and Prejudice* is a literary masterpiece." Her voice was strained, and she busied herself plumping the already plump sofa pillows.

"Don't a lot of women think Mr. Darcy is some kind of sex symbol?" Luc set Bingley down and held his hands to his face in a vain effort to stop laughing. Cat was cute when she was embarrassed, as well as dangerously sweet and appealing.

"So?" Her tone was prim. "Amy?" Her daughter's name came out in a bellow.

Luc jumped. For a small woman with a soft voice, she could sure project it when she wanted to.

"What?" Amy appeared in the living room doorway with a cardboard box.

"If you want to show Coach Luc your trophies and cards, you need to get a move on. It'll be bedtime soon." Cat refolded a pink knitted throw with jerky motions.

"It's only seven." Amy set the box on the coffee table in front of the sofa and pointed at a brass clock on an end table. "I don't have to go to bed for a whole two and a half hours yet. Coach Luc can stay for ages." She looked between him and Cat. "After I show you my hockey stuff, do you want to play Clue? It's Mom's favorite game because she likes solving mysteries."

Luc sat on the sofa with a bump, and the cats followed him. "Clue's a great game. I used to play it with my sisters."

"Mom?" Amy sat on one side of Luc and motioned Cat to his other side.

"I ... Amy ... " Cat's voice was strained.

"Clue's way more fun with an extra player." Amy pulled the game box from a shelf beside the sofa. "Mom likes to win," she added to Luc, "but she feels bad if she beats me."

Luc blew out a breath and then clamped his lips together to hide a smile. Amy wasn't exactly subtle, but he couldn't be mad at her. He swallowed a laugh and turned to the two cats who looked up at him with identical amber eyes. He was trapped by a pint-sized matchmaker and a pair of arthritic fur balls. He should make his excuses right now and leave. Except, he didn't want to. His blood thundered in his ears as the truth zapped him with laser-like intensity.

When he lost Maggie and then hockey, he'd lost the two most important things in his life. Although his family and friends had tried to understand, they couldn't, not really. He'd pasted on a smile and gone through the motions of life on autopilot, while the months had turned into one year and then two. Until now.

In this snug apartment with its soft lighting, happy colors, purring cats, and a faint, tangy rose smell that was unique to this woman, he'd found something special. It was something he'd once have grasped with both hands and held onto tight, but he wasn't the man he'd been back then. He couldn't be that man again because life and tragedy had changed him. Even if he'd still had a whole heart to give, he couldn't let himself risk giving it to anyone again.

Chapter Ten

❧

It was a routine Wednesday morning, but Cat had made an extraordinary find. She took off the gloves she'd worn to handle the fragile documents and rubbed the kinks in the back of her neck. The inn's archive had a treasure trove of material for the kind of popular history book she longed to write. Unlike the book based on her dissertation, or the academic articles she'd proposed in her application for the research grant, it would be a book that her family and people in town would be able to read and enjoy. A story of Firefly Lake.

Her heart beat faster before the excitement faded. If she didn't get a permanent job soon, she'd be back teaching from contract to contract, and any research, let alone the kind she enjoyed most, would have to wait.

She stared out the window at the silvery icicles that hung like teardrops from the wooden eaves. The small archive was tucked into a room high up under the roof in what had once been the quarters for the inn's maids. From here, she had a bird's-eye view of the white-tipped pine trees that girdled the snow-covered shores of the lake. The sky was a robin's-egg blue, and in front of the inn, sunlight flashed against the blades of the lone skater who made loopy figure eights on the cleared ice surface. The same place where she'd temporarily taken leave of her senses and kissed Luc in full view of the inn staff, guests, and anybody from town who might have been passing by. And since that earth-shattering kiss, she hadn't been able to think of much else.

"Cat?"

She jerked upright and almost fell off her chair. Did she only have to think about Luc to conjure him up? "What are you doing here?" The words came out in a rush with a prickly edge she hadn't intended.

"I had a meeting with the chef and her team." He ambled farther into the room, Vermont business casual in black dress pants and a blue button-down shirt the same color as his eyes. He filled the small space like he'd filled her apartment that night after dinner at the Pink Pagoda. Although he'd only stayed for an hour, the crisp scent of his aftershave had lingered and tempted her more than she wanted to admit. "The inn is Simard's biggest customer in town, so I have to find out what they what."

His words tumbled into Cat's heart and lodged there like a thorny truth she also didn't want to admit. She wanted this man, but she couldn't have him.

He glanced at the photos and papers she'd spread out on the long table. "I bumped into Georgia in the lobby. She said you were up here."

"I'm working." She made her tone cool. She was a

busy, professional woman, and a serious scholar doing work people were paying her for.

Luc dragged the only other chair in the room around the table to sit beside her. "I need to get to work too, but if you can take a break for a few minutes, I'd like to see those hockey pictures you talked about before I head back to the creamery."

"Okay." She sucked in a breath. It would only be for a few minutes. As soon as she showed him the photos, he'd be on his way. She reached for a box at the far end of the table, brushed his forearm, and reared back. "Here." She handed him a bigger pair of gloves. "No fingerprints on the pictures." She wouldn't let herself think about how her skin had sizzled from that brief touch, only his thin shirt and her sweater between them, instead of the barrier of winter clothing.

He flexed his hands as he pulled the gloves on and gave her a teasing smile. "Fingerprints would be bad."

"Very." Her mouth went tinder dry.

She put her gloves back on and fumbled to open the box. "I put all the hockey pictures in here. They're not organized yet."

"These are fantastic." Luc's voice was a mix of reverence and excitement. Exactly how Cat felt when she looked at a hidden stash of old photos or letters for the first time, like they held a puzzle or mystery she was on the cusp of solving. "It's amazing some of these guys didn't get killed. See?" He gestured to the top photo. "This group isn't wearing helmets or protective gear. If you got a puck to your head or neck dressed like this, it'd be game over."

Cat studied the picture and, inside the gloves, her

palms went damp. It wasn't only the heat radiating off him, it was his scent, too. The familiar aftershave mixed with a compelling masculinity.

"That team's the Firefly Lake Flyers." She made herself focus on facts instead of on the bubbling volcano of sensations erupting inside her. "They won a New England championship in the nineteen twenties. There was a women's team too, the Lady Flyers." She dug in the box for more photos. "These were taken around nineteen seventeen. Can you imagine how the women played in those long skirts?"

"No, I can't." Luc's eyes shone with the same enthusiasm she suspected was mirrored in hers. "The women I invited to do demos at the carnival have to see these." He leaned closer, and Cat bit back a breathy sigh. "They're all Olympic medalists and now they're involved in girls' hockey camps. I can't wait for them to meet Amy. Those camps offer scholarships and, if you give the go-ahead, I want to recommend Amy for one."

Cat's body cooled and, all of a sudden, she had no problem focusing on facts and the harsh reality that went along with them. "Wouldn't any scholarship take into account school grades?"

Luc set the photo aside. "I don't know for sure."

"To play hockey on the team in Boston, Amy had to meet a certain academic standard. She wasn't meeting it. I tried to help her, but it wasn't enough." Cat swallowed the fear at the back of her throat. "If we'd stayed there, she'd likely have been off the team by now. If she hears about a hockey camp or a scholarship application...she'll get her hopes up...and I can't...it would break her heart if she couldn't go because of her schoolwork." Cat would be heartbroken too because if she couldn't pay for extra tutoring, she sure couldn't pay for hockey camp fees.

"I see." He tented his hands on the desk, the strong fingers dusted with light brown hair.

Except, despite the concern in his eyes, he couldn't see, not really. He couldn't see Amy's frustration when the learning that came easily to other kids was so hard for her. He couldn't see Cat's frustration either as she'd battled to get Amy the help she needed, and her ever-present sense of failure because the best help cost more money than she earned. And she had no way of telling Luc or anyone else how much she worried about making sure her daughter got the bright future she deserved.

She laced her fingers together and tried to steady her breathing. "If there's an academic requirement..." Her throat clogged.

Luc's brow furrowed. "Amy wouldn't meet it."

Cat twisted her hands tighter. "No, at least not right now, even though so far she's doing better at school here." For Amy's sake, Cat should stay in Firefly Lake for the next few years, but she needed a job and it wasn't like one was going to pop up either here or within commuting distance.

"I'll find out more about those scholarships." Luc's voice had an encouraging tone that would have given Cat hope if she could only let herself believe in hope again. "In the meantime, why don't you talk to Scott? He's not her homeroom teacher, but he got drafted in to teach sixth grade math this year."

"I already did. Although Amy's doing better in math than most other subjects, she's so far behind she'll still be doing well to pass her year."

Scott had told her the truth and had promised to help Amy all he could, but would it be enough? An icy trickle of dread slithered up Cat's spine. If her daughter wasn't promoted to seventh grade, what would that do to her already fragile confidence?

"So the hockey program here works for her because it isn't linked to school grades. Any kid who wants to can play." Luc gave her an assessing look. "No matter what happens at school, Amy has one place where she can feel good about herself."

"Yes."

Luc was perceptive like he'd always been, but even though she didn't need to spell Amy's situation out for him, that didn't make it any easier.

"There has to be something else she would qualify for." There was a new determination in Luc's face and voice. "Even if they're not dyslexic, a lot of kids who excel at sports have a tough time at school. Between us, there must be a way we can make this right for her."

The tension in Cat's shoulders eased a fraction. What would it be like to have someone like Luc on her side? He was the kind of guy who helped the people he cared about fight the battles that life threw at them. Being around him made her feel stronger and a lot less alone.

"I appreciate that you want to help, but how?" It wasn't like either of them could wave a magic wand and Amy's academic challenges would disappear.

"Hang on." Luc leaned back and one of his big legs brushed against hers. "Maybe we aren't looking at this the right way. Everybody sees Amy's dyslexia as a disability, but when it comes to hockey, perhaps it's actually an ability. It could give her that sense of the ice that makes her such a special player. And because of her dyslexia, she might also want to prove herself so she'll work harder."

Although every cell in her body urged her to move closer and sink into all that warm strength, Cat forced herself to draw back and sit up straight. "Even if you're right, Amy will never be tested on that." After sixth grade, her daughter had six more years of school to get through, including the tricky middle and high school years. "I have to think about her future." Amy was her responsibility, and as her mom, she had to make the best choices for her that she could.

"Why can't Amy have a future in hockey?" The warmth in Luc's voice ebbed.

"Maybe she could, but it's a big risk." And Cat wasn't good with risks. "Hockey worked out for you, sure, but how many kids, boys—let alone girls—grow up to play pro?" She wrapped her arms around her chest as if she could physically hold herself together. "I don't want that kind of uncertainty for Amy."

He raised an eyebrow. "Amy's tougher than you think. She's so driven, she reminds me of you as a kid."

Cat hugged herself tighter. "Promise me you won't say anything to Amy about a hockey camp or scholarship. Not yet."

"Of course. You're her mom. I'm only her coach. It's your decision. Always." Luc studied her for several beats before he bent over the pictures again.

Cat shivered. Amy was driven, but she was also more vulnerable than she looked. And what if hockey didn't work out for her? She had to make sure her daughter had lots of choices, and school was a means to do that.

She stared at the old photos. What had life been like for those women? Separated in time from her by a hundred years, their world was gone forever. A world where even though they played hockey, they hadn't had the choices she did. A world where because they were women, they were vulnerable.

Cat stole a glance at Luc's firm lips and the strong column of his neck above his shirt collar. Then, as now, vulnerability got you into trouble. The kind of trouble she could get into with him.

"Cat's sure a hard worker."

Luc dragged his gaze back to Liz Carmichael, who stood beside his booth at the North Woods Diner, a speculative gleam in her brown eyes.

Why had it taken him all these years to notice that Cat McGuire was hot? Even with her back to him, seated at a front table with Amy, Gabrielle, and Ward, he hadn't been able to keep his gaze off her. And all of a sudden, she was everywhere. Even if he didn't actively seek her out, as he had three days ago at the inn, he'd bumped into her twice this week at the bakery. She'd come into the drugstore when he was on his way out, and she'd also happened to be crossing the town green when he'd taken Pixie for a walk one day after work.

"Michael says Cat's got a smart head for business on her, too. Sales are up and, for the gallery in January and early February, that's saying something." Liz refilled Luc's coffee cup from the pot that was like an extension of her arm.

"Oh?" Luc dumped creamer into his coffee. Liz wasn't making offhand conversation. In a small town, even the most casual of glances didn't go unnoticed by somebody, somewhere.

"Cat's real pretty, too." Liz rested a hip against the table, and the paper Valentine heart that hung from the ceiling brushed her hair in a gentle caress. "Not as showy as some, but with the quieter types, you know more what you're getting." She paused and Luc tensed. Those pauses of hers always meant something—usually something he didn't want to hear. "You should ask her out."

"On a date?" Luc set his coffee mug down with a thump, and hot liquid sloshed over the rim and onto the table. "I'm not ready to date anyone."

"If you keep saying that, you never will be." Liz grabbed a handful of paper napkins and wiped up the spill in several deft motions.

"I'm also Amy's coach."

"So?" Liz gave a throaty chuckle. "Hockey season doesn't last forever, does it?"

"No, but..." Even though it seemed like Amy had been trying to push him and Cat together, Luc couldn't let himself get any more involved than he already was. He also couldn't let Cat or Amy think he could give them something that wasn't in him to give.

"See Michael over there at the counter? If you aren't careful, you'll end up like him. He's made a success of that gallery, sure, but what else does he have?" Liz's voice was gruff. "Apart from some cousins over Burlington way, he's all on his own." A wistful expression flitted across her usually bright face.

"Maggie's only been gone two years." He wasn't anything like Michael. His sisters might not live in Firefly Lake, but they were still a close family. *Except my folks won't be around forever, and then what?* He stared into his coffee cup, the dark brew the same color as his wife's hair. How could someone who'd been so alive and vibrant all of a sudden be gone?

"Nearer two and a half." Uninvited, Liz sat across from him in the booth. "Nobody's saying you should forget Maggie, but she'd be the first one to tell you to live the life you've got." She nudged his bowl of porridge. "Eat up. Fiber keeps you regular."

Luc glanced around the half-empty diner. A medley of sixties hits played from the jukebox that was older than he was. Liz's prized Boston ferns still hung in their baskets, as lacy and green as when he'd been a kid. But even though everything looked the same, he was different. Maybe it had been a mistake to come back here. People here didn't only know your name. They also concerned themselves with every aspect of your life and made it theirs. "I *am* living my life."

"You call walking around most of the time like a dog with a drooping tail living?" Liz snorted. "When you danced with Cat at Nick and Mia's wedding, it was the first time in I don't know how long that I've seen you look happy."

"Cat's a friend." Except, he didn't think about other female friends the way he'd started to think of her.

"So you say, but maybe you're using Maggie's memory as an excuse." Liz got to her feet as the bell that hung over the diner door jangled. "You and Cat would make a sweet couple, and little Amy needs a father. Who'd be better than you?"

The oatmeal he'd eaten congealed into a stodgy lump in Luc's stomach. Any number of men would be better for

Cat and Amy than him. Men who'd have been there for their wife and unborn child when they needed him most, and who hadn't made a bad choice that meant they still lived under a crushing load of guilt and grief.

"Hey, Coach."

Luc started at Amy's voice, and he reached out automatically to return her high five.

"Grandma and Ward took Mom and me out for breakfast." She gave him a cheeky grin and flicked a glance at the remains of his porridge. "Grandma made me eat oatmeal, too. She said it's so cold today oatmeal will stick to my ribs."

Luc laughed. "She's right."

"Grandma and I are going shopping with Aunt Mia while Mom works on the history display for the carnival." Amy's eyes lit up. "You should help her. She has to go out to the inn, and I bet she'd be finished a lot quicker if you went along."

"Amy." Cat stopped at Luc's elbow. "Too much information." Her coat was slung over one arm, and, although her blue sweater wasn't the least bit revealing, his mouth still went dry.

He gestured to the other side of the booth, and Amy slid into it. "Cat?"

"No, we're interrupting your breakfast." She glanced at Amy, who eyed Luc's last piece of toast with the same expression as Pixie when she wanted a dog cookie. "I'm going to the inn to take some pictures for a 'then and now' storyboard. Firefly Lake has hardly changed since those old pictures I showed you were taken."

Luc swallowed and forced himself to look at her face instead of how the soft wool of that sweater hugged the gentle curve of her breasts. Or at how its hem cupped the curve of her hip above her jeans. "Go ahead." He gestured to his toast, and Amy grinned. "Like Amy said, why don't I come to the inn with you? I could bring my hockey gear so you're not taking pictures of an empty lake." He'd picked up on Amy's blatant suggestion for no other reason than because it was friendly and neighborly. The lie burned his gut.

"I guess that would be okay." Cat's gaze darted to Amy. "I mean, if you're not busy or anything."

"I'm free until the game this afternoon." For a guy who wasn't part of a couple and who didn't have kids, Saturdays in a town as small as Firefly Lake had a lot of empty hours to fill. The crew building his house didn't work weekends, so although he went out to the site to check progress most weekdays, it wasn't as if there would be anything new to see today, and he'd met with his contractor yesterday. "It's only fair I help you out. I'm the one who suggested that display in the first place." And helping her would give him a perfect reason to spend more time with her without Amy around. The truth burned his gut even worse than the lie had.

"That's right, you did." A small smile hovered.

"Great." Amy spoke around a mouthful of toast. "I won't be back until I have to dress for the game, so you have lots of time." She swallowed and wiped crumbs off her face with the back of her hand.

"Amy, how many times have I told you to use a napkin?" Cat's face flushed, and she plucked at her daughter's arm. "Grandma and Ward are getting ready to leave."

"Okay." Amy gave Luc another high five, then kissed

Cat as she exited the booth. "See you later. We're gonna kick that other team's butt for sure."

Cat sat in Amy's vacated seat as if her legs wouldn't hold her up any longer. "I don't know what's gotten into her lately. She used to be so quiet I had to encourage her to talk, but now she never stops talking. And what comes out of her mouth..." She crumpled a paper napkin. "She doesn't get it from me."

"Don't worry about it." Luc took a mouthful of coffee so he wouldn't laugh. "Amy's a great kid, real spunky."

"She's that all right." Cat frowned. "And what's that about kicking butt? All I've ever told her is to do her best and enjoy the game. I want her to be a good sport and team player."

"Uh..." He drank more coffee he didn't want. "I'm a guy. Except for Amy, I coach guys. We kick butt."

"Oh." Cat's frown deepened. "Well, I'd appreciate it if you didn't use that expression around her anymore."

"Would you rather I told her to kick ass?"

"Of course not, but I've taught her that physical violence, whether it's in words or actions, is wrong. Besides, she's picking up a lot of other hockey talk, too. Like the jokes she comes home from practice with." Cat made a pained face.

"Okay, no kicking butt." Luc tried to keep the smile out of his voice. "But she's a hockey player so, whether you like it or not, she's going to pick up hockey talk. That's one of the ways she fits in with her team. Don't you want that?"

"Sure I do, but I also want her to fit in at school." Cat twisted the wide, silver band on her right ring finger. "Over the past few weeks, between practices, games, and extra coaching with you, she's hardly had enough time for her homework."

"Have any of her teachers said there's a problem?"

"No, but that doesn't mean there isn't one." Cat didn't meet Luc's gaze. "All Amy talks about is hockey, and I want her to have other interests."

"Has she shown an interest in anything else?" Something more than hockey had Cat worked up, but what?

"Not really." Cat's shoulders slumped. "But over the past few weeks, it's like she doesn't care about anything else. Not our movie nights or board games..." Her mouth opened but no more words came out, and she pressed a hand to her throat.

"Hey, it's okay." As understanding dawned, guilt pricked him. "You aren't losing Amy. She loves you. She talks about you all the time when she's with me. You're the most important person in her life."

"Now that you're coaching her, she listens to you more than me." Cat bit her bottom lip and her face got a pinched expression. "That's never happened with any other coach." She hugged herself.

Luc fought the urge to slide into the other side of the booth and take her in his arms. "I had no idea." Although he should have guessed because Amy looked up to him, and when she was on the ice, she did everything he asked her to and more. Coaches were role models and could have a big influence on kids. "I'm her coach, so I'm teaching her sports skills, but you'll always be the one who cherishes her heart."

Cat straightened and pushed back her shoulders. Which also pushed out her breasts under that way-too-tempting sweater. "That's why I need to fix it."

"Why? It sounds like I'm the one causing the problem. You don't have to do everything by yourself."

"I always have. It's who I am."

Her voice was high and strained, like the little girl Luc remembered. Although he'd been too young to fully understand it then, that little girl's world had been turned upside down when Brian McGuire skipped town. And she'd grown up into a woman who was afraid to trust or depend on anybody, maybe even herself.

"I want to help you. Let me talk to Amy before practice this week." Mixed with desire was that protective urge she'd always brought out in him.

"Okay…thanks." Her voice was still high but less taut, which he guessed was a victory of sorts. She got to her feet and looked at him, feisty but uncertain like she didn't know where they went from here.

He didn't either, but he slid out of the booth and patted her stiff shoulder. "We'll take my truck out to the inn. We got freezing rain overnight, and the truck's safer than your little city car." His hand tingled from that one brief touch.

"My little city car has snow tires." Her anxious expression faded, and her voice held a teasing note. "It's also more fuel efficient than that monster truck of yours."

"Which would be real important if you skidded off the road and halfway across the lake, wouldn't it?" Luc left money on the table for his breakfast and shrugged into his parka. "It's not a monster truck, either. Those have bigger tires."

Her tongue darted out to moisten her lower lip. "Noted, but I can still drive myself."

Luc wrenched the zip up on his parka to hide the front

of his jeans. Fuel efficiency wasn't a sexy subject, so what was it about this woman that turned him on, even when she pissed him off? He fumbled for his gloves and took a deep breath. "How many times do I have to say this? Let somebody help you. Me."

"All right." Her voice was unexpectedly—and deceptively—meek. She took a filmy blue scarf from her coat sleeve and wrapped it around her neck before slipping a matching hat on her head. All of a sudden, her eyes got a lot bluer and held a twinkle that made him catch his breath. "But I want to drive."

Unlike a lot of guys, a showy vehicle didn't mean much to him, but his truck was different. It had seen him through some long days and hard times, and if a big hunk of metal could be considered family, Buddy was like a brother. "Have you driven a truck before?"

"Grandpapa Brassard taught me. I started out driving his old Chevy around a farmer's field outside town and then on all the back roads between here and the Quebec border." She gave him a cheeky grin. "Laverne sure was a great truck. I still miss her."

He dug in the pocket of his jeans and handed her Buddy's keys. "You're full of surprises, Minnie."

"So are you." Her fingers brushed his as she snagged the key chain. Her teasing expression disappeared and something primitive sizzled in the blue depths of her eyes. She held his gaze for several beats, then turned away.

Luc's head whirled and he followed her to the diner door on autopilot, part of his brain registering the gentle swing of her hips, even sexier because the movement was natural, not put on.

"You're not regretting letting me drive already, are you?" She pushed the door open and tossed another cheeky grin over her shoulder.

The hairs on the back of his neck stood up, and not from the frigid blast of February Vermont air. He wasn't ready to get serious, but memories cast long shadows. Maybe it was time to venture out of those shadows and make some new memories alongside the old.

"Look!"

His head jerked up at Cat's excited voice.

"Sun dogs. I haven't seen those in years. Aren't they supposed to mean good luck?"

Luc squinted at the wintry sky where shards of golden light danced and sparkled around the sun. "A snowstorm in the next twenty-four hours is more likely."

Her laugh rang out. "There's no poetry in your soul."

"Us hockey guys aren't good with poetry." Luc laughed too, a big belly laugh that was both unexpected and instinctive.

Since that day two Novembers before when life as he'd known it had stopped, he'd chuckled and he'd even managed what passed for a laugh, at least to everyone except him. But until now, none of that laughter had come from his heart. In a morning of surprises, that was perhaps the biggest one of all.

Chapter Eleven

❧

Slow down, you're making me dizzy." Cat waded through a snow drift to the edge of the frozen lake.

"You said you wanted an action shot." Luc skidded to a stop and snow flew up from his skates. He leaned on his hockey stick and grinned at her. His brown hair gleamed with gold in the bright winter sun, and in his dark blue hockey jersey he stood out in sharp relief against the white landscape.

"It's a woman's prerogative to change her mind." There was something about his smile that always made Cat smile back. She snapped the photo and checked the image on the screen. Perfect. Luc had replicated the poses from several of the old photos. The same place, but a different time and a much different man. A man with whom she had to keep it light because if she didn't, she'd be pulled even deeper into this irrational, illogical, but oh-so-tantalizing thing between them.

He skated over to where she stood. "If you've got

enough pictures, I want to show you something." His voice was tentative and, at least for him, almost unsure.

"I've got more than enough for the carnival display, but..." She worried her bottom lip. She should work on her book before Amy's hockey game. She should do laundry, along with a million other household chores. Her to-do list oozed out in as many directions as the tentacles of an octopus.

"You're doing it again." Luc propped his stick in a snowbank, then sat on the bench by the lake to unlace his skates and replace them with his winter boots.

"Doing what?" Cat tucked her tablet into her bag.

"Thinking too much. You need to have more fun. Go with the flow and stop rushing. You even drive like you're going against a clock." He slung the bag with his hockey gear over one shoulder and picked up his stick again.

"I have a busy life. Besides, I'm a mom." And the only time she'd gone with the flow, it had resulted in her daughter.

"Your mom is more of a free spirit than you are." He softened his words with a gentle touch on her coat sleeve. "Besides, aren't you curious about what I want to show you?"

More than she wanted to admit. "I guess so." One of the perils of having an academic mind was that she was curious about everything. However, over and over again, life had taught her to be measured and cautious.

"This way." Luc put his free hand under her elbow and guided Cat up the small snowbank away from the lake and toward the cluster of outbuildings behind the inn. "Through here." He pushed the snow-covered branch of a pine tree aside and stood back to let her pass between the narrow gap in the trees.

As Cat eased through it, a shower of snow landed with a soft rustle on her parka hood. A hard-packed trail of snow curved into the forest. "What is this?"

"Don't look so worried, Minnie. It's for snowmobiles. The inn keeps it groomed." Luc followed her and let the branch fall back into place.

"I'm not worried." Her voice came out in a flat monotone, and her heart was like lead in her chest. She wasn't worried about the trail, but every time he called her Minnie, it made their relationship, which wasn't a relationship, more intimate. And with that intimacy came expectations, hopes, and dreams that couldn't be fulfilled.

Another one of Luc's way-too-appealing smiles spread across his face. One in which there was only good humor. "Follow me, then."

She nodded, even as her heart constricted. If she wasn't careful, she could fall in love with this man, but she wouldn't. Instead, she'd treasure each of these little moments for what they were, instead of brooding about what they weren't.

"I spot that little fellow every day when I come out here to see the work the guys are doing on my house." Luc gestured to a plump, red squirrel perched on a low tree branch. He made a soft chirping noise, and the squirrel darted down the tree and disappeared into a tunnel in the snow, reappearing moments later with a pine cone clutched in its tiny paws.

"Are there any other animals back here? Big ones?" Cat drew closer to him. Under the cathedral of tall trees, the sun poked through the branches to tint the snow a silver blue. A soft wind whispered in the treetops and brushed her face.

"No, we're still too close to the inn." His deep laugh rumbled out. It was a new laugh, without the undercurrent of sadness she'd grown used to hearing. He pulled her into the shelter of his body. "My great-grandfather on Mom's side was a trapper in Quebec. He took me into the bush with him when I was a kid. I never liked hunting, but he taught me a lot about animals and surviving in the woods. Wild animals don't like to be around people any more than we want to get close to them."

"I come from a family of mill owners and lawyers." Snug in the curve of Luc's body, Cat was warm and more at ease than she'd ever been with any man except Nick. But she was also more aware of Luc than she'd ever been of any man in a way that wasn't at all fraternal.

"I'm a business guy myself now that I'm behind a desk at the creamery from Monday to Friday." Luc guided her along a side trail that led deeper into the woods, going ahead of her to make a path through the heavy snow that was unmarked, apart from tracks made by little animals. Halfway along a thick wall of trees, he lifted a branch and motioned her under it.

Cat sucked in a breath of frosty, evergreen-scented air. A small, snow-covered pond made a perfect circle edged by trees, and steam rose from a dome near the opposite shore. "It's a beaver pond. There's the lodge." She put a mitten-clad hand to her mouth and looked at him.

"It sure is. What do you think?" His voice was gruff.

"It's magical." The scene in front of her could have come out of one of the picture books she'd read to Amy when her daughter was small.

"There's been a beaver pond back here as long as I can remember. When Maggie came to Firefly Lake the first time, I brought her here. It's one of my favorite places. I haven't..." He stopped and cleared his throat. "I haven't been here with anyone but her."

And now you. His unspoken words fluttered between them as gentle as the wind that swayed the treetops.

"I have to find my way back to me again. That's why I came home to Firefly Lake. But Maggie..." He dropped his hockey gear and stared at the pond, a wistful expression clouding his face. "She was the biggest part of my life from when I was eighteen. I met her my first day of freshman year in college."

"You won't ever forget her." Cat forced the words out through cold lips. "She'll always be in your heart, along with your memories." Precious memories he was lucky to have. Like he was lucky to have given his heart to someone who'd given him hers back.

"I brought you here because I like you. I didn't plan it, but after we finished taking the pictures, I thought...I didn't want to go right back to town or to the inn. I wanted to share this with you. It's hard but..." He stopped and scrubbed a hand across his face. "Maggie's gone, but you...you're Nick's sister and Amy's mom. Our families have been friends forever." He paced to and fro in the snow at the edge of the pond. "It's complicated."

It was, but she was thirty-four, and the women she studied were more adventurous than she was. Right here in Firefly Lake women had played hockey, worked alongside men in her family's mill, and single-handedly kept the inn and a lot of other businesses in town going when their menfolk were at war. Yet, unless she drove that change herself, she'd stay stuck and never be like any of those feisty women she admired. Despite the sick feeling in her stomach, she had to stop thinking and start living.

"I like you, too." There, she'd said it. If liking involved a lot of lust, she didn't have to tell him that part.

"I should have apologized for kissing you, but I can't." His voice was thick. "I want to kiss you again but—"

"Why don't you?" The opportunity to start living and make a different choice was right in front of her. If she didn't grab it now, maybe she'd never have that choice— or the courage—again.

Luc took a breath. His pupils dilated, and his warm breath fanned the tendrils of hair that framed her face around her parka hood.

She quivered, then moved closer and stood on tiptoe to wrap her arms around his chest. She wasn't the girl she'd been back in high school. Even if she wasn't fearless, she could still be brave. And if making a choice resulted in a mistake, she'd own that mistake and move on. From now on, she wouldn't let the fear of making choices—or mistakes—define her life.

"Cat." Her name was torn out of him in a low growl and, almost as if he couldn't help himself, he reached out and touched her jaw, his glove soft against her skin.

Sensual awareness rippled along her nerve endings. Before she let herself analyze it, she pulled him down for a kiss.

He stilled. "I..."

"I kissed you. Don't even think about saying sorry." While she might be sorry for a lot of things, she wasn't sorry for this. She had to take a chance on what she could get, even if it was only one perfect moment.

His rough laugh was laced with sexual promise. "Who said anything about being sorry?" He pulled her hard against his body and dipped his head.

After that, analyzing was the last thing Cat wanted to do.

Luc hadn't been avoiding Cat, but was she avoiding him? Until today, and except at hockey practice, he'd hardly seen her since last Saturday. However, after that explosive kiss by the beaver pond, a kiss that had ended much too soon, thanks to snowmobiles—and people—approaching on the trail, she'd been on his mind night and day. Especially during those endless quiet nights at Harbor House when his bed was too big and he had too much time to think.

"I've never been to a winter carnival before." Amy bounced beside him in Old Harbor Park like an excited puppy. "Mom and I have wanted to go to the one in Quebec City for years, but something always happens. Last year the car broke down. Mom says we need a money tree so we can do more fun stuff."

"Amy." From the girl's other side, Cat made a shushing motion. "We have to stick to a budget, that's all."

A tight budget. The troubled expression on Cat's face at Amy's innocent excitement was yet another reminder how different her life was from his. He looked at Amy and resisted the urge to tug on the ponytail that waved from beneath her knit hat. "This carnival hasn't changed since your mom and I were kids. The ice sculptures, dog sled races, and hockey tournament are all still the same as I remember when I was your age."

"Except you played in the hockey tournament and I didn't." Amy's tone was heavy with sarcasm.

"Those boys were huge." Cat's voice was firm, as well as more than a bit scared. "For the first time in my life, I was glad girls were banned from taking part in something."

"It's still unfair." Amy frowned before she gave Luc a dimpled grin. "Maybe by next year there'll be enough girls playing hockey here to have at least one girls' game."

"We don't know if we'll be here this time next year." Cat's face got a tense look. "Besides, wasn't skating with those Olympians better than any tournament?"

"Of course, but playing in the tournament would have made a perfect day even better." Amy bounced again and pointed in the direction of a wooden warming hut at the edge of the park, where it met Firefly Lake. "There's Kylie. I said I'd meet her over there to go to the snack bar. Uncle Nick gave us money to share. See you." She darted into the crowd.

"Wait...Amy—"

"She'll be fine. It's Firefly Lake, remember? Besides, we can keep an eye on her from here."

"I worry about her." Cat's voice was small.

"Of course you do." Like he'd have worried about a kid of his. "But most of the town is here, so she's got a lot of folks watching out for her."

A smile hovered around Cat's mouth. "And if she takes one misstep, somebody will tell me about it."

"Sooner rather than later." Luc's laugh got stuck in his throat. Even bundled up in winter gear, Cat was sexy. Yet, if he so much as reached for her hand, it would be as good as making an announcement in the "Social Notes" section of the *Kincaid Examiner*. Firefly Lake's informal but highly efficient network of friends and neighbors would jump into action and within an hour, his mom would be on the phone asking him why he hadn't told her what he had going on with Cat. And since he couldn't explain it to himself, he had nothing to say to his mom.

"You're doing a lot for Amy with the coaching and now with the women's hockey demonstrations. She may not truly appreciate it yet, but I do. You gave her a wonderful day."

"Today wasn't only for Amy. It was also for all the other girls around here who might be interested in hockey." His heart gave a painful bump because, although he'd never tell anyone, not even Cat, today was for Maggie, too—his way of keeping her memory alive.

"No matter who it was for, Amy looks up to women like your friends. Meeting them and skating with them is something she'll remember for the rest of her life." Cat's voice caught. "You made a dream come true."

"Mom." Amy skidded to a halt on the snow-packed path between him and Cat. "Kylie invited me to sleep over tonight. I don't even have to go back to the apartment because they have stuff I can borrow. Even a toothbrush. It's okay with Aunt Mia. Can I? Please?" Her eyes shone.

"Sure." Cat smiled at her daughter. "It sounds like fun."

"You're the best mom ever." Amy's words tumbled over each other. "Aunt Mia's making sloppy joes, and we're gonna have ice cream and watch movies and do hair and makeup and take selfies." She hopped from one foot to the other. "Kylie and me are staying up real late to watch the fireworks. Uncle Nick says we can sleep in as long as we want tomorrow morning."

"Kylie and I." Cat's voice held a hint of laughter.

"Whatever." Amy glanced at Luc. "Without me around, Mom won't have anything to do. You should have supper with her. She really liked it when we went to the Pink Pagoda that time."

"Amy." Cat made a choked sound. "I'm sure Luc has plans for tonight. Since you're having a sleepover, I can work and... well—"

"Great idea, Amsey." Luc swallowed a laugh. The girl was cheeky, but she was also a sweetheart, and if he didn't watch it, he'd get more attached to her than a coach should. Cat threw him a look. "What? We have to eat, and why should we eat alone?" He didn't have any plans for Saturday night, except watching the Islanders game and choosing bathroom tile. Maybe Cat could even help him with the tile. From what he'd seen of her place, she was good at decorating.

"Amsey?" Cat's voice was hesitant.

"It's what the guys on the team call me. It's a nickname." Amy shrugged.

"I named you after Amy in *Little Women*. It's a beautiful name, but Amsey?"

"Mom." Amy rolled her eyes. "Only you would name a kid after somebody in a book. A pretty dumb book, too, if it's anything like the movie. As for that Amy, she was such a girlie girl. I'm nothing like her."

"No, but I love you anyway." There was a smile in Cat's voice and a teasing twinkle in her eyes. "Go on and have fun. Don't forget to brush your teeth with that toothbrush."

"I won't." Amy hesitated. "I have to talk to Coach Luc first, though." She looked from side to side. "In private."

"Okay." Cat hugged Amy, then stepped away. "I'll be over by the bandstand with your uncle Nick."

"What's up?" Luc looked at Amy. A guy would be lucky to have a daughter like her. She was good at hockey, sure, but she had the makings of a good person off the ice, too.

She leaned in close. "I think my mom likes you."

"I like your mom, too. She's a friend." Which was the truth, or at least part of it, and the only part that Amy needed to know.

"No, I mean she *really* likes you." Her voice was a stage whisper.

Luc took a step back. This conversation was getting way too personal, way too fast. "I really like your mom. I've known her since I was younger than you. Your whole family's like family to me." Another half-truth. Luc's stomach heaved.

"No, I mean my mom likes you how Melanie Grant likes Kieran Cormier." Amy's face was serious.

"Who?" Luc glanced around. In a small town, people always seemed to pop up the instant you wanted privacy, but when you needed an interruption, folks went about their business like you weren't even there.

"Kieran, the guy who plays right wing on our team. Melanie's in my class. You must have seen her hanging around at games staring at him? Long brown hair and lots of blue gunk on her eyes?" Amy wrinkled her nose. "Kieran stares at her, too, and whenever she's around, he shows off. I think it's weird. They're only in sixth grade, but if, like... you know... you wanted to look at my mom like that, I guess that'd be okay with me."

"Your mom's great, but..." Luc stopped. If he couldn't

explain his feelings for Cat to himself, how could he explain them to Amy?

"She *is* great, and she's also smart, pretty, and kind." Amy's expression was earnest. "She'd be a great girlfriend for you."

"I'm sure she would, but I'm not looking for a girlfriend right now." He tried to smile. "Besides, I think I'm too old for one, don't you?"

"Of course not. Look at my grandma and Ward? He's way older than you. And I think my mom's boss likes Mrs. Liz a lot. Age is only a number. That's what Grandma says." Amy smiled at him.

"She's right." Luc hesitated. Anything he said would either give Amy false hope or hurt her, and he couldn't hurt this sweet girl. "Go on. Kylie's waiting for you."

"Okay, but if you want to know anything more about my mom, just ask me. She's kind of serious, but she can be really funny. And even though she doesn't think so, Mom looks great in a bikini."

"Amy…" By the time Luc got his tongue unstuck from the roof of his mouth, she'd darted away.

It was February in Vermont. It wasn't like he'd have the opportunity to see Cat in a bikini anytime soon, so he shouldn't even think about it. Except, he *was* thinking about it and, although he couldn't give Cat the kind of commitment she needed, it was getting harder and harder to deny what he wanted.

If the way she kissed him by the beaver pond was any indication, Cat wanted it, too.

Chapter Twelve

Cat slipped into her winter coat as Luc held it out for her. Despite the intimacy of the Pink Pagoda, where red paper lanterns had cast a rosy glow over their table for two, this dinner hadn't been a date.

"See you again soon." Katie Wong, one half of the husband-and-wife team who'd owned the restaurant as long as Cat remembered, held out the brown paper bag with their leftovers and gave her a knowing smile. "It was busy tonight because of the carnival, but next time I'll make sure you have a quieter table." She glanced at Luc. "More romantic."

"Our table was fine." Cat took the bag, then fumbled in her coat pocket for her mittens. Despite her newfound determination to truly live her life, she couldn't expect romance with Luc. Romance was about love, and that was for books and movies, not real life.

"Great food, too." Luc's voice was warm. "That's the

best meal I've eaten outside of Chinatown in San Francisco."

"Thank you." Katie bobbed her head. "A picture for our wall?" She gestured to the framed photos that hung along the entryway wall above a tank, where several enormous goldfish swam in lazy circles.

"Sure." Luc moved closer to Cat.

"I don't..." Cat stopped because Katie had already whipped out her phone and was clicking away.

"Luc is very good for business." Katie bobbed her head again. "He will bring us great fortune. Smile, Cat. You look nervous."

Luc squeezed her shoulders through her coat. "Sorry," he whispered into her ear.

Cat gritted her teeth and smiled through tight lips. There was no reason for her to be nervous. She didn't like having her picture taken, that was all. It had nothing to do with the easy familiarity of the dinner she and Luc had shared, lingering until the restaurant was empty. Or the sensual spark in his blue eyes that had made her heart hammer, and that had meant she'd been so caught up with him she'd barely registered any of the other diners.

"Much better." Katie put her phone away and patted Cat's arm. "You need to smile more. It's not good to be so serious. Besides, smiling makes good wrinkles." She held open the street door and cold air rushed in, together with a shower of snow. "Walk her home fast, Luc. It's stormy tonight." Her dark eyes twinkled before she closed the door behind them.

Cat shivered as snow pellets stung her face. "You don't have to walk me home." She swayed in the icy wind that buffeted them. "My apartment's only a few blocks away."

"Of course I'm walking you home." Luc gripped her arm and steered her across Main Street, breaking a path with each effortless stride. "I'd drive you if I had my truck and you hadn't insisted we walk here from the park. The truck will be buried in snow by now."

"It wasn't snowing earlier."

But while they'd been in the restaurant, pillow-like clouds had blotted out the stars. The wind had risen to make a high, keening sound, and snow had drifted across the street like a thick blanket of marshmallow fluff.

"That's a Vermont winter for you. My dad jokes he's put more miles on his snow blower than his car." Out of the darkness and swirling snow, the streetlights along Main cast a pale glow. "There won't be any fireworks in this weather."

"Amy will be disappointed." Cat panted to keep up with him. Snowflakes kissed her nose and tongue before eddying around her legs.

Luc glanced at her, then slowed his steps as they passed Nick's darkened law office and the Cozy Corner Craft Shoppe. "I'm sorry about Katie. People taking my picture came along with playing in the NHL, but it made you uncomfortable."

"It's okay." Cat's boots slid in the new-fallen snow. "I bet she'll edit me out. You're the star."

"I never wanted to be." Luc's voice was serious. "From the time I was in first grade, I wanted to play pro hockey, but when I did, I had to become this whole other person off the ice. I'm not comfortable with people taking my picture, either, but it was part of the job, so I had to learn to live with it." He stopped at the corner of the cross street before the gallery.

"Is that why you came back to Firefly Lake? Because most people here treat you like a normal person?" Until now, Cat hadn't suspected that Luc was such a private guy, maybe even as private as her.

"Apart from helping my family with the creamery, yes. Having a normal life is something you can't put a price on. I'll even put up with this weather." A smile creased his cheeks and with his eyebrows and lashes etched white, he was a sexy and way-too-appealing Jack Frost.

Cat stepped off the curb and sank into deeper snow, over the tops of her boots. "Doesn't the town still plow?"

His chuckle wrapped around her like a warm hug. "It's late. We closed the Pink Pagoda. The town won't plow again until morning."

Cat stumbled sideways. "Why did I ever leave Boston?"

"They get snow there." Luc laughed harder, then he lifted her into his arms and carried her the rest of the way across the street.

"Of course they do, but what…no…put me down." Cat wriggled, but he held her tight.

"And have you disappear into a snowbank?" He stepped onto the sidewalk in one smooth motion and continued toward the gallery.

"The snow isn't that deep. I can walk." Cat hung onto Luc's broad shoulders.

"With wet snow in your boots?"

"Not a lot." She wiggled her toes. Which was a mistake because one of her boots slipped off, and her bubble-gum-pink Minnie Mouse sock ended up almost level with his nose.

Barely breaking his stride, Luc bent to pick up her

boot. "You have a pair of those socks for each day of the week?"

"No. Amy only had three pairs." Cat squeaked as Luc swung her over his shoulder.

"Keys, Minnie?"

"In my left coat pocket...oh..." She squeaked again as he rummaged in her pocket. The security light went on, and he started up the outside stairs beside the gallery.

"You can put me down now." She pushed at his rock-hard chest through his parka.

"Your feet are wet." His voice went tight.

"Your hair is, too." Beneath his woolly hat, strands of golden brown hair were damp against her cheek. "Come in and I'll get you a towel to dry off. You should warm up before walking back to my mom's. I can make hot cocoa and..."

She stopped as they reached the top of the stairs. Luc slid her down on the small landing, the movement slow and arousing.

"I'm already warm, and if I come into your apartment, it won't be for cocoa." His voice roughened, and he kept her clasped tight against his body.

She looked at him and blinked, winded by the naked want in his eyes. She respected that he wanted to give her a choice, but they'd led up to this moment for weeks. It wouldn't be a vacation fling like she'd had with Amy's dad, a guy she barely knew. This was Luc. He couldn't give her forever, and she was okay with that. She also didn't have a head full of romantic dreams or unrealistic hopes. "I want this, you."

He covered her hand with his and they unlocked the apartment door together. When the door swung open.

Bingley and Darcy wound themselves around their ankles with loud meows.

She didn't need forever, but she needed what Luc could give her. Comfort, however brief, and a sense of the woman she'd never had a chance to be because she'd had Amy so young and supporting her daughter had been her only focus outside school. A woman who wasn't so serious and who could take a risk without it changing the rest of her life.

She moved into the apartment foyer and gestured to him to follow. "I'll find you a towel." She pulled off her remaining boot, the wet socks, and curled her cold toes against the hardwood floor.

His eyes flashed blue flames as his gaze connected with hers. "You're sure?" He cleared his throat. "I think Amy's looking for something permanent. She talked to me earlier and asked if I liked you. I do, you know that, but I can't...do permanent anymore." His voice was all of a sudden flat.

"I've never needed permanent." She was independent and self-sufficient, skills she'd learned early on when her dad left. Cat pushed down the little flicker of something that might have been doubt. Could her life have been different? Maybe if she'd found the right man a long time ago, but she hadn't, so she wouldn't let herself think about it.

"Amy's never had a dad, so she's looking for a father figure. You're her coach. It's natural she's turned to you." Her daughter was growing up, and sharing her with someone else was a natural part of that process. "She's never had a coach before who wasn't the dad of one of her teammates."

And none of those dads had been like Luc. They didn't have his charisma or the star factor that lingered from his playing days. They also hadn't focused on Amy like he did. As for Cat, she'd never reacted to any of them, even the divorced ones, like she did Luc.

She slipped off her coat and hung it on the stand, then took Luc's parka and sweatshirt. "Amy can't know about this."

Luc's gaze was steady. "I don't want to hurt her. Or you."

"You won't." Cat didn't let herself get hurt, and if Luc's only role in Amy's life was as her coach, he couldn't hurt Amy, either. She went into the kitchen to put the leftover food in the fridge, then padded back into the entry hall, where Luc still stood and watched her, his gaze intent and his breath rising and falling beneath a thin T-shirt. She opened the linen closet to take out a towel. "Here you go." She held it out.

He took one end of the fabric and used it to pull her close to him again. "You do it."

"Do what?" Her fingertips tingled where they touched his.

"Dry my hair." With a gentle tug, he propelled her into the living room and sat in the armchair near the fireplace.

"I..." She let out a husky breath as he eased her onto his lap. "I was going to make cocoa and—"

"I'll warm you up." His voice got thick, and the towel dropped to the floor.

Her body flushed with heat from the top of her head to the tips of her toes, and she twined her fingers with his. "I haven't done this in a really long time." She shifted on his lap and her legs slipped apart.

"Me neither." His fingers tightened on hers. "I was a one-woman guy."

Cat trembled. "I thought…in high school you were popular and—"

"You thought wrong." He pulled her into the curve of his chest, and her hip brushed his erection through his jeans. One of his hands slipped to her breast, the nipple already taut beneath her sweater and bra.

"Maybe I think too much." She moaned as his finger traced her nipple.

His laugh was wicked as his other hand slipped beneath the hem of her sweater and traced a circular path upward. He undid her bra by its front clasp with unerring accuracy, and his warm hand covered one of her breasts.

Cat rocked into his touch. For one of the few times in her life, she couldn't think. She could only give herself up to sensation and him.

Luc eased Cat's sweater over her head and sucked in a harsh breath. In the muted light of the living room lamp, her skin was creamy white, tinged with pink, and, for such a tiny woman, her breasts, tipped with hard, darker buds, were lush and curvy.

"What?" Her expression was wary.

"You're beautiful." He slipped her bra off and touched each of her breasts in turn, his fingertips skimming across her skin to linger on her nipples.

She quivered. "I—"

He put a finger to her soft lips. Despite the raw need that thundered through him, his heart was filled with sudden tenderness. "You're smart *and* beautiful." He traced the ripe swell of her breasts again and then drew her off his lap to toss several throw cushions and a blanket on the floor in front of the fireplace. "Here." He patted the impromptu bed.

"Not in my bedroom?" Her voice hitched.

"The fire's all ready to light." He pointed to the stacked wood and kindling in the grate.

"Michael says the power still goes off a lot here in winter. He told me to help myself from the woodpile out back." Cat shot him an unexpectedly flirty grin and nibbled her plump bottom lip. Her breasts rose and fell with her rapid breathing.

Luc grabbed a match from the holder, lit it, and touched the flame to the kindling. Although he'd had opportunities, he hadn't been with another woman since his wife. He slid the screen in front of the fireplace with an unsteady hand and pulled off his T-shirt. It was more than time. His body throbbed and, as he turned back to Cat, he caught his breath. Lying on a pink pillow, her blond hair tumbling around her head, she looked sexy, wild even. Not the cautious, buttoned-up woman he was used to seeing. "Where were we?"

She reached out and ran a hand along his forearm, and his skin tingled. Her eyes were dark and aroused and she gave him a slow smile. "You asked me to dry your hair."

"Yeah, I did." Before he'd distracted her, distracted them both to give himself a last chance to think about what he was doing and why. He grabbed the towel and passed it to her.

"Here." She sat up, held his gaze, and opened her arms wide.

Then the towel and her hands were in his hair, her

gentle touch an almost unbearable mix of sensuality and healing. As he relaxed into her embrace, the tightness in his shoulders he'd carried even before he'd gotten hurt eased. And he couldn't help it, he moaned—loud, guttural, and turned on.

Cat stilled. "Am I hurting you?"

"No." He clenched his hands briefly, then released them. "It's so good you could do this massage thing professionally. Guys would line up."

"I doubt it." She gave a soft laugh and leaned even closer.

Then the towel dropped to the floor, and her hands were everywhere; in his hair, on his face, and clutching his back. "Don't sell yourself short." Luc moaned again as her fingers connected with his bare chest and teased the springy tendrils of hair.

Except, he didn't want Cat touching any other guy but him. The thought bounced off him like a rogue slap shot. He wanted her all to himself. Her sharp mind, gorgeous body, and sweetness—everything that made her the woman she was. But he couldn't go there, not now and not ever. This thing between them was physical and to satisfy a need they both had, nothing more.

The pebbled tips of her breasts brushed his chest and he shuddered against her. Her gaze met his in a searing moment of truth before she traced the zigzag scar tissue that ran along his right shoulder blade, her touch featherlight.

Luc quivered with pleasure. "Pro hockey's a tough game." He ground out the words as her tongue replaced her finger, to leave a trail of liquid fire across his bare skin.

"Too tough." Her hands drifted lower to the buttons on his jeans.

His breath came in short, harsh bursts as she undid each button in turn, her touch delicate against his hardness. "Cat..."

"What?" Her voice was throaty and her tongue darted out to lick her lips.

"You're killing me." He helped her tug his jeans over his hips and down his legs and off.

"Like you're not..." She stopped and let out a hiss. Then her hands inched back upward to graze the curve of his bare hips. "You aren't wearing any underwear."

"No." He shivered as her fingertips glided across his inner thighs.

She stared at him, and her body tensed. "You're big." Her face went red. "Really big." She pulled her glasses off and buried her face in one of the cushions.

"We'll fit together just fine." He made his voice gentle and eased the cushion away to cup her chin in one hand. "I won't hurt you, I promise."

"Will you stop if...?" She trembled.

He moved closer and brushed kisses along her jaw. "You set the pace. If you want to stop, we stop." Even though he was harder than he'd been since college, this was her call.

"No, I want this. I want you." She set her glasses beside the matches, then undid her jeans and wiggled out of them until she was naked, apart from a pair of pale pink panties edged with creamy lace.

Beneath her serious demeanor, she was so feminine, much more so than he'd first expected. He fingered the edge of her underwear, and she gave a breathy sigh and rocked against his hand. "Cat..." When her hand covered his erection, his breath almost burst out of his lungs.

"You said I can set the pace." She gave him a half smile and pressed her breasts against his chest. Her lips parted before she bent her head to suck his lower lip into her mouth.

He juddered as an electric current of sensation shot through him. "Hang on." He eased her panties off before reaching for his wallet in his jeans. Her skin shimmered in the flickering firelight. Luc's pulse sped up as he found the condom he carried around out of habit and handed it to her.

She tore open the package and together they rolled it on. He settled her against the cushions and sought her breasts with his mouth. The fire crackled, and the zest of the wood smoke mingled with her lighter rose fragrance. She made a sharp sound deep in her throat as he tugged at her nipple and rolled his tongue around it.

Her fingers tangled in his hair, and she arched into him.

He tore his mouth away from her breast, then looked into her eyes, shiny and dark blue with desire. He was so turned on, and it had been so long that, for a brief moment, he was dizzy. Her face and body, the firelight, and the soft lamplight all melded together in a golden haze. "Yes." It was a statement rather than a question. He held his breath.

"Yes." Her voice was tight as he eased between her legs and braced himself on his forearms above her. Her hands gripped his hips, lightly at first, then harder, and her tongue delved deep into his mouth.

Luc forgot about being gentle, and he forgot about being tender as she moved beneath him and urged him on with inarticulate cries. But he didn't forget about looking at her as he eased into her body. As his gaze held hers, it wasn't only physical. He was also giving her a small part of his soul.

Chapter Thirteen

Snow hit Cat's bedroom window with a gentle hiss, and the gray light of a winter morning crept through the slatted blinds. She squinted at her trusty, battery-powered alarm clock on the night table. It was only nine. Amy would be at Nick and Mia's for a few more hours, so she didn't have to get up yet and could savor this, Luc, for a little while longer.

Luc still slept beside her. Brown stubble darkened his jaw, and he looked both relaxed and younger. Sex with him had been everything she'd ever imagined and more. But even as they'd shared their bodies, she'd been careful to hold the core of herself back, the part that could get hurt.

"Morning, Minnie." His voice rasped in her ear.

She started and swallowed the emotion lodged in her throat. "Morning." She'd gotten what she wanted. It had to be enough. "I thought you were asleep."

"I wake up fast, thanks to all those years of early morning practices." One of his arms looped around her and pulled her close to the heat of his body. "You don't regret last night, do you?"

"Of course not. It was great." Except, it could only be last night and, after glimpsing the woman she might have been, she wanted more.

"It was sure great for me, too." He settled her into the crook of his shoulder, and his tone had more than a hint of satisfaction. "If we'd had another condom, I'd have wanted to do it all over again."

She would have too because his body had been a perfect fit for hers. After they'd made love, they'd snuggled together in her bed where they'd touched and talked for hours. It had been intimate and tender—and it had irrevocably changed how Cat thought about herself.

She traced one of his hard biceps. His big body bore the scars of the game he'd played for almost his entire life, and each one mapped who he was. What she'd felt for Amy's dad had been lust, but her feelings for Luc were deeper, maybe even love—if she still believed in love.

"Since you don't have to pick Amy up until noon, why don't I make us some breakfast and then I can drop by the drugstore as soon as it opens. I think we need more practice, don't you?" His fingers slid through the strands of her hair to zero in on the sensitive spot behind her ear.

"The drugstore near the town green?" Her stomach clenched. Although she wanted to make love with him again, she couldn't let herself get in any deeper. He'd been honest. He could give her this, whatever it was, but nothing more.

"Is there any other drugstore in town besides

Doucette's?" Luc's hand drifted from her neck downward to her bare breast.

"No, but you can't go there." Cat quaked as he tweaked her nipple. "If anyone sees you buying condoms, they'll know you're having sex, and they might guess it's with me. Half the town saw us together at the carnival and then the Pink Pagoda." After she'd been the focus of town gossip once, the hurt had gone deep. Ever since then, all she wanted was to keep a low profile. "I was in Doucette's last week and bought two boxes of tissues and a vaporizer. Twenty minutes later, one of my mom's friends stopped me in the market to ask if Amy was sick."

"Was she?"

"No. The stuff was on sale."

"That's living in a small town for you." Luc's soft chuckle vibrated against her breast. "With all the snow, the road to Kincaid will be impassable until the plows get through. I guess we'll have to be creative. What do you say?"

Cat quivered as his mouth captured her breast. "Creative is good." If last night had shown her anything, it was that she'd never been creative enough. His hand tracked the curve of her hip, and her legs fell apart.

An instant later, she stilled and surfaced from the haze of sensation Luc was evoking with his fingers and mouth. "What was that?" She rolled into a sitting position and shivered as cold air hit her bare skin.

"What?" Luc raised his head.

"I heard a noise." She fumbled for her glasses on the bedside table.

"It must have been the cats." He gave her a sexy grin.

"No, voices."

"Michael's probably downstairs. He comes in early, doesn't he?" Luc outlined a sensuous path between her ankle and instep.

"Never on Sundays." Cat groped for her pajamas, but she hadn't worn them.

Footsteps echoed on the staircase landing outside the apartment. "Cat? Are you in there, honey?" Her mom's voice. "The power's out and cell phone coverage is down." There were several sharp raps on the door before a key turned in the lock. "I brought you a mug of tea." The door squeaked open, and her mom's voice came closer. "We're all over at the diner. Amy too. The generator has kicked in, so you come right over to keep warm and get something to eat. Hey, kitties, where's…"

In the sudden silence, Luc swore under his breath and fumbled in the comforter.

"Quick, in there." Cat scrambled for her bathrobe on the floor by the bed and gestured to the half-open closet door.

"I'm not hiding in the closet." He found a towel from Cat's laundry basket and wrapped it around his hips. "We don't have anything to be ashamed of."

Except, they were both naked and most of their clothes were still scattered across the living room floor. It also wasn't *his* mother out there. Cat suppressed a groan. "I just woke up. I'll be out in a minute."

"Cat?" Georgia's voice this time. "Mia sent you an extra sweater. She knows how you feel the cold." She made a sound that was almost, but not quite, a laugh.

Floorboards creaked in the hall. "Do you know where Luc's got to?" Her mom was in the living room on the other side of the wall from Cat's bedroom. "He didn't come back to the house last night after the carnival. With no cell service, his mom can't reach him, so Chantal asked me to...oh."

Cat gestured toward the closet again. "Get in there, now." Her words came out in a hiss, and she shoved Luc's buttock through the towel.

The guy was hard in all the right places.

Yanking on her bathrobe, she tied the belt tight. She'd never hear the end of this, and it wasn't like she could pass it off as some kind of misunderstanding. Even if her mom and Georgia didn't actually see Luc, the evidence was out there as plain as day, right down to the empty condom wrapper. Nobody else in town wore a Winnipeg Jets sweatshirt, either, and that sweatshirt was still on the hall stand where she'd left it with his coat the night before.

"I'm..." She raked her fingers through her hair, then caught her reflection in the mirror over the dresser. Her skin was flushed, and her eyes were bright. Her hair was tousled, and she looked more relaxed than she had in years, maybe ever. She also looked like she'd had sex with a man who knew exactly how to do it.

"Take your time, honey." A gentle clatter followed her mom's words. "I've left the tea on the table for you. I'll tell Amy you're fine and that she doesn't need to come up. She's in the gallery with Ward and Michael checking the security system. She gave me her key and said it was okay to come right on in."

Her daughter. Cat's mouth went dry. Amy could have walked in on her with Luc. She glanced at him, where he stood in front of the closet door.

"I'll leave Mia's sweater on the table, too." Her mom's

footsteps moved farther away. "And I'll tell Luc's mom he hasn't gotten stuck in a snowbank somewhere and frozen to death. Chantal's a worrier like me."

"You can tell her he's snug as a—" Georgia's voice shook with laughter.

"Georgia McGuire, you stop right there and wipe that look off your face. You may be a grown woman, but you'll never be too old for me to—"

The apartment door shut behind her mom and Georgia with a bang. Cat fingered the belt of her bathrobe. The silence pressed in on her as cold and impenetrable as an Atlantic sea fog.

"I should find my clothes." As Luc gestured toward the closed bedroom door, the muscles in his forearm rippled.

"Yes, me too." Cat shoved her feet into the snowman slippers Amy had given her for Christmas. She glanced at the dresser mirror again. Luc was reflected behind her, and the pink bath towel hung low on his lean hips. His chest was still bare, and her mouth went dry. "I'm sorry... my mom and Georgie didn't think... I'm not... I don't usually..."

She'd never brought a man home before and, apart from that long-ago spring break, she'd never had what amounted to a one-night stand, either.

"Why do you need to be sorry for anything?" A rueful smile tugged at one corner of Luc's sensual mouth, and he scrubbed a hand through his hair. "It sounds like your mom's pretty cool with everything. Once my mom knows I'm not lying in a ditch somewhere, she'll be fine, too. We're both adults. We're allowed to have a life. It's not like that was Amy out there."

Except, in a small town where nothing much happened

in the winter, people talked and Amy might hear something that would hurt her. There was a sick feeling in the pit of Cat's stomach and she sat on the edge of the bed with a bump.

"If the power's been out for a while, I guess it's too much to hope there's enough hot water for a shower." The towel slid lower on Luc's hips.

She shook her head. "There's never a lot of hot water here anyway."

"Hey." Luc came around the end of the bed and sat beside her. "It's not the end of the world. Maybe it didn't seem that way when we were kids, but people have sex in Firefly Lake. Sure, their mom and sister don't usually walk in on them, but it isn't a big deal. I'm not embarrassed by what happened between us. Are you?" His blue gaze sharpened.

"No." She wasn't embarrassed. She'd have sex with Luc again if she had the chance. But sex with him had taken her out of herself, and now she had to put herself back together again before she faced Amy, as well as half the town over at the diner. "Amy can't guess what happened."

"How would she? It's not like your mom or Georgia are going to tell her, are they?"

"No." Cat rubbed her hands.

"Besides, as soon as I can get to a drugstore in Kincaid, I want it to happen again, don't you?" He wrapped an arm around her and gave her what, under any other circumstances, would have been a comforting squeeze.

She did, but, despite the warmth of his body next to hers, Cat shivered. She wanted more than sex. She wanted everything that came along with making love. And after last night, she also wanted more of Luc's heart and his life than he could ever give her.

"Your mom looks different." Kylie nudged Amy's arm across the table. They were tucked into a two-person booth in the middle of the North Woods Diner, a plate of French fries topped with gravy and cheese curds between them. Her grandma called the dish "poutine," and Amy had never eaten it before moving to Firefly Lake.

"Mom looks exactly the same to me. Aunt Mia's sweater looks pretty on her, though." Amy wrapped her hands around her warm mug of cocoa.

Mrs. Liz made the best cocoa, the best poutine and, given the aroma of meat, vegetables, and spices that wafted from the diner kitchen, she must make good chili, too.

"No, she's got a new look to her." Kylie grinned. "Like Mia looked when she and Nick got together. Once they had s-e-x." She dropped her voice and spelled the word out.

Amy stared at the marshmallows bobbing in her mug. Even though spelling was hard for her, she knew that word. "My mom doesn't even have a boyfriend." Although she'd tried to get her mom and Coach Luc together, the two of them were friends, nothing more.

"You don't have to have a boyfriend to have sex." Kylie pointed to Amy's mom, who was behind the diner counter with Mrs. Liz. "Look at her and then look at Coach Luc." She jerked her head in the other direction, where the coach sat with Amy's uncle Nick and a few of the hockey dads by one of the diner's curtained front windows. "It looks like they're ignoring each other, but they're actually looking at each other every chance they get. That's a sign something's going on."

"Even if there is, it's none of your business." Amy's stomach got tight, and she moved to the end of the booth, as far away from Kylie as possible. Her mom hated people talking about her, and she always said that gossiping was wrong. She needed friends, but she didn't need a friend who said things that would make her mom feel bad.

"I thought you wanted them to have dinner together last night." Kylie's gaze was still fixed on the coach. "If they went on a date, maybe they did *it*." Kylie's voice rose above the diner clatter.

"Butt out." She tried to make her voice match the tough words because if anybody from school heard Kylie, they might talk about her mom and the coach and that would make Amy feel bad, too. "It wasn't a date." Amy gulped some hot cocoa. "Besides, my mom says sex is special. You should only have it with someone you really care about and who cares about you."

"Mia says that too." Kylie's expression was thoughtful. "But if your mom and Coach Luc did have sex, and if they keep having it, he might become your dad. Then you'd have to share your mom with him, wouldn't you? She might love him more than you."

Amy's chest got as tight as her stomach, and it was hard to breathe. She'd wanted her mom and the coach to get together so she could have a dad, but until Kylie said it, she'd never let herself think that the coach could take her place in her mom's life. "The coach isn't gonna be my dad. He and my mom don't have anything in common." She shrugged like it wasn't important.

"You never know. For an old guy, he's hot, and your mom might like that. Have you heard what the high school girls who hang out at the rink after school say about him?" Kylie gestured with her hands. "A six-pack or what."

"He's the coach. They shouldn't talk about him like that." The backs of Amy's eyes stung. Her mom loved her. She knew she did. She wouldn't love Coach Luc more, would she? And why had she ever asked Kylie to help her with that dumb dad list? Kylie was only a year older than her, but sometimes she seemed really old, almost like she was already a grown-up.

Kylie rolled her eyes. "Why not? The hockey moms talk about him like that, too. I heard them that day I was with Mia when she picked you up after practice."

Amy picked at a hangnail on her thumb. "So? The moms shouldn't talk, either." But she'd heard the same talk. And she'd also heard her teammates' moms talking about her mom. How smart she was, as well as a bunch of stuff Amy hadn't exactly understood but that had something to do with her mom's dad and her grandma.

"I think the coach would be an okay stepdad, but you never know. Some guys are nice until they hook you in, but after that they change big-time. I knew this girl in Burlington whose mom's boyfriend was fine with her at first, but as soon as the mom got pregnant, the girl was packed off to live with an aunt over in Maine somewhere. The guy said he didn't want a kid who wasn't his around. What if your mom and the coach had a baby?" Kylie shrugged. "You're my friend, so all I'm saying is you have to watch out."

Amy didn't think Coach Luc would ever do something

like that, but what did she know, really? She took a deep breath. "I don't want to talk about this anymore. Not now and not ever." Despite the burning sensation behind her eyes, she was almost as strong and powerful as those women who'd come here for the hockey demonstrations. Even when they were her age, she bet those women hadn't been scared to kick butt when they needed to. "You shouldn't talk about it, either, because gossiping about people is mean." If she'd learned anything from being bullied at her old school, it was that she had to stand up for herself. But knowing she had to was still easier than actually doing it.

"I'm sorry." Kylie's voice had a little wobble in it. "I didn't mean to make you mad. Nick says I have to watch my mouth, but sometimes I forget. Still friends?"

"I guess so." The tightness in Amy's chest loosened a bit.

"You're real lucky, you know that? Your mom loves you a lot." Kylie's green eyes clouded. "I bet she'd do anything for you."

"Yeah, she would." And Amy loved her mom. Although it was only the two of them, she had the family by birth that Kylie had never had. "Uncle Nick and Aunt Mia love you a lot, too. I heard Uncle Nick say he couldn't love you any more than if you were his very own daughter."

"Really?" Kylie's eyes got shiny.

"Yep." Amy nudged Kylie's arm. "He's the best."

"He sure is." Kylie's voice cracked. "I got lucky with him and Mia. There aren't a lot of folks out there like them." Kylie moved the plate of poutine closer to Amy. "Hey, you've hardly eaten anything. Aren't you hungry?"

Amy shook her head. Although she'd been really hungry a few minutes ago, she wasn't now. She studied her mom more closely. Kylie was right. Her mom *did* look different, almost like she was lit up inside, and so did Coach Luc.

When she'd thought about fixing up her mom with the coach, it had been so she'd have a dad like all the other kids and fit in. If she was looking for a dad, she'd wanted one she could share her sport with. But she hadn't thought about having to share her mom with him, or that he might not want a kid around. And what if Kylie was right? What if it turned out her mom loved Coach Luc more than she loved Amy?

Amy took a soggy French fry and ate it without tasting it. Unlike in Boston, nobody here called her dumb and, for a while, she'd almost forgotten she was. But if her mom was having sex with Coach Luc and she'd never spotted it, she must be really dumb. Her stomach knotted and she blinked to hold back the scalding rush of tears.

She glanced between her mom and the coach again. They *were* looking at each other. She looked at him like he wasn't a coach, and he looked at her like she wasn't a mom. It was the kind of look that shut Amy and everyone else out. They liked each other all right, and unless she came up with something fast, that look could change her life in a whole bunch of ways she didn't want.

She tore her paper napkin into small pieces and stared at the plate, where several cheese curds blurred with the tears she fought to hold back. Her mom didn't want her to kick butt on the ice, but she'd never said anything about kicking butt off it.

* * *

A spoon clanged against a glass, and Luc looked up from his bowl of Liz's fiery Texas chili. Ward, Gabrielle's partner, stood at the front of the diner, with Gabrielle by his side. Nick, Cat, and Georgia were clustered behind them.

Ward hit the spoon against the glass again and the buzz of conversation quieted. "Because of the storm, almost everyone we care about is here, so Gabrielle and I thought it was the perfect time to tell you that Nick and Mia won't be the only newlyweds in town for much longer." He paused and glanced at Gabrielle, who smiled and nodded. "Last night, Gabrielle made me an even happier man by agreeing to be my wife."

Gabrielle rested a hand on Ward's arm. "At our age, we won't have a big wedding, but we'll have a party afterward, and we hope you'll all join us to celebrate."

Luc got to his feet to join in the cheers and congratulations. Of course he was happy for Gabrielle and Ward, so why was there that pinch around his heart?

"I never thought Gabrielle would get married again, but turns out I was wrong." Beside him, Josh Tremblay gave a wry laugh. "As soon as that silver fox rolled into town, she was a goner. Now I owe Georgia fifty bucks."

"Gabrielle better not know that you and Georgia had a wager about whether she and Ward were going to get married." Luc eyed Josh long enough to make the guy sweat. He liked him, and he'd made sure his contractor had hired him to do some work at the new house, but if Josh had upset Gabrielle, that contract was off.

"Of course not." A faint flush tinged Josh's cheeks beneath the dark beard stubble. "It was Georgia's idea, and I went along with it for a joke. That girl's as crazy as she ever was."

And nowadays it seemed she was Josh's kind of crazy. Luc bit back a smile. "There wasn't anything more to it than a dumb bet?"

Josh grinned. "Nope. I'm smarter than I used to be."

"At least one of you is." He glanced to the front of the diner again, where Cat and Georgia hugged their mom. While Cat had always been conservative with a capital *C*, Georgia was trouble with a capital *T*. He'd suspected, though, that Georgia had a big heart beneath that wild-child exterior. Cat wouldn't be so close to her sister otherwise.

"Great surprise, huh?" Nick joined them. "Mom told us the news earlier, and we're all happy for them. Ward's a good guy and he looks out for Mom, but he still lets her be independent like she wants."

"They're sure good together." Luc's heart gave an agonizing thud.

Ward had loved his first wife and grieved when she'd passed. Somehow, though, he'd found the courage to let himself love again. How had he done it? Unlike sports, grief didn't come with a playbook.

"The contractor says my house will be done by Memorial Day at the latest, so unless Georgia sticks around, Gabrielle and Ward can have their privacy in Harbor House." And even though he couldn't let himself love her, after last night and what they'd done in front of the fire and in her bed, Luc wanted that kind of privacy with Cat.

"You're building an awfully big house for a guy on his own." Josh's voice was contemplative. "Unless maybe you're thinking of having company?" He glanced toward Cat and Georgia still huddled with Gabrielle.

"Give the guy a break." Nick raised a dark eyebrow.

"With all that extended Simard family, he needs the space. Besides, there's a lot to be said for having more room than you need. I thought that, with an addition, Mia's house would be plenty big for all of us, but it's still a squeeze. Who knew a bunch of females had so much stuff? Mia needs a separate closet for her shoes alone." The happy sound of his laugh grated on Luc's ears.

Josh still eyed Luc. "How long is Cat staying in Firefly Lake?"

"I don't know." Luc eyeballed him right back. The guy might think he'd seen something, but even if he had, Luc wouldn't give anything away—especially not in front of Cat's big brother.

"Amy's been great for the team. Connor has learned a lot from her." Josh grinned. "I'm real proud of my boy for admitting he can learn something about hockey from a girl. It's tough being a single dad, and although I want to raise Connor to respect girls and women, it's sure harder than I thought it would be."

Okay, maybe Luc was paranoid. Or maybe it was the guilt that needled him. He'd had sex with a woman who wasn't his wife, and everybody must have guessed. His dad had, that was for certain. It was in the look he'd given him when Luc had come into the diner fifteen minutes after Cat, like they'd agreed. But his dad knew to mind his own business, and he'd make sure Luc's mom did, too.

Maggie had been gone for more than two years. There was no reason for Luc to feel like he'd cheated on her. But it was more than that. Even before he'd had sex with Cat, he'd started to feel something for her that he'd never felt for anyone except Maggie.

He held out his coffee mug to a passing waitress. He

needed caffeine and lots of it. Then he needed another bowl of Liz's chili. And when the crew got the power back on, he needed a shower, a hard workout, then another shower.

After all those things, maybe he could figure out these feelings he had for a woman who couldn't have been more unlike his wife but who'd curled herself around his heart in the exact same way. Even more than the sex, that was what he had the most guilt about.

Chapter Fourteen

"Only ten minutes or so until you can breathe normally again." Her mom patted Cat's arm, then pointed to the remaining game time as the luminous, red seconds ticked down on the scoreboard mounted high on the arena wall.

"I didn't know I was that obvious." Cat blew out a breath and tried to uncurl her tense fingers inside her mittens. It had been a week since she'd had sex with Luc. Since then, they'd circled around each other and, by unspoken agreement, avoided what had happened between them. But whether it was in her mom's kitchen, or today behind the home team's bench, each time she saw him, her heart clenched a little tighter and she wanted him again a little bit more.

"I remember what I was like with your sister and brother." Her mom picked up a Thermos and poured more tea into Cat's mug. "When Georgia went through her gymnastics phase, I died a thousand deaths every time she flung herself off that balance beam. Even now, whenever

Nick goes skiing, I picture him lying unconscious at the bottom of a mountain, every bone in his body broken." She gave Cat a wry smile. "It's a dangerous business being a mom. At least I never had to worry about you and sports."

But her mom had worried about Cat in other ways, and she still did. She'd never mentioned that morning of the snowstorm in Cat's apartment, but it was still there between them, along with everything else that had piled up over the years.

Cat sipped the hot tea and tried to focus on the action on the ice. Even to her untrained eyes, it was obvious Amy was good and Luc's coaching had made her better. She was a faster and more polished skater. Her turns were crisper, and she handled her stick with more confidence.

"Luc's been good for Amy." Her mom looked at the ice, too. "And she's been good for him. I worry about Luc almost as much as I did about Nick before Mia came into his life. But since you and Amy moved here, Luc's eyes aren't sad anymore. He even laughed twice in one day this week."

"He likes coaching Amy, and she sure likes him." Cat's fear of losing her daughter was groundless. Although Amy had been unusually mouthy this past week, she was growing up, and the teenage hormones were starting to kick in.

"I think Luc's good for you as well." Her mom's tone had a hint of amusement, but her gaze remained fixed on the ice. "You have a lot in common. For a start, both of you are focused and determined—and hurting."

"I'm not hurting." At least not like Luc was. He'd lost the only woman he'd ever loved, his soul mate. Whereas she'd only lost the man who'd fathered Amy, a man she'd barely known. Besides, that loss was years ago and she'd moved on.

"If you say so." Her mom looped an arm around Cat's stiff shoulders. "But you're both at points of transition in your lives. He's making a future for himself after hockey and Maggie, and you're—"

"Still making the same future I always planned on." She had to give it time, that was all. "As soon as I get a permanent job, I'll be able to give Amy everything she needs. A girls' hockey league, tennis lessons in the summer, a real vacation, and maybe even private school." Cat set her mug of tea on the bleacher with an unsteady hand.

"All Amy needs is a mom who loves her and wants the best for her. Thanks to you, she already has that. Tennis lessons and private school are nice, sure, but they're not the most important things." Her mom's voice was neutral.

"I want her to have the best opportunities, too." Cat's stomach rolled. "Like you did for us after Dad left. You said not to worry, you'd give us everything we needed, and you did."

"Maybe I was wrong." Her mom tugged on her fluffy gloves. "Maybe what you really needed, I couldn't give you—time with your dad."

"It wasn't your fault Dad left, and it wasn't as if any of us kids wanted to visit him, either. He didn't want us, not really. If he had, he wouldn't have done what he did." Cat tried to keep the little-girl quiver out of her voice. "It's over."

"As long as you carry around all that hurt and anger, it will never be over." Her mom's voice was loving but also firm. "Meeting Ward changed me for the better. Since I've finally faced my fears and agreed to marry him, it's like a big weight's been lifted off my chest. He's a different man than your dad, and he deserves not only my love but my trust. I don't want to interfere in your life, or tell you what to do—"

"I don't…what's…Amy?" Cat stumbled to her feet and her gaze zeroed in on the pile of heaving bodies near center ice. The moment she'd taken her focus away from the game, the hockey version of hell had broken loose. She made her legs move along the bleacher toward the steps leading to the ice. Despite the arena's numbing chill, sweat trickled between her shoulder blades beneath her sweater and parka.

"Wait." Her mom's voice came from behind her. "Luc and Scott are right there. You won't help Amy if you fall and crack your head open."

Cat slowed and picked her way down the steps. Amy couldn't be in that pile of bodies. As she reached ice level, her vision blurred.

"Here." Her mom pulled open the gate for Cat to go through and gripped her arm.

"You're not allowed on the ice." The male voice was young and hesitant.

"Just try to stop me." Cat half-turned to face the teenage referee who hovered at the edge of the melee, his whistle useless. "My daughter's there. I have to get to her."

"If you stop her, you'll have to stop all of us." Stephanie and a group of the other hockey moms surged onto the ice behind Cat, an unlikely but solid phalanx of support.

Cat's heart hammered. Luc, Scott, and the other team's coaches pulled boys off of each other. A streak of red darkened a patch of ice next to a first aid kit and stack of towels.

"Amy...I still don't see her." She wasn't on the home team's bench or with the small group of players huddled at the end of the rink by one of the goal nets. And she wasn't in the tangle of arms and legs still piled up on the ice. No number five and no familiar dark blond hair sticking out from beneath a helmet.

"Stay here." Her mom pulled at her sleeve. "If you get in the middle of a fight, you'll only make things worse."

"But Amy, she..." Cat swallowed a sob. "At her age, there's no body checking in hockey. It's noncontact. Luc promised me." Her voice came out in a high wail.

"Boys of this age don't know the meaning of *noncontact*." Stephanie stopped at Cat's shoulder. "Believe me, I have two of them. As for men's promises, they're not worth much. Even Luc, and he's one of the good ones." Although Stephanie's voice was hard, her light touch on Cat's back was kind.

"Amy will be okay." She had to be because if she wasn't...Cat stopped that train of thought with an effort, only to see Scott pull off the last boy, a big player from the opposing team, and the small, still figure on the ice beneath him.

"Oh my God. Mom...she's not moving...she's..." Cat slid across the few feet of ice that separated her from her daughter.

"I've already called the paramedics and they'll be here any minute." Luc's voice was steady. "Scott is a certified hockey trainer and first aider."

Cat's eyes swung to Scott, who knelt on the ice on the other side of Amy. "What happened?"

"She took an illegal body check even before most of the two teams landed on top of her." He turned back to Amy. "You're going to be fine, Amy. It's Coach Scott. I need you to stay as still as you can and tell me where you hurt."

Amy whimpered. "Everywhere." Behind her face mask, her blue eyes were unfocused and she blinked up at the bright, overhead lights. "My head."

"She's still wearing her helmet. I bought her that one because it was supposed to be the safest. I researched it. I compared all the facts."

Amy's hair stuck out from underneath it like the limp tresses of a doll.

"It protected her from the hit, but no helmet's concussion-proof." Luc crouched on his knees beside Cat. "I tried to get to her in time, but it all happened so fast."

Cat's chin shook. "It'll be okay, sweetie. I'm right here. Grandma is, too, and Coach Luc. Don't move and do what Coach Scott says." She glanced at him again as he wrapped a strip of gauze around Amy's left hand, where blood spurted onto the ice.

"She's got a deep cut, but it's clean. And she's lucky. Skate blades can do a lot worse damage." He tied the makeshift tourniquet tight, then went back to touching Amy's arms and legs.

"I really kicked spaghetti out there, didn't I, Mom?" Amy's voice was so soft Cat had to strain to hear her.

"Spaghetti?" Cat's insides were in a viselike grip. "I don't understand, honey."

"You didn't want me telling the kids to kick butt, so since then they've kicked spaghetti instead." Luc's voice was rough. "It was Amy's idea, and the guys went for it."

"You sure kicked something out there." Cat swallowed the lump in her throat. "It looks like you got kicked, too."

"I'd have scored another goal if that big guy hadn't hit me." Amy winced as Scott put a blanket over her. "But did you see how my whole team came to help?" Her smile was crooked and so childlike that Cat's heart splintered further.

"I don't think a bench-clearing brawl can be called helping." She stroked the ends of Amy's sweat-matted hair with a gentle finger.

"It didn't start off as a fight. It just...it happened, I guess." She looked at Cat and her expression was anxious. "We have to finish this game and there's another one tomorrow and—"

"You don't need to worry about any of that." Luc's voice was calm. "I already told the referee to call this game so nobody else gets hurt." He glanced at Cat. "He's only seventeen. He's never had to deal with something like this before."

"And you won't be playing in the next game." If Cat had her way, Amy wouldn't play hockey with boys ever again.

"I have to." Amy looked at Luc. "I can't let my team down. We were winning this game and I want to keep winning."

"But—" Cat stopped at a warning glance from Scott. "Let's wait to hear what the doctor says," she said instead.

Focused on Amy, the pain in Luc's blue eyes was unmistakable. He brushed a hand across his face. "I promised you...I let you down, both of you."

"It's not your fault." Cat's body shook. "You couldn't know this would happen." She stopped and tried to swallow the tight knot of anxiety.

Apart from the kid who'd tackled Amy, if it was anybody's fault, it was hers. She was the one who'd said Amy could play on the boys' team. Even though she'd done it to make her daughter happy, she'd still put her at risk.

Behind Luc, Stephanie stood with her boys, arms looped together in an uneasy embrace, flanked by the rest of the hockey parents and players.

Cat's gaze connected with Stephanie's. The other woman's expression was etched with pain, as well as concern. "Thanks," Cat muttered.

Stephanie's face went red. "If you need anything…" She cleared her throat. "All of us, we…" She gestured to the group. "Here, hockey means family." She pulled at her coat collar. "You and Amy are part of that family."

Cat gave a jerky nod and her stomach dropped as she looked at Amy huddled under the blanket. Even though the accident wasn't Luc's fault, it was still a reminder of why she couldn't give any man her heart—or her trust. Like Stephanie had said, and Cat had almost let herself forget, she knew the worth of men's promises and had already paid a bitter price. She might be smart, but when it came to her heart, she also had to be wise.

"I'm looking for the X-ray department." Two hours later, Luc stopped beside an information kiosk at the county hospital in Kincaid. The place was a confusing mix of old and new architecture with mazelike corridors in every direction. It also had that sterile hospital smell he associated with sickness and death.

"It's back the way you came." A petite, white-haired woman in a blue sweater above beige slacks took his elbow in a gentle clasp. "Why don't I take you there?"

"Thanks. If it's not too much trouble." All Cat's text had said was Amy had gone from the ER to X-ray. He tried to steady his breathing and blinked at the woman's name tag. Betty. A name from an older generation and as comforting as a kindly grandmother or great-aunt.

"No trouble at all. I'm a volunteer. It's my job to help folks like you who get turned around in here." The woman had dark eyes set in a face as wrinkled as a raisin. "You look like you could use a cup of tea." She stopped at a machine and inserted a plastic card. A cardboard cup popped into a holder and brown liquid streamed into it.

Although he was usually a coffee drinker, Luc took the cup Betty held out and wrapped his cold hands around it, nodding his appreciation.

"You're that hockey player, aren't you? The Simard boy?" She took his elbow again and guided him down yet another long corridor with closed doors on either side.

"Yes. Are you a hockey fan?"

"Nope. Baseball all the way for me. It's those uniforms, don't you know?" Betty's dark eyes gleamed with fun. "But I remember your grandparents. They were fine people." She turned into another hallway. "Here you go. X-ray's through that glass door at the end. If you need anything else, holler." Her smile warmed him more than the drink had. "You did your family proud, you did all of us around here proud, but it's right you came home."

Home. Luc glanced at Betty, who barely reached his elbow. Home had been where Maggie was, but Vermont was home, too, and somehow, almost without him noticing, it had also become that curious sense of comfort he got with Cat.

Betty grasped his arm with unexpected firmness. "It'll be all right, son. Whatever's troubling you will all come out in the wash. Hearts heal, if you let them. They take a bit longer than broken bones is all." Her steady gaze held his.

"I...thanks." Luc stopped as a jolt went through his body. In that instant, for the first time in months, he had a sense of hope. A sense of purpose and rightness too, as well as a rock-solid conviction he was exactly where he was meant to be.

With another smile and fluttery wave, Betty disappeared around a corner like a benevolent, geriatric angel.

Luc tugged open the door to X-ray. Although the room was full, he only had eyes for Cat hunched in a chair at the far end. "What's happening?" He ignored the covert looks and low murmurs and sat in the chair beside her.

"They took Amy in a minute ago. I couldn't go with her." She clutched her purse, and her gaze darted from side to side. "She has a mild concussion, and the ER doctor put a few stitches in her hand, where the skate blade caught it, but they want to take a closer look at her left arm." Her voice cracked.

Oblivious to the onlookers, Luc set the tea aside and wrapped an arm around her. "I got here as fast as I could. Scott took over most of the after-game stuff, but it's snowing again and that road from Firefly Lake is treacherous. Where's your mom?"

"Ward came to get her a little while ago. He booked a room for the two of them at a B&B a few blocks away." She gave him a small smile. "Mom wasn't happy about leaving, but although she wouldn't admit it, she needed to rest, and it's not like she can do anything practical here.

Georgie's at work. She said she'll come after her shift finishes, but if the roads are as bad as you say, she might not make it back to town from the inn, let alone here." Cat's eyes were purple-shadowed and her body rigid.

"She won't." Luc pulled out his phone from his jacket pocket and unlocked it. "Text her. The number's in my contacts. Tell Georgia I'm here and I'm staying with you and Amy as long as you need me to."

"You don't have to do that." She scrubbed a hand across her face and blew out several short breaths.

"I want to." He pressed his phone into her other hand. "I feel responsible for what happened. I sent Amy out on that shift. I knew the guy who hit her was a troublemaker, but I never thought . . ." His throat got thick. "I made a bad call." He'd replayed what had happened all the way here. Amy breaking away with the puck. The kid coming up on her right side. The sickening thud when he hit her. Then an uproar followed by eerie silence.

Cat's fingers shook as she sent the text and handed the phone back to him. "It's because of me Amy was playing with boys in the first place. Besides, when she's on the ice, Amy gives as good as she gets, but that kid was so big." She blinked and her eyes were too bright.

Luc put his phone away and tucked his hand into hers. "I know it doesn't make it any easier, but injuries are a part of hockey." But not this kind of hockey. This kind was supposed to be fun. He stared at his feet.

Cat stiffened and her hand was clammy. "You said there wouldn't be any body contact."

His heartbeat was loud in his ears. "There shouldn't have been, and I made sure that kid got suspended, but there are risks in any sport." Even before the words were out of his mouth, it was clear he'd said another wrong thing.

"Amy wouldn't have been tackled by some overgrown kid if she'd been swimming or doing ballet, would she?" Cat's voice was high and she pulled her hand away from his.

"Has she ever expressed an interest in swimming or ballet?" Luc kept his voice low, because all conversation in the waiting room had ceased.

She flinched and gave him a fixed stare. "No, but that's not the point. The point is—"

"X-rays are all done." A guy in green scrubs pushed Amy in a wheelchair to a stop in front of Cat. Amy looked smaller than usual, and her eyes were half closed. Above a blue hospital gown, her face was almost as green as the guy's scrubs. "You need to wait to see the doctor again." He flicked a glance at Luc. "Hey, you're Luc Simard. I'm a huge fan. It was a sad day for hockey when you retired."

The words hit Luc like a punch. It had been a sad day for him, too, and he missed the team more than he'd ever let on, that sense of community and camaraderie he'd taken for granted until, all of a sudden, it wasn't there.

"Can I get your autograph?" The guy's expression turned hopeful. "The name's Kevin." He pulled a blank sheet of paper from behind Amy's chart and fished a pen out of his breast pocket.

"Sure." Luc took the pen and paper and scrawled his name. "Do you think you can find us a room to wait in for the doctor? We could use some privacy." He glanced at Cat. Her face was ashen and her arms were crossed in front of her chest. The murmur of conversation had started up again, and if he didn't get out of here fast, he'd be signing autographs and posing for fan pictures for the rest of the night, instead of being there for Cat and Amy like he wanted to.

"You bet." Kevin pocketed the autograph Luc handed him and, in one deft motion, turned Amy and the wheelchair around. "Follow me." He whisked them down a short hall and into a small room behind a reception area. "Anything for you, Scooter. The doc will be with you as soon as she can." He gestured to two chairs by a desk, then disappeared.

"Scooter?" Cat tucked a white hospital blanket around Amy's legs before she slumped in one of the chairs.

"It's Coach Luc's nickname from when he played in the NHL." Amy's voice was slurred. She had a reddish-purple bruise on her neck above the gown, and her left hand was wrapped in gauze and surgical tape. "Everyone called him that because he was fast and could get the puck out of tight spaces."

"I see." Cat's smile was forced, and she glanced at Luc as if she didn't see him.

Amy gave a hollow cough, and Luc's insides twisted. "Did the doctor say if I can play tomorrow?" She squinted in the bright overhead light and put a hand to her head.

"The doctor hasn't said anything yet, but I say you're not playing." Cat tucked Amy's blanket tighter.

"I only bumped my head." Amy stuck her bottom lip out and shoved the blanket away. "A few stitches and some bumps and bruises aren't a big deal."

"Your mom said the bump on your head's a concussion. You know that's serious."

Amy had so much promise, and Luc had to make sure

it could be fulfilled. He clamped his hands together and grimaced as more guilt smote his chest.

"I'm feeling okay now, honest." Amy's freckles stood out against the greenish pallor of her face. "I'm the best goal scorer on the team. They need me."

"Even if that's true, scoring goals doesn't make up for getting hurt." Cat's voice was gruff and laced with worry.

"You don't understand anything." Amy's voice got louder and she rocked back and forth. "When I'm on the ice, it's the only place I feel like me."

"Honey." Cat stopped and sucked in a breath. "Please believe me when I say I'm trying to understand. I know hockey's really important to you, but you got hurt. We don't know about your arm yet, but a concussion and stitches are enough to keep you off the ice for a while."

"Coach Luc played through lots of injuries." Amy's gaze swung to Luc, and her eyes were cold.

"Yes, I did, but that doesn't mean I made the right choices." There was a buzzing in Luc's head. From today, back through all the years before, he'd made a lot of bad choices, and playing when he was hurt was only one of them. "You can't play with a concussion. Your mom says so, as your coach I say so, and I'm sure the doctor will say so, too."

"Fine." Amy's expression was sulky. "But nobody can stop me from watching games or helping the guys."

"What do you mean?" Cat's eyebrows went up into her hairline.

"Some of the guys on the team are hopeless at hockey." Amy let out a heavy breath. "I've been coaching a few of them at lunch and recess. Not on skates, but I've been showing them stuff, and then they've been helping me."

"Helping you how?" Like her eyebrows, Cat's voice went up, too.

"With math." Amy rolled her eyes. "Connor Tremblay can barely skate from one end of the rink to the other, but he's like a math genius. Coach Scott's got him doing seventh grade work already. Jeez, Mom, what did you think?"

"Since you've never mentioned anything about this before, what did you expect me to think?" She flicked a glance at Luc. "Did you know?"

"No." Although, it explained why Connor had all of a sudden at least managed to stay upright most of the time. Luc tapped his fingers on the arm of the chair. "If your mom and the doctor are okay with it, I'm happy for you to help out with coaching more officially, but now you need to take it easy so you can heal."

"When I'm not on the ice, you can't tell me what to do." Amy's head jerked as she looked between him and Cat and her expression hardened. "You're my coach, not my dad."

"Amy . . ." Cat's voice was a distressed moan. "Hurt or not, I won't have you speak to Luc like that."

"Why are you taking his side? I'm your daughter, and you always say we're a team."

"We are a team—"

"It sure doesn't feel like it. Maybe you like him better than me? Because he's—" Amy's mouth twisted and she leaned forward in the wheelchair. Then she threw up. All over Luc.

Chapter Fifteen

❦

Cat stopped outside the door of the room where the doctor had found Amy a bed for the night. "I'm sure Amy didn't throw up on you on purpose. The doctor said kids can be sick with a concussion. As for what Amy said, she was upset and scared, that's all." Except, the expression on Amy's face as she'd looked between her and Luc was stamped on Cat's heart. It was both furtive and almost as if her daughter thought Cat had betrayed her. And why would Amy think Cat would take Luc's side, or that she'd ever like him best?

"Don't worry about it." Luc shrugged and his abs rippled beneath a yellow T-shirt with TRUST ME, I'M ALMOST A DOCTOR on it in green letters.

Cat's gaze followed the tight shirt down to the black scrub pants, which stopped in the middle of his muscular calves. Even with Amy asleep in a hospital bed ten feet away, the man could still turn her on. She made an effort to focus. "Still, your clothes are ruined. I'll replace them, of course."

"Forget it. I never liked that shirt or those jeans much anyway." Luc gave her a half-smile. "The most important thing is Amy's going to be okay. Her arm's bruised, not broken, and if we weren't in the middle of a blizzard, the doctor would have sent her home tonight. She's one tough kid."

Tough kid or not, Cat shuddered at the indelible memory of her daughter's still body crumpled on the ice. "Of course she'll be okay, but that's not the point. I don't want her playing on a boys' team anymore."

"Didn't she ever get hurt playing with girls?" Luc's voice was low, and he took Cat's arm and eased her along the corridor, farther from Amy's room. "She was in a competitive league, and girls can be aggressive, too."

"Maybe I don't want Amy playing hockey at all." Cat stared at the framed watercolor hanging on the wall until the muted tones of the Green Mountain landscape scene blurred together.

"Do you really think you can stop her? She loves the game, like all the great ones do." Luc looped an arm around Cat's hunched shoulders. "If you don't want her playing with boys, fine. There aren't many games left in the regular season, anyway, and Firefly Lake never had a hope of making the playoffs. However, you have to give Amy another option. What about one of those hockey camps? When Maggie's friends were here for the carnival, I talked to them about Amy. If I recommend her, she'll get a place, no question. Also, because of her dyslexia, they may consider her case separately and waive any standard academic requirements for a scholarship."

"That would be great, too good to be true, but..." Cat's breathing sped up. "Even if she goes to a hockey camp, it's a one-off. I need to help Amy see that she has lots of choices—ones that won't get her hurt."

"From what I've seen, she's already made her choice." Luc's gaze was as steady as his voice.

He was right, but what he didn't know, and what Cat didn't plan on telling him, was that every time Amy skated onto the ice, Cat was reminded of the man who'd fathered her—the kind of person she didn't want her daughter to become. "It's great of you to want to help Amy, but right now I can't . . . " Her voice cracked and she swallowed around the thickness in her throat.

"You're a mama bear protecting her cub, and my timing sucks. Come here." Luc pulled her into his arms. "You've had a rough day. You don't have to decide anything now."

"Okay." Cat buried her face in the T-shirt that Kevin from X-ray had lent him. Luc hadn't worn it long, but it had already taken on his warm and comforting scent, and his chest rose in a steady rhythm under her cheek. "I should go. Amy needs me." She stood on tiptoe to touch the strong column of Luc's neck.

"Of course." He bent his head to brush her lips with his, a brief whisper of a kiss that helped heal her heart and brought solace to her soul. "I'll be in the waiting room at the end of the hall if you need anything. Food, a magazine, whatever."

"Thanks for coming here and staying with us . . . thanks for everything." Cat curled her toes inside her boots. From when she was six, she'd convinced herself she didn't need a man in her life, at least not permanently. But now the evidence stared her in the face, bigger than any of those facts her logical mind set such store by. She did need a man, the one who was right here, still protecting her and looking out for her, like he'd done when they were kids.

What she felt for Luc now, though, wasn't a childish crush. Even though she hadn't planned to, she'd fallen in love with him. While it might have seemed like a spur-of-the moment decision, she'd only slept with him because he meant something important to her.

His eyes crinkled at the corners as he smiled. "It's not the first time I've spent the night in a hospital waiting room. When I played for Vancouver, a guy I roomed with ended up in the ER at least once every road trip."

"I hope that's a joke." Cat tried to smile back, even as her knees went weak.

Love. She took a deep breath to savor the word. Although she could never tell him, for the first time, everything she'd read in books or seen in all those romantic movies made sense. The world seemed brighter because Luc was in it. And when she was around him, she didn't only feel safe, she felt complete.

"Nope." His grin broadened and the drawstring pants slipped lower on his hips. "After he married the ER doc who sewed him up a couple of times in LA, he got a lot less accident-prone."

"Oh." Cat's laugh was forced and her pulse raced as she backed toward the door of Amy's room. "Well, thanks again."

Luc couldn't love her back, or give her what she truly needed. Nobody could. The world seemed to slow down, and her chest ached.

"Night, Minnie." His expression changed, and heat replaced the teasing. "See you in the morning."

"Good night...Scooter." Her voice hitched, and she held his gaze for several endless seconds before she pushed open Amy's door and slipped behind the curtain that encircled her daughter's bed.

"Mommy?" Amy's voice was heavy with sleep and so childlike that Cat's heart turned over.

"I thought you were asleep." She sat in the chair next to the bed and smoothed Amy's hair away from her pale face.

"I was, but when I woke up, you weren't here." In the soft glow from the night-light plugged into the wall, Amy looked smaller, and she cuddled a corner of the blanket with her bandaged hand.

"I only went out into the hall for a minute."

"Were you with Coach Luc?" Despite its softness, Amy's voice held a sharp edge.

"Yes, and now he's in the waiting room. It's snowing too hard for him to drive back to Firefly Lake tonight." Except, no matter what the weather, Luc would still have stayed here. He was that kind of man.

Amy reached for Cat's hand. "Lie beside me so I can go back to sleep."

"Sure." Cat pulled off her boots, then eased onto the narrow bed beside her daughter.

"Tell me a story." Amy rolled onto her side and into the curve of Cat's body.

"What kind?" Cat's breath brushed the soft tendrils of hair near Amy's ear.

"About when I was little." Amy's blue eyes were fuzzy from the painkillers the doctor had given her. "About us. You, me, and our family. The story you always tell me."

A dense mass settled on Cat's chest. "Once upon a

time there was a little girl called Amy Gabrielle. She lived with her mommy and two cats called Darcy and Bingley. They lived in Boston in a brick building near a park."

"Her mommy loved her more than anything." Amy's words were muffled.

"I do."

"Even though Amy's daddy went far away before she was born, she didn't miss him because she never knew him. All she ever needed was her mommy." Amy snuggled into Cat's neck and her breathing steadied as she slipped into sleep.

Cat lay still. She'd had to be everything for Amy because Jared had lied to her from the moment they'd met. Then when he'd gotten himself killed, Cat had no choice but to go on alone, so she'd done the best she could, like she'd done after her dad left.

"Mom?" Amy nuzzled Cat's cheek.

"I'm right here. I'm not going anywhere." Although Amy was all Cat had, she was all Amy had, too. The heaviness entrenched itself in her heart. No matter what she felt for Luc, even if it was a love that went bone-deep, Amy had to come first.

His skate blades cut into the ice with a hollow whoosh as Luc rounded the corner of Firefly Lake near Old Harbor Park. The frozen lake, enfolded by the small town and dark green hills, sparkled in the Sunday afternoon sunshine. Even when everything else in his world was upside down, Firefly Lake had always been as solid as Vermont hard rock maple. It still was. And today, like it always had, the same tinny sound system belted out a mix of country and pop tunes, and the same friends and family still thronged this outdoor rink. Two weeks after Amy's accident, it was March, and there wouldn't be many more days of skating on the lake left this winter.

Luc waved at Liz, who stood near the snack bar with Michael, before circling back toward the other side of the rink near Carmichael's Marina. Sean and Charlie sat on a park bench by the edge of the ice with little Lexie bundled up in a pink snowsuit and tucked into a sleigh. His heart squeezed. Lexie was still too young, but in a few more winters, she'd be out here laced into her first pair of skates, gliding along beside her mom and dad. Like he'd once imagined skating with Maggie and their child. He made himself wave and smile, then sped up until the wind stung his nose and cheeks.

"Slow down. I'm not as young as I used to be." His mom's dark blue eyes, the same color as her puffy blue parka, twinkled beneath her white stocking cap as she skated up beside him.

"You still caught me." Luc skidded to a stop and gave her a one-armed hug.

The woman who'd had him on his first skates on this same rink hugged him back, then studied him. "I left your father with Gabrielle and Ward so I could talk to you alone. You've been avoiding us these past few weeks."

"I see Dad at the office every weekday. You too, whenever you can leave the creamery store and drop by." Luc stroked forward across the ice and his mom followed. "Between coaching and work, I've been busy." The lie clogged his throat. Because of whatever this thing was with Cat, he *had* avoided his folks, not because he cared what they thought, but because he didn't want to talk about something he didn't understand himself.

"You're so busy you've only come to dinner once since the winter carnival. Your dad tells me you hardly say two words all day long." His mom's skates made a crisp sound as she kept pace with him. Beneath her cap, wisps of silver-blond hair fluttered in the wind.

"I'm learning the business, so I need to focus." He softened his voice. "You know what Dad's like. He's such a details guy, and he wants me to know Simard's inside and out. I don't want to let him down—let either of you down."

"You'd never do that." His mom pivoted to skate backward in front of Luc, which meant he couldn't escape her searching gaze. "I know what you're like, too." She paused and looked him up and down. "That's why I want you to invite Cat and Amy to join us for dinner next weekend. Saturday or Sunday, whenever all of you are free."

"How...why..." Luc stared at his skates. Any denial would be pointless and make him feel worse than he already did. "Cat has a lot of work right now." Which was true, plus he couldn't make himself take that next step to ask Cat to join his family for something as significant as dinner. If she sat next to him at his folks' dining room table, it would be like she was taking Maggie's place in his life and heart.

"Cat still eats dinner, doesn't she? She's a sweet woman, and I'm so proud of you the way you're helping Amy. Gabrielle says Amy can get back on the ice this week." His mom's eyes clouded. "I'm glad you aren't playing anymore. Every game, I worried about you getting hurt, and when you did, I worried even more."

"Mom." He let out a breath and it made a swirl of steam in the frosty air. He'd been hurt far worse off the ice than on it—the kind of hurt he'd learned to live with but that would never fully heal.

"I know it's none of my business." His mom's expression was both worried and tender. "But I want you to be happy again, and Cat—"

"Cat's a friend, like she's always been." Luc turned away and stared at the bluish-white expanse of the lake.

He was a truthful guy, but now he'd lied to his mom twice in less than five minutes. His stomach rolled. Cat was a whole lot more than a friend, and, although he was trying to be patient, never being alone with her was driving him crazy. Amy was attached to her like a baby kangaroo snug in its mom's pouch, and because before this weekend Michael had been away on a buying trip, whenever he dropped by the gallery, Cat was too busy to stop and chat.

"If you say so." His mom quirked an eyebrow and said, "I didn't know Cat could skate," before she went into an elegant spin as easily as a woman half her age, and with the same grace as the champion figure skater she'd once been.

"What?" Luc blinked as his mom spun in front of him. "She can't, not really."

His mom came out of the spin and took his arm. "Maybe not, but she's over there with Amy. See?" She gestured to the town side of the lake.

Cat stood at the edge of the rink close to shore. She held Amy's hand and teetered in a pair of white figure skates.

"Even if she can't skate yet, she's sure giving it a good try." His mom gave him a speculative look. "When are you going to admit to yourself how you feel about her?"

"I don't know what you're talking about." There was lie number three. Bile rose in Luc's throat as the sound system sputtered into the Beatles' "Yesterday."

"If you don't, you're not the son I raised." His mom's voice had a sharp edge to it that Luc guessed he deserved. "Folks are talking about you. Maybe you spent so long in the fast lane you forgot what it's like here, but if you're spending time with a woman like you're doing with Cat, you either make a commitment to her or you don't. Is she your girlfriend or whatever you call it nowadays?"

"I...not exactly. It's only been a few months. We're taking things slowly." Luc glanced across the ice.

Cat put one foot in front of the other like he'd taught her all those weeks ago. Then she loosened her hold on Amy and marched forward in small steps all by herself. Fierce pride and an unexpected, but familiar, warmth welled up inside him.

"Even though he couldn't skate back then either, I knew within five minutes of meeting your dad that he was the one for me." His mom's eyes softened. "He said the same thing about me. When you know, you know, and there's no reason to hide it. Or hide out." She patted his arm before she spun around and skated away.

Luc's stomach went rock hard. He could never love anyone as he'd loved Maggie. She wasn't only his past. Even though she was gone, she was still part of his today and she'd be part of all his tomorrows, too. He wasn't hiding out in Firefly Lake. He was fond of Cat, sure, but it was way too soon to go public with anything as official as calling her his girlfriend. Besides, a "girlfriend" was someone you dated in high school or college, not in your thirties.

Yet, as Paul McCartney sang on and the words of "Yesterday" echoed in Luc's heart, he wove through the skaters, pulled toward Cat as if by an invisible force. "Hey." He stopped at her side.

"Luc." She stared at the ice.

"Where did you get the skates?" He softened his voice. Her rigid body stance told him something was up, but what?

"They're an old pair of Georgia's. They were packed away with stuff she left in Mom's attic." She raised her head to look at him and squinted in the sunlight.

"I'm teaching Mom to skate." Amy wedged herself between him and Cat. "Even though I can't get back on my skates for a few days yet, she says I'm a great teacher."

"You're sure a great coach, the way you've helped me out with the team over the last few practices." Luc smiled at Amy, but she didn't smile back. Instead, she looked through him like he wasn't there.

"Amy, please." Cat's voice was tired and her eyes were gray-shadowed.

"What?" Amy glared at Luc.

"Why don't you go and talk to Grandma for a minute?"

"Are you trying to get rid of me?" Amy crossed her arms in front of her chest.

"Of course not, but Grandma could use your help." Cat gestured toward Gabrielle, who stood at the edge of the lake with a wriggling Pixie in her arms. "If you hold the dog, she can skate for a bit."

"She should have thought of that before she brought Pixie with her, shouldn't she?" Amy's voice was sullen and she scraped her boots against the ice.

"Amy." Cat's tone was firm. "You know that's not the way to talk."

Amy made a sulky face. "Whatever, but I'm coming right back." She gave Luc a hard stare. "In five minutes."

"You'd think she was already a teenager, wouldn't you?" Cat's brittle laugh turned into a sigh. "I'm trying to make allowances because not being able to play hockey is hard for her. The doctor also said concussions can make kids sad and angry. Ever since Amy got hurt, though, it's like she's an entirely different girl. She's never been this mouthy and rude before."

Luc glanced at Amy as she stomped away from them, stealing sly glances over her shoulder. Amy hadn't been herself at the rink, either, but he hadn't said anything to Cat because he didn't want to worry her more than she already was. But the expression on Amy's face was clear. Stay away from my mother. Or else.

Chapter Sixteen

Cat rested her chin in her hands and stared at the computer without seeing the text on the screen. What was wrong with her? Amy was at school, the gallery was quiet apart from the soft strains of an Irish ballad, and Michael was unpacking a delivery in the storeroom. She got a lot more satisfaction than she'd expected from her work here, and she thrived on the challenge of helping make Michael's business thrive, but today her head was as fuzzy as if it was filled with cotton batting, and she couldn't put two coherent sentences together. Although it was Tuesday, this was Monday morning brain fog on steroids.

Outside the gallery, fat icicles dripped from the overhanging eaves. Despite the snowbanks that still lined Main Street, the sun was warmer than it had been only a week ago, and she'd put a trio of wooden Easter rabbits and several wicker baskets filled with colorful eggs in the gallery's front window earlier. If she didn't get her head together soon, she'd be back teaching from contract to contract before she knew it, and so much for that security she wanted to give Amy.

She looked up as the bell over the front door jangled. "Liz?"

"Something's happened to Michael." The older woman wore a red diner apron dusted with flour.

"What do you mean?" Cat got up from the desk and met Liz by a table of local pottery. "He's back in the storeroom."

"He's not answering his phone, and I have a bad feeling." Liz's voice cracked.

"I'm sure he's fine." Cat took Liz's arm and steered her toward the back of the gallery. "If something was wrong with him, I'd have heard it. I've been here all morning."

Beneath her apron, Liz's chest heaved. "I know what I'm feeling. My Scottish grandmother had second sight."

Cat pushed open the stockroom door. "He..."

"Michael!" Liz dropped Cat's arm and darted to where he lay on the floor beside the worktable, colorful quilts scattered around him.

"I fell." His right arm was twisted. "One minute I was standing there unpacking a box, and then I got dizzy and had this pain and... I don't know how I ended up down here."

"I'll call an ambulance." Cat sped back to the desk and found her phone. If she'd been paying attention, she'd have heard something. Her stomach heaved as she made the emergency call, then ran back to the storeroom, her heels tapping on the wood floor. "The paramedics are on their way."

"We have to get ready for the exhibition. It's opening in May." Michael tried to sit up, but Liz eased him back.

"Don't worry, I'll take care of it." Cat grabbed a quilt and tucked it under Michael's head.

"I'll help you." Fear pooled in Liz's brown eyes as she patted Michael's cheek. "You're all sweaty and cold." She grabbed another quilt and covered him from his chin to his tasseled loafers.

"I'm fine." Michael winced. "I don't need you two fussing over me."

"You're not fine. You haven't been fine for weeks, and I should have insisted you see a doctor before you went on that last buying trip. I can't lose you." Liz's voice broke. Tendrils of hair escaped from her neat French twist and, with her free hand, she scrubbed at her face.

Michael levered his good arm above the quilt to snag Liz's wrist. "You're not going to lose me." His voice was faint.

Liz gulped and rested her face against Michael's arm. Silent tears coursed down her face to leave a damp patch on the quilt.

Cat stood frozen in the storeroom doorway, her knees shaking. "The paramedics . . . I'll wait out there for them." She made herself step back. This was a private moment, too intimate for her to share.

"No." Liz's voice was thick with tears. "Don't go. If something happens to him . . . I can't . . ." She gulped and her eyes were desperate. "I've been so silly."

"If anybody's been silly, it's me." Michael raised his hand and brushed the tears off Liz's cheeks with a gentle finger.

"We live in different worlds. We always have. Your mother hired mine to clean that fancy house of yours up on the hill." Liz's smile was wistful.

"They're both gone and most of those old prejudices with them." Michael made a feeble sign of the cross. "I loved my wife like you loved your husband, God rest their souls, but that fancy house is empty and...if you could...it's not too late for us."

With a soft sob, Liz buried her face against Michael's neck.

Cat's eyes watered. Although he hadn't said the words, Michael's expression was full of tenderness and love. What would it be like to have someone look at you that way?

"Oh, Michael." Liz's voice was muffled.

"I don't have any intention of dying just yet, so let's look ahead, not back. I've always hankered to go to Australia. What do you think, Lizzie?" His laugh was weak, but it was still Michael's laugh.

"I'd go to the moon if that's where you wanted to go, but Australia sounds mighty nice. I'd have to get a passport and some new clothes, but...oh..." Liz raised her head and her brown eyes shone like stars in her careworn face. "Can you see me in Australia?"

"I can see both of you there." Cat's heart squeezed tight against her ribs and she pressed a hand to her chest. The happiness on Liz's face was palpable. The same happiness that was on Nick's face when he looked at Mia, and also between Charlie and Sean. The kind of happiness her romantic, childish heart had once yearned for until she'd grown up and, except in the pages of books, logic trumped romance and her head ruled her heart.

"No waterworks from either of you." Michael's gaze swung from Liz to Cat and back. "If you're going to cry about anything, cry about putting two Maura Fitzpatrick quilts on this dirty floor. Maura's the best quilt designer Vermont ever produced and thanks to you two, my head's lying on several thousand dollars' worth of fabric, and there's another few grand on top of me."

"You're worth more than any quilt." Liz touched Michael's ashen cheek. "Besides, this floor isn't dirty. Cat swept it yesterday and she's as neat a housekeeper as me." She sat back on her heels and fumbled in her apron pocket for a tissue.

Michael grunted. "That may be, but I'm still lying under 'Evening Rest,' aren't I? It may sound like a funeral home, but there's no need to start planning for my passing anytime soon."

A siren keened, and Cat's tense breathing eased.

Michael turned back to her. "You always were a good girl, and you've turned into a fine woman. I'm leaving you in charge."

"I'll do my best for you." Cat pushed the words out.

"Of course you will." Michael's voice was gruff. "For someone with so much book learning, you have a lot more sense between your ears than I expected."

Cat tried to smile. Despite his waxy skin and the bluish tinge around his mouth, Michael could still tease her. "You get better, okay? Do what the doctors tell you."

"He will." Liz got to her feet as two paramedics came through the door. "God will take care of the first, and I'll make sure of the second."

"You have to eat something." Luc slid a sandwich wrapped in brown paper across Cat's desk. The door had just swung closed behind Gabrielle and Ward, and the gallery was finally empty.

"I'm not hungry." She fingered one corner of the paper. "I appreciate you getting this food, but I can't eat when I'm stressed."

"Not even the Vermont BLT?" He lifted part of the wrapping to release a whiff of bacon and fresh-baked bread.

"How did you know?" She licked her bottom lip.

"Georgia was in the deli at the same time as me. She said the Vermont BLT's your favorite—rustic bread, local cheese from Simard's creamery, and extra crispy bacon." He leaned his elbows on the desk and studied her wan face. "Michael's going to be fine. Remember what Liz said when she called?"

"A heart attack's still a heart attack, no matter how mild it was." Cat broke off a small piece of cheese and toyed with it. "He also cracked two ribs and strained his wrist when he fell."

"Yes, but if you and Liz hadn't found him right away, it could have been a lot worse." Luc broke off a corner of the sandwich. "Here, I told Liz I'd make sure you were fed."

"It was Liz who knew something was wrong. She got this feeling." Cat shivered. "It's not logical, and I can't explain it, but she was right." She took the piece of sandwich, chewed, and swallowed, as if by rote.

"Not everything in life can be explained by logic and facts." He glanced toward her laptop and the stack of paper beside it. "How's your research going?"

"Fine." Cat's voice was flat. "I've finished my book, and I've got enough material for the articles I pitched to get that grant in the first place. I've started writing them, too."

"That's great." He hesitated and a leaden silence stretched between them. "Isn't it?"

"It still might not be enough for me to get a permanent job." She picked at the sandwich again, then put a hand to her mouth to cover a yawn.

"Why? Any college would be lucky to have you." Except, when she got that job, she wouldn't be living in Firefly Lake, and she and Amy would be as good as gone from his life. His insides quivered.

"Thanks for the vote of confidence, but it's not that simple." She gave him a sad smile. "It's a tough job market and, with all those temporary teaching contracts I had to take on to support myself and Amy, I couldn't keep up on the research side. I've been out of my PhD for a few years, too, so I'm not new and interesting anymore. Until this year, I only applied for jobs in New England because I wanted to stay near Mom and not uproot Amy too much, but there weren't a lot of those and now . . ." She shrugged. "Even though it's gotten to the point where I'd go anywhere, I might not even be able to do that anymore."

"That's not fair." He might not want Cat to leave Firefly Lake, but he still wanted her to succeed. Not only was she smart, she was the hardest worker he'd ever met.

"Maybe not, but we both know that a lot in life isn't fair." Her eyes were bleak and yet another yawn almost split her face in two.

He did, so he swallowed the words he could have said, along with the sour taste in his mouth. "Why don't I cover for you here so you can go upstairs and lie down for a few hours? In addition to the shock, you've had half of Firefly Lake in here over the past two hours asking about Michael. You're worn out." Although Cat never looked robust, her skin wasn't usually so translucent, nor the dark circles under her eyes so pronounced.

She shook her head. "Michael left me in charge. Besides, don't you have to get back to work this afternoon? It was great of you to leave the creamery when you heard the ambulance siren, but you don't have to stay."

"I texted my dad. Since I started early and worked half of last Saturday, he's not expecting me back at the office today." He reached for Cat's hand and, even with that simple touch, heat sizzled up his arm and straight to his groin. "Let me help you out."

"I want to, but…it's difficult." She pushed the mostly uneaten sandwich away.

"Try me."

"I've looked out for myself almost my whole life." Her voice was tight and she took off her glasses and covered her face with her hands.

She was afraid to let anyone in. Tenderness replaced Luc's desire. Cat had built up a shell around herself because she was scared, and maybe she'd built it so high and thick she didn't know how to tear it down, even if she wanted to.

"Hey." He came around the desk, pulled her to her feet, then took her in his arms. "What is it?"

"I don't know." She sniffed, and he grabbed a handful of tissues from the box on the desk. "I'm not usually so emotional, but with Amy's accident and now Michael, it's like everywhere I turn, disaster is waiting to strike."

"That's not true. You've had a run of bad luck is all." Luc chose his next words with care. "I'll keep coaching Amy as long as you're here, but have you given any more thought to that summer camp?"

"Sure I have, but Amy has only ever been away for me for a night, not a whole week." Cat's voice broke again. "I don't want her to think I'm sending her away because I want to get rid of her. She has to know she comes first in my life. I'd never abandon her."

"Why would she think that? Despite what she said that night at the hospital, Amy knows you love her and sending her to the camp would show her you care about what she wants." The hairs on the back of Luc's neck stood up as he studied Cat's woebegone face. Everything with Cat went right back to her dad's desertion. Although she was an adult on the outside, on the inside, a big part of her was still that scared little girl who'd been abandoned by the first man she should've been able to count on.

"You're right. Amy's not me." Cat managed a wobbly smile. "I hated summer camp. Nick and Georgia loved it, but it was my worst nightmare. All those sports and organized activities were like torture for me, and the only time I could read was just before lights out. My dad paid for it, though, so I had to go. The year I got chicken pox and was sent home the second day was the best. I don't think I was ever so happy as when Mom's car stopped in front of the main building."

Luc pulled her against his chest. Cat had only opened the door to her guarded heart a crack, but it was far enough for him to glimpse a woman still haunted by her past, a woman who, like the lost and insecure girl he remembered, he still wanted to look out for and protect. However, he was drawn to the woman in a way he'd never been drawn to the girl.

"I don't know what this is between us, but I want to be part of your life." His stomach fluttered as he reached for her hand to link her fingers with his. "I'd never have made love to you otherwise."

Her breath hitched.

With his free hand, he traced a circular pattern on the front of her sweater. "Amy won't be back from school for a few hours, will she?"

Cat shuddered as he stroked her breast through the fine wool. "It's an early dismissal today, but Nick's picking her up and taking her to an event at the riding stable with Kylie and Emma. They won't be back until after supper."

Luc dipped his head and feathered kisses into her hair. "If you take a nap now, we'd still have some time after the gallery closes?"

"Yes." The word came out in a throaty whisper.

He tilted her chin so she looked at him. "I want you, this, whatever we have."

"I'm not that tired." Cat's voice was thick and her pupils were dilated. "Michael always closes the gallery for half an hour at lunch." She trailed a hand down his chest to his belt buckle. "Thirty minutes isn't much, but I could take a late lunch."

He trembled as her hand swooped lower. "I don't need a lot of time." He covered her lips with his. He didn't even want to wait to take her upstairs. The stockroom was private enough.

"I don't either." Her body convulsed as she pressed herself into him. "Hang on while I lock the door and—"

"Mom?" The bell over the door clanged like a fire alarm.

Cat jerked away from him. "Sweetie…I…you… you're supposed to be with your uncle Nick."

Amy came to a stop by the desk and flicked a glance at Luc. "He's outside in the car." Her voice was shrill.

Luc ran a hand through his hair and his legs went weak. "It's not...your mom and I...we were—"

"I may be dumb, but I'm not that dumb." Amy's face was as white as her fuzzy scarf. "You...you and my mom—"

"You're not dumb, not ever." Cat reached for Amy, but the girl pulled away. "What happened to your jeans? They're wet and—"

"Like you care." Amy's tone was insolent.

"Of course I do." Cat's mouth worked. "I care about everything that happens to you."

"A kid pushed me into a snowbank—after I pushed him first." Amy's mouth was set in a hard line and her eyes were filled with both pain and anger.

"What kid? Why? You know we don't solve problems with physical violence in our family." Cat caught Amy's wrist.

"One of the guys in my class, Mason, said you were having a thing with Coach Luc. He laughed and said some other things too, bad things. I pushed him, and he pushed me back." Amy pulled away from Cat. "I guess I shouldn't have bothered. He was right. You're a real—"

"No." Luc reached for Amy but she whirled away from him, too.

Mason didn't play on the team, but he hung around hockey practice, and Luc had already called him out for bullying a few of the smaller, less able players. He was a sharp kid and, like a hunting dog on the scent of prey, he must have picked up on something between him and

Cat. If only he'd spotted what Mason was up to sooner, he might have stopped this.

"You stay out of this, and don't tell me what to say or do. I already told you you're not my dad, and from now on, you're not my coach, either." Amy launched herself at his midriff, and Luc covered his groin with one hand and caught her arm with the other. "Mason also said the only reason you were coaching me was because of her. Because you want to—"

"That's not true." Luc froze and he glanced at Cat, who stood in the middle of the gallery with a stricken expression. "I'm coaching you because you're talented. Why would you think anything else?"

Amy slipped from his grasp, then her fist connected with his stomach. "Why wouldn't I? I saw you with Mom a minute ago. Anybody in town could have seen you."

Luc winced and drew in a sharp breath. The kid packed a hell of a punch for twelve. "I—"

"Stop it, Amy, right now." Cat tugged her away from Luc, but Amy spun toward a shelf of glassware and sent a fruit bowl crashing to the floor.

"I hate you." She stumbled toward the gallery entrance, yanked open the door, and collided with Nick, who stood outside, a hand half raised to his open mouth. "I hate both of you."

Then the door slammed shut. The bang mixed with the sound of shattering glass to spear Luc's heart.

Chapter Seventeen

I...she...she's upset and..." Cat brushed past Luc on shaking legs. She had to go after Amy and try to explain. She pulled open the gallery door and ran into a puddle of icy water to her ankles.

"Hang on." Nick caught her arm.

"Where's Amy?" Cat scanned Main Street. The afternoon sun momentarily blinded her and she stumbled against her brother.

"In my car." Nick gripped her shoulders and flicked his head toward his silver Lexus parked by the curb two doors down.

"I have to talk to her." Water trickled into Cat's shoes. Her suede pumps would be ruined, but that didn't matter. Nothing mattered except Amy. To her dying day, she'd never forget the expression on her daughter's face when she'd walked in on her and Luc.

"Do you think she'd listen to you right now? She's

a McGuire. We act first, say a bunch of stuff we don't mean, then calm down later."

Not Cat. She contemplated every step before she took it and never spoke before she thought. Except, she'd let herself tumble head over heels for Luc almost without thinking—just like she'd done with Amy's dad all those years ago. "Amy saw Luc with me and..." Her chest heaved as panic spiraled.

"Unless you were having sex on the desk, which you weren't, Amy didn't see anything to scar her forever." Nick's tone was dry. "You're allowed to have a life."

"Amy has always come first. I promised myself I wouldn't be like Dad. I thought I was special to him, but he left and..." She made a choked sound.

"Your whole world fell apart." Nick eased her back across the slushy sidewalk toward the gallery door. "Mine did, too, and it took meeting Mia to show me I was still hung up on what Dad did. Whether you talk to him or not, you have to make peace with what happened. As for Amy, nobody would ever question she comes first with you, but you also need to put yourself first sometimes. You're a mom, not a nun."

"I..." Cat swallowed another sob. She wouldn't cry, because if she did, she might never stop. Nick didn't understand; nobody did.

Her brother's blue eyes were filled with warmth as he looked at her. "Amy didn't mean it when she said she hated you."

"You heard that?" Cat's voice shook.

"Only because she yelled it on her way out the door." Nick gave her a half-smile. "She's mad, and puberty's looming. She's also not used to sharing you with anyone.

I bet she's got a lot of feelings right now she doesn't know how to handle. Try not to take it personally."

Cat's mouth dropped open. "When did you start talking like a parenting handbook?"

"I want to be the best dad I can." Nick's voice was solemn. "I'm reading some books Mia suggested. She's helping me a lot, too. I don't want to be like Dad."

"You couldn't." Cat's eyes smarted. "Mia's girls and Kylie are lucky to have you."

"I'm sure lucky to have them." Nick gave her shoulder a comforting squeeze. "Now get in there, Muppet, and tell Luc he's not going to be on the front page of the *Kincaid Examiner* for public indecency. Amy's hurt and embarrassed, that's all. You remember being her age? How would you have reacted if Mom was doing it with a guy who wasn't Dad? Or even with Dad? I like Ward, but I don't like thinking about Mom doing it with him either, and I'm nearly forty."

Cat shuddered. "As Amy would say, TMI."

Nick's smile teased her. "I'll still take Amy to the riding stable with Kylie and Emma and bring her back after supper. We'll swing by my place first to pick up dry clothes for her to change into. I doubt she'll say anything to the girls, but if she wants to talk to Mia or me we'll listen. If she doesn't, we'll ignore the whole thing and let her settle. We McGuires are good at ignoring stuff, too."

Cat curled her icy toes inside her shoes. Maybe she was more like the rest of the McGuires than she thought. And maybe she needed to take a bigger leaf from her mom's family. Although they argued—a lot and loudly— the Brassards and Pelletiers still talked to each other and, even when they disagreed, they never hid how much they loved each other.

"Thanks, Big Bear." Several fat tears oozed out to trickle down her cheeks as she gave her brother a self-conscious hug.

"This whole thing with Amy will blow over. As for me, I'm glad you're finally getting some action. Luc's a good guy who can teach you stuff you won't learn from books." Nick hugged her back. "Just remember, I want to be the one who walks you down the aisle."

"I...Luc and I...we're not...but even if I was, with anyone, I can walk myself down the aisle." Or if it ever came to that, maybe she'd elope and skip the whole church wedding thing entirely.

"Of course you can, but I want to be there for you— always." Nick's expression softened. "Now go." He grinned and swiped her arm.

She brushed away more tears and swiped him back.

"Cat?" The gallery door swung open, and Luc held out a lap quilt patterned with green and blue dragonflies. "I couldn't find your coat. You must be freezing."

Cat shook her head and turned away to stare at Nick's car. Amy was hunched over in one corner of the back seat, her head bowed. Even as the car pulled away, she never looked back.

"Here." Luc wrapped the quilt around Cat's bent shoulders.

Her eyes burned as she followed him back into the gallery and flipped the sign on the door to CLOSED. Water squished out of her sodden shoes onto Michael's prized oak floor. She slipped off the shoes and left them by the door. The broken glass was gone—Luc must have swept it up—but the big empty space on the display shelf mirrored the big empty space in Cat's heart. She pulled the quilt tighter and tried to stop shaking.

"I boiled the kettle." Luc took her arm to steady her, and she leaned into the stability and comfort he offered. "You need to get something hot into you." He gave her a half smile and guided her toward the stockroom. "I know. I'm turning into a cross between my mom and Liz."

"Or my mom." Motherly advice passed from generation to generation. Yet today, all that advice had failed her, and she didn't have any words to talk to her daughter about what mattered most. Cat moved into the stockroom on rubbery legs and stumbled to the worktable. What had she done? And how could she fix it? She pulled out a stool and sat.

Luc took two mugs from the cupboard over the small sink in one corner of the room. "I'm sorry. I didn't think. Anybody could have walked in on us, not only Amy."

"I didn't think, either." Because she'd been so caught up in how Luc made her feel. Guilt rolled over Cat like a tsunami.

"I'm not sorry about wanting to make love to you again, but I shouldn't have started something here." Luc filled the mugs with hot water, then dropped a chamomile tea bag into Cat's. "Do you want me to talk to Amy?"

"Not yet." Cat rested her elbows on the table and the lap quilt pooled at her sides. Dragonflies symbolized change and looking beyond the surface of life. She'd read that somewhere and filed it away along with all the other facts crammed into her head—facts she'd focused on to avoid feelings. Being with Luc had changed her enough, though, to tell him the truth. "Before I came back to Firefly Lake, I was hiding out. From life, men, everything."

"Why?" Only one word, but the gentleness in Luc's voice almost broke her heart. He carried the mugs to the table, then sat on the stool next to hers.

Cat worked moisture into her dry mouth. "I met Amy's dad in Florida during spring break my senior year in college. It was a last-minute trip with a few girls from my dorm. Someone canceled, so there was an extra space. I took it. We all went to a beach party one night and started talking to this group of guys. Jared... I liked him, and I thought he liked me, too, so I slept with him. For once in my life, I wanted to be like other girls. I'd never been before. Not in high school, not during my gap year with Mom's family in Quebec, and not in college, either." She rubbed a hand across her face.

"And?" Luc's compassionate gaze met hers.

"We'd had too much to drink. He had a condom, but we were messing around, and I guess he put it on too late. Nine months later, I had Amy." Her stomach knotted.

There was no condemnation in Luc's expression, only kindness. "Did you tell him you were pregnant? He should have taken responsibility."

"It turned out Jared had a fiancée back home in Minnesota he never mentioned." Cat took several deep breaths. "I found out about her the last night we were there. One of his friends was joking around and I heard... He and the other guys had made a bet with Jared and..." Her stomach lurched with the same hurt and humiliation she'd felt back then. The same sense of betrayal as when she'd huddled in the shadow of the palm trees at the dark end of the motel parking lot and thrown up over her pink sandals until there was nothing left in her stomach.

"Aww, honey, you—"

"No." Cat shook her head. She had to finish this. "Even so, I'd have told him, but the week I found out I was pregnant, he was killed in a farm accident. One of my dormmates hooked up with one of Jared's buddies that same trip. She told me." She stared into the mug of tea without seeing it. "For a smart girl, I made a stupid mistake."

"Because you're a smart girl, you didn't let that mistake, or one stupid jerk, ruin your life." Luc's voice was rough and he covered one of her hands with his. "Despite what happened this afternoon, you're a good mom, and Amy's a good kid. Don't ever think otherwise."

"Out of something bad, I got the most precious gift ever. Amy." Cat studied their joined hands. His knuckles were dusted with light brown hair, and his skin was pitted and dented with the wounds of the game he'd played his whole life. Her hand was pale with long fingers, a scholar's hand. "But she's never been so mad at me before. What if she never forgives me?"

"Of course she will, but right now, maybe it's good that she's not bottling up her feelings."

His voice would have soothed her if Cat could have been soothed. Maybe Amy would forgive her, but could she ever forgive herself? "She hit you. Hitting isn't ever acceptable. That's what I've taught her."

"She's sure going to be able to look after herself if anybody goes for her on the ice again." Luc rubbed his midriff.

"She pushed one of her classmates, too." Cat's hands shook and she wrapped them around the mug.

"From what I've seen of Mason, I doubt Amy's the first kid to push him."

"That doesn't make it okay." Cat might not want to, but she had to tell Luc the rest of the truth and make him understand. "Amy's dad played college hockey. His friends called him an 'enforcer.' Back then, I didn't know what that meant. Now I do, and that's why at first I didn't want Amy to play hockey. But now that she loves hockey so much, I have to teach her fighting's wrong."

Luc's smile slid away. "Just because her dad was a tough guy on the ice doesn't mean Amy will be. Nature versus nurture, remember? Whether you think so or not, you have a big influence on her." His voice was his coach voice, calm and logical. "As for Mason, she shouldn't have pushed him, but she was protecting you. When you get a group of twelve- and thirteen-year-old boys together, before you know it one of them says something and they're punching each other out."

Cat stiffened and pulled her hand away from his. "Not every boy is like that."

"No, but from what I've seen coaching, a lot of them are. Amy will calm down. You can talk to her when she gets home. Nick's right, we weren't having sex on the desk, so she didn't see anything that'll mess her up for life." Amusement sparked in his eyes.

"You weren't supposed to hear that." Cat's face heated.

"A woman who blushes is very sexy."

"It's embarrassing." Cat put her hands to her face.

Luc tugged them away. "I want to know more about you, Cat." His expression turned serious. "All of you."

"You do know me. You've known me since I was born." She touched her throat.

"But until now, you've hidden the most important parts of yourself." His voice was low and promised intimacy that was not only physical but emotional. "I want you to let me in. What do you have to lose?"

She gulped, then gave a jerky nod. Nothing. Or maybe everything.

Luc shifted on the sofa, and the two cats curled together on his lap like inverted question marks meowed in protest. He scratched two sets of brown tabby ears, and two sets of amber eyes drifted shut again. In the oasis of Cat's quiet apartment, Amy walking in on him kissing Cat seemed like days ago instead of mere hours.

"You're spoiling my cats." Cat sat beside him and tucked her legs beneath her.

"I don't hear either of them complaining." He rubbed Bingley under his chin, and the cat rewarded him with a loud purr. "Besides, after I shut them out of your bedroom earlier, I have to make sure there aren't any hard feelings."

"Hence that cat jungle gym or whatever it is?" She pointed to the climbing tree that now occupied one corner of her living room, before giving him a naughty grin that reminded him why he'd scooped the cats off her bed, then followed her into it. "You were supposed to be picking up the pizza."

"Len's Hardware is on the way to Mario's." Luc gave her his most beguiling look. "Besides, Len was practically giving that climbing tree away." He snagged the remote and clicked the TV on. "Darcy and Bingley like it, don't they?"

"Of course they do." A smile hovered around Cat's

mouth. "And Amy will love it. She's been after me to get one of those things for ages, but you don't need to give me presents."

"It's not for you. It's for Darcy and Bingley." He flicked to a sports channel. It was good hanging out with Cat, more than good, if he was honest. "If I leave in an hour, I'll be gone before Amy gets home so you'll have lots of time to talk to her."

"She hasn't called." Cat's expression clouded.

"If there was a problem, Nick would have called or texted you."

"Yes, but maybe I should have called him." She bit her bottom lip.

"He told you she needed time to cool off. You're giving her the space she needs right now, so try not to worry." Luc pulled her into his shoulder. "Let's watch some hockey. There's a replay of the Bruins game from Saturday night."

"Didn't you already see that one?" There was a teasing lilt in her voice.

He tickled the soft curve of her side. "How many times have you watched *Pride and Prejudice*?"

"That's different." She laughed and tickled him back. "It's a classic."

"Like the Bruins versus the Penguins is classic hockey." He looped an arm around her. "Tell you what. You watch hockey with me now, and tomorrow night I'll watch one of those bonnets and ball gowns things with you."

She sent him an outraged look. "Deal. I have a Jane Austen box set."

"Why am I not surprised?" He chuckled and tweaked

her nose. "You still look pretty tired." She was even paler than she'd been earlier and her mouth had a grayish tinge. "Rest your head on my shoulder. If you fall asleep, I'll wake you up when I leave." He pulled a throw from the back of the sofa and wrapped it around her legs.

"Thanks." She snuggled into him, and Luc's heart tripped. This was right. Here, Cat, and the two felines. Not doing anything special, but still the most special time he'd spent with anyone since Maggie died. He was almost happy, at least his new happy.

"Luc?" Her voice was a low murmur against his shoulder.

"What?" He muted the sound on the TV. He didn't need the game; all he needed was her.

"I won't be able to sleep until Amy gets home." She fingered the tassel on the edge of the throw. "Tell me about Maggie's death. If...you can talk about it." There was no idle curiosity in her voice, only gentle concern. "You said you wanted to know all about me. I want to know about all of you."

His heart thudded and blood roared in his ears. "Didn't your mom tell you?" He stared at the screen, where players darted to and fro across the ice.

"Yes, but that's not the same." The kindness in her voice gave him courage, and when she curled a hand into his, he held onto it as if it were a bulwark against the riptide of emotion her words had unleashed.

"Widowers are supposed to be older, not thirty-three. At that age, you should be decorating a nursery, not picking out a funeral plot. You should be starting a college fund and planning for your family's future." His voice caught as the band around his chest almost suffocated him.

"I can't imagine how hard that must have been." Cat gave his hand a little squeeze.

"Most people don't want to talk about death." After they'd sent flowers and cards, or made a big donation to the USA Hockey Foundation in Maggie's memory, almost all of the people he'd thought he could count on had disappeared from his life as if what had happened to him was somehow catching. "My folks helped me as much as they could, but..." He stopped and fought for control.

"They must have been grieving, too." Cat's soft voice was a healing balm to his tortured soul.

"Yeah." For the first time in his life, his mom and dad couldn't make things better and, like Maggie's parents and sisters, they'd been as broken and bewildered as he was. "Maggie wasn't sick. She ate healthy, exercised, and never smoked or did drugs. She was a US Olympian. Her picture was even on a cereal box."

Cat leaned forward and clicked off the TV. "And?" The crack in her voice paralleled the crack in Luc's heart.

"She was thirteen weeks pregnant when she had a brain aneurysm at the side of the rink one afternoon in the middle of practice. I was on the road with the team, and by the time I got back it was all over. I failed her." His words were infused with the bitter taste of guilt. "I wasn't there when she needed me. If I'd been there, maybe she would have made it."

Cat rubbed his back and shifted so her knees bumped against his. "Why? From what Mom said, the EMTs did everything they could." Her gentleness unlocked the layer of grief he'd hidden deep in a vain attempt to forget it was there and helped him tell her what he'd never told anyone, not even his mom.

"Maggie wasn't feeling well the day before I left for the road trip. She had a headache." Luc stroked the dozing cats and stared at his feet. "I was distracted. The team was on a losing streak, and I was more worried about the slump than I was about my wife and child. What kind of a husband does that make me?"

"Exactly like husbands everywhere." The compassion in Cat's voice almost undid him. "Most people who have headaches don't die of brain aneurysms. I had lots of headaches when I was pregnant with Amy, and the doctor said it was normal. You had no way of knowing Maggie's headache wasn't."

"I wasn't there, so I didn't know the headache must have gotten worse. She was only coaching that day to help a friend. Why did she even go to the rink?" He'd replayed those hours over and over again in his head, but the outcome was always the same. The woman he loved was gone, and he hadn't even said good-bye.

"Maggie made a choice, but she could have died at home all alone." Cat scooted even closer to him. "At least she had people with her when it was her time."

"Maybe it wouldn't have been her time if she hadn't been pregnant. She was worried because she'd already had three miscarriages, but she'd had a lot of tests. When the doctor gave us the all clear, I pushed her to try again. Me, even though I was the one who'd promised to love and protect her. And when it...she...I was thousands of miles away."

He dropped his head into his hands. When the phone call from an unknown ER doctor had come, for endless seconds he'd tried to convince himself it was a sick joke. He'd stared out of his hotel room window at the sparkling blue of the pool, where everything still looked like it had two minutes before, even though his world had imploded.

"I didn't listen." His throat was as sore as if he'd swallowed a carving knife. "We didn't have to have our own kid. We could have adopted. I as good as killed her."

"No, you didn't." Cat's voice was firm. "Maggie did what she did. You did, too. Do you really think she'd blame you for what happened? Didn't she want her own baby?"

"She did, but—"

Cat put a soft finger to his lips. "From what you've said about her, Maggie would never for one minute have blamed you."

"It doesn't stop me blaming myself."

"Is that fair?"

"That's not the point. Since I'm still here, I have to live with what I did for the rest of my life." He sagged into the sofa cushions.

"You'll always love and miss Maggie, but you don't have to let needless guilt eat you up inside. She loved you as much as you love her, and that kind of love is bigger than guilt or blame." Cat looked deep into his eyes. "For Maggie's sake, even if not your own, you have to forgive yourself."

His eyelids burned and the pain in his chest got worse.

"Here." She eased the cats aside to pull him into her arms. "It's okay. Let it out."

He buried his face against her soft sweater, and the scorching tears he'd never let anyone else see spilled out unchecked.

"I'll call you later." Cat handed Luc his coat. His body was stiff and his expression shuttered. His grief wasn't a secret, but she'd never guessed he blamed himself for Maggie's death. Unless he got past that, and no matter how much she let him into her life, how could there ever be a real place for her in his?

"Tell Amy—"

Her cell phone shrilled with a tune from the *Muppet Show*. "Sorry, I have to take this. It's Nick." She grabbed the phone from the coffee table and patted Luc's shoulder.

"What do you mean?" Her heart raced as she tried to make sense of her brother's words. "How could Amy have disappeared? She's twelve, not two."

"She went to the bathroom, but she didn't come back." Nick's voice echoed with horrible resonance. "We've looked everywhere. I've already called the police and—"

"I'm on my way." The phone slipped from Cat's hand and Luc caught it.

"What?" His mouth shaped the word.

Her ears rang, and the living room tilted like a fairground ride as Luc disconnected Nick's call and grabbed her arm to steady her. "Amy was at the stable with Nick and the girls, but now she's gone. I have to—"

"I'll drive you." He found her coat and bundled her into it. "After the last time, I thought she'd learned her lesson about wandering off."

"I thought so, too." Cat snatched her purse from a chair. "I've never heard Nick sound so frantic."

"Have you got a picture?" Luc's blue gaze was somber.

"Do you think someone's taken her?" Cat's voice rose as she fumbled in her purse for her keys. "If she's run away...no...she must have taken a wrong turn coming back from the bathroom. It's dark and with the snow..."

"I'm not thinking anything because we don't know

what's happened yet. The stable isn't on a busy road, and it's probably a fuss about nothing, but the cops will want a picture just in case." Luc took the keys from her, then glanced around the living room and plucked a framed school picture of Amy from a bookshelf. "Does she have any money on her?"

"Not more than five dollars. She always has a bit in case there's something she needs to buy at school." Cat stuck her feet into her boots and jammed her winter hat onto her head. Amy couldn't be missing again. Any minute now, Nick would call her back to tell her it was a mistake.

Luc took her arm again, locked the apartment door behind them, then led her down the outside stairs past the dark gallery. "Where would you go if you were Amy?"

"She still misses Boston, but it's too far away. How would she get there? And who would she run to there? We have friends but...all her family is here." Cat swallowed a gulping sob. "Unless she hitchhiked, how would she get to the Greyhound stop? And the bus doesn't run from here very often." She pressed a hand to her mouth.

"When she wants something..." He stopped and bit his lip, but the truth was in his eyes. He was all too afraid Amy was headed for Boston.

Cat pressed a hand to her midriff. Her daughter had a reckless streak. Cat had seen it on the hockey rink, and she'd seen it again when Amy had stormed out of the gallery earlier. Like the man who'd fathered her, it was a streak that could hurt her in hockey—and hurt her even more in life.

"Let's check the arena first. That's where she went before." When they reached the bottom of the stairs, Luc shepherded her toward his snow-covered truck.

But even if she was at the rink, how had she gotten there? Someone would have had to drive her. Cat held back a cry and scaled a snowbank to slide into the truck's passenger seat. Ice pellets hit the window in a quick staccato, and the wind shrieked as it blew a thick curtain of snow across Main Street. Amy couldn't be out in this weather. She clutched her stomach. There might not be a place in Luc's life for her, but maybe there wasn't one for him in hers, either. No matter how much they wanted it.

Chapter Eighteen

❧

When Amy left the stable it was still light, but dusk had come on fast and now night was closing in. It was colder, too, and the snow that seemed pretty earlier from inside the warm riding stable tumbled from the overcast sky thick and fast, erasing the few familiar landmarks.

She looked all around, especially behind where her footprints were already half covered by fresh snow. She couldn't stay in Firefly Lake now, not with how things were between her mom and the coach. And she couldn't ever go back to school here. Not after what Mason had said. Once she made it back to Boston, she'd figure out what to do from there. Maybe her mom's friends who were renting their apartment would let her stay with them.

Amy stopped at the edge of the trees and curled her clammy fingers inside her mittens. If she went into those dark woods, she might never find her way out again. It would be better to stay close to the road. The Greyhound stop was at the gas station on the outskirts of town. If she remembered the schedule right, there was a bus in an hour. Town hadn't seemed far away before, but it had been daylight then and she'd been in a car.

At a rustle in the woods behind her, she flinched. The tracks in the snow at her feet were small, a rabbit maybe, but that noise was bigger. She hadn't thought about wild animals out here. Heading away from the woods, she turned back toward the road and wrapped her hand around Uncle Nick's wallet in her coat pocket. She'd pay him back, but he must be missing both the wallet and her by now. She'd slipped it from his jacket while he watched Kylie and Emma in the riding arena. Her stomach growled and she dug in her other pocket for the half-eaten Dove bar she'd stashed there earlier.

The narrow country road wasn't much lighter than the dark forest that lined it on either side. Her heart racing, Amy walked along the shoulder, where snow had drifted into soft mounds. Was town this way? Her legs shook. That noise had scared her so much she'd lost all sense of direction. She slipped on an icy patch, dropped the chocolate, and fell butt first into the ditch to land atop a snowdrift.

Above her, yellow light shone around the curve in the road, and she crouched low to wait until the car passed. She wouldn't hitchhike. Bad things happened to people who hitchhiked, and her mom had told her to never do it.

But the car didn't whoosh past. Instead, it slowed, and Amy was trapped in the beam of light. She tried to scramble to her feet and run, but the snow was wet and heavy and she couldn't get traction. As she flailed right, then left, her coat caught on something. Was it that animal? She screamed and lurched forward, her breath coming in short gasps.

A car door slammed, and a dark shape moved toward her. "Amy?"

At her aunt Georgia's voice, Amy's legs went out from under her again, and she tumbled farther back into the snowy ditch. "Yeah."

"What are you doing out here all by yourself, honey?" A different voice, one that belonged to Charlie Carmichael, Aunt Mia's sister, who, as a big-shot journalist, was almost as great a celebrity in Firefly Lake as Coach Luc.

"I screwed up." Amy's voice was a whimper. "Now I think I need some help. I'm stuck. I can't..." She yanked at her coat and a piece of fabric let go with a ripping sound.

"It's good we came along, isn't it?" Charlie knelt at the edge of the ditch and held out her gloved hands. "Hold on tight. Let me pull you out."

With two strong tugs, Amy hurtled up the sloping bank onto the shoulder of the road to land next to Charlie's boots. She lay there panting and tried to catch her breath.

"The last time I did that was in the French Alps." Charlie's brown eyes twinkled in the car lights. "You're a lot lighter than my photographer was."

"Amy...sweetheart...thank God you're safe." Aunt Georgia bent down to wrap her in a hug. "Your mom's frantic."

"You talked to her already?" Amy tried to sit up. Her head spun and her heart felt like it was going to explode right out of her chest. Her mom would be so mad. She'd be lucky if she wasn't grounded until high school.

"I called her while Charlie was pulling you out." Her aunt's voice sounded like she was going to cry, which was weird because Aunt Georgia was the most chilled-out person Amy knew.

"I'm sorry." Amy shook so badly she couldn't unzip her coat.

"Let me." Aunt Georgia pulled off Amy's wet coat and mittens, then replaced them with her own warm ones. "You're frozen. Get in the car."

Amy huddled into the backseat, where her aunt gestured, and took the blanket she held out. Next to her, baby Lexie slept in a car seat.

"Here." Aunt Georgia waved her phone. "Your mom's waiting. You have to talk to her."

"I can't." The words came out more like a cry, and she tried to make herself as small as possible. "Tell Mom I'm fine and I'll talk to her real soon, but I can't, I have to..." Amy didn't know what she had to do, but if she talked to her mom right now, she didn't know what she'd say except for stuff that would make everything a whole lot worse.

Aunt Georgia turned around and said something into the phone that Amy couldn't hear. Then she swung back around again and her words tripped over each other. "I should be mad at you, but I can't be. Not right now, anyway. Nick's looking for you everywhere and, to top it all off, he can't find his wallet. It's lucky he went to high school with one of the cops so he didn't have to prove his identity. You wouldn't happen to know anything about that, would you?" Her eyes narrowed as she looked Amy up and down.

"I kind of like...took it. It's in my coat pocket." She gestured to the coat her aunt still had a hold of. "I didn't mean to. It just happened." The mistakes had piled up as dirty and messy as the snow the plows left in the big field at the edge of the arena. "I'm sorry."

"You can save the apologies for your mom and Nick. If Charlie hadn't seen something on the side of the road…" Her aunt's voice cracked as she took out the wallet. "She thought an animal had been hit so we stopped. You could have been killed, sweetheart, out here alone." She rubbed a hand across her face.

"I guess you were running away, huh?" From the driver's seat, Charlie started the car and turned up the heat.

Amy stared at the melting snow that dripped across the car mat from her sodden boots. "I didn't mean to, at least not exactly." Inside the cozy mittens, she dug her nails into her palms.

"But you wanted to leave Firefly Lake?" Aunt Georgia got in on the passenger side and turned to look back at Amy. Her voice was kind and, in the half-light, her expression was understanding.

"Yeah." Except now that she thought about it, the problems wouldn't be so easy to leave behind, no matter where she was.

"I can't count the number of times I wanted to leave Firefly Lake when I was your age, but here I am right back where I started." Aunt Georgia fingered her beaded necklace and her laugh was as tinny as the canned laughter on a TV show.

"Sometimes you have to go all the way around the world before you find your way back home. In my case, it took a lot longer than it did for Georgia." Charlie's voice was so soft Amy had to strain to hear her.

"I never said I was staying, did I?" Her aunt glanced back at Amy and made a disbelieving face.

"You never know." Charlie pulled the car back onto the road, then grinned at Amy in the rearview mirror. "Did you know your fabulous aunt is teaching yoga to a group of senior women for free? I'm doing my bit by writing a story for the local paper. That's why we were out here. The class is at a farm a few miles beyond the stable."

"You should come with me next time." Aunt Georgia's face went pink and her smile was unexpectedly sweet. "The older ladies would love you right up."

"Sure." Amy muttered the word, then tucked her head into the collar of Aunt Georgia's fake fur coat, soft like a cuddly teddy bear. Her mom probably wouldn't let her out of the apartment unless it was for school. She might not even let her play hockey. Her stomach turned over. She'd messed things up so bad with Coach Luc, though, he'd probably never speak to her again, let alone want to share a rink with her.

Her eyes watered and she stared at Lexie still asleep beside her. Life was easy for babies. All you had do was eat, sleep, play, and poop. Everybody loved you and said how cute you were.

If you were a baby like Lexie, you had a mom and dad who were crazy about you and about each other. Nobody would ever say your mom was banging your coach, or that you got special help not because you were special but only because of your mom. If your parents were kissing, it might still be weird and disgusting, but they were your parents. They were supposed to be weird and disgusting; Kylie said so.

Even though Amy wasn't cold any longer, she shivered again as the outskirts of Firefly Lake came into view. Through the snow, lights twinkled from the big houses up on the dark hill where her grandma lived. Not only had she messed up with her mom and Coach Luc, she'd messed up with everyone, and now she had to face the music.

"We've all made mistakes." Aunt Georgia reached back and squeezed Amy's hand. "Me, Charlie, and even your mom, despite her perfect GPA. The most important thing is that you learn from those mistakes. Nick and your mom will be okay with everything, you'll see."

Amy jerked her chin and bit down on her bottom lip. Her aunt wanted to help, but she couldn't. The only mistake her mom had made was getting pregnant. But until today, she'd never thought that meant *she* was a mistake. But Mason had yelled it out so loud all the kids waiting for the buses must have heard. Coach Scott was there, so he must have heard it, too. It was a gazillion times more humiliating than anything that had happened to her back in Boston, and now she couldn't get those words out of her head. How could she face all of them again? And how could she face her mom and Coach Luc?

Lexie opened her big, blue eyes and waved her chubby hands like she'd never seen them before. Then she made a gurgling sound that turned into a belly laugh.

Yep, life was easy for babies. Amy slipped off one of Aunt Georgia's mittens and hooked her pinkie finger with Lexie's, then hunched back in her seat. She'd been so determined to escape everything that had gone wrong, she'd taken what she thought was the only way out. But like Aunt Georgia said, she'd ended up exactly where she started, except this time in a whole lot more trouble than ever before.

* * *

"Georgia and Charlie should be here with Amy by now." Cat pushed back the drapes that covered the big bay window in the living room at Harbor House and peered out into the night. The snow still fell and enveloped the trees that lined the drive like a shroud.

"It's only been fifteen minutes since Georgia called." Her mom joined her at the window and wrapped an arm around Cat's tight shoulders. "The riding stable is way out of town, and we don't know exactly where they found her."

Each minute felt like an hour or even a day. Cat shifted from one foot to the other. Maybe she should have gone home, but Georgia had thought it would be easier for Amy if she brought her to Harbor House first. Now Cat wasn't so sure. They'd have an audience here.

"What was Amy thinking? I know we had a fight, but why would she run off again?" And why wouldn't Amy talk to her when Georgia called? Did she think Cat wouldn't forgive her? Couldn't she understand Cat would always love her, no matter what? Pain speared Cat's chest, and she pressed her nose against the window to look out into the swirling snow.

"Twelve-year-old girls can get worked up real fast. You and Georgia were the same when you were Amy's age." Her mom rubbed Cat's back in a gentle circular motion.

"My daughter was, too." Ward joined them and held out a mug of tea. "For a few years there, it was like I was living in a permanent hurricane. If my wife hadn't died, she'd have known how to handle Erica better, but I sure didn't. All you can do is your best."

Except, Cat's best never seemed to be good enough. She shook her head at the tea. She couldn't drink or eat anything past the fear in her throat. "Georgia and I never ran away." But they hadn't seen their mom kissing one of Cat's teachers or Georgia's gymnastics coach.

"One of my sisters ran away once." Luc completed another circuit from the front hall to the living room with Pixie at his heels. "She was thirteen and mad because Mom wouldn't let her buy this bikini she had her eye on. She made it as far as the railroad tracks at the edge of town before a neighbor spotted her. It was only a swimsuit, but from the way she carried on, you'd think the world had ended."

"For a thirteen-year-old girl, it probably had." Her mom pressed Cat's arm. "Amy loves you. It'll all work out, you'll see."

Cat wished she could be so sure, but this problem was too big and had gone too deep for everything to magically be okay. "Is that Charlie's car?" She rubbed at a foggy patch on the window.

"Yep." Ward moved toward the front door, but Cat reached it first and wrenched it open.

"Amy." She ran across the porch in her sock feet and down the steps. She reached her daughter by the snow-laden maple tree at the front of the house and held out her arms.

Amy stumbled into them. "I'm sorry." Her words came out in a hiccup. "I messed up so bad."

"You're safe. Everything else we can fix." Whatever it took, no matter how long it took, Cat would find a way. She touched her daughter's cheek, then her hair and hands, all reassuringly familiar. Amy smelled the same too, a faint whiff of lemon shampoo mixed with spearmint.

"Thank you." Cat looked from Georgia, who hovered behind Amy, to Charlie still in the car. "Thank you both."

"It's okay." Georgia gave Cat's hand a brief clasp. "The weather's getting worse, so Charlie has to get home with Lexie. If you need to talk, she said to call."

After Charlie's car slipped out of the drive, Cat turned back toward the house. "Let's get you both inside. You must be freezing." She rubbed Amy's hands between hers. "And Georgie, your coat and mittens...you gave them to Amy."

"She needed them more than I did." Georgia shrugged and shuffled her feet.

Cat took one arm away from Amy to hook it around her sister. "You're a big softie. Teaching yoga to older ladies for nothing and rescuing lost girls. What's next?"

"I'm not the one who rescued her." Georgia's bottom lip wobbled. "When I realized it was Amy, I panicked like I always do. Charlie pulled her out of the ditch."

"Don't talk like that. You called me and stayed with Lexie." Cat made her feet move up the porch steps and back into the house.

"I wasn't lost, not really." Amy voice was muffled as she was folded into her grandmother's arms.

"Lost or not, you're home now and safe." Cat's gaze connected with Luc, who stood farther back in the hall with Ward. His expression was so sad that her heart turned over.

"Coach Luc?"

"Yes?" His tone was gruff.

"I'm sorry I hit you and said that stuff about you and my mom." Amy's voice was high and thin—a little girl's voice.

"Apology accepted." Luc moved toward the sweeping staircase. "I'm glad you're okay. I'll see you at the rink whenever you're ready."

"You mean you'll still coach me? After everything?"

Cat's stomach knotted at the hope and regret in Amy's voice.

"I promised, didn't I?" Luc's smile was strained. "As long as you're in Firefly Lake and the arena has ice, I'll coach you. If it's okay with your mom." His smile disappeared and he glanced at Cat, like she was any other hockey mom. "Give me a call."

"Yes." Although the initial fear in Cat's throat had eased, it had been replaced by another kind entirely. One that had nothing to do with Amy's safety, but everything to do with what Cat's love for her daughter would mean for her secret love for Luc.

Chapter Nineteen

Cat patted Amy's legs through the green and white quilt with the starburst pattern they'd chosen together for her twelfth birthday. "You need to eat something."

Amy toyed with a strip of toast, then set the plate on the nightstand beside the bed. Her eyes were puffy and red-rimmed from crying. She picked up the tattered sock monkey toy she'd had since she was a baby and stroked its tail. "I'm not hungry."

Cat shifted on the single bed beside her daughter. She had to focus on Amy, not on the look in Luc's eyes before he'd turned away and gone up the stairs at Harbor House, each footfall on the uncarpeted steps like a bittersweet but irrevocable good-bye.

"About this afternoon..." She stopped and glanced around Amy's bedroom. The cream-painted walls were covered with hockey posters. Schoolbooks, clothing, and sports equipment were scattered across the floor. "I never meant for you to see Coach Luc and me kissing." Her throat closed.

"You always say we're a team, but now with him…" Amy pleated the edge of the quilt between her fingers. "It's not like I didn't know you were having dinner with him and stuff. You never hid that from me, and at first, I even wanted you to like him."

"But that changed?" Cat needed Amy to be honest about her feelings, no matter what it might mean.

"Nothing worked out like I thought it would." Amy rubbed at her eyes with her pajama sleeve. "I wanted the two of you to go out because I thought…I don't have a dad, and I wanted to be like all the other kids." Her eyes were haunted and desperate. "I thought Coach Luc would be great because he understands about hockey, and he also made me feel special."

"Special how?" Why hadn't Amy already felt special?

"Hockey's the only thing I'm good at. Here, I don't have to be good at school to stay in hockey, and when Coach Luc started coaching me, that made me special. Even though some of the other kids and their parents didn't like it, for the first time in my whole life, I had something other kids wanted. It was nice, you know?" Her voice shook, and Cat's heart broke a little bit more.

"When Luc and I started seeing each other, although that's what you thought you wanted, you didn't feel special anymore?" Cat tried to keep the wobble out of her voice—and the fear.

Amy twirled the monkey's tail. "Kylie said if you and Coach Luc got together, you might love him best, not me."

Cat let out an unsteady breath. "Love doesn't work that

way, honey. The human heart stretches like a big rubber band so there's always enough love to go around. How I love you is different from the way I love your grandma or Uncle Nick and Aunt Georgia, but it doesn't mean I love you any less."

Although there was no question that what she felt for Luc was love, it was a secret love and always had to be. He couldn't love her back the way she loved him. Even if he did, they couldn't be together because it made Amy so uncomfortable. "No matter if I someday fell in love with a man, it wouldn't take anything away from my love for you."

"But Mason, as well as a bunch of the other kids at school, said Coach Luc was only working with me because of you." Amy's voice caught and fresh tears rolled down her face. "That means I'm not special at all."

"Mason and all those kids are wrong. A lot of them are probably jealous of how good you are at hockey. Do you honestly think someone like Coach Luc would spend so much time helping you if you didn't have talent?" Cat grabbed a handful of tissues from the box and patted at Amy's tears.

"I guess not, but even though you've never said so, I don't think you like me playing hockey. What I'm good at doesn't make me special to you, either." Amy's words came out in a wrenching sob.

"Of course you're special to me, and for all sorts of reasons that have nothing to do with hockey." How had Amy not known how much she loved her? "You're the best daughter I could ever have hoped for. You're loving, kind, funny, and smart, and that's only the start. We're still a team, and we always will be."

"But hockey..." Amy stared at the quilt. "Is it something to do with my dad?"

From the day that Amy had put on her first pair of hockey skates and moved onto the ice with such passion and purpose, Cat had known this moment was coming. But like an ostrich, she'd avoided it and pretended Amy would never ask much about the man who'd fathered her beyond the bare facts Cat had already shared. Somewhere along the way, she should have learned that avoiding problems only made them bigger.

"Your dad played college hockey for the University of North Dakota." Cat sucked air into her lungs. "He was good at it, but he played rough, and I'm scared you...for you..." She stopped and swallowed hard. Although she hadn't meant to, and as Luc had already pointed out, she'd transferred some of her feelings about Jared to their daughter. Now she was paying the price.

Amy let out a huff. "You need to trust me, Mom. I got your genes, too. I know I messed up today, but I'm not my dad. I don't want to be like him, either. He sounds like a real loser. Why did you hook up with him in the first place?"

"I messed up, too." Even though she'd been a lot older than her daughter back then and had almost finished college, Cat had wanted to fit in as much as Amy did now. "But out of that came the best thing in my life—you." She smoothed Amy's tangled hair.

"Mason said I was a mistake." Amy spit the words out.

"I never thought that, and I never said it, either. Neither would Grandma, Uncle Nick, or Aunt Georgia. They're your family, and although you were a surprise, they all love you as much as I do, and they did from the very start." Cat made her voice strong and certain. Amy had to believe her, but if she didn't, Cat would keep telling her the truth over and over for as long as it took.

"Even if Mason's a big liar, he yelled it out real loud." Amy's voice was hoarse from crying. "Everybody must have heard, and they'll think I..."

"No, they'll think he's the one who *made* a mistake." Cat tried to steady her breathing. "I'll go to school and talk to your teachers and Coach Scott and everyone to make this right."

"You'd do that for me?" Amy sniffed.

"Of course. I'd do anything for you." Even if it meant she had to give up Luc forever. Cat's stomach plummeted like it was in freefall. "As for hockey making you special to me, it does, but it's only one part of it."

"Really?" Amy's voice cracked.

"Really." Cat wrapped her in a hug. "As far as hockey goes, though, Luc told me about this summer hockey camp for girls in New York State. He thinks you could get a scholarship if he recommends you. That should tell you how special he thinks you are. What do you say?"

"Me?" Amy's mouth dropped open. "You'd let me go?"

"Yes, you, and yes, I would. Despite what happened today, I trust you and believe in you." Cat rubbed her temples. Between worry about Amy, Luc, and her never-ending job search, she'd had a headache for days, a dull, persistent throb behind her eyes. "If you could continue with Coach Luc and go to the camp, would that make up for not playing on a team right now?"

"Like yeah." Amy blew her nose into a tissue. "Hockey season's almost over anyway." Her eyes, the same light blue as Jared's, became thoughtful. "But Coach Luc said there's a good girls' team an hour from here. They play in tournaments and everything. If I could keep working with him and also play on that team next season, I wouldn't care about not going back to Boston. Once you fix things at school, we could stay in Firefly Lake."

Cat stared at her hands. If nothing came through from all those job applications she'd sent out, what would she do? Amy couldn't go back to her old school, but the research grant funding only ran until the end of June. She didn't want to uproot Amy again, but she might not have a choice. And if she didn't get a better job, she might not have enough money to pay for hockey anyway. If Amy played on that girls' team, there would be gas money and lots of other costs. Around and around her thoughts circled, but she was never any closer to an answer.

"Only a few hours ago you were running away from Firefly Lake." Cat laced her fingers with Amy's. "Although I've said yes to that hockey camp, you have to understand that running away from problems is never a solution. You have to face the consequences of your actions." Cat's stomach turned over. She needed to take her own advice, starting with Luc. "I was frantic when your uncle Nick called and said he couldn't find you. He was frantic, too. As for taking his wallet, you know better than that."

"I didn't spend any of his money, and even if I had, I planned to pay everything back." Amy's expression was too innocent. "Are you going to ground me?"

"Maybe." But a simple grounding might not bring home to Amy the seriousness of what she'd done. "You and I are going to sit down tomorrow and talk about the right consequences for what you did."

"You mean I have to help you come up with a punishment?" Amy rolled her eyes.

"Why not? It'll mean more that way, don't you think?" Cat didn't want to go through this kind of worry ever again.

"Why do you always have to be so smart?" Amy grinned and dimples dented her cheeks. "I love you, Mom, and I'm sorry."

"I love you, too, so very much." Cat reached over to flick off the bedside light and kissed Amy's forehead.

"What about you and the coach?" The bed frame creaked as Amy slid farther down under the quilt.

"I'll call him tomorrow, but you're my priority and you always will be." A half answer, but the truth was staring Cat in the face. After what had happened today, there couldn't be anything more between her and Luc. She'd been the focus of town gossip once and, although the hurt had faded, those old wounds were still there. She should have paid attention to logic and never gotten involved with her daughter's coach in the first place. Putting Amy first meant making hard choices.

"Kylie also said that if you and Coach Luc got together, you could have a baby. You wouldn't do that, would you? With him or anyone?" Amy's voice was small.

"Of course not. Whatever gave Kylie that idea?" Although Cat would have liked to give Amy a sister or brother, being a single mom to one child was hard enough. And with Amy on the brink of adolescence, it was too late.

"Everybody loves babies best. Look at Lexie." Amy rolled onto her side and curled up into a ball.

"No matter how old you are, you'll always be my baby." Cat eased off the bed and tucked the quilt around her daughter like she had when Amy was small.

"What if the kids at school don't stop talking about me?" Amy's shoulders stiffened.

"They will." Cat had to make sure of it. "Now stop worrying and go to sleep. Everything will look better in the morning."

For Amy, it probably would. For Cat, however, the problems went too deep for one night of fitful sleep to fix.

Luc shot the puck from center ice toward the net, where it hit the goal cage with a clang that echoed in the empty arena. Even though the doctor had cleared Amy to skate, she hadn't turned up for coaching since the day she'd gone missing, or to help out at the last few practices of the season. After almost a week, and apart from one brief phone call when she'd asked him to give her space, Cat was communicating with him by text messages and only if it had something to do with Amy's hockey.

He fired another puck. This time it hit the glass.

"If you break it, you pay for it." Scott's head popped up from behind the penalty box.

"It's shatterproof." Unlike his heart. Luc skated over to the boards and skidded to a stop. "What are you doing here?"

"I swung by to pick up some paperwork." Scott's gaze sharpened. "You doing after-work target practice?"

Luc shrugged and leaned on his stick. "What's it to you?"

"Amy didn't show again today?" Behind his glasses, Scott's eyes were wise.

"No." Each day that went by without him seeing Cat and Amy, Luc's heart hurt a little bit more. Only a few short months ago, he hadn't thought he could feel much of anything again or take pleasure in everyday life, but almost without him noticing it, that kid and her mom had changed him.

"Cat was at school earlier." Scott came around the penalty box to meet Luc by the boards. "The first day Amy went back to school, some of the kids gave her more grief about you coaching her. Their folks aren't much better. Now Amy doesn't want to go to school or even leave the apartment."

"That poor kid." Anger seared Luc, quick and hot. "Anybody who has seen Amy play has to recognize she's got potential."

"It doesn't have anything to do with seeing her play. If a parent thinks another kid's getting an unfair advantage, they'll make an issue of it. Since Firefly Lake's such a small town, talk spreads faster here than it would most other places." Scott's jaw went tight. "You must remember what it was like for you."

"You mean when I didn't wear my jersey until I had to go on the ice because a couple of the parents would boo me? That was mostly at away games." But it had still hurt because all Luc wanted was to play the game he loved as well as he could.

"Some home games, too." Although Scott's voice was even, Luc flinched. "You're the big hero around here now because you were an Olympian and NHL all-star, but back when you were Amy's age, it was different."

"Yeah, it was." And it had taught Luc early on who he could and couldn't trust.

"I talked to Cat, and she's going to send Amy back to school again tomorrow. The other teachers and I will do everything we can to stop the talk during school hours, but you can't police kids every minute. Amy's a great girl, and she was doing so well. It's a shame this stuff blew up and dented her confidence again."

Luc's stomach rolled. "How can I help?"

"Are you and Cat still seeing each other?" Scott stared at a point above Luc's head.

"What makes you think that's your business?" Luc sucked in a breath. He respected Cat's need for space right now, but he wanted to help her and Amy, too.

"It's not, but when even a few folks make it their business, kids pick up on that." Scott's tone was neutral, not judging. "Then, before you know it, the rumors are swirling. I love Firefly Lake, and I never wanted to live anywhere else, but it's not the kind of place where you can keep to yourself."

"I'll talk to Cat." She couldn't avoid him forever. "All this must be tearing her up." The place that Luc had counted on to give him sanctuary and stability to regroup had turned out to be as complicated as anywhere else.

"Cat looked rough earlier. Amy's her whole life, and the main reason she moved to Firefly Lake was to give Amy a fresh start. It's only a guess, but I think she's blaming herself for what's happened."

There was a grim twist to Scott's mouth, and sweat trickled between Luc's shoulder blades. "If Amy isn't going to school, what's she doing?"

"Cat's mom's keeping an eye on Amy at the apartment

so Cat can work." He paused and gave Luc a pointed look. "The doctor told Michael he can't come back to work until the middle of April. Cat's running that gallery by herself. On top of everything with Amy, she's sure got her hands full."

Luc suppressed a groan. Cat hadn't told him she needed help, and she must have sworn Gabrielle to secrecy, too. But that didn't matter. He was going to help her, no matter what. If it weren't for him, she wouldn't be in this mess in the first place.

"Thanks, buddy. It was lucky you came by."

"Lucky?" Amusement twinkled in Scott's hazel eyes. "Luck's got nothing to do with it. I guessed you'd be here. Some guys head to the bar when life dumps a load of crap on them. You head to the ice. The paperwork was an excuse for Stephanie out there. Unlike you, I haven't forgotten how small towns work."

Luc grinned. "Smart ass."

"Takes one to know one." Scott clapped Luc's shoulder. "Go find Cat. At the very least, you'll get my wife off my case. She loves a happy ending."

He'd had his happy ending once. Another one wasn't in the cards.

Scott eyed him up and down and gave him another meaningful look. "You won a Stanley Cup and an Olympic medal. You also faced the biggest enforcers the NHL could throw at you. Don't tell me you're too much of a chickenshit to talk to one woman."

"Dickhead." Luc grinned.

Twenty minutes later, he'd lost the grin. He wasn't scared to face Cat, but it had been a long time since he'd had to make his case with a woman. And whenever he'd messed up with Maggie, he'd known what made her tick. With Cat, he barely had a clue.

Luc parked his truck outside the gallery and strode inside with a box of Cat's favorite muffins from the Daily Bread bakery. Baked goods weren't as obvious as flowers, and she didn't seem like the kind of woman who'd appreciate him turning up with a bunch of roses.

"I'm sorry, but we're about to close." Cat looked up from behind the desk and her expression froze.

"Great timing then." He went back to the door and flipped the CLOSED sign over to face the street.

"My mom's upstairs with Amy, but she needs to get home. It's her book club night." Cat's gaze darted from side to side.

"My mom's in that book club, and it doesn't start for two hours. I only need ten minutes." He pulled out a chair across the desk from Cat and sat. "I heard there's a lot of stuff going on with Amy and school. Why didn't you call me?"

"I couldn't." She plucked at the tie on the box of muffins Luc set on the desk between them. "Scott told you?"

"Yes." He paused. It wasn't only the dark shadows beneath her eyes or more prominent cheekbones. She was also hunched in the chair like she was somehow broken. "You said you needed space and time, and I've given you that. But I'm a big part of the reason Amy's upset, so I want to fix it."

"It's not only Amy, it's me." She pushed the muffin box aside. "I shouldn't have gotten involved with you. You're her coach, and since I don't want you to stop coaching her, we can't see each other anymore."

A weight pressed on Luc's chest. "Isn't that a bit extreme? It was a kiss, that's all. True, we didn't show the best judgment and should have been more discreet, but—"

"But what?" Cat rested her chin on her hands. "I like you. I like what we had together, but Amy comes first. I moved here to help get her back on track, but now she's refusing to go to school because the other kids won't stop talking about her. It's like it was in Boston, only ten times worse."

"Because they're talking about you, too? About us?" Luc's heart ached.

She gave a quick jerk of her chin. "In Boston she was teased for her dyslexia, but here everyone's talking about my family." She gulped and pressed her hands to her face. "The details are different, sure, but it's still exactly like it was all those years ago with my dad. It's…I can't…" The gulp turned into a choked sound. "I promised myself no child of mine would ever have to go through what I did, and now…"

"Back then, you didn't have anybody to stand up for you." A slow anger burned in Luc's gut and spiraled upward. "Now you have me and lots of other people in town. I bet it's only a few who are talking. Most people don't care if we see each other or not."

She raised her face, and the lost expression in her eyes shredded his heart even more. "I don't know whether most people care or not, but I care. Amy does, too. As long as you and I spend time together, and even if Amy knows it isn't the case, folks will keep saying she's getting special treatment because of me."

Luc's pulse sped up. "Anybody who says that is jealous because their kid doesn't have the talent Amy has. In hindsight, maybe you and I getting involved wasn't the best decision, but it's too late to change that now. If we make it a big deal, it looks like we're ashamed. I'm not ashamed of what's between us. Are you?"

"No." Her voice broke.

"Apart from everything else, we're friends. I don't want to lose your friendship." He didn't want to lose everything else either, but he couldn't see a way clear to have it. "Running away from a problem never solved anything. You can't let the bullies win, either."

She gave him the ghost of a smile. "That's what I told Amy."

"See?" He tried to steady his breathing. "Maybe we need to step back for a while so Amy doesn't feel threatened and the gossip dies down. I'll do whatever's best for her. I care about both of you."

"We care about you, too." Cat's mouth worked and her eyes were filled with pain. "For Amy's sake, we have to step back. And I can't promise that will ever change."

Chapter Twenty

Three days later, Cat rang the doorbell beside the front door of Michael's charming New England clapboard. Although it was the end of March, snow still fell in a soft whisper to edge the porch railing, and the low shrubs near the house were tipped with frost.

The door swung open, and Michael appeared dressed in a pair of dark cords and a cream-colored sweater. "Since my doctor has grounded me, thanks for coming here." He ushered her into a cozy hall lined with art, then took her coat.

Cat pulled off her boots, followed him into the living room, and sat where he gestured in a plump armchair up-holstered in a bright berry color. "How are you feeling?" She tucked her tote bag under the chair.

"Fine, although you'd never know it the way Liz carries on." He sat in a matching chair to the right of a stone fireplace, where a cheerful fire danced in the grate. "At least she let me out of my dressing gown in honor of your visit. She even went to work for a few hours today."

"Liz loves you. She wants you to be around for a long time." Even as she smiled, Cat's heart hurt.

Michael's expression softened. "I'm not going anywhere unless Liz comes with me. We were a pair of fools for too many years. To think it took me having a heart attack for us to be honest about what we really feel for each other." He shook his head and poured Cat a cup of tea from the pot on a tray on the table between them. "We might have gone to our graves thinking the silly things that supposedly divide us were more important than what brings us together. Who cares what anybody else thinks?"

Cat's hand trembled as she took the cup Michael held out. "Liz said pretty much the same thing to me about you."

Along with "don't sweat the small stuff, and if you have a chance at happiness don't let it pass you by." Not only Liz's words but the unusually serious expression in her brown eyes had stuck in Cat's head. Although she hadn't mentioned Luc, Liz's meaning was clear. Except, what was between Cat and Luc wasn't the same as that between Michael and Liz. There was a child involved, for a start, and Amy was still upset and mixed up.

Cat pushed the troubling thoughts away. "I brought the books from the accountant for you to go over." She set the cup back on the tray and laced her fingers together. "Sales are up again."

"Thanks to you." Michael's smile was warm. "I'll take a look at the books later. I want to talk about something else first."

"What?" Cat's stomach lurched and she pressed her joined hands over it. Michael wouldn't fire her, but maybe he wanted someone else to take on the day-to-day management of the gallery, someone who had business experience and knew more about art and craftwork than she did.

"I want to offer you a partnership in the gallery with a view to full ownership when I'm ready to retire." Michael sat back. "You're a smart woman, and my business couldn't be in better hands."

"I..." The room spun, and Cat pressed harder on her roller-coaster stomach. "I appreciate your offer, but I'm still looking for a university job." That was what she'd set her mind on since her sophomore year in college. Despite the doubts that niggled, it was what she wanted. Wasn't it?

"How's that working out for you?" Michael's sharp blue gaze held hers.

"Not so good." There was no use trying to sugarcoat it. For the first time in her life, she'd set her mind on a goal she might not reach. Cat scrubbed a hand across her face. "It's a bad job market. I keep applying, but there's not a lot out there for someone like me." Her jaw got tight. "I applied for one job at a small college in New Mexico over a month ago, but I haven't heard anything."

"There must be a lot of idiots on those hiring committees." Michael gave her a half smile. "But New Mexico? What would you and Amy do so far from family?"

"Have you been talking to my mom?" Cat's stomach pitched again.

"No, but it stands to reason you wouldn't want to be

a continent away from the folks you care about." He set his teacup on the saucer with a clatter. "I wanted to be an art historian, but when I finished college, there weren't many jobs in my field, either. I'd worked in galleries in the summers and liked it. My wife was a textile artist and wanted to stay in New England, so when my dad offered to help us start the business here in a building he owned, I thought why not? It's more than forty years ago now, but that bend in the road has made me happy. Maybe even happier than I'd have been if I'd followed the first path."

"I..." Cat stopped. She'd only always seen one path, but what if that path wasn't all there was for her?

Michael reached across the table to pat Cat's arm, his touch gentle, almost fatherly. "Apart from my wife passing so young, I've had a pretty good life. If my ticker keeps ticking, I've got a lot more life to look forward to. Firefly Lake's home, and I've built a decent business here." His grin was boyish. "Not bad for one of those 'artsy-fartsy' types, as some people around here still call me."

Cat managed to smile back. "Decent" was an understatement. She'd seen the books and, even when the economy was tough, the gallery had gone from strength to strength. "I like the work, and you're a great boss. I've never thought about going into business myself, though."

"You're good at it." Michael's voice was tinged with unexpected pride. "There are lots of ways you can use that brain of yours without half starving yourself while doing it."

"Sure, but..." Cat bit her bottom lip. What would her

life be like if she all of a sudden chose a different path? Her heart raced and excitement surged through her.

"But what?" Michael's voice was husky. "You may have taken that grant and moved here for Amy's sake, but you love the work you're doing over at the inn and, unless I miss my guess, you'd like to do more of it. You could if you worked with me. I can afford to pay you what you're worth and with full benefits. You wouldn't be working twenty-four/seven like you are now, either."

Cat caught her breath. The gallery would be a steady job. No more of the uncertainty that came with teaching from contract to contract. No more juggling as many contracts as she could and working from dawn to dusk because it was the only way she could support herself and Amy. She'd have security, stability, and work she enjoyed. Although she wouldn't write the books and articles she'd thought she would, she could write the popular history she liked best instead. The history of people who'd shaped places like Firefly Lake. She'd also have more time for Amy, and a life that wasn't so caught up in work she'd actually have time to live it.

"I...wow...you..." She stopped as her vision blurred.

"You don't have to let me know right away. Take whatever time you need to think about it." Michael smiled. "I'm not doing this out of charity. You're the right person for the job."

"I didn't think...charity...no." Cat's tongue got thick in her mouth.

"Maybe not now, but the thought would have crossed your mind at some point." He grunted. "Don't think I don't know you're a hard person to help. It takes one to know one." His eyes twinkled. "But the help wouldn't be all on one side. You'd be helping me, too. I want to travel, and now I have Liz to go with me. Leaving the gallery with you would be a load off my mind."

"I don't know what to say." Cat's thoughts spun like the snowflakes that still tumbled softly outside the leaded-glass window. What did she want, not only for Amy, but for herself? Could stepping off a path that wasn't working give her what she wanted after all? Had she been so focused on a single goal she'd forgotten there was a whole world of opportunities out there?

Michael's expression turned wistful. "You can spend a lot of time looking back in life and that can keep you from going forward. If you're knocking on a door that's staying closed, climb through an open window. Maybe you think people will imagine you've failed or sold out because you couldn't get a university job, but why? Nobody who truly cares about you is going to think any less of you for doing something different. All they'll see is that you're taking charge of your life. As for anybody else, what does it matter?"

Except, Cat had spent most of her life caring what other people thought, ever since her dad had made her family the talk of Firefly Lake. Achieving at school had become a way of proving herself. Old habits were hard to break, but that didn't mean she didn't need to try. Her muscles went weak and she gripped the arms of the chair. "You're right."

"I usually am." Michael grinned. "Don't tell Liz, though."

Despite her jumbled thoughts, Cat laughed. "I won't."

"If I'd ever had a daughter, I'd have wanted her to be

like you. Not only smart and independent, but a good person through and through." Michael gave her another fatherly pat. "Talk to Amy. See what she thinks. I appreciate that you need to think about her as well."

Snow hissed against the window and, despite the warmth of the comfortable room, Cat shivered. She was thinking about Amy, and she already had a good idea what her daughter would think. If she accepted Michael's job offer, she could afford that girls' hockey program Amy had talked about. And if she stayed right here in Firefly Lake, she wouldn't have to uproot her daughter from a school where she was finally settling in.

Except, now Cat wanted more. She wanted happiness that had nothing to do with work or Amy. A sick recognition lodged in the pit of her stomach. She wanted the happiness that came from being with Luc, too. Despite the excitement of Michael's job offer and how it might make her life easier, the price of getting true happiness—and a lasting love—might be too high for her to pay.

"You're doing great, but take it easy. You haven't been on the ice in a month." Luc clapped Amy's shoulder, and she gave him a wary smile from behind her helmet—the first smile she'd given him since she'd finally reappeared for her usual after-school coaching session. "Ty Carmichael's going to take you through a couple of drills while I talk to your mom." He waved at the blond teen on the far side of the ice, who towered over three tiny girls bundled up like miniature snowpeople—Firefly Lake's future girls' hockey players, according to their parents. "Ty wants to work toward his coaching certification, so I'm helping him."

"Okay." Amy stared at her skates.

"Is there a problem?" Luc studied her bent head and stiff stance.

"It's nothing to do with Ty." Amy finally lifted her head. "But you can't upset my mom. She gets upset really easy these days." Her expression was earnest, defensive, and protective all in one.

"I won't upset her. I want to talk about that hockey camp for you." He wanted to talk to Cat about a lot of other things, too—the small things as well as the big things that made up the fabric of everyday life and he'd gotten used to sharing with her. And now he missed.

"Oh." Amy's voice warmed slightly.

"Go on with Ty, but tell him if you get tired, okay?" Luc's heart twisted. He cared for Cat, but even if they somehow took their relationship further, having a child with her wouldn't ever be in the cards. He couldn't take that risk again.

"Hockey never makes me tired." Amy gave him a real smile this time before she skated off to join Ty and the little girls.

"Cat." He glided to the boards. She sat in the first row of the bleachers with Pixie on her lap. "Can I talk to you for a minute?"

"Sure." Her face was whiter than her winter-white hat. "How's Amy doing?"

"Great. She's such a trouper, she'll be back to her usual fitness in no time." He opened the gate, then sat beside her. "The hockey camp application's almost ready. All you need to do is sign it and supply copies of Amy's medical records. I left the package in reception with Stephanie."

"Thanks." She coughed and her breath made a cloud in the cold air. "I appreciate you continuing to coach Amy and recommending her for the camp, too."

"Why wouldn't I?" He reached over to rub Pixie's ears and tried to smile. "Someday I expect to be known as the coach who discovered the next US women's hockey star."

"A lot can happen between now and then." Her voice was flat and her eyes were dull.

"Of course, but there's no harm in thinking big." It wasn't like Cat to not think positive. "What's Pixie doing here?" At least the dog, in a pink coat trimmed with white faux fur, was her usual perky self.

"Mom's shopping in Burlington. Since Ward's in Boston, I said I'd look after Pixie today. She's Mom's baby." Her smile was faint.

"I had Pixie in my office at the creamery yesterday when your mom was in Kincaid. I took her with me when I went out to check on my house, too." Although Luc couldn't put his finger on it, something was off with Gabrielle. She usually stuck close to Firefly Lake, but she'd been out of town two days in a row this week.

"It's great to see Mom happy and with so much energy." Cat coughed again.

"If you've got the cold that's going around, this is the worst place for you. Go home and I'll drop Amy off in an hour."

"Thanks, but I'm fine." Cat straightened and fiddled with Pixie's pink rhinestone collar.

The hair on the back of Luc's neck prickled. Cat wasn't fine, and he had to get to the bottom of what was going on. He grabbed the clipboard he'd left on top of the boards and opened it. "I also want to talk to you about Amy's scholarship application. I've filled out as much as I can, but there are two sections you need to complete."

She looked at the areas he'd flagged and a sneeze shook her slight frame. "I'll fill these out tonight. I can leave this form with Stephanie tomorrow when I bring in the medical records." She dug in her coat pocket for a tissue. "You really think Amy will get a scholarship?"

"I don't see why not." He glanced toward the ice, where Amy was focused on a passing drill with Ty. "She has a special quality about her. I bet that after this camp a few scouts will show interest."

"She's only twelve." Cat's voice held a hint of panic.

"Kids start to get scouted around fourteen, but if and when that happens, you don't have to handle it alone. I'll help you."

"Thanks." Cat held the dog close. "It looks like I'll be staying in Firefly Lake for good. Michael offered me a partnership in the gallery. I've talked to Amy, and I'm going to accept."

"That's great." Luc raised an arm to hug her, then stopped. No public displays of affection, not even a friendly, innocent one. "Assuming the gallery's what you want?"

"When I first moved here, I'd have said no. But now…I guess you never know what's around the bend." She shrugged and gave a wry smile. "I like the work, and I like and respect Michael. It feels right. Besides, it's best for Amy. Her confidence took a real blow with what some of the kids at school said, but now that the talk is starting to die down, I don't want to move her again." She hesitated. "We can be friends, and I need your help with Amy's hockey, but as for anything else, I'm sorry." She let out another hacking cough.

Luc's heart skipped a beat. Amy had to be the priority for now, but with Cat staying in Firefly Lake, he'd have plenty of time to convince her it was worth seeing where this thing between them might go. His gaze settled on the delectable curve of her mouth and, despite the cold, his palms started to sweat.

"Did you see me, Mom?" Amy skidded to a stop on the other side of the boards. "I was faster than Ty."

"I'm sorry, honey, I missed it." Cat didn't look at him. "Can you do whatever it was you did again?"

"I thought you were watching me." Amy's eyes narrowed. "I can't do it again. I'm tired and hungry." Her voice had the hint of a whine.

"Then there's fruit and a muffin in your backpack." Cat's tone was firm. "Coach Luc and I were talking about your hockey camp application. I can't watch you every minute."

"Was that all you were talking about?" Amy's voice was sulky, and she gave Luc a challenging stare.

"Amy, you know that isn't acceptable. You'll be polite and respectful to your coach and to me. Otherwise—"

"I get it, okay?" Amy made a little girl face and cracked her knuckles.

"I don't think you do, so we'll talk about consequences of that behavior when we get home." Cat's tone was calm and resolute.

Amy clomped over to her backpack, then turned her back on them and pulled a banana from her bag.

Luc drew in a breath. "It'll be okay. Amy's had a rough

go of it. You have, too." He ached to take Cat in his arms to comfort her. And help her and be there for her when she needed it.

But he couldn't do any of that right now, and he didn't know if he ever could. Would Amy ever accept him in her mom's life?

Chapter Twenty-One

Something's up." From her perch on the footstool beside Cat's chair, Georgia poked Cat in the ribs and gestured around the living room at Harbor House. "Why else would Mom invite the whole family here on a Saturday afternoon?"

"Because you're working tomorrow and Aunt Josette and the cousins made a surprise visit?" Cat huddled into the depths of the wing chair, sick as well as tired. Night after night, she lay awake worrying about Amy, who seemed to have regressed to a much younger child. When she wasn't eyeing Cat with suspicion, Amy clung to her almost like she'd done as a toddler. After they'd talked at hockey practice three days earlier, Cat worried even more about Luc, too, and the mess she'd made of things with him. The only thing she wasn't worried about was taking on the gallery partnership. Her new job had given her a fresh sense of purpose and excitement.

"That's another thing." Georgia leaned closer. "Why is Mom's family here now? I thought they were coming for Easter. It's only a few weeks away."

"I don't know." Cat put a hand to her head.

Mia played softly on the piano, and between the music and chatter of her assorted relatives, Cat's head ached. Her gaze drifted to the fireplace, where flames curled upward into the chimney. Luc stood with Nick and Ward in front of the brass fire screen. Even the sight of him made her heart give an agonizing throb.

"What's wrong with you?" Georgia nudged Cat's arm. "If there's a mystery, you're the one who always wants to figure it out, not me."

"Nothing. I'm fine." Cat rubbed her temples against the swirling notes of "Rhapsody in Blue."

Georgia snorted. "If everything's so fine, why are you looking at me like you did at my sixth birthday party before you were sick all over the cake?"

"I'm..." Cat pressed a hand over her mouth, then darted to the powder room at the end of the hall and locked the door behind her.

"Cat?" Georgia's voice echoed through the door, followed by a sharp knock. "Let me in."

"No." Cat raised her head from the toilet to study her reflection in the beveled mirror over the vanity.

"I'm your sister." Georgia banged on the door again.

Cat slumped to the tiled floor. She couldn't be. Except, all the signs were there. Signs she'd put down to worry, tiredness, stress, and being distracted.

"If you don't let me in, I'll break down the door." There was no teasing in Georgia's voice, only worry.

Given it was Georgia, breaking down the door wasn't

an empty threat. With numb fingers, Cat released the lock.

"You look awful." Georgia squeezed into the powder room beside Cat and closed the door again. "Is it the stomach flu?"

Cat shook her head and sat on the closed toilet seat. What were the odds of having a birth control failure twice? Likely a statistical improbability, but it figured. The only subject she'd never been good at, she turned out to be an expert in the way she didn't want. The tiredness could have been because of that cold that had hung on and on. But the nausea, dizziness, irritability, and how she cried at TV commercials with kids and animals wasn't. Why hadn't she put the pieces together sooner?

"Oh." Georgia's tone was cautious. She grabbed a washcloth from the cupboard under the sink, wet it with cold water, and dabbed at Cat's face. "Have you told him?"

"No." She didn't need to use Luc's name. Nobody else could be the father of this child. Cat knew it, Georgia knew it, and, in a few months, the whole town would, too. "I didn't figure it out until now."

"Oh, honey." Georgia dropped the washcloth in the sink and wrapped Cat in a hug. "I'm here for you. Like Mom and Nick will be."

Although, her brother would likely want to kill Luc first and ask questions later.

Cat shuddered. "I don't think Luc wants kids." Even if he could commit to another woman, which was doubtful, the expression on his face when he'd told her about Maggie's death was etched into Cat's soul. He thought the pregnancy had killed her. No matter what Cat had said, he still blamed himself.

"Luc's a good guy. He'll do the right thing. Why would you think he wouldn't?" Georgia's voice was firm.

"Of course he would, but I don't want to be an obligation. And what about the baby? How would it feel to know your dad only stepped up because he had to?" Cat dropped her head into her hands.

"It was different with Amy's dad. Jared died before you could tell him, but Luc's right here. He won't let you down." Georgia crouched to Cat's level and her worried blue eyes swam before Cat's face.

"I'll have to tell Luc sometime, but first, I need to think. You can't say anything to anybody. Promise me, Georgie."

"Of course I won't, but—"

"No, not a word." Cat gripped her sister's hand. "I have to be able to trust you. I just started my new job, and Michael…" She tapped down the panic and swallowed another wave of nausea.

"Michael will understand." Georgia squeezed her hand. "I want to help."

"You can help me most right now by keeping your mouth shut and keeping everybody else from guessing there's anything wrong. As well as Mom, there's Aunt Josette. She doesn't miss anything, either. And Mia…" Tremors racked Cat's body.

"I promise. I'm not good at a lot of things, but I'm good at creating distractions." Georgia's expression turned sad. "I wish…"

"I wish, too." For years, Cat had wished her dad hadn't

left. Now she wished she'd never slept with Luc, no matter how great the sex had been.

"Georgia? Are you in there?" Nick's voice came from outside the powder room door. "And have you seen Cat? Mom and Ward are looking for both of you."

"I'll be out in a minute. Cat's in here with me. We're touching up our makeup." Georgia made a face. "He's such a guy," she added in a stage whisper. "He won't notice neither of us wears much makeup to touch up."

"Thanks, Georgie." Cat got up from the toilet seat. Georgia was reflected next to her in the mirror. She and her sister didn't look anything alike physically, and she'd never thought they were anything alike as people either, but maybe she'd been wrong.

Georgia's smile was wobbly. "You've never asked for my help, ever, but now...let me help you. I want to. The past couple of weeks, I didn't think I'd stick around Firefly Lake beyond the summer, but now I will. I'll even be your labor coach if you need one. Unlike you, I've never been the squeamish type."

Cat's eyes smarted. "Not that your life's a disaster like mine, but I'm here for you, too." She'd been so focused on why she didn't need her dad she'd forgotten who and what she did need. Starting with her sister.

"You're a great mom to Amy, and you'll be a great mom to this baby." Georgia smoothed Cat's hair.

Even though Amy wouldn't pick up on anything right away, what would this news do to her? Cat bit her lip. "You don't think anybody out there will guess? Luc?"

"Like Nick, he's a guy. How would he guess?" Georgia looped her arm through Cat's.

"I hope you're right." Cat studied her pale and drawn face reflected back at her in the mirror.

"Sure I am, but if anybody asks, say you ate something that disagreed with you. I'll back you up. I spotted Aunt Josette's lobster bisque in the kitchen earlier and it looks as awful as ever." Georgia's eyes were shiny, but she gave Cat a teasing grin. "Now, let's go out there and be fabulous."

Five minutes later, standing in front of the fireplace with her brother and sister, Cat had never felt less fabulous, but Georgia was right about one thing. Something was up, and if whatever it was didn't happen soon, she'd be back in that bathroom even before she'd taken an obligatory taste of Josette's infamous bisque.

Ward cleared his throat, and Mia stopped playing the piano. "Gabrielle and I invited you here today for a special reason." He held out his right hand and Cat's mom took it. "You know we didn't want a big fuss over a wedding, so we thought what better way than to invite our family and friends for a meal and add getting married to it."

"Mom—"

Ward raised his free hand to silence Nick. "This is what your mother wants, and I'd do anything to make her happy. I hope you'll be happy for us." Ward tucked Gabrielle into the curve of his shoulder.

Nick's dark brows drew together. "Of course I am, but…"

Cat bit back a smile. Her overprotective brother didn't like surprises any more than she did.

"We're all happy for you." Mia moved to Nick's side and took her husband's arm in a firm grip. "I think it's a wonderful idea. If it hadn't been for the girls, I remember you said before our wedding that you wanted to elope and go straight to the honeymoon."

Nick gave his wife a grudging smile as laughter rippled around the room.

Gabrielle reached for Nick, then turned to Cat and Georgia. "All of you, come here and stand beside me."

"Like my family will stand with me." Ward gestured toward the stairs. "I kept them out of sight until now, but I had to let them in on the secret so they could fly in from Seattle."

A tall and slender woman with a visible pregnancy bump descended the stairs, followed by a broad-shouldered man who kept his hand at the small of her back and looked like the Navy pilot he was. A fair-haired toddler clutched the man's other hand and, when she caught sight of the onlookers, buried her chubby face against her dad's pant leg. Ward's daughter, Erica, and her husband and little girl.

Cat's heart was like lead in her chest. What would it be like to be part of that kind of family unit? To be loved and adored in the way Erica's husband adored her? Or cherished in the way he cherished his little girl and would cherish the new baby, too?

"Great surprise, huh?" Luc's deep voice came from Nick's other side. "They even kept the minister hidden away until the last minute." Luc waved toward Reverend Arthur, who'd come down the stairs behind Ward's daughter and her family.

Cat's stomach heaved as the sharp scent of Luc's aftershave mixed with smoke from the fireplace. She *was* happy for her mom, but the surprise was also a reminder of what Cat didn't and wouldn't ever have.

"Mom." Amy pulled on Cat's arm. "See the dress Grandma gave me? When she asked me to change into it, she said it was because of a secret. What do you think? I don't usually like dresses, but this one's pretty." Amy gave a little twirl and the dress's filmy purple skirt floated around her slim figure like the petals of a flower.

"You look beautiful, sweetie."

"Ward says that if I want to, I can call him Grandpa Ward. I think I'd like that." Amy twirled again, and Luc nudged her shoulder to ease her away from the fireplace screen.

"If you keep that up, you'll make your mom dizzy. She's already swaying a bit." He took Cat's elbow to steady her.

It wasn't Amy making her dizzy. It was Luc's baby. Although he or she was still only the size of a peanut, they were already making their presence known.

Mia launched into an impromptu wedding march, and there was laughter, good wishes, and the high-pitched voice of Aunt Josette organizing everyone in a mixture of English and French.

And then there was silence, and only Reverend Arthur's voice saying the solemn words of the marriage ceremony. Her mom's voice quavered as she said her vows, but as she looked at Ward, her eyes were filled with love. There was an answering roughness in Ward's voice as he promised to love and cherish Gabrielle all the days of his life, and then only tenderness as he slipped the diamond-studded platinum wedding band on her mom's ring finger.

Baby Lexie gurgled, and Cat glanced across the living room. Until now, she hadn't spotted Charlie and Sean

here, but it was fine. Everything was fine except for the
Stanley Cup final going on in her stomach. She teetered
again, and Georgia touched her waist.

And then Gabrielle Brassard was Ward Aldrich's wife.
Above her elegant, silver-gray dress, Gabrielle's face
glowed, and Ward beamed back at her.

There was hugging, kissing, and more organizing from
Aunt Josette, who herded everyone into the dining room
to eat. People took pictures, and Cat smiled like she was
expected to and hugged everyone who hugged her, even
Luc. Someone had tied a white bow to Pixie's collar, and
the little dog scampered underfoot and barked.

It was everything a wedding should be. Everything Cat
had once wanted her wedding to be, back when she'd
thought she'd wear her mémère's dress, a frothy confec-
tion of white lace and tulle, and float down the stairs at
Harbor House into a happy ever after.

Getting pregnant once by accident was bad luck.
Twice was something else. As Cat looked at her mom
and Ward together, a piece of her heart froze. She'd
given up on the romantic fantasy a long time ago, but
deep inside, in a part of herself she'd never truly ac-
knowledged, she still hankered after that white dress.
Yet, even though it was packed away in a trunk in Harbor House's attic, the dress was as dead as the dream it
had once represented.

The noise of Gabrielle and Ward's wedding party still
hummed one floor down, but soon after Cat had left with
Amy, Luc made his excuses to the bride and groom and
slipped upstairs to his room.

He sat on the edge of the queen-size bed and stared

at the blank, pale gray walls. Cat hadn't lived in this room for a long time, and it had been painted before he'd moved in late last summer, back when his house had only been a folder with an architect's drawings and a newly poured foundation. Now that house was almost finished, and it was everything he'd imagined it would be, but without the woman he'd counted on to make it a home. However, as Gabrielle and Ward had exchanged their vows, it had hit him—a truth so obvious he should have thought of it before. But before he talked to Cat, there was something he needed to do first.

He got up from the bed and went to the closet on the far side of the room, his footfalls heavy on the carpet. At the very back, on the top shelf behind a neat stack of sweatshirts, he found the wooden box he hadn't been able to make himself open since Maggie's funeral. The one he'd made for her twenty-first birthday, using the wood-working skills his dad had taught him. The one she kept her most treasured possessions in.

Luc took a deep breath and set the box on the bed. Even though his chest ached, he lifted the lid and took things out one by one.

First were the cards he'd given Maggie for each birth-day and Valentine's Day from when they'd met as college freshmen until her death. His touch lingered on a wedding picture of the two of them looking like the kids they were. Beneath it was the blue velvet box that held her engage-ment ring, with the small diamond cluster, the best he'd been able to afford back then, and she'd never wanted him to replace it. Then flowers she'd pressed from her wed-ding bouquet and the charm bracelet he'd given her for college graduation.

His vision misted as he fingered the tiny charms, each a symbol of their life together. As he lingered on the silver baby rattle, his throat closed. What would their baby have been like? He'd never know, and the more he thought about it, the more he tortured himself.

At the bottom of the box, beneath more pictures, were the diaries Maggie had kept from junior high on. Maybe he should have burned them, but he couldn't because they were part of her, a last tangible link to her life. He sat cross-legged on the bed and flipped through pages at random.

The doctor says lots of women have a miscarriage, and there's no reason I can't have a healthy baby. When I'm ready, Luc and I will try again.

He glanced at the date, his lungs burning. They'd been married almost two years then, and the time had seemed right to try for the child they both wanted. They'd graduated from college, and he was in his second season with the NHL. The money was rolling in, and life was good. He swallowed and Maggie's beloved handwriting blurred. That first miscarriage was supposed to have been a blip, but then it was followed by another and another.

His hands trembled as he opened a book with balloons on the cover.

The doctors can't find anything wrong with me, or Luc either. Luc says it's bad luck, but I can't help thinking it's somehow my fault. He's always away. I know the team needs him, but I need him, too.

Even though guilt rose up to suffocate him, Luc kept reading.

I have a good feeling about this pregnancy. After all, I've made it to twelve weeks this time, the longest yet. I'll never forget my lost babies, but this time everything will be okay. I'm sure of it. Luc gave me a charm for my bracelet to celebrate. The doctor says I can help coach as long as I don't skate. As if! I'm too scared to wear heels, let alone my skates. But even from behind the bench, it'll be a reminder of what I love best. Apart from Luc and our baby, of course!

Underneath, she'd drawn two big hearts and one smaller one. The rest of the book was blank.

Luc traced the curve of Maggie's handwriting, as familiar to him as his own. His eyes stung as he piled things back into the box and lingered again on the wedding picture. He stared into Maggie's dear brown eyes, looking for an answer to the question he could never ask. Would she have blamed him for wanting to try for a baby one last time? He didn't think so, but he'd never know for sure. Maybe it wasn't a matter of blame, though, but forgiveness. Maggie would have forgiven him, no question, and she'd have wanted him to forgive himself.

Luc tucked the photo on top of the box and closed the lid with a soft click. He leaned forward and gently laid his head on it. The pine was smooth beneath his cheek, except for the bumps where he'd carved her initials. Maggie was a gift, and he'd always cherish the time he'd had with her, but Cat was another gift and he was a different man now. One who was finally ready to put the past where it belonged and make a life with Cat and Amy.

He straightened and let out a shallow sigh. Maggie had been his first and forever love. But maybe the friendship, caring, comfort, and a bone-deep sense of closeness, all mixed with the unexpected but sizzling sexual attraction he had with Cat, would be enough. Lots of couples made a life together with less. It might not be the quiet life he'd first planned, but it would be better because Cat and Amy would be in it.

Cat would understand why he didn't want kids. She already had Amy, and she'd never said she wanted another baby. In time, Amy could be his kid and he'd be the best dad he could to her. As soon as Cat agreed to marry him, they'd be a family, and nobody in Firefly Lake would dare talk about her or why he was coaching Amy. He'd give them both everything he had. His loyalty and devotion, as well as all the security and stability money could buy.

Cat could even help decorate his house so it was her house, too. Although they'd never talked about it, most women liked choosing paint colors, curtains, and all the rest of it. Luc lay back on the pillows and tucked his hands behind his head. He'd give Cat a few days for the excitement of her mom's wedding to subside before he talked to her. He'd invite her out to the house and ask her to share his life. He wouldn't buy her a ring because she was a woman who'd want to have a say in choosing her own ring, but as soon as she said yes, they could start planning.

It was the perfect solution. Cat was as practical as he was, and neither of them was a starry-eyed teen caught up in the first flush of love. Heat radiated through his chest.

Love. The word hit him with the force of a puck to the head. Was it love that he felt for Cat? His body shook and his mouth went dry. He'd only known love once before, and this feeling was different than what he'd experienced with Maggie.

But it must be love because it felt right and, for the first time in more than two years, Luc was truly content. Laughter drifted up from the party downstairs and he smiled. He had a good plan, a sensible plan. Nothing could possibly go wrong.

Chapter Twenty-Two

Cat drove through the wrought-iron gates that marked the entrance to Luc's house and continued along a gravel driveway between two rows of century-old maple trees. The drive curved into old-growth forest before it widened out near the lake, where the house was tucked into a small bay. Cat parked beside Luc's truck in front of the house. Apart from Amy's coaching session, she'd managed to avoid him in the four days since her mom's wedding. All she had to do now was show him a few quilts, like Michael had asked her to, and then she could leave. For the money Luc was prepared to spend, Michael had insisted she make a personal visit.

She levered the heavy quilt box from the trunk and picked her way across the icy path to the house. It was vintage New England architecture, with a rambling front porch and white clapboard frame, but modern too, with the triple garage off to one side and floor-to-ceiling windows bare and waiting for the decorator's touch. Although patches of snow still lingered, the air was soft and warmer than it had been for months. Water dripped from the bare branches of the trees clustered by the porch.

She had to tell Luc about the baby, but how? Maybe once she'd seen a doctor it would be easier to find the words. As she raised her hand to a brass knocker shaped like a moose, the front door swung open and Luc stood on the other side.

"Here, let me." He took the box out of her arms and gestured her inside.

"Thanks." She stepped into the hall. He was so big, but she was small. If this baby took after him, she might be in trouble. She pulled off her wet boots and left them on the tray in the empty hall that still smelled of wood and fresh paint.

"I don't have any furniture yet." Luc gave her a half smile as he took her coat and draped it over the carved banister that led to the upper floor. He wore faded jeans and a flannel shirt the same blue as his eyes.

Cat swallowed the lump in her throat. Would the baby have those eyes? She made herself focus on the light-painted walls and cathedral ceilings as he led her through what would be the formal living and dining rooms to the great room at the back of the house.

"It's beautiful." She moved to a set of French doors that opened onto another porch and overlooked Firefly Lake. Although most of the lake was still frozen, an area of open water near the shore glistened in the afternoon sun. She gestured to the left of the porch, where a big patch of muddy ground had been marked off with stakes and yellow tape. "Is that going to be a tennis court?"

"That's the plan." Luc's laugh was strained and, for him, uncharacteristically nervous. He set the box on the floor by a window.

The quilts. She was here to talk about quilts, not to admire this stunning house that reminded her yet again how much money someone could earn by shooting a rubber disc across a sheet of ice. "Is this the room you want to hang a quilt in? Michael said you were interested in a statement piece." She bent to open the box's flaps and pulled out the edge of the top quilt, a woodland design in shades of green, blue, and brown.

"This room's as good as any." He crouched beside her. "I didn't know anything about quilts or statement pieces until yesterday when I bumped into Michael at the bakery."

"Oh." Cat bit her bottom lip. "Well, if you choose a wall quilt as the statement piece for this room, you need to make sure your decorator sees it first to match upholstery and pillow colors. I brought three quilts in different color palettes, but if you don't like any of them, why don't you send your decorator into the gallery with fabric swatches? We have a lot more designs there."

"I don't have a decorator—yet." He covered her hands atop the box and there was an expression in his eyes Cat had never seen there before; soft and maybe even loving. "Why don't you choose the quilt you'd like to hang in this room?"

Cat rocked back on her heels. "It's your house, so you need to—"

"No." Luc took the quilt out of her hands, then eased her gently to her feet. "I want it to be your house, too. Our house. You, me, and Amy. That's why I asked Michael if you could come out here. You seem to like quilts, so when Michael mentioned...I thought...oh hell, I'm not good with words like you are." He tightened his grip on her hands. "I want you to make a life here with me."

Hope mixed with giddy joy fizzed in Cat's chest. "You mean...you want me to..." She couldn't say the words, could hardly even think them. Luc wanted to marry her because he loved her like she loved him. Not because of the baby. He didn't know about the baby. Shy Cat McGuire was loved by Firefly Lake's all-American golden boy.

"I want you to marry me." He took one of his hands away and put a tender finger to her lips. "Wait, before you say anything, I need to explain."

A rainbow starburst erupted behind Cat's eyes. He could explain all he wanted and, for the first time in her life, she'd be happy to be quiet and listen. Not question or analyze but accept this miracle. The embryonic baby in her stomach did a little tap dance. If she'd been anywhere else, Cat would have gone looking for the nearest bathroom, but not now.

"It makes sense, don't you think? If we get married, we can be together like we both want and nobody will talk about us or Amy. It's because of her and folks talking that you said we can't see each other anymore. When your mom and Ward got married, I thought, why not? You and I are good friends, and the sex is sure great." His blue eyes were earnest, and Cat's excitement was doused as if he'd tossed a bucket of cold lake water over her. "We're both heading toward forty and it's not like we want to have a family. You already have Amy, and I...I don't want children of my own. Amy can be my kid. I mean if that's okay with you." He gave her a hopeful look.

"What…" Cat licked her dry lips and her stomach lurched. Maybe she should find that bathroom after all. "Children are a big responsibility, sure, a lifelong responsibility—"

"I knew you felt the same way," he broke in as his expression changed to one of relief. "Amy's twelve, and now you've just taken on the gallery. You wouldn't think of having another baby. We can keep using condoms, but maybe you should go on the pill so we're extra sure we won't get pregnant. Or I could take care of it. I'd do that for you."

That was like closing the barn door after the horse has bolted. One of her mémère's favorite sayings popped into Cat's mind like an evil imp. She'd been wrong. Luc didn't love her. He'd never even used the word *love*. He liked the idea of marriage because it was convenient, and, whether he was aware of it or not, this was one more way he wanted to help her and Amy.

"I can't marry you." She pulled her sweaty hands out of his. She'd been afraid he'd want to marry her out of duty because of the baby, but this was much worse. Even though Luc didn't know about it yet, he didn't want the baby. And he only wanted her because it was practical. He didn't want to live in this huge house all by himself. Friendship and great sex weren't the same as love. Not even close. Anger spurted and she knelt to fumble with the quilt box.

"Why not? I thought it would be a perfect solution. You're the most sensible woman I know. That's one of the things I like about you. I hate it that folks talking

makes you sad. I want to give you and Amy everything."
He waved his big arms. "Besides, I...I care about you so
much." His voice was gruff.

Sadness made Cat's body heavy. He thought he could
give her his heart, but it was buried with Maggie and always would be. He wanted to give her everything except
what mattered most. "Marriage isn't a business arrange-
ment." And she not only needed and deserved to be loved,
but she loved him too much to marry him this way. She
was used to the hard path, and although being a single
mom was tough, it wasn't any tougher than marrying a
man who didn't want a child, who didn't love her.

She clutched her stomach. What if he thought she'd
gotten pregnant on purpose to trap him? Or because she
was after his money? Her thoughts spun as her usual
clear-headedness deserted her. Or maybe it had deserted
her the moment his supersonic sperm had met her egg.
Pregnancy brain was real, and she had it. All she knew
was she had to get out of here before she started to babble
and let her heart rule her head.

"I know marriage isn't about business. And I want to
share my life with you." His tone beseeched her.

"I'm sorry, but like I said, I can't marry you." She
hated the coldness in her voice, but she couldn't help it. If
Luc ever guessed how she really felt, she'd be in an even
bigger mess than she already was. When she couldn't
wait any longer to tell him about the baby, maybe Nick
would help her. He was an attorney. Whoa. She took two
steps back across the expensive wood floor. She was an
independent woman and an adult. She didn't need her big
brother to fight her battles.

"But why?" The wounded expression in Luc's eyes infiltrated her stupor and almost crushed her. "We're good together. You and Amy would make this house a home." His voice cracked and he turned to look out at the lake. "I thought you cared about me, too."

She did, and they were good together, but even with the stability he was handing her on a plate, she couldn't take the risk of getting her heart broken any more than it already was. A chill coursed through her body as a long-ago memory surfaced. She'd stood on the front porch at Harbor House, and the door of the moving van with her dad's things had slammed shut with an awful finality.

"I want to be part of your life, kitty cat. This doesn't have to change things much." Her dad had smiled his special smile for her. *"Don't tell Georgia or Nick, but you've always been my favorite. My little princess."*

Then when she hadn't said anything, his voice had become cajoling. *"You're a practical girl. You understand why I can't live with your mom or in Firefly Lake, but as soon as I get settled, you can live with me and make my house a home."*

Cat blinked as her dad's image dissipated like a wisp of lake fog. In all the years that followed, he'd never been settled and the only house she wanted to make a home was her own. Hers and Amy's and this new baby's. She'd count on herself like she always had. Her body was hot and it was hard to swallow.

"No matter how I feel about you, I can't marry you." The stilted words left a sour taste in her mouth and the nausea worsened. To break eye contact, she bent to pick up the box with the quilts, but Luc was too quick for her.

"This is heavy. I'll take it out to your car." His voice rasped. "I don't want a quilt after all."

On top of everything else, she'd lost the gallery a big sale. "I..." She pressed her lips tight together.

"It doesn't matter." Luc moved back through the house toward the front door. "Choose a quilt for your mom and Ward and send me the bill. Call it a wedding present. You came all the way out here." His voice was clipped and devoid of emotion.

Cat grabbed her coat from the banister and found her boots. The coldness had moved from her voice to settle in her bones.

When Luc opened the front door for her, she clicked the remote on her keys for him to put the quilt box back in the trunk. She could get through the next few minutes, then she'd stop and call Georgia and ask her to stay longer at the gallery. Not only did she need to be away from Luc, she also needed to be alone. Her stomach somersaulted as if to remind her that because of the baby, she'd never truly be alone or apart from Luc ever again.

She followed him to the car and got into the driver's seat, her muscles all of a sudden as stiff as an elderly woman's. She couldn't think about the baby right now. She couldn't think about Luc or how much she loved him, either.

"Cat?" Outside the car his sensual mouth shaped her name.

She turned the key in the ignition and powered down the window. "Yes?"

"Drive safe."

"I will." She always did. As well as practical and sensible, she was careful and conscientious, especially when it came to her heart.

She started the car and pulled into the circular drive. When she glanced in the mirror, he stood watching her, his expression somber, until she turned into the curve of the road to take her back to town.

And take her back toward something she should have faced long ago. Her dad's farewell words reverberated in her head as hot tears coursed down her face. Even though he was in faraway Nevada, her dad still loomed large over her life. She'd moved on with work, but if she wanted to move on with everything else, she had to put her dad's desertion to rest once and for all.

Her mom was right. She had to let go of that mess of hurt and anger she carried and stop letting it shape her choices. She wasn't the abandoned little girl she'd once been. Cat sniffed and took one hand away from the steering wheel to wipe it across her face. She was a strong, capable woman, and the security and stability her dad had taken away—the security and stability she'd searched for ever since—had been inside her all along.

Luc rounded one corner of the arena at speed. His skates threw up chipped ice, and his lungs burned as adrenaline rushed through him. He hadn't thought it possible to feel any worse than he had when Cat turned down his marriage proposal but now, two days later, the truth was all too clear. He felt a hell of a lot worse.

"Whoa." Nick raised a hand over the boards near the blue line.

"What?" Luc skidded to a stop.

The last thing he needed was Cat's brother sticking his nose in. The woman had said she didn't want to marry him. End of story.

Except, it wasn't. Not when Cat was on his mind day and night.

"Take it easy, buddy." Nick leaned over the boards, all corporate in his black wool coat half unbuttoned over a suit and tie.

"Why?" Luc tried to steady his breathing. Not even the punishing skate had gotten Cat out of his mind.

"You'll give yourself a heart attack." Nick's voice was amused. "That's your business, sure, but if you keep it up, you'll give Amy one, too."

"Amy?" Shit, he'd lost track of time and forgotten he was due to coach her in a few minutes.

"I sent her to the locker room to change." Nick grinned. "When she comes back, stay downwind of her. You're sweating like a pig."

"Says the guy who sits behind a desk all day." Luc swore under his breath.

"Hey, if you were a girl, I'd say you had PMS." Nick took a step back. "What did I ever do to you?"

"Nothing. Forget it." Luc tried to smile. "Why did you bring Amy here today? Where's your sister?"

"Georgia took her to the doctor. Cat's got bronchitis or something, so Mia, Charlie, and Liz are helping out at the gallery to get ready for Michael's big quilt exhibition." Nick gave him a grudging smile in return. "If Ward hadn't whisked Mom off on a surprise honeymoon to Florida, I bet she'd be there, too. Those women stick together like glue."

Sweat that wasn't from his workout trickled between Luc's shoulder blades under his jersey. Would Cat tell her sister and the others what had happened between them? Maybe not, because she was a private person. And a sick one. His stomach clenched.

"I hope Cat's okay." He wanted to be there for her. To

love her and have her love him back. Although it was a kind of love he hadn't ever felt before, it was still love. He'd never have proposed to Cat otherwise. Didn't she understand how hard it was for him to say what was in his heart? She should know he loved her and that he didn't take marriage lightly.

"She'll be fine, but me, Sean, Josh Tremblay, and a few other guys from pool night at the Moose and Squirrel are swinging by the gallery tonight to lend a hand. You should join us." Nick's eyes narrowed. "Cat didn't already let you know?"

"I haven't checked my phone in a while." The lie burned Luc's tongue. He'd checked his phone obsessively, but none of the texts or calls had ever been from Cat. He hadn't thought he could love again, but he'd been so wrong. His stomach fluttered.

"I admit I wasn't totally thrilled at first with you and my sister getting together, but you're good for Cat. You calm her down and make her laugh. She hasn't been as serious lately." Nick crossed his arms in front of his chest. "Is everything all right with you two?"

"Why don't you ask Cat?" Luc swallowed.

Nick had his court face on and that was never a good sign.

"I did, but she told me to stay out of her business." Nick's don't-mess-with-me voice was another bad omen.

"Then I can't tell you anything more." Luc kept his voice even. "She's a grown woman."

"Fair enough." At Nick's hesitation, Luc sweated even more. "However, if you do anything to hurt Cat, I won't stand by. Our dad leaving nearly destroyed all of us, and Cat has never really gotten over it. Then there was Amy's dad. If I'd ever gotten my hands on that rat bastard ..." Nick flexed his fingers, as if to remind Luc that, although he sat behind a desk all day, Nick had a trainer on speed dial.

Luc gave what he hoped was an offhand, no-comment kind of shrug. Except, maybe he had hurt her. His knees wobbled. He hadn't said he loved Cat because everything about her threw him so off-balance he hadn't been able to get the words out. He thought she'd know how he felt. Which made him a bigger dumbass than he'd ever thought he could be.

"Hey, Coach." Amy skated onto the ice and waved at him. "You ready for me?"

"Sure." At least he'd make himself go through the motions, and Amy was a distraction from her way-too-sharp uncle. The guy had worked in New York City for years, and despite settling into Firefly Lake and a cozy life with Mia two weeks out of every four, he hadn't lost either his big-city savvy or his ability to cut through bullshit and read people. "I gotta go." Luc gave Nick the smile he'd perfected through dealing with nosy reporters his entire adult life; slick and meaningless but with a carefully honed air of sincerity.

"I have to take care of some paperwork, Amy, but I'll be right up there in the bleachers." Nick shot another speculative gaze at Luc. "Let me know if you need anything, or if Coach Luc works you too hard."

"Okay." Amy blinked at Luc. "Why would you work me too hard?"

"No reason." Except, her uncle had a stick up his ass, and, like a hound tracking a scent, he guessed something was up and wouldn't rest until he'd figured out what it was. "Let's do a few laps to warm up. I'll skate with you." Even though Luc didn't usually do laps with Amy, and he was already warmed up to the boiling point, he wanted to keep an eye on her for Cat. It had nothing to do with keeping as far away as possible from Mr. Hotshot Attorney.

"Good job, Amsey." Twenty minutes later, Luc's breathing had eased. Hockey was his place and still, to his surprise, coaching got him into almost the same zone playing once had. Especially coaching Amy, because she was magic on the ice. Except, the thoughts of Cat were still there. The love was, too. A love that he'd been too stupid to tell her about.

"Coach?" Amy glided to a stop beside him. "I know we're not done with practice yet, but can I talk to you for a minute?" She glanced at Nick, who was on his cell and focused on his laptop screen three rows back from the ice. "Kind of in private?"

"Sure." Luc gestured to the away team's bench on the other side of the arena from Nick. "Is here okay?"

"I guess so." Amy undid the strap on her helmet and pulled it off. Her hair was plastered to her head, and her usually rosy face was white.

"Do you need a rest?" Unease pricked Luc. She wasn't sick, was she? She was so keen that he sometimes forgot to slow down. "You should have said so earlier."

"I'm not tired." She licked her chapped lips. "I've made a big mistake, and I don't know how to fix it." She sat on the bench and her shoulders slumped inward.

"Have you talked to your mom?" Luc sat beside her.

Nick was still on the phone, but once he got off, the guy would be over here sticking his nose in like the best of the Firefly Lake gossips.

"Mom's part of the mistake, so I can't." Amy's words came out in a burst.

Luc's stomach quivered. "Are you or your mom hurt or in some kind of trouble?"

"Not exactly." She laced her fingers together. "But I've done something really dumb, dumber than anything I ever did before. And I've made Mom sad and maybe even sick. Aunt Georgia took her to the doctor. Mom didn't want to go, but Aunt Georgia made her."

"How could you have made your mom sick? Your uncle Nick said she's got bronchitis or something." Luc's tight breathing eased.

"Even though she's still coughing a lot, I don't think it's bronchitis. When Aunt Georgia told my mom she had to go to the doctor, Aunt Georgia also said Mom couldn't leave *it* any longer, but I don't know what *it* is. Mom would be mad if she found out I talked to you, but you're part of the problem." Amy's eyes were anxious.

"How so?" Luc tried to make his voice gentle.

"Mom doesn't want to see you anymore because of me." Amy's voice wobbled. "Even though I said I was sorry and you're still coaching me and everything, it's because you're coaching me that Mom doesn't think she can go out with you. I was afraid Mom would like you better than me, so I said some bad stuff to her."

"Aww, Amsey, it's not your fault." Luc put a hand to his head. "Your mom will always like you best. As for me coaching you, it's my privilege. It doesn't have anything to do with your mom."

"I get that now, but even though Mom likes you a lot, she won't go out with you because people talked about her and you coaching me. If you don't coach me anymore, you can date Mom again and she'll be happy, like she was before, instead of so sad." Amy's trusting expression made another fissure in Luc's heart. "Even though the kids at school haven't said anything since Coach Scott talked to them, I'm scared they still could. If you're not coaching me, I wouldn't have to worry about that, either."

"It's not that simple." Luc's stomach clenched. What had he said to Amy once? He wouldn't have any bullies on his team. "I appreciate that you're trying to help, but you're only twelve."

"Twelve and a quarter. I'll be thirteen in nine months." She let out a long breath. "If I had to, I'd even give up hockey for my mom, not only coaching with you."

"Even though your mom is anxious about you getting hurt, she wouldn't ever want you to give up hockey." Luc rubbed his forehead. The bullies might not be on his team, but they were still out there. No matter what happened between him and Cat, he had to take a stand.

"But . . . Mom's not happy, and I don't know how to fix it." This time Amy's voice broke. "She also made tuna noodle casserole twice this week."

"What does tuna noodle casserole have to do with any of this?" Luc gave Amy's shoulder a rough pat.

"Mom knows I hate tuna, but I ate three helpings of that casserole anyway and she never noticed." Amy made an aggrieved face. "And she's watching really lame movies over and over. *Pride and Prejudice* and a whole bunch of other ones she borrowed from the library. Then she cries, except for when she's being sick."

Luc's legs shook. "What do you mean she's being sick?"

"Throwing up sick. She says it's because of Aunt Josette's lobster bisque, but that was ages ago. Even though that soup was gross, why would Mom still be sick now? When I had food poisoning last year, I was sick as sick but it didn't last long."

Cat couldn't be pregnant, could she? Luc's head got light. They'd used a condom every time. New condoms. Apart from the first time. The condom he'd had in his wallet. The trembling spread from his legs to his chest and then his hands. He'd told her…oh crap…he'd said he didn't want kids. He'd as much as made it a condition of marrying her.

"Are you okay, Coach? You look almost as sick as Mom." Amy's voice was worried.

"I'm not sick." At least not sick in the way Amy meant. Luc tried to work moisture into his desert-dry mouth.

"You said your mom's crying a lot?" When Maggie was pregnant, the slightest thing would set her off.

"Yeah, it's weird, because Mom doesn't cry usually." Amy shook her head. "I hope I never get like that."

"You wait until somebody puts an Olympic medal around your neck." Luc tried to smile through his anesthetized lips. "Then you'll want to cry, for sure."

"You think that will really happen?" Amy's eyes widened.

"As long as you keep on the way you're going, I don't see why not." He cleared his throat. "And I'll be there cheering you on."

"That's years away. Right now, I want to make Mom feel better, but I don't know how." Amy leaned against his shoulder, and, although Luc wasn't usually a crier either, the warmth and trust in that gesture made his eyes smart. Or maybe it was also the thought of Cat, the woman he loved, pregnant, alone, and still so determined to handle everything by herself.

"You did the right thing to tell me." He might not have wanted to risk having kids, but if Cat was having his kid, he'd be there for her whether she liked it or not. And even if she didn't love him like he loved her.

"You think you can help Mom?"

"I'm sure of it. I'm also sure I won't have to stop coaching you, either." Luc's heart swelled with that new and still bewildering love, along with worry and a whole lot more. Cat must be so scared and confused. "How do you think I measure up to that Mr. Darcy guy?"

Amy studied him. "You're okay-looking, almost as good as the one in the movie." A small, sweet smile tugged at one corner of her mouth.

Almost. Luc would take that. He'd take anything if it meant he could get Cat back. "What else?"

"Mr. Darcy did some dumb stuff, but he made it up to Lizzy in the end. He was also real rich, so maybe that helped, and he had a great house. Mom likes his house."

The band around Luc's ribcage pressed tight. He'd done more dumb stuff than Mr. Darcy ever had, and Cat didn't care how rich he was. Although, before the dumb stuff, she'd seemed to like his new house.

"I guess it hasn't always seemed that way, but I'd kind of like it if you and Mom got together." Amy's voice was low. "Before I got jealous, I made this list of stuff I thought a great dad should do. You ticked every box."

Luc's eyes stung. "If I had a great daughter list, you'd tick every box on it, too. How do you feel about that?"

"Okay." The word was a soft whisper, then Amy reached for Luc's hand and looped her fingers with his.

"Good." He folded her small hand in his. "I'll talk to your mom, but I might need your help." If Cat froze him out, he'd have to use everything he had to reach her.

"How could I help you?" Amy's expression was puzzled.

"Your mom doesn't want to talk to me right now." Which he deserved, but if Cat gave him another chance, Luc would spend the rest of his life making it up to her.

"Oh." Amy's voice was small. "I'll try to help, but you can't tell Mom I talked to you." She gripped his hand. "Promise?"

"I promise." Luc spoke around the pulsing emotion in his throat. Amy's trust was a precious gift he'd never abuse.

"There's something else, maybe even worse." Amy's mouth worked. "I told Mom...I made it sound like if you two ever got together, I'd hate it if she had a baby, because everybody loves babies best. But if someday...I mean...it might be okay." She hesitated. "Besides, Mom says hearts are stretchy and there's always more than enough love to go around."

"Your mom's right." The truth reverberated in Luc's head like the big Chinese gong in the party room at the Pink Pagoda. He'd never stop loving Maggie, but his heart was plenty big enough for Cat, Amy, and dozens of babies. "Baby or not, you'll always have a place in my heart, Amsey. Your place. No baby could ever take that away." Luc rubbed his free hand across his eyes. "Besides, a baby couldn't play hockey for years and years. Maybe it wouldn't be athletic at all."

Amy let out an infectious giggle. "It could be exactly like Mom."

But no matter what their baby was like, Luc would love it with everything he had to give. Like he loved Cat and had assumed she knew but had been too caught up in himself to tell her. Given that half-assed proposal, no wonder she'd turned him down. He'd make this right, no matter what and how long it took. He'd make things better for Amy, too. He gave her hand one last squeeze. "We're a team, Amsey."

"And we're gonna kick spaghetti." She knocked the heels of her skates against his.

Nick appeared by the bench with his laptop under one arm. "Is practice over already?"

"No, we were talking strategy." Luc winked at Amy. "If you're going to play the game, you have to know strategy. Right, Amsey?" He gave Nick a bland smile.

"Right." Amy gave Luc a high five and grinned.

"Now we have work to do." Luc stood and rolled his shoulders.

"Very important work." Amy clomped over to the ice and fixed her helmet back on her head. "Wanna race, Coach?"

"You bet."

"But…" Nick stared at Luc a little too long.

Luc stared back.

Amusement twinkled in Nick's eyes. "I'll be damned." He made a wheezing sound that might have been a laugh, then clapped Luc on the back. "You've sure met your match in my sister."

Luc hoped like hell he had. "I…" He stopped. He wouldn't tell Cat's brother anything before he talked to the woman herself.

"I'm happy for you, really." This time Nick did laugh. "But if you've pissed her off, Cat has sharp claws."

Like Luc didn't already know that. He glanced at the ice, where Amy waited for him. He had an unexpected ally in Cat's daughter, though, and he wasn't afraid to use it.

"Good luck, bro. I can't help you out. Cat has always known her own mind, and she's never thanked me for getting involved in her business, but I won't stand in your way."

"Thanks." Luc skated onto the ice with new determination. The only person standing in his way was Cat herself. And a whole team of guys chasing after the Stanley Cup would be less formidable.

Chapter Twenty-Three

Cat cupped a hand over her nose and moved across the arena lobby toward the reception desk. The scent of stale beer, sweat, and hockey equipment never dissipated, despite the almost around-the-clock efforts of the cleaning crew.

"Amy? Hurry up, honey." She glanced at her daughter several steps behind her, then nodded at a guy with a mop and bucket outside the home team's locker room.

He gestured with his mop and grinned. "Coach Luc's in his office."

"Thanks, but we're here to see Stephanie." Luc was the last person Cat wanted to see. She rummaged in her tote bag and pulled out a sheaf of papers. She'd already dropped off Amy's medical records once, so why Stephanie couldn't find them was a mystery. As was why she wouldn't accept scanned copies and insisted both Cat and Amy had to come in.

"I'm just leaving." Behind the reception desk,

Stephanie pulled a coat on over her cozy pink sweater and tailored jeans. Unlike Stephanie's usual, several-sizes-too-small wardrobe, the outfit was one Cat might have chosen for herself.

"I thought you said you'd be here until five thirty." Cat glanced at the wall clock above Stephanie's desk. It was only a few minutes past five, and she'd closed the gallery early and raced over when the other woman had called to make sure she'd have plenty of time to fix whatever had gone wrong.

Stephanie made an apologetic face. "Something came up."

"No worries, I'll leave the paperwork here. Call me Monday morning if you need anything else. I dropped off copies before, remember? And why do you need to see Amy? She was in the middle of homework." She gestured to her daughter, who seemed intent on avoiding Cat's gaze.

Stephanie shrugged. "Bureaucracy. I have to tick all those little boxes, you know?"

"Well, now that you've seen her we can go. Ready, Amy?" If she could get out of here before Luc came out of that office, she could avoid talking to him for one more day.

"Mom." Amy shrugged away Cat's touch. "There's no rush. Since we're here anyway, why don't we get a snack? Maybe there's a figure skating practice or something going on. It's Friday. I have all weekend to do homework."

"You don't like figure skating—"

"You can't leave the paperwork here." Stephanie's tongue clicked against her teeth. "It's confidential. You have to talk to Luc." She turned to Amy. "Go right in, honey. The coach wants to talk to you as well."

"No...Amy...come back here." Cat bit her lip as the door of the coaching office banged shut behind her daughter. "I'll come back first thing Monday morning." As soon as she retrieved Amy, they'd review what listening meant.

"The camp deadline's tonight." Stephanie came around the desk and made another apologetic face. "Luc's right through there. He's expecting you."

"But I..." Cat tightened her grip on the papers. There had to be another option.

"No exceptions." Stephanie's face went as pink as her sweater and she stared at her boots. "I said that to you before, didn't I?"

"It doesn't matter, I—"

"Yes, it does matter." Stephanie fiddled with the strap of her enormous handbag. "If I don't say this now, maybe I never will. How I treated you when we were kids wasn't right. What happened to Amy at school...it wasn't right, either. I just wanted to say...you know...I'm sorry."

"Thanks." Cat's face heated.

"You were always going places. I wasn't. The biggest thing in my life was going to the state cheering championships." She hunched her shoulders. "My mom and I went on a bus trip to Nashville last summer when my ex had the boys, but that's it. I've never even been to New York City. Every New Year's Eve when the boys are asleep, I sit on the sofa and watch that big ball in Times Square on TV and I..." Her mouth trembled.

"Stephanie, you—"

"No, I promised myself I had to tell you this. I try to teach my boys to be kind, so I should take my own advice, starting with you." She held out her right hand. "Whether you believe me or not, ever since you turned up here with Amy that day to register her for hockey, I've been thinking about you and me and how things were between us. I'm a single mom, too, and my ex...well, this job is all I've got. Sometimes...it's hard, you know?"

"Yes, it is." Cat took Stephanie's hand in hers. One handshake wouldn't wipe out almost thirty years of animosity, but it was a good start. And since folks who lived in Firefly Lake tended to stay here, she and Stephanie might have another thirty years or more to work things out.

"As for Luc, even though I might have wanted there to be, even back in high school, there was never anything between us. And now, well...I hope it works out for the two of you."

"It...he..." Cat's thoughts spun.

"You're the icing on his cupcake, sugar." Stephanie gave her a tremulous smile.

"What?" The word popped out before Cat could stop it. "Sorry, I—"

"No, it's me." Stephanie put a hand to her cheek and her face went even pinker. "When I get nervous, stupid stuff comes out of my mouth. Maybe it's because of all the old movies I watch. I've been stuck here my whole life, so they're like an escape. Real dumb, huh?"

"No." Even though she hadn't been stuck in Firefly Lake, Cat got that need to escape. It was why she'd spent the past few weeks buried in the historical romances on her e-reader—after she'd borrowed every movie from the library's small collection that had promised a distraction from her real life. "I like movies, too."

Stephanie's brown eyes got shiny. "I have to go, but maybe sometime we could...I mean if you're not busy... we could hang out...catch a movie together."

"I'd like that."

"Me too." Stephanie gave Cat another bashful smile, then darted past her and almost ran out through the arena's reception area, her boots clattering on the tile.

Cat pressed a hand to her stomach. Who would have thought she and Stephanie had anything in common, let alone a second chance to start fresh and try to make things better between them? She hadn't, but if Stephanie could make that effort, so could she.

Like she had to do with Luc. She studied his closed office door. She was an adult. Luc was too. And this was about Amy, so she could talk to him for five minutes, fix whatever had gone wrong with the hockey camp application, and be on her way. Once she told him about the baby, she'd have to talk to him for the rest of her life anyway. Although this meeting wasn't a second chance, it might at least help break the ice.

She rapped on the door.

"Cat." Luc pulled the door open, his voice low.

"Here." She shoved the paperwork toward him. "Amy's medical files."

He looked at her but didn't move to take the papers. "I'm sorry." A pulse in his throat worked and his blue eyes were somber.

"Mistakes happen, but Amy would be so disappointed if she missed out on the camp because some paperwork had gone missing. Stephanie said the deadline's tonight." Cat pressed harder on her stomach with her free hand. Morning sickness was a misnomer. It was all-day sickness and all night, too, but it wasn't the baby's fault. She'd love it enough for two parents, like she did Amy. And where was Amy anyway? Apart from Luc, the cramped office was empty and the connecting door to the training room was shut.

"This isn't about the hockey camp application." Luc's gaze dropped to her hand, then jerked back to her face. He gestured her into the office. "I've already heard informally that Amy's in. Despite her dyslexia, it's likely she'll get a full scholarship."

"Then why?" Cat stuffed the papers back in her bag, then covered her nose again. If anything, the arena smell was worse in here. "And where's Amy?"

"With Scott and the team in the training room for an impromptu end-of-season party. I had to find a way to talk to you." Luc's voice was raw, and he took her arm to ease her into a chair. The same chair she'd sat in all those weeks ago before she'd let herself love him, and he was nothing more to her than an old family friend and childhood crush.

"There's nothing for us to talk about." She stared at her scuffed, winter-weary boots.

"I wouldn't call a baby nothing, but I didn't make it easy for you to tell me." He crouched beside the chair and rubbed her back through her coat. "I was wrong. I thought you knew how I felt about you, about us, so I didn't...I'm sorry." His voice was sad, but not angry.

"How did you find out about the baby? Georgia promised me she wouldn't say anything." Cat's eyes burned.

"Georgia didn't tell me. Nobody did. I guessed." His breath rasped by her ear. "I love you, Cat, and even though I took a wrong and mixed-up way to do it, that's why I asked you to marry me out at the house. I didn't know you were pregnant then, but I knew I loved you. I still do. And baby or not, I still want to marry you." His hand moved from her back to her face to trace the curve of her chin.

"Maggie was the love of your life." Luc was doing the right thing like Cat had known he would, but even though he sounded sincere, she didn't want to be second best. As well as a man who would be there for her and their child, she wanted her own love story.

Luc sat back on his heels. "I fell in love with Maggie when I was a kid. If she'd lived, we'd have grown old together. But I lost her, and although she'll always have part of my heart, you have my heart, too. Like you tell Amy, hearts are stretchy and big enough to love more than one person."

"How…Amy…she?" Her voice faltered and Luc moved closer on one knee.

"Amy loves you and, like me, she wants you to be happy." He cupped her chin to make her look at him.

"I…" Happiness flickered then was quenched. "You said you don't want children. I didn't get pregnant on purpose. You have to believe me that I didn't try to trick you."

"As if I'd ever think that. You're not that kind of woman." The expression in Luc's eyes was loving and honest. "There were two of us, remember? If anybody's responsible, it's me. It was my condom."

He stood and pulled Cat to her feet like she was a piece of thistledown. "I said I didn't want children because I vowed I'd never risk putting any other woman I loved through what Maggie went through." His voice cracked and his big body shook. "And now you...if anything happens to you...I couldn't...God, Cat, feelings go deep for me, and it was hard to say it right away, but I love you so much. I can't lose you, too. I don't want to go through the rest of my life without you by my side." His eyes were grief-stricken.

Cat wrapped her arms around him. "My pregnancy with Amy was fine, and this one's starting off exactly the same way. The doctor says everything's okay so far." She took a deep breath. Instead of sweat, beer, and dirty hockey gear, she smelled him. Clean and safe. The man she wanted and who also wanted her.

A tender smile lifted one corner of his mouth. "I never thought I'd get so lucky twice in this lifetime. Maggie's my past, but I want you, Amy, and our baby to be my future."

Happiness broke inside Cat like water surging through melted ice on Firefly Lake when winter gave way to spring. "Amy? She...did you talk to her?"

"That's between Amy and me. I promised her I wouldn't say anything to you. Don't be mad, but along with Stephanie, Amy helped me get you here today."

"I..." Cat's heart bumped against her ribs.

"I want to fix things with you." Luc's voice was gruff and he held her tight. "I was wrong the way I handled things before. Let me make it right."

"I love you, Luc. A part of me always has, right back to when I was a lost and bullied little kid, but I didn't think you could ever love me back."

"I love you, too." His voice vibrated with emotion. "You've made my world right. You helped me come out of that wasteland of grief I was stuck in and hope and look forward to the future. I need you, Cat. Do you believe me?"

"Yes." She didn't need to analyze any evidence or think things through. She only needed to listen to her heart.

"I don't deserve you, but if you give me a chance, I'll spend every day for the rest of my life showing you what you mean to me." His voice was filled with love.

Cat raised her head. "You can't change your past, like I can't change mine. I called my dad a few days ago, and you know what?"

"No, what?" Luc's expression was guarded.

"I've spent so many years being angry with him. For a lot of those years, I also missed him, at least when I wasn't hating him for what he did to Mom and all of us. But when I called him, it was strange. I couldn't feel anything except pity. He didn't even seem like my dad, just someone I once knew."

Although she'd cried after she'd hung up the phone, tears dredged from the depths of her soul, they were tears that helped her begin to finally heal and move on, as if she'd washed away all the bad things and given the good a place to grow. "I've made my share of mistakes, but we've got a future ahead of us. I want my future to be with you."

Luc had given her a priceless gift. Not only love but acceptance. As well as the kind of security that had nothing to do with money and everything to do with what she'd needed since that childhood day when her dad's betrayal had ripped away her trust forever.

Luc's breath got short and emotion almost choked him.

Cat had given him another chance, and now he had to make the most of it. To give her the love story she needed and deserved. The kind of love story she'd only ever read about in those books of hers or seen in movies. "Come here." He tucked her into his side and moved with her out the office door, through the deserted reception area and toward the rink.

"Where...why?" Her eyes were puzzled.

He gave her a brief smile, then tugged open the door to the ice and led her to the home team's bench. It was edged with the tiny, white lights he'd set up earlier that now glowed in the darkness of the arena.

"What...?" She sucked in a breath.

"Shush." He eased her onto the bench and got down on one knee in front of her. "I made a big mistake before, but I want to do things right this time."

"Okay." In Cat's steady blue gaze was all the love he could have ever wanted and more.

He stuck his hand under the bench and pulled out a box wrapped in shiny, pink paper. "I love you, Minnie, and I want to look out for you."

"You've always looked out for me." Her words came out in a soft whisper. "Even when I didn't want you to or think I needed it."

"I want to keep doing it, but from now on, I also want us to look out for each other." He took the lid off the box and Cat drew in a breath.

"How did you...?"

"Liz makes whole quilts. She said a wedding dress for little Minnie Mouse here was easy." Luc set the plush toy on the bench between them. "Don't worry, I swore her to secrecy." He dug in the box again and pulled out Mickey dressed as a groom.

"I..."

He swallowed and, still on one knee, set Mickey beside Minnie and took Cat's hands in his. "I love how smart you are, but I love your sweetness and kindness even more. I love you with every fiber of my being." He paused and his throat tightened further. "If I ask you again, will you marry me?"

"Yes."

Only one word, but it was enough.

"I won't let you down. Or Amy and the baby, either. I swear it." Luc's voice was raw and his hands shook in hers. Cat's beloved face swam together with the twinkling lights. "Even if you hadn't agreed to marry me, I wanted to make sure nobody around here ever hurt you or Amy again." He took one hand away to flip a switch beside the bench and the arena lights went on.

"What do you mean?"

"It's Friday night. Family skating, remember?" Luc gestured to the far end of the arena where Amy, Scott, Amy's teammates, and half of Firefly Lake skated onto the ice. "Since you're sticking around, I want you to be sure you know you're welcome."

"But everybody's here. Why?"

Luc's gaze swung from Amy to Gabrielle and Ward, who held Pixie, to Nick, Mia, and the girls to Georgia with Josh beside her, Charlie and Sean, with Ty rolling Lexie along in a stroller, his folks, Stephanie, and her boys, and even Mason and his parents.

"Michael dropped by my office at the creamery last week. We were talking about Chamber of Commerce stuff, and he said something that made me think. He said that what brings us together is more important than whatever we might think divides us. I took the opportunity to remind a few folks of that."

"You...I..." Cat's eyes shone. "Michael said pretty much the same thing to me once."

"He's almost as smart as you." Luc grinned. "It kind of snowballed from there. The only advantage to being a little bit famous is people don't want to offend me. Pretty much the whole town's coming out tonight. There's pizza from Mario's, Chinese food from the Wongs at the Pink Pagoda, and cold meats and salads from the deli. All the businesses in town chipped in so there's free skating and skate rentals all night."

Luc leaned toward her and, despite the clang of skates, he lowered his voice. "There are good people here, but a lot of them have had a tough time. People like Mason and his family. His dad's been out of work for almost a year, and although Mason wanted to play hockey, his folks couldn't afford it this season. He's a good player, so that's why Amy became a target. He resented her."

"You did all this for me...for my daughter...I..." She put a hand to her mouth.

"I did it for all of us. You, Amy, me, and everyone in this town." Luc drew her hand to his and gave her knuckles a gentle kiss. "Most people want to do the decent thing, but sometimes a few of them need a nudge in the right direction. Or in Mason's case, a pair of skates and next year's hockey registration fee once I'm sure he understands his words have consequences."

"And you...you were the one who gave that nudge in a way that included rather than divided people." Cat's smile was full of so much sweetness and love that Luc's heart skipped a beat.

He shrugged. "I didn't do a whole lot. It was Michael's idea, really. I only pointed folks in the right direction." Luc searched the crowd to find Michael standing with Liz by the boards. The older man gave him a small, knowing smile.

"Don't be so modest." Cat squeezed his hand. "No matter whose idea it was, you made it happen."

Luc slid onto the bench beside her and dipped his head toward hers.

"You can't kiss me here. Not with everybody looking." Cat's face turned that pretty shade of soft pink he loved, sweet and oh-so-sexy.

"That's the point. I want everybody to know we're together, so you better get used to it."

But even as his mouth covered hers, and his hand settled on the curve of her waist to pull her and their baby close, Luc knew, to his bones, that he'd never get used to it. And he'd never take it for granted, either, because this wasn't only a happy ending he never thought he'd find again but a brand-new chapter in a lifetime of living and loving together.

Epilogue

❦

Three weeks later

"Tradition is that it's bad luck for the groom to see the bride before the ceremony." With her hands on her hips and elegant in her pale-pink bridesmaid's dress, Mia stood at the top of the sweeping staircase at Harbor House and blocked Luc's path. Despite her stern expression, her tone was amused.

"Please? Just for a few minutes?" Luc glanced beyond Mia to Charlie, who stood behind her sister in a matching dress.

"Around here, weddings are all about tradition." Charlie's brown eyes twinkled. Through the half-open window beyond, a warm wind fluttered the lace curtain and birds sang a springtime chorus.

"They're right," Georgia chimed in. As Cat's maid of honor, she wore a darker pink dress that matched the Celtic knot tattoo on her forearm.

"I thought you'd at least take pity on me, Georgie." Within the small confines of Firefly Lake, there wasn't anybody less traditional than Georgia. "All I want is to see Cat first, without a crowd of people around. There's even a reporter and photographer at the end of the driveway."

"Only from the local paper." Mia gave him a teasing look before she turned to the other two. "I suppose we could make an exception."

Charlie and Georgia grinned and stepped aside.

"Five minutes and I have to time you." Georgia gestured to her phone. "Mom will freak if we're even a minute late getting to the church. She's waited years to be a mother-of-the-bride, then she's a bride herself and a bride's mom in less than two months. She has another grandchild on the way, too. You're lucky she doesn't have heart problems. If she did, this much excitement could kill her." Her laugh was warm and so infectious that Luc, Charlie, and Mia laughed, too.

"Thank you." Luc moved to stand in a circle with the three women, all of a sudden serious. "Thanks for everything. You've put this wedding together so fast, and you're all helping Cat at the gallery since she's so tired and sick." Which scared him so much that he'd called the doctor's office three times a day until Cat had made him stop.

"Although you're the reason she's tired and sick, you're okay." Georgia elbowed him.

"And we love Cat, so we love you, too." Peacemaker Mia patted his arm.

"Get in there before we have to come and get you." Charlie gave him a gentle push toward Gabrielle's closed bedroom door. "Gabrielle and Ward left ten minutes ago, so, apart from Amy, the coast is clear."

Luc smiled his thanks and rapped on the door.

It eased open, and Amy's head popped through the narrow gap. "Hey, Coach. Am I ever glad to see you. Mom's a wreck." She grabbed Luc by the lapels of his suit jacket and hauled him through the door, then slammed it shut behind him.

"Luc?" Cat sat on a small bench in front of a mirrored dressing table. Reflected back at him, her face was almost as white as her grandmother's wedding dress, which billowed out around her tiny figure.

"I'm right here." His heart twisted at the panic-stricken expression in her eyes.

"See?" Amy tucked an arm through his and marched him toward Cat. "I've never seen her so nervous. She's all twitchy, even worse than Bingley and Darcy when there's a thunderstorm."

"What is it?" Luc crouched on the floor at Cat's side as Amy hovered behind. "Is it the baby? Do I need to get Dr. O'Brien? She's downstairs in the living room. I asked her to ride to the church with you."

"It's not the baby." Cat fingered the pearl necklace her aunt Josette had brought from Montreal, and her smile was sweet mixed with annoyed. "As for Jessa O'Brien, if you keep on like this, she'll be moving in with us after the wedding."

"Do you think she'd do that? She's single, isn't she?" Why hadn't he thought of it before? The new house was more than big enough, and if she didn't want to stay right in the main house, there was a guest cottage. Cat and the baby would be even safer. Amy, too, because kids got sick all the time. Or so he'd heard.

"Yes, Jessa's single, but no, she's not moving in with

us." Cat laughed and put a hand to the gentle mound of her stomach, still slight, but Liz had nevertheless needed to make a few invisible alterations to the wedding dress. "I'm fine. So is Scooter Junior, who, miracle of miracles, seems to have decided to give me a day without throwing up. I'm scared half to death, though, because in a few minutes, I have to go out there and have everybody looking at me. I don't like being the center of attention."

"Aww, honey." Luc rested his head on her shoulder. "You look beautiful, and I'll be right there beside you the whole time."

"Me too." Amy's face above her blue junior bridesmaid's dress met his in the mirror. "Well, maybe not all the time, because I'm not going on your honeymoon, but I'll stick to you like glue the rest of the time." She grinned. "Right, Coach?"

"Right, Amsey." He reached back to give her a high five.

"I've been thinking..." Amy worried her bottom lip. "After today, I can't call you Coach anymore. That kind of sucks, but I was wondering...I think Dad would be an even better name, don't you?"

Cat faced him, and her big, stretchy, loving heart was in her eyes. "It's a perfect name."

"I think so, too." Luc's voice was gruff and he blinked as he put his hand over Cat's, the one that wore the Art Deco sapphire and diamond ring they'd chosen together from a dealer friend of Michael's in Boston. It wasn't a traditional engagement ring because she wasn't a traditional woman, but she was *his* woman and he was her man. And today was about sharing that with the whole world. "Now, what do you say we go get married?"

Amy put her hand on top of his. "That sounds great, Dad." Her voice was thick.

Cat's eyes glistened. "I don't care what anyone says. I promised Nick he could walk me down the aisle, but until then, I want to walk out of this room with you and keep you beside me all the way to the church, both of you." She turned to include Amy.

"I wouldn't have it any other way." He wrapped Cat in a hug, then caught Amy, too. "What do you say, kiddo?"

"Let's kick some butt out there." Amy grinned at him.

"Please." Cat's voice was threaded with laughter. "No hockey talk on my wedding day."

"You're scared, aren't you?" Amy's gaze swung between him and Cat.

"Not anymore." Cat's soft smile was for Luc alone. A promise and a vow as important as those they'd say at St. James Episcopal in half an hour—vows that would bind them together for life. "In fact, I don't think I'll ever be scared again." Her smile broadened. "Not now that we've got Scooter on our team."

"Always, Minnie." He got to his feet and held out one hand to Cat and the other to Amy.

"And forever." Cat took his hand, linked her fingers with his, then stood on tiptoe to pull him in for a kiss.

"Mom. Dad." Amy rolled her eyes. "I'm still here."

"Exactly where you belong." Luc's heart swelled with the kind of love and happiness he'd never thought he'd feel again, so strong they took his breath away. "With each other, that's where all of us belong, back home at Firefly Lake."

Charlotte Gibbs just wants to put the past behind her. But now, back at Firefly Lake, she is overwhelmed with memories of sun-drenched days, late-night kisses, and the one man she could never forget...

Sean Carmichael doesn't know why Charlie disappeared all those years ago, but he's never gotten over her. She left him once when he needed her most. How can he convince her to stay now?

A preview of *The Cottage at Firefly Lake* follows.

Chapter One

Sean Carmichael balanced the canoe paddle on his knees, scanned the lake and sandy shoreline, and lingered on the cottage hugged by tall pine trees.

"Dad?" Ty brought the rental canoe alongside his. The white Carmichael's logo gleamed with fresh paint. "You want to deliver this canoe to the Gibbs place or sit in the middle of the lake all afternoon?" His fifteen-year-old son flashed a teasing grin.

"Just waiting for you to catch up," Sean teased back.

"Race you?" Ty's blue eyes twinkled.

"Sure."

Shadow, their black Lab wedged into the hull, thumped her tail as Sean dipped the paddle and the canoe shot forward through the pristine water of the Vermont lake. Twenty feet from shore, Sean slowed to let Ty cruise past him.

Ty scrambled out of the canoe and waited for him in

knee-deep water. He pinned Sean with an accusing look. "You gotta stop doing that."

"What?" Sean jumped out of his canoe and dragged it to the sandy beach. Shadow loped by and splashed Sean's board shorts and T-shirt.

"Letting me win." Ty pulled the other canoe onto the beach, then fisted his hands in his T-shirt. Big broad hands like Sean's that could already do a man's work. "I'm almost sixteen. I'm not a kid anymore."

"I know." Sean swallowed a sigh.

"Some car." Ty pointed to a black BMW parked by the cottage under the pines. "New people renting the Gibbs place this summer?"

"Not that I heard." Sean tugged on his baseball cap to shield his face from the July sun. Not much ever changed in this little corner of Vermont's Northeast Kingdom.

Ty tossed a stick for Shadow to chase. "Why's it called the Gibbs place anyway? There've never been any Gibbses around Firefly Lake."

"Not since you'd remember." No Gibbs had been back here in years. Eighteen years, if anybody was counting. Which Sean wasn't. "We better get a move on. After we deliver this rental, we have to paddle back and do some more work on the racing canoe before your mom picks you up."

"I've got other stuff I want to do. Can't the work wait till tomorrow? Or I could call Mom and ask her to pick me up later." Ty's voice was hopeful.

"Sorry, but no. Your mom likes to keep to a schedule." And his ex-wife's schedule was the kind Sean had never managed to live up to. "Besides, the work can't wait until tomorrow. We made a commitment to the customer."

Ty's mouth flattened into a stubborn line. "*You* made a commitment to the customer, not me."

Sean grabbed one end of the rental canoe and Ty the other, lifting it above their heads. "You're as much a part of this business as me."

"What if I want something else?" Ty's voice was sharp.

Sean's chest got heavy as worry for his son sparked memories of what—and who—he'd once wanted. "I have a good life here. All I want is for you to have a good life too. This business is part of our family. I wanted to take on Carmichael's when I was your age."

"I'm not you."

"I know you're not, but unless you talk to me, how will I know who you are or what you want?" Sean stopped by the patch of grass in front of the cottage, and he and Ty eased the canoe to the ground.

"Whatever." Ty clumped up the steps to the wide porch. White clapboard walls rose behind to a second story.

Sean bit back the frustrated words he might have said before he pushed his son away. He couldn't lose Ty. His father and grandfather were the past, but his son was the future. The future of the business they'd built together. A legacy.

Following Ty, he rapped on the screen door. A radio inside was tuned to a news station, and light footsteps tapped down the hall. "Son, I want the best for you—"

"Uh, Dad." Ty's voice cracked.

Sean's head jerked up and the world fell away.

A girl in her early teens stood on the other side of the half-open door. She wore an aqua bikini top with a white sarong tied around her hips. And she had long brown hair and big brown eyes like melted chocolate drops.

Sean took a step back and bumped into Ty. No, it couldn't be Charlie Gibbs because Charlie was seven months younger than Sean. But she had Charlie's face and hair and those eyes that had always seen straight through him.

Forgetting the past was up there with all the other things Sean was good at. Except, sometimes, that past caught him when he least expected.

"Can I help you?" The girl had a slow drawl, Southern definitely, Texas maybe.

Ty edged forward, and there was a smile of pure masculine appreciation on his son's face. "I'm Ty Carmichael, and this is my dad. Somebody here rented a canoe from us." He pulled off his fishing hat and stuck it into the back pocket of his shorts. "We own Carmichael's, the marina and boatyard next door."

"I'm Naomi Connell." The girl smiled back and showed a mouthful of braces. "I don't know anything about a canoe rental."

"Maybe your dad booked it?" Sean's voice was higher, like it belonged to some other guy.

Naomi studied him. "My dad's not here, but I can ask my—"

"No!" Sean broke in. "If there's been a mistake, my brother will pick the canoe up later." Sweat trickled down his back, beneath his shirt.

Naomi quirked an eyebrow, and what was left of Sean's heart, the heart Charlie had ripped out of his chest and shredded, thudded against his ribs.

Inside the cottage the radio stopped. "Who's at the

door?" It was a woman's voice, and her words were clipped. An accent Sean couldn't place. His stomach churned.

Naomi, the girl who was and wasn't Charlie, spoke back into the shadowy hall where beach bags and summer shoes were piled in an untidy heap. "Some guys are here about a canoe rental."

She turned again to Sean and Ty and opened the door wider. "You want to come inside? We made iced tea." A smile flowered across Naomi's face. A smile that was sweet, innocent, and so much like Charlie's it made Sean's heart ache.

"Sure." Ty's smile broadened. "Iced tea sounds great." He shook sand off his feet and moved toward Naomi as if pulled by a magnetic force.

"We have to get going." Sean grabbed Shadow's collar as the dog nosed her way into the cottage.

"Sean?"

He froze, and the past he'd spent eighteen years forgetting slammed into him.

Charlie's brown eyes met his, surrounded by the thick, dark lashes that had always reminded him of two little fans spread across her face when her eyes were closed. Instead of being laughter-filled like he remembered, though, her eyes were wary, framed by brown hair cut into an angular bob, which sharpened her heart-shaped face.

"Charlie." He forced her name out through numb lips. Above loose white pants, her lemon tank top molded to her lush curves like a second skin. His body stirred, and awareness of her, and everything they'd once meant to each other, crashed through him.

She gave him a bland, untouchable smile. The kind her mom and sister had perfected. Not a smile he'd ever expected to see on Charlie's face. "It's good to see you again."

"Really?" Sean drew in a breath.

Charlie's smile slipped. "We were friends."

"Friends?" Sean caught her dark gaze and held it. Her jaw was tight, but her skin was burnished like a ripe peach.

Shadow strained forward, tail wagging a greeting.

"It's been a long time." Her voice was cool, but when she bent to pat the dog her hand shook.

Sean opened his dry-as-tinder mouth and closed it again before he said something stupid. Something he'd regret. In that time, he'd built a life. And the girl who'd been his best friend, his first love, and his whole world wasn't part of it.

He glanced at his son and Naomi where he and Charlie had once stood, Charlie tilting her face up to his for a good-night kiss. His stomach knotted at the look on Ty's face. Long ago, he'd looked at Charlie that way. Like she was the prettiest girl in the world. The only girl in the world for him.

"Let us know what you want to do about the canoe." Even though his pulse sped up, his voice was as cool as Charlie's as he pulled the rental agreement from the pocket of his shorts and held it out. He was thirty-six, not eighteen, and he'd made sure he never thought about those good-night kisses or any other memories he'd buried deep.

Charlie took the paper at arm's length. "I'm sure there's an explanation for the order."

"Ty?" He inclined his head toward his son.

"But, Dad—"

"No."

With a last look at Naomi, Ty vaulted over the porch railing and landed on the ground below.

Sean turned, his steps deliberate. This time he planned on being the one who walked away.

Sean Carmichael looked good, too good, and he was as self-contained as always. Unlike her. Charlie sucked in a deep breath against the volcano of emotion that threatened to erupt from her chest.

"Auntie Charlotte?" Naomi whispered. "Are you okay?"

"Fine, honey." The comforting lie she'd make herself believe. She forced her feet to walk across the porch and stop by the railing. "Sean?" Firefly Lake was a small town. She'd have to face him sooner or later and tell him a truth she'd rather avoid. At least one of them.

He paused at the bottom of the steps, and his big body stiffened. "What?" Voice tight, he half turned, his dark-blue eyes fixed on her in the way that had always unnerved her because she was sure he could tell what she was thinking.

"Wait." She scanned the piece of paper he'd given her.

"Why?" The black dog by his side looked at her and then back at Sean, eyes wise.

"The rental's fine." She wouldn't fall apart. Even though the sight of him almost brought her to her knees. "Can your son leave the canoe in the boathouse? Naomi will get the key and help him."

He glanced at Ty. The boy had Sean's sandy-blond

hair, thick, rumpled like he'd just rolled out of bed. He had Sean's height, but his eyes were a lighter blue, his face thinner. The memory of what might have been squeezed her heart.

In profile, Sean's nose still had the bump from where he'd broken it playing hockey the winter he'd turned sixteen, but his sensuous mouth was bracketed by fine lines, no longer the face of the boy she'd known.

"Of course." Sean's eyes were shuttered. Like Charlie was any other customer.

Naomi darted into the cottage and reappeared seconds later holding the boathouse key by its red cord. "Auntie Charlotte?" She looked at Ty and tossed her hair over her shoulders.

"Please unlock the boathouse and then wait on the beach." The past reared up and choked Charlie and made it hard to breathe. It reminded her of when she'd been a girl like Naomi and head over heels in love with Sean. Her whole life ahead of her, no mistakes yet. No regrets either.

"Sure." Naomi skipped down the steps.

"Auntie Charlotte?" Sean rested one bare foot against the bottom step, his legs muscular and dusted with dark-blond hair. At eighteen, he'd still been lanky, but now he was a man, all lean, long-limbed magnetic strength.

"Naomi is Mia's daughter. You remember my sister?" Charlie's legs trembled, and she wrapped a hand around the porch railing to steady herself.

"Yes." Sean's voice was deeper than she remembered, rougher, with an edge to it that set her nerve ends tingling. "But Charlotte? You hated that name."

"People change." When she'd left Firefly Lake, she'd

left Charlie behind and turned herself into Charlotte. A person who wasn't the scared girl she'd been, who'd convinced herself she'd made the only choice she could.

Sean tapped one foot on the step. "If you say so."

"Ty, your son?" Her tongue tripped over the words. "You and your wife must be proud of him." She pushed away the stab of pain sparked by the thought of Sean's wife. Pain as sharp as it was unexpected.

"He's a good kid." Sean's expression softened to give her a glimpse of the boy he'd been. "He's working with me for the summer."

"You've done some building." Charlie gestured toward the beach that narrowed at the point, still framed by the trees and rolling hills she remembered from childhood summers. Carmichael's was on the other side, and an unfamiliar tin roof glinted in the sun.

"We put in a new workshop last year. I built a house there a while ago too. Moved out from town." Sean smoothed the bill of his ball cap, and Charlie couldn't help but notice there wasn't a wedding ring on his fourth finger.

Sean must be married. He had a son and he'd always been a conventional guy. Loyal and true. Her heart twisted tighter and there was a sour taste in her mouth. "So you stayed here."

"I always wanted to take on Carmichael's." Sean paused. "But since we're taking this trip down memory lane, what about you? Did you get what you wanted?"

When you ran out on me and on us. The words he didn't say hung heavy between them.

"I'm a foreign correspondent for the Associated Press, based in London, but I travel all over. Wherever the next story is, I go." It was the life she wanted and had worked hard to get. And she loved it. At least until four months ago.

"You always wanted to see the world." Sean's voice was flat.

"Yeah, I did." She looked at the beach where Ty and Naomi tossed a Frisbee. The dog darted between them. Naomi laughed at something Ty said and he laughed, too, Sean's laugh.

Charlie's stomach rolled. She had to get a grip. Focus on who she was now, not who she'd been. She wasn't looking at herself and Sean on that beach.

"Must be an exciting life." Sean's voice had an edge of steel.

Excitement wasn't all it was cracked up to be. Charlie's hands were clammy. She sat on one of the Adirondack chairs Mia had found in the shed and crossed her right leg over her left. Her pants covered the scar tissue that stretched from her left knee to her ankle. "It pays the bills." But there wasn't much left over to save for the future and she wasn't getting any younger.

"Charlotte..." He hesitated, and the name he'd never called her rang in her ears. "Why are you here?" His eyes narrowed into blue slits, framed by spiky lashes several shades darker than his hair. "You could have put that canoe in the boathouse as easy as Ty."

Her heart thudded, a dull throb that hurt more than the ache in her leg. "I didn't expect you to turn up on the doorstep, but since you did, I don't want you to hear this in town."

"Hear what?" He tugged on his T-shirt and smoothed it over a still-taut stomach, although his shoulders were bigger, the muscles more defined.

"Mia and I and her two girls, we're here for a month to sell the cottage." She swallowed the lump in her throat. Selling was the right choice, the only choice.

"Your folks, they..." Sean yanked off his hat and sat sideways to face her on the middle step, the weathered boards creaking under his weight.

She nodded. The only sounds were the buzz of the cicadas and the whisper of the wind in the pines.

"I'm sorry." His voice was gruff.

"We lost Mom last Christmas. Cancer." Charlie blinked as tears pricked the backs of her eyes.

"That's rough." He paused for a heartbeat. "My condolences. My mom will be sad to hear about your mother."

And the cottage was her last tangible link with her mom, and the place Charlie had always thought of as home. It was the only constant in her life after the summer she'd turned ten and they'd left Montreal for her dad's new job in Boston. But she had to be practical. The money from the cottage sale would secure that future she worried about.

Sean put his hat back on and looked out at the lake. "What about your dad?"

"He died five years ago." Charlie shivered. "He had a heart attack on the golf course."

"My dad went like that a little over a year ago. Over in the marina." Sean's voice caught and he tented his hands on his knees, the strong, capable hands that had taught her how to paddle a canoe and build a campfire. Hands that had comforted her when she'd been scared of the bear with the sharp yellow teeth Mia told her lived in the boathouse. And hands that had loved her and taught her how to love back.

"He was a good man, your dad." Honest, upright, and devoted to his family. Everything Charlie's dad wasn't.

"He had a good life." Sean gave her a brief smile. "Even though he went too soon, he went doing what he loved, with the family he loved around him. A man couldn't ask for more." His face changed, tenderness wiped away, and a muscle worked in his jaw. "You're here to sell the cottage."

"Yes." She'd made her decision and wouldn't go back on it now that she was here. "It's the last piece of Mom's estate." All the beauty, vibrancy, and love that had been her mom reduced to a dry sheaf of papers.

"You could have sold the cottage from anywhere." Sean's voice rasped.

Charlie hugged herself. "This place was special to Mom. I owe it to her to come back one last time." Maybe she owed it to herself too.

"There should be a lot of interest." Sean got up from the step. "It's the biggest cottage on Firefly Lake. Since it's only a few hours from Burlington and Montreal, it's easy to get here on weekends. Even from Boston like you did. It'll be sold before you know it, and you'll be back on a plane."

Charlie pushed herself out of the chair and stood. "We might not sell it in the way you think. You see, there's a developer interested."

"A developer?" Sean moved toward her so fast Charlie rocked against the porch railing. Pain radiated up her leg.

"They haven't made us an offer yet, but they're talking about a tasteful little resort." Pinned between Sean and the railing, the top of her head level with his broad chest, Charlie reminded herself to breathe. She'd forgotten how big Sean was, how male. "They'd give us a good price."

"What do you mean a good price?" Sean's expression hardened. "Firefly Lake hasn't changed in generations. People come here because it hasn't changed."

"A resort development won't change things much." Charlie avoided his gaze.

Sean's laugh was harsh. "You really believe that? Everywhere else, life has sped up, everybody rushing without knowing what they're rushing to or why. Here things stay pretty much the same. At least the same in the ways that matter. Don't you care about keeping it that way?"

"Yes, but in this economy not as many people are buying summer cottages." Her heart raced, and she pressed a hand to her chest. "Besides, Vermont has legislation to protect the landscape, and developers have to meet certain criteria before they can get a building permit."

"Keep renting the cottage out until the economy gets better." His blue eyes blazed with the anger she'd only seen once before. "That seemed to work fine for the last eighteen years. Don't talk to me about some law. You can't sell all this to a developer." He raised an arm to take in the cottage, the forest behind it, the beach and the lake, hazy blue in the afternoon sun.

"That's not your decision to make. I need to let the cottage go." And she needed to forget about sentiment and think with her head, not her heart. Let the past go and use the money she'd get for the cottage to live the rest of her life, a life she'd almost lost.

"You were good at that, weren't you?" His face reddened. "Letting go of things you no longer wanted."

"That's not how I remember it." She forced a calmness she didn't feel. "But if you mean what was between us, that was a lifetime ago, like the cottage is a lifetime ago."

"You really think so, Sunshine?"

Charlie flinched as Sean's old nickname for her drove a spike through her battered heart.

"In all your talk about this place being special to your mom, it sounds like you've forgotten how special it was to you, too."

He whistled for his dog, the shrill sound slicing through the air. And when he walked away, this time Charlie didn't try to stop him.

About the Author

Jen Gilroy grew up under the big sky of western Canada. After many years in England, she now lives in a small town in eastern Ontario where her Irish ancestors settled in the nineteenth century. She's worked in higher education and international marketing but, after spending too much time in airports and away from her family, traded the 9–5 to write contemporary romance to bring readers' hearts home.

A small-town girl at heart, Jen likes ice cream, diners, vintage style, and all things country. Her husband, Tech Guy, is her real-life romance hero, and her daughter, English Rose, teaches her to cherish the blessings in the everyday.

You can learn more at:
  www.jengilroy.com
  Twitter: @JenGilroy1
  http://facebook.com/JenGilroyAuthor

Fall in Love with Forever Romance

RENEGADE COWBOY
By Sara Richardson

In the *New York Times* bestselling tradition of Jennifer Ryan and Maisey Yates comes the latest in Sara Richardson's Rocky Mountain Riders series. Cassidy Greer and Levi Cortez have a history together—and a sizzling attraction that's too hot to ignore. When Levi rides back into town, he knows Cass doesn't want to get roped into a relationship with a cowboy. So he's offered her a no-strings fling. But can he convince himself that one night is enough?

Fall in Love with Forever Romance

THE HIGHLAND GUARDIAN
By Amy Jarecki

Captain Reid MacKenzie has vowed to watch over his dying friend's daughter. But Reid's new ward is no wee lass. She's a ravishing, fully grown woman, and it's all he can do to remember his duty and not seduce her...Miss Audrey Kennet is stunned by the news of her father's death, and then outraged when the kilted brute who delivers the news insists she must now marry. But Audrey soon realizes the brave, brawny Scot is the only man she wants—though loving him means risking her lands, her freedom, and even her life.

Fall in Love with Forever Romance

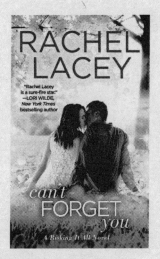

CAN'T FORGET YOU
By Rachel Lacey

Jessica Flynn is proud of the spa she's built on her own. Now that the land next door is for sale, she can expand her business...Until Mark Dalton, the man who once stole her heart, places a higher bid on the property. Mark doesn't want to compete with Jess. But as he tries to repair the past, he realizes that Jess may never forgive him if she learns why he left all those years ago.

BACK HOME AT FIREFLY LAKE
By Jen Gilroy

Fans of RaeAnne Thayne, Debbie Mason, and Susan Wiggs will love the latest from Jen Gilroy. Firefly Lake is just a pit stop for single mom Cat McGuire. That is, until sparks fly with her longtime crush—who also happens to be her daughter's hockey coach—Luc Simard. When Luc starts to fall hard, can he convince Cat to stay?

Fall in Love with Forever Romance

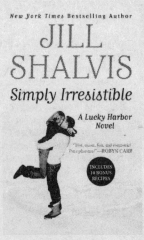

SIMPLY IRRESISTIBLE
By Jill Shalvis

Now featuring ten bonus recipes never available before in print! Don't miss this new edition of *Simply Irresistible*, the first book in *New York Times* bestselling author Jill Shalvis's beloved Lucky Harbor series!

NOTORIOUS PLEASURES
By Elizabeth Hoyt

Rediscover the Maiden Lane Series by *New York Times* bestselling author Elizabeth Hoyt in this beautiful reissue with an all-new cover! Lady Hero Batten wants for nothing, until she meets her fiancé's notorious brother. Griffin Remmington is a mysterious rogue, whose interests belong to the worst sorts of debauchery. Hero and Griffin are constantly at odds, so when sparks fly, can these two imperfect people find a perfect true love?

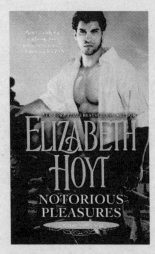